AN OLD

C0001 98896

The first in the Retribution se
gangland

Three families… One prize…
A live-in carer. A retired dancer from a Soho club. The notorious Powell firm.

Teagan Fraser had no idea what she was getting herself into when she took on an assignment as a live-in carer for Dulcie Adams – a retired dancer from a Soho club. Dulcie has waited forty years for her lover, Michael Pointer, to return, but she's been living in hope for a time that never came and left looking after something important, which Jonah Powell and his firm want back.

In addition to the notorious Powell firm, there are others wanting to claim what they believe is rightfully theirs and they'll do anything to get it back. If only Dulcie wasn't around it would be a lot easier, but she's difficult to shift…

A lot can happen in two weeks and sometimes it's better not get involved.

"Edie Baylis has delivered a belter. Expertly plotted and full of amazing characters. Gripped until the last page." – Caz Finlay, Author of *Bad Blood* series.

What readers are saying about *An Old Score*:
- *"Gritty gangland thriller…"*
- *"From page one this book had me hooked…"*
- *"A great contribution to this genre…"*
- *"Another fast-paced, brilliant read…"*
- *"Full of lies, deceit and so many plot twists…"*
- *"One fast-paced, thrilling read…"*

Also by Edie Baylis

Retribution Series
Finders Keepers (Retribution #2)
The Final Take (Retribution #3)
The Retribution Series Box Set

Allegiance Series
Takeover (Allegiance #1)
Fallout (Allegiance #2)
Vendetta (Allegiance #3)
Payback (Allegiance #4)

Hunted Series
The Status Debt (Hunted #1)
The Family Legacy (Hunted #2)
The Target of Lies (Hunted #3)
The Hunted Series Box Set

Downfall Series
Until the End of Time (Downfall #1)
Escaping the Past (Downfall #2)
Vengeful Payback (Downfall #3)
The Downfall Series Box Set

Scarred Series
Mirrors Never Lie (Scarred #1)

AN OLD SCORE

RETRIBUTION #1

EDIE BAYLIS

A✝HAME
press
- LONDON -

ISBN 978-1-9161627-3-0
e-ISBN 978-1-9161627-4-7

Athame Press
Unit 13230 - PO Box 6945 – London – W1A 6US

For my son
My superstar, best mate and right-hand man
I love you more than pins
xx

1965

DULCIE HEFTED HERSELF UP onto the pillows and sighed contentedly. Her painted eyebrows formed a frown as Michael moved to the edge of the bed, reaching for his clothes hanging over the back of the dressing table chair. 'You're leaving already?'

Standing up, Michael pulled on his trousers and smiled. 'You know I have to, but it won't be for much longer.' Leaning down, he pressed his lips on Dulcie's.

'But Michael,' Dulcie said breathlessly, already ready for a second helping of the man she found irresistible. 'How long before... before...'

'Before we can do this for real, you mean?' Michael said, placing one of his large hands gently on Dulcie's belly. 'Like I said, not long.'

Dulcie's eyes narrowed. 'You've been saying that for ages.' She winced, feeling a strong kick from within. 'This child of yours won't wait around much longer. I've already left my job and moved away, like you wanted, but all you're bothered about is how it looks to everyone else? It wasn't an issue putting this one in me whilst my husband's body was still warm, was it?' she snapped, knowing she was pushing her luck by speaking this way, but she loved Michael. Loved him desperately.

Michael swallowed his rising irritation. 'I'll pretend you didn't say that Dulcie,' he said, his voice, although soft held a distinct note of warning. 'Like you wanted, I ensured Peter was taken out of the way, didn't I? But we have to leave a reasonable time before we move things forward.'

Dulcie pouted. 'I know you did and I'm grateful for that.' Her husband's unfortunate death outside The Feathers under the wheels of a car whose out of control driver hadn't even bothered to stop had certainly freed her from her unwanted marriage, leaving the way clear for her to be with the man she truly loved, but months on and she was still on her own. And she didn't like it. It wasn't supposed to be like this.

She glanced around the large bedroom – the bedroom in this massive house Michael had moved her to; the place where she'd imagined waking up next to him every day, but instead, several months on, she was still rattling around alone in his absence. 'I'm sick of being your bit on the side.'

Michael reached for his crisp white shirt and shrugged it on. 'The solicitor is wrapping things up with my divorce as we speak,' he said. 'But don't worry. As promised, it's all in hand. I just need to make sure everything's done properly.'

His name would be mud when it became known he was divorcing his wife. *Everyone* had a bit on the side, but it wasn't the done thing to ditch the wife and mother of your children in favour of a mistress – especially in Jacky Powell's eyes.

Michael had worked for the Powell firm for years and Jacky, the head honcho, had a strong set of principles when it came to family. Michael knew full well he would lose a lot of kudos and respect when it got out that he was leaving his missus. A few of the other lads already knew, thanks to his mouth getting loose after too many drinks the other night, but Dulcie Adams would also shortly be the mother of a child of his too. The difference between her and Sophie, his wife, was that

ONE

2005

JONAH POWELL YELPED as the burning drops of coffee scorched his skin where he'd let the angle of his cup tilt too far. 'Fuck's sake!' he roared, hastily mopping at the liquid soaking through the front of his once pristine white shirt. 'NERO? Get in here NOW!?'

Jonah scowled. He couldn't believe this. He just couldn't fucking believe it. After all this time? All this time he'd listened to how this had slipped through the firm's fingers. He'd been brought up with tales of what would happen when the truth finally came out. But the truth had never come out. Not in his father's lifetime anyway.

Until now.

Jonah's eyes flicked around his wood-panelled office situated near the rear of The Feathers Club. A plethora of framed accolades and certificates adorned the walls, signifying the almost 100-year popularity of the place – many of which stemmed from after his father took ownership.

His father had loved this club – loved everything about it. Aside from it being a legitimate front for several of the other interests the Powell firm had, there had always been a deep-seated love for The Feathers; it's staff, the show and the whole atmosphere. But Jacky's happiness and unrivalled loyalty to everyone – both involved in the firm and the club itself had been blown out of the water by what had happened in 1965.

Jacky Powell went to his grave thirty years later still seething about being wronged – by not one, but *two* of his trusted men and on top of that, witnessing his eldest son being sent down because of the connected fallout.

Because of this, Jonah had made the promise to his father that he'd find a way to get even. That was ten years ago. Ten years since his father had passed and now – here it was. Right in bloody front of him.

Anger like a thick miasma seeped from every single pore and only the grating noise of the heavy door to his office opening stopped him from spontaneously combusting.

Jonah glared at Nero Banks, his most trusted right hand man, standing in the doorway. 'I thought I told you to get that fucking sticking door fixed!'

Nero eyed Jonah warily. He didn't know what had happened but one thing was for sure and that was his boss was not in a good mood and he'd bet the reason he'd been called in wasn't to discuss the state of the door.

'Look at this!' Jonah snapped, jerking his head towards his computer screen.

Nero stood to the side of Jonah, the rage emanating from the man making his skin bristle. He looked at the screen and frowned. Ok, so it was a news website – the video section. Bending forwards slightly, he peered at the computer. *What the hell was this and why was Jonah watching it?*

'Well?' Jonah barked, waiting for a response. 'What does *that* tell you?'

Nero blinked. 'It tells me you're watching an old bat doing the goose step.'

Jonah slammed his fist down on his desk and spun around in his chair, his face forming into a ferocious snarl. 'It's not just *any* old bat. Look closer and listen.' He pressed 'play again' on the video clip.

Nero watched the old dear prancing around on the screen for the second time. So, she was spritely for someone of her age, but what was he supposed to be noticing? Was there something obvious that he'd developed a blind spot for? *Oh no, Jonah hadn't developed a fetish for the oldies, had he?*

Nero tried not to display his confusion. When Jonah was in a mood like this, it was akin to inadvertently brushing against an unexploded bomb and he didn't want the grief, but when the voiceover filtered into his brain, his attention sharpened fourfold. The word *'Feathers'* was enough. He peered closer; his ears finely tuned to the female narrator.

Jonah paused the video and faced Nero, raising his eyebrows questioningly.

Unable to quite believe it, Nero leant against the wall in shock. 'Fuck me! That's Dulcie Adams?' he whispered. *'The* Dulcie Adams?'

'How many Dulcie fucking Adams who headlined the Feathers club in Soho do you think there are? That's her. That's fucking *her*!'

Nero blew out between his teeth. 'Jesus Christ!' Twenty years he'd been with this firm after being brought in at the age of eighteen to work alongside Jonah and his father. Everyone knew of the outstanding debt. The actual situation might have occurred twelve years before he was born, but the quest to reclaim what was lifted by Michael Pointer had never gone away and it was something that every single member of the Powell firm was well acquainted with.

It hadn't taken long for Jacky Powell to work out that Pointer had lifted a lot more than he'd told them. Pointer had clearly underestimated exactly how on the ball Jacky Powell was when it came to knowing exactly where and what everything was.

Apparently, Jacky had relished allowing Pointer to think for a short amount of time that he'd got away with it – allowed him to think there was no suspicion and let him walk straight into the trap – and of course he had. The minute Pointer had said he was retiring, coming out with some bollocks about not wanting to upset his wife or offend Jacky's family values by divorce, that had been the needed confirmation.

After that, it had taken a very short time to despatch the man, but the jewels had remained elusive. Presuming Pointer was keeping them at his home somewhere had been wrong – a thorough going over of the man's house uncovered nothing but a terrified wife with no clue. Sophie Pointer hadn't been party to any of it, so Dulcie, as Pointer's long term mistress, was the next obvious choice. But she'd disappeared, and had done so long before the actual heist had taken place and somehow the woman had given them the slip ever since.

The firm had been looking for this woman since 1965 and despite using more manpower than the police would allot to a serial killer investigation, they'd always drawn a blank.

But if anyone had thought that when old Jacky Powell died the search would be scaled down or perhaps even laid to rest along with his body, they'd soon realised they were wrong. Taking over the reins from his father in the absence of his elder brother, Jonah had made it clear from the off that what Pointer had done would never be forgotten. They had, of course, managed to retrieve the couple that O'Hara had possession of, but it still left the majority with Pointer's tart – wherever she was lurking.

As time had worn on the firm had other things to deal with – plenty of them, but the possible link with that heist and Dulcie Adams had remained forever floating in the background.

Nero locked eyes with Jonah and frowned. 'So now what?'

Jonah grinned, exposing his straight white teeth. 'That clip you just saw was connected to a business of some other slag – I'm presuming it's the daughter – something to do with an estate agent. Bring Keith up to speed with what I've told you.'

Nero's heart sank. 'You want me to work on this with Keith?'

Keith Grogan was a great enforcer – the size of a house, but the collection side of the business was chock-a-block at the moment and he didn't want that to slide. Furthermore, Keith was hardly the most subtle of characters.

Jonah eyed Nero. 'Yes, I do. Do some digging and see what you can find.' He folded his arms across his wide chest. 'This time we're finally going to fucking find that old bitch and discover for definite whether she was the one. You know as well as I do how much what she might have stashed is worth. And if she's got it...' He twirled his pen around between his fingers, '...then we're getting it the fuck back from her.'

• • • •

'WHAT ON EARTH WERE YOU THINKING?' Robert asked, his stance tense as he stood stiffly next to the huge fireplace, his wide frame all but blocking the mantle from sight. He glared at his mother; his cold eyes hard. As much as he loved her, she wasn't making things easy. 'Why would you feel the need to do that?'

'Oh Robert,' Dulcie sighed. 'What exactly is the problem? The woman was nice and we got chatting, that's all.'

'She was a bloody journalist! She came to do that interview with Helen.'

Dulcie shrugged. 'Did she? I can't remember now. It was ages ago.'

Robert's eyes narrowed. 'It wasn't ages ago! It was only a fortnight past. Have you completely lost your mind?'

Dulcie laughed. 'So Helen keeps telling me.'

'She'll go berserk when she sees this,' Robert muttered. 'You've made the nationals too – there's clips of you on their news channel website.'

'Their news channel *what*?' Dulcie exclaimed, her blue eyes twinkling. 'Website? Oh, you mean like the TV? Ooh, how exciting! I haven't been on a newsreel since 1964. Can I see it?'

'No you can't! I could barely bring myself to watch it myself. Christ. How embarrassing. You're sixty-five, not eighteen!'

'The girl asked if I could remember any of the routines from back in the day.' Dulcie smiled proudly. 'Well, of course I can, so I showed her and she said I still had it.'

Robert paced around the room fuming silently. He wasn't so much angry with her, just annoyed that her doing things like this made it harder to fight her corner where Helen was concerned.

'Have you seen yourself?' Dulcie laughed. 'You looked just like your father then.'

'I wouldn't know,' Robert barked. 'If you remember, I never met him and I don't need constantly reminding of that. I can't see why you want to keep all of this rubbish either.' His arm gestured to the framed photographs and posters adorning the walls; some black and white, others colour of old music advertisements and celebrities. 'Why would you want to showcase memories of the places and people connected with where my father – your husband, died? I don't understand you.'

Dulcie's eyes narrowed. 'You don't know what you're talking about. I don't know *what* killed your father or if anything ever did!'

Robert stopped pacing. 'What you do you mean, you don't know? You were the one who told me he got run over outside that goddamn club where you worked.'

Dulcie staggered and reached for the back of the chair to steady her bird-like frame. 'I-I don't feel well,' she muttered.

Robert stared at his mother, his mouth forming a thin line. Whether he liked to admit it or not, her mental health was definitely worsening. He watched her take a seat on one of the chairs, patted her shoulder and smiled calmly. 'Please don't do any more of this sort of thing. It will only give Helen added reason to think you're going dotty.'

He resented Helen constantly going on about their mother going nuts. She wasn't nuts, she was just getting on and becoming forgetful in the process. But whether he wanted to admit it or not, it was getting worse and it was only fair to warn

Helen that this article and web stuff was doing the rounds.

Two

NERO GUNNED IT ALONG THE M40. After confirming they had ID'd the one lead they had – Helen Shepherd, they'd got on the road back to London. There was no point hanging around. It was obvious they'd get no further with this tonight, but now it was a question of where they went from here.

He shot Keith a glance as he sat squashed into the passenger seat, shovelling one of the many sandwiches he'd bought from the Spar into his mouth. The man's massive hands made the sandwich look the size of a postage stamp. No wonder they always had to buy several of the damn things each time.

It had been a pain in the arse trekking up to Maidenhead. Bloody posh bastards this side of the Home Counties never failed to get on his tits; thinking their shit didn't stink - the birds poncing around like Stepford Wives. *No thanks.*

Neither had Nero in any way enjoyed sitting through the brain-numbing interview about Helen Shepherd's 'successful and elite' estate agency business – catering to people who 'wanted country homes with a touch of splendour…' *Jeez, have a day off! What a load of bollocks!* Tell a posh twat that a shed was the thing to have and they'd fall over their designer shoes to buy one. But the interview had at least given them all the relevant information where this estate agency was and who ran it.

The TV interview had also proved that Helen Shepherd was, as Jonah suspected, Dulcie Adams' daughter. The woman hadn't looked overly pleased when the reporter asked for an opinion of her mother's dancing skills – the expression on Helen's face had been reminiscent of a slapped haddock.

Nero bit back a grin. The silly cow would be even less pleased to realise her all-so-important interview had inadvertently reignited the Powell's search to get their hands on Dulcie Adams and what she'd most likely got stashed. Helen Shepherd's need to get ahead in the world had given them a direct lead to what had been overdue for four decades.

'Here, that Helen bird's alright looking, isn't she?' Keith mumbled through a mouthful of cheese and onion.

'Not my cup of tea,' Nero muttered as he sparked up a fag and jabbed at the button for his electric window, opening it a crack.

Keith brushed a buttery chunk of bread off his jeans, leaving a greasy smear down his left leg, then casually wiped his fingers on the seat belt. 'I'd do her!'

Nero chuckled to himself. Keith would shag a corpse providing the face hadn't rotted away too much, but to be fair, even in her forties, the woman was a decent looker, but she had too much of an 'I'm above everyone' sneer across her nicely made up face for his liking. Certainly not the sort he'd put his cock in for a quickie, but at least forcing himself to sit through that interview had made sure he'd known straight away that the woman who'd left the estate agents this afternoon was the one they were looking for. The only problem being they hadn't been able to confirm an address for the elusive Dulcie Adams.

It had been a bit too much to hope for that the very day they rolled up to watch her, Helen Shepherd would leave the estate agents and conveniently lead them straight to her mother. There had been a small chance of that, but it hadn't happened. He'd half expected to end up following her back to her hubby –

presuming she had one, but tailing Helen's Mercedes had only led them to a poxy-looking wine bar. After an hour of watching a group of snooty bastards sipping from wine glasses, and desperate for a drink himself, Nero had made the decision to head back. The chance of Helen Shepherd going on to her mother's now was slim.

Taking a long drag on his cigarette, he veered out into the outside lane to overtake a car hogging the middle lane. Giving the female driver the finger as he passed, he grinned at her refusal to look in his direction.

'What's the plan now?' Keith asked.

Nero shrugged. 'I haven't got a clue, but Jonah will tell us soon enough.' He suspected Jonah would have much preferred for them to have been able to confirm the old bat's address straightaway, but life was very rarely that simple.

With a sigh of resignation, he accepted there would more than likely be several more trips up to Maidenhead required before even the first leg of this new discovery was wrapped up.

• • • •

HELEN SHEPHERD SLAMMED her knife and fork down on the table and looked at her husband. 'What do you mean, it's not that bad? Of *course* it's that bad!' Her forehead creased. 'How many times do I need to explain that my mother is ruining my business with the things she does and this has got to be the worst one yet.'

Although it showed that her plan was working, it wasn't supposed to infringe on her bloody business. She removed her linen serviette from her lap and dabbed at the corners of her mouth, inspecting the cloth to make sure she hadn't inadvertently transferred any lipstick onto it.

James studied his wife for a flicker of emotion but found none. *As usual.* 'What does Robert think about it?'

Helen raised an eyebrow and laughed – a hollow, tinny, sarcastic laugh. *Yes, Robert... Robert always had the most inept timing.* He'd have known calling her to inform her about this latest example of their mother's ridiculous behaviour would wind her up. And it had. Even then he'd waited a full day before telling her!

More than anything, she wished she'd stayed for a few more drinks after work, but receiving that phone call halfway through her first glass had put paid to that. After hearing what Robert had to say she'd been in far too much of a foul mood to even think about remaining there and trying to act normal.

This really was the very last thing she needed and gave her even more impetus to get her mother out of the way before she screwed things up even more. It had taken *months* to get that interview set up and she was counting on it bringing new clients into the business.

Sales had been gradually sliding with Shepherd, Percival and Proctor for a couple of years now, but last year was by far the worst. Unbeknown to James, she'd already remortgaged the house to plough the money into the business. She could hardly not do her part, being as both the other partners had contributed to the firm's shortfall, but since Neil Percival had died, it only left her and Bob Proctor and she just hadn't got any more funds, which was becoming embarrassing.

And all James could think about was Robert's opinion?

'It's not Robert who will be affected, is it? It's my business that will,' Helen snapped. 'But at least he's finally beginning to accept that our mother is going nuts.'

And Robert *had* to accept their mother was going crazy because getting her out of the way was the only bloody chance she'd got of getting more money for the business.

Robert didn't want to accept it. Oh no, he wouldn't because he'd always been the favourite out of the two of them. It was ok for him; he didn't have to worry. His job as a computer consultant brought top money in with no overheads to speak of.

Her plan was working, she acknowledged that, but it was slow – too slow. And a side effect of it was damaging her business further, which wasn't supposed to happen.

Listening to Helen ranting, James sighed. He'd heard

nothing but the state of Dulcie's mental health for months. Aware Helen hadn't spoken for several minutes, he fiddled with the remainder of his steak. 'You should get a doctor involved if you think she's developing something such as dementia.'

'Yes, I'm intending on doing that.' Helen watched James cram another piece of steak into his mouth and felt like punching him in the face. Why had she bothered marrying him in the first place? It wasn't like he'd contributed to anything. It was *her* who had got somewhere in life. It was her who had made the business work with no help from him, but this was probably why. He couldn't get his priorities right. Why was he even bothered about her brother's opinion? It was hardly massive in the large scale of things, unlike her business' reputation, which if her mother's antics became too erratic, would be in jeopardy. She'd lose clients hand over fist and she wasn't putting up with that. The sooner her mother was out of the picture, the better.

Helen glared at James. Contrary to what he believed, she *was* doing something about it and it wouldn't be too much longer before everything would come together. He could push in any direction he liked, but she'd got everything in hand.

She forced a smile in her husband's direction. 'Can we talk about something else?'

James picked up his wine glass and sighed inwardly. Personally, he liked Dulcie and from what Helen had said, it did sound like the poor old girl was beginning to lose her marbles, so both Helen and Robert needed to act on it sooner rather than later before things got really bad. And as much as he didn't have much time for the insular, miserable creature that was Robert, he did understand the man's unwillingness to accept the situation, but he'd do what Helen asked and change the subject. He never got anywhere reasoning with her – it only ever made her angry.

As for her blowing her top over a news clip regarding the old days, he couldn't see where the harm was in it. She was just stressing because the clips came off the back of that interview about her estate agents. Clients wouldn't have an issue with it, surely? If they saw it, they'd probably think it was nice – showing that Helen had a family – a nice mother. But James knew she didn't see it like that.

He studied his wife's crease-free brow. If Helen's theory was correct, she should be more worried about the dementia, rather than the possibility of offending a few toffee-nosed clients. He knew he would be if Dulcie was *his* mother.

Despite his underlying concern, James remained upbeat. *It was easier.* 'By the way, a parcel arrived for you this morning. I've put it on the table in the hallway.'

'Ok, thanks,' Helen muttered, hoping James wouldn't question what she'd ordered. She'd been starting to think the order was lost in the post and that would not be good. Not now she was nicely on track, but James didn't need to know the details. He didn't need to know *anything*.

Hearing the phone ring, James smiled as he got up from the dining table. 'I'll get that. You finish your wine.'

Helen breathed a quiet sigh of relief as he left the room. It was only a few days before her meeting with an old flame from the property business to set the wheels in motion. Before long, her mother would be purchasing one of those flats for elderly people whose minds had gone west, leaving *her* free to sell that massive house and plough the profits into the business she'd worked so hard to make successful.

That way she could match Proctor each time he suggested investing more money or pursuing new avenues, with no fear of not being able to find the cash.

Her mother would be unable to argue about the new living arrangements. She'd be making sure the woman would be too far gone in the head by then. And even if she did moan, it would be too late. James had no say in it, and Robert... Well, Robert would eventually go with whatever she said - like he always did.

She just had to hope her bloody mother didn't trash her business' reputation before this got wrapped up. Once it was done, then and only then could she quit this poxy charade of playing the 'good daughter'. And it wouldn't be a moment too soon either.

THREE

TEAGAN FRASER hadn't been overly enamoured to receive the details for her next job from the agency, but on the other hand, she needed the money.

Twenty five years old and *still* living at home. She felt like the only person in the entire world who was. Temping as a carer wasn't the best for career progression, but it was better money than a permanent job doing the same thing and a *lot* better money if the job entailed living in and that was the only reason she'd accepted this assignment.

Sighing despondently, she absentmindedly watched the houses flash past as the taxi continued. Spring had quickly turned into summer, the weather perking up dramatically, but now she'd be stuck inside. Apart from her half-day a week off, it would be 24/7 in some old dear's house with no contact with the outside world – apart from Facebook.

Teagan frowned. Everybody seemed to be joining Facebook. She'd been reluctant at first and now she really wished she'd given it a miss. It did her no real favours. All it achieved was reminding her what she was missing, who was getting married, promoted, holidaying – whatever, you name it – *they* were doing it. Everything she wasn't.

But she had a plan.

Hearing her phone beep, Teagan pulled it from her bag and opened the text message:

```
You there yet? xx
```

Quickly, she typed a reply back to Joe:

```
Not yet. Text u when I can later. This better
be worth it 😊 x
```

And that was the plan. Well, *Joe's* plan. After three years of being together, they'd *talked* about moving things forward or rather *she* had. Not marriage or anything, although she'd hoped he might have at least mentioned that by now, but Joe had never as much even hinted that was on the cards.

Teagan sniffed. It wasn't so bad for him – he shared a house with two other guys, but their place was like student halls - or what she imagined them to be like, anyway.

Just picturing Joe with his surfer-look, carefree ways and laid back happy attitude, her heart fluttered. The moment she'd met him her heart had crash landed. He'd been a breath of fresh air, as well as being exciting and gorgeous. That feeling hadn't wavered and she loved him desperately, but wanted them to live together. Just *them*. Like a *proper* couple.

The trouble was, there was no way they could afford to buy, not around here, but they could *rent* somewhere, like Joe did with his mates. With their joint wages they could just about afford it, but saving for the equivalent of two months' rent, *plus* a months' rent just to enable them to get through the door seemed a long way off. That was until Joe came up with this idea…

Teagan frowned. She hadn't been over the moon with his suggestion, considering it would be down to *her* and her alone to pull it off, but after thinking about it, it made sense. Besides, if she wanted their relationship to move forward, it was the only viable option.

Like Joe said, all it would take was one live-in placement and within weeks they'd have the extra money needed. Put like that, it sounded good, but it also meant weeks without seeing him. Still, as soon as she'd got enough money, she'd think of a suitable excuse to leave.

Teagan pulled a mirror from her handbag and gave herself the once over. She looked presentable enough; a light pink top with a scoop neck and a pair of nicely fitted black trousers. Her long dark brown hair fell with a slight wave just past her shoulders and she'd done a decent job of not overdoing the makeup; a bit of light brown eyeshadow and a small amount of eyeliner, just enough to set off her hazel eyes. A decent covering of mascara and some dusky pink lip gloss had finished off the casual, yet professional look.

'It's somewhere along here, Miss,' the taxi driver said, snapping Teagan from her thoughts.

Teagan glanced out of the window. She hadn't noticed the taxi slowing down and had no idea exactly where the place that she'd been sent to was.

'Do you know which one it is?' the driver asked gruffly, eyeing Teagan in his rear view mirror.

Teagan scanned the large detached houses. 'Erm... not exactly,' she mumbled. 'I'm a carer and this is my first day at a new placement. The house is called 'Footlights'.'

'What kind of a house name is that?' the driver griped, peering at name plaques as the car crawled along the side of the kerb.

Teagan shrugged. 'I'm sure that's what the email said.' Pulling her phone from her bag again she located the email from the agency. 'Yes, it's 'Footlights, Frogmore Road.' That's all it says.'

Spotting the signal bar in the corner of her screen struggling in and out, her heart sank. Bad signal? *Jeez, that was all she needed.*

'Carer, you say?' the driver asked. 'Maybe with a house

name like that this old dear you've been sent to look after is a retired chiro... podo... Oh, I dunno, what are the people called that deal with feet?'

Teagan blinked. 'I've no idea,' she muttered. And that was half the problem; she knew very little about who she'd been sent to look after.

The agency usually sent tons of info about the person - things like medical history, previous notes from prior carers, likes and dislikes, that sort of stuff. This was normally received well in advance of starting the placement so that she could 'get to know' her new client before arriving. But this time the information was sparse to say the least.

She scrolled down the email once more:

To: Teagan <tfraser622@gmail.com
From: booking@bellevuecarers.co.uk
Date: 5 June 2005
Subject: New placement

Hi Teagan,
Details for New Placement:

This placement is for Mrs D Adams. Lives alone. 65. No previous carers supplied by this agency. Job booked by client. Reticent to give any in-depth background on herself and stated there is no relevant medical history that we need to be aware of.
Placement is for 6 months initially (providing she likes you - her words!) and there's half day a week off.
Rate: Live-in £680 per week
Start date: 3pm. 10th June
Address: Footlights, Frogmore Lane, Maidenhead

Good luck
Sheila

Teagan was nervous. She hoped this Mrs Adams wasn't one

of those cantankerous people. She'd had a few of them in the past and it was demoralising as well as hard work. But there was no way she could turn this one down. The pay was too good for that and she could pull together the money for the rental deposit in no time, but whatever happened, there was no way she was staying for six months! A month should do it. Six weeks, tops.

The driver jerked to a stop. 'This is it, by the looks of it.'

Teagan stared at the tall, dilapidated house; out of character compared to the other pristine dwellings on the road. The place towered up three storeys and, judging by the ornate parts visible, the building was Victorian. Based on the overgrown front garden and the dirty and chipped once white render, the property didn't look well maintained.

Oh well, it is what it is, she thought, paying the taxi driver his fare.

Getting out of the car, Teagan waited while the driver popped the boot and lifted out her wheeled case. 'Thanks,' she said, pulling out the metal handle from the case.

'Good luck, love.' He raised an eyebrow and glanced up at the imposing property.

Smiling weakly, Teagan dragged the case up a flight of stone steps, some almost covered by thick weeds pushing through the cracks of the thick stone blocks. Reaching the top, she glanced at her watch. A couple of minutes early. She looked at the thick wooden door; the edges of its rusted iron brackets covered with paint where the door had, at some point, been repainted. The paint job must have been some time ago as the bright pillar box red of the door was chipped and faded.

Tentatively, she pressed down on the doorbell housed in an ornate brass surround. A deep tinkling was heard from within, signifying this was one of the old fashioned type; a bell on a wire, suspended somewhere in the hallway beyond.

Hearing no movement from within, Teagan waited. *What if this was the wrong place?* Panic stirred. If she was in the wrong location, then she would be late by the time she found the right one. And the taxi had gone too.

Procrastinating whether to ring again, she raised her hand to do so, but heard heavy footsteps from inside approaching the door.

• • • •

JONAH MADE A POINT of cutting one of his legendary scowls at the prison officer, who not being one he'd seen previously, must be a new one, whose colleagues had little time for, considering they hadn't given him the lowdown about the treatment of particular visitors.

Squaring his shoulders, mentally removing the humiliation of being searched along with every other Tom, Dick or Harry before being granted access, Jonah manoeuvred his 6' 3" frame through the doorway into the visiting room, immediately spotting his brother seated near the back.

Acknowledging the nods of greeting from the other convicts and visitors alike, Jonah moved confidently through the tables to where Saul Powell sat.

'Should I even ask?' Jonah said with a half-grin as he took his seat on the plastic chair opposite his brother.

Saul cocked an eyebrow, the movement causing the stitches above his eye to pucker. 'Whatever happened to me is nowt compared with what happened to the other one.'

Jonah grinned. That, he did not doubt. It was guaranteed that for every mark his brother had, anyone else involved would have at least twenty more – that's if they'd been lucky. He watched Saul crack his massive knuckles as he flexed his fists. 'I presumed something had gone down for my last visit to be cancelled at the last minute.'

'Yeah, not much I could do about that. The Governor couldn't override this one; too much pressure from the board at the moment.' Saul shrugged his massive shoulders. 'Still, a few days down the block isn't an issue.'

'And? How much longer added now?' Jonah waited to hear the inevitable.

'Dunno. Probably another six months at a guess. The Gov's not stupid. He knows the score, but he's got to at least be seen doing *something* otherwise everyone would kick off.'

Jonah sighed. Saul just couldn't help himself. The brief had already told him he'd be looking at an extra six months on his sentence, at the very least. And that was more than lenient for slashing another prisoner's throat.

Saul had already got his sentence added to so many times since the original sentencing he'd be in here for ever at this rate. On one hand it was frustrating, but on the other hand it was also preferable. Saul running the firm would have meant chaos and devastation – not what their father would have wanted.

Jacky Powell had been devastated when Saul got fifteen years for the slaughter of Sean O'Hara back in '88. His elder son's incarceration was the second casualty to his family, courtesy of Michael Pointer's stunt, but what Sean had done added more salt to the already raw wound. To discover twenty years after the robbery that O'Hara had been party to ripping the firm off along with Pointer was doubly difficult to accept. Especially being as the man had remained under the firm's wing – acting as put out as everyone else about Pointer's disloyalty.

O'Hara's part in it had only come to light when the stupid fuck thought twenty years was long enough to leave it before putting the feelers out to sell the couple of gems he'd filched. But twenty years was *nowhere* near long enough – not for the Powells not to get wind of it on the grapevine. Jewellers just about anywhere in the entire world knew it wasn't worth any amount of commission to risk having the Pointers on their back.

Unsurprisingly, it had been a matter of hours after Sean O'Hara had made contact with a back-street jeweller - one not even one on their usual radar for dealing with knocked-off clobber, before the Powells were alerted. And from that second on, Sean O'Hara had signed his own death warrant.

Jonah clenched his jaw. O'Hara, along with Pointer had both been trusted enforcers in the firm. Pointer's betrayal was bad enough, but to find out that O'Hara was another one of them made it even worse.

O'Hara's brother - also an enforcer, had done a runner back to Ireland once it kicked off with Sean and had never been seen of again. The man wasn't stupid enough to think he'd be allowed to remain working for the firm with his connections, but there had been little point going after him; he'd had nothing to do with it. Besides, word had it that he'd cracked and was now certifiably loony.

Of course, Saul had kicked off. He'd gone straight out – mad as a hatter, as was his style and butchered Sean O'Hara. He hadn't just butchered the man - he'd butchered him in full daylight in front of hordes of people in the King's Arms in Soho. No amount of witness intimidation could have kept him out of nick that time, especially as Saul had all but decapitated O'Hara in front of several off-duty detectives having a casual lunchtime drink.

No, Saul was fucked as far as his freedom went, but at least he hadn't taken the firm down with him. He should have been out by now, but his psychotic temperament followed him inside and the vicious attacks on any prisoners who wronged him added several more chunks on his stretch. His release date had gradually moved from 2003 up until 2007 - still a long way off and if Jonah knew his brother at all, it wouldn't stop there either.

As the eldest son, Saul should have taken over from his father in running the firm, but due to his enforced absence, Jonah got the job. And secretly, Jonah thought his father was pleased about that, in as much that *he* was more like his father in temperament and attitude than Saul – who was definitely on the psychotic spectrum in anyone's opinion.

Saul was incapable of running a fair ship. The firm would have been run on fear, loathing and devastation – not the way Jacky Powell would have ever been happy with. But it was a double-edged sword. The pain of seeing his son banged up because of Pointer's legacy and the newly revealed snake-in-the-grass, O'Hara, was a further insult and Jonah firmly believed that these combined things had directly led to his father's death. And that was something he'd not have forgiven *either* of those two for.

Jonah eyed Saul. He had a good idea of what his brother's reaction would be to the latest news and it wouldn't be pretty. 'We've found her...'

The plastic cup of rancid tea from the drinks machine froze half-way between Saul's mouth and the table. A nerve in his neck twitched frantically. 'Are you talking about who I think you're talking about?'

Jonah nodded almost imperceptibly. 'Yep... Dulcie Adams...'

Saul smashed his cup down on the rickety table, the plastic concertinaring under his fist, tea spraying everywhere. 'Don't mention that fucking cunt's name out loud!' he roared.

'Oih! Powell!' A screw yelled. 'Calm it!'

Saul's rabid glare turned on to the screw – the same one who Jonah had taken an immediate disklike to. 'Shut it, you bastard!' he yelled, scrambling to his feet.

As the visiting room fell into worried silence, all eyes on them, Jonah casually watched another prison officer rush towards the offending screw and say something under his breath. At this point, the screw paled and allowed himself to be quickly ushered over the other side of the visiting area whilst another screw gave Saul the nod to sit down.

'Keep it down, will you?' Jonah hissed out of the corner of his mouth. 'You don't want even more time on top of your latest extension!'

Wild-eyed, Saul begrudgingly parked himself back in his chair. 'He's a fucking wanker that one. Don't know his arse from his elbow and needs a damn fine kicking.'

Jonah sighed. 'Just ignore him. Now do you want to know what's happened or not?' He waited until the visiting area's usual background chatter resumed before filling his brother in on how Dulcie Adams had been finally located.

• • • •

'YOU'RE ON TIME.' A man's large frame blocked most of the doorway, his expression not relaying any pleasure at Teagan's punctuality.

'Oh, erm...' Teagan stuttered, taken off guard. There was no mention of a man in the brief. And although not great at gauging ages, she'd put him to be in his early 40s. Thick, dark hair, flecked with grey, his eyes scrutinised her. *Did she have the wrong place after all?* 'Erm... I'm Teagan Fraser... I-I'm looking for Mrs Adams? She telep...'

'Yes, yes,' the man snapped impatiently. 'We've been expecting you. You'd better come in.'

As the man turned on his heels and walked away, Teagan faltered, before heaving her bag over the high doorstep and into the porch. Presuming it was the done thing to close the wooden door behind her, she did so, quietly admiring the beautifully coloured thin panes of stained glass either side of the front door which closed both heavily and loudly. Cringing, hoping the reverberation wouldn't cause the stained glass to fall out, Teagan awkwardly stepped through the inner door to a dark hallway and glanced around nervously.

The hallway was long with a Milton tiled floor, parts of which were raised, others cracked. She looked up at the high ceiling, spotting the doorbell, its brass bell hanging from a coiled loop of wire just behind the inner door. The area was made gloomier by dark wallpaper; plain green at the lower level and a dark green, overlaid with a busy gold pattern above the dado rail. There were several doorways leading off and she realised with a rising sense of dread that she had no idea which one the man had disappeared into.

'Hurry up!' the man barked suddenly, his head appearing from one of the doorways further along. 'Are you standing there all day?'

Fighting the overwhelming urge to disappear, Teagan instead dutifully made her way towards the room, admiring the ornate archways along the length; the base of each arch festooned with the head of an angel.

Nerves fluttering, she entered a large, what would be described as a drawing room, with once opulent velvet curtains now faded and frayed, draped from a huge rear-facing bay window, the swags covered with a liberal helping of dust. The room had countless framed pictures on the walls and ornaments on virtually every flat surface. Small dark wooden occasional tables with turned legs housed more ornaments and a huge cast iron fireplace stood in the centre of one wall, surrounded by beautiful patterned tiles.

Aware that she was staring, possibly with her mouth hanging open, Teagan looked for the man, finding him next to a mustard-coloured upholstered chair with a woman sitting in it. Seeing this lady was of similar age to the man, Teagan knew she couldn't be the client either. Smartly dressed in a dark trouser suit, the woman's perfectly styled fair hair hung in a chin-length bob.

'This is the girl,' the man's voice boomed, his tone having lost none of the previous contempt. His eyes fixed on Teagan. 'I can't remember what you said your name was?'

Teagan forced a smile. 'Teagan Fraser. 'I'm from the Bellevue Agency and...'

'Hello Teagan,' the woman smiled. 'Please excuse my brother. He has a habit of making people feel about as welcome as leprosy.'

Teagan found herself returning the smile, relieved that at least, unlike the man, the woman didn't appear to hate her on sight. She risked another glance at the man, finding him scowling openly in the direction of his sister.

The woman motioned to a matching chair opposite her own. 'Come and take a seat.'

'She's not paid to sit down,' the man snapped.

The woman flapped her hand. 'Oh for God's sake, Robert. The girl has only just arrived and is probably wondering who on earth we are.'

Teagan tentatively sank into the chair, the springs having seen much better days. She tried not to think too much about how she would get up again without looking like a drowning beetle. 'Erm, I…'

'Let me explain,' the woman interrupted. 'I'm Helen Shepherd, Mrs Adams' daughter, and this is Robert Adams, my brother. Our mother is wh…'

'She doesn't need a live-in carer!' Robert barked.

Helen gave her brother a disparaging look, then turned her attention back to Teagan. 'As you can see my brother isn't happy about, well, shall we say, your engagement… No offence is meant… we realise you're only here at the request of the agency.'

Teagan's heart sank. She was getting the boot? *The shortest job in history.* 'Oh, I see… I…'

'Our mother had a lady, well, we've arranged several over the years that came in for a few hours on a daily basis,' Helen explained. 'You know, to do cooking, cleaning, that sort of thing and…'

'Not that you could tell,' Robert interrupted. 'The place is like a bloody junk shop!'

'Yes, well,' Helen frowned. 'But anyway… Mother recently took it upon herself to tell the people we organised that they were no longer required.' She glanced at Robert. 'We couldn't believe it actually, but anyway… We were lining something else up, only to be told two days ago that she had sorted it herself! She phoned the agency and… well, here you are…' She smiled sadly. 'She's not quite as she used to be… We think she may have dementia, but she won't go to the doctors even though she doesn't know what she's saying half the time, will she Robert?'

Robert remained silent, his angry expression fixed on the hearth.

'I know it sounds awful, what with her being our mother and everything, but she talks rubbish and sometimes it gets embarrassing,' Helen continued.

'You don't need to go into details, Helen!' Robert said, his voice curt.

Teagan smiled consolingly. 'Any form of dementia is difficult,' she said. 'Especially for the family.'

'Glad you're such an expert!' Robert snapped.

'Robert!' Helen cried. 'He doesn't mean to be rude, Teagan. It's just that your arrival has been very unexpected. We need to give serious thought about moving her to a proper care home before long.'

'So you keep saying.' Robert glared at his sister.

'What sort of things will I be expected to do?' Teagan asked, eager to diffuse the clash of opinions between the siblings where their mother was concerned.

'Are you not qualified?' Robert snapped, looking Teagan up and down. 'This is a bad enough situation without having someone who doesn't have a bloody clue!'

Teagan for once felt both insulted and incensed. 'I'm both qualified and experienced, Mr... Mr Adams. I've been doing this job for seven years.'

Raising his eyebrows questioningly, Robert made a harrumphing sound. 'You don't seem sure of what's expected.'

'To be honest, I received scant details from the agency. There was little instruction or specifications from Mrs Adams,' Teagan explained.

Helen sighed. 'As I said, I'm afraid our mother doesn't have much concept of reality.'

'I wish you'd stop talking about her as if she's a raving lunatic!' Robert glared at Helen. 'You don't need to keep shouting about it to all and sundry.'

'I'm just being upfront,' Helen said calmly, giving Teagan a sideways glance before handing her a business card. 'Feel free to call me with any questions or concerns.'

'Oh yes, how could anyone forget that our mother is completely mad when you constantly remind everyone?' Robert snapped.

Teagan cleared her throat uncomfortably. The man was so rude, it was embarrassing. She smiled at Helen and took the card. 'I probably haven't explained myself very well,' she said, keeping her voice light. 'I'm presuming the usual things will be required. Cooking, cleaning, laundry etcetera. Does Mrs Adams need any additional support, for instance getting washed, dressing, medicine - that sort of thing. I'm happy to undertake anything that is required.'

'Just her vitamins. They're the most important thing at the moment,' Helen said. 'At least we can keep her body as healthy as possible until we get a formal diagnosis about her mind.'

'As far as I'm concerned, you can clear all of *this* stuff out!' Robert snapped, waving his arm around the cluttered room. 'Most of the rooms are like this. Some are even *worse*. She's such a hoarder and…'

'I do *not* require that, thank you!' boomed a voice from the doorway. 'Whatever you're planning, fair children of mine, think again!'

Teagan stared as the owner of the loud commanding voice moved into the room. Small, almost bird-like, the woman looked far too tiny to own a voice like that.

Moving closer, the woman's beady, yet alert blue eyes focused on Teagan. 'Ah-ha! You must be my new girl.'

Teagan rose to her feet. 'Mrs Adams? Pleased to meet you, I'm…'

'Yes, Teagan. They told me. Don't take any notice of my children.' Laughing loudly, the older lady lowered herself onto a high-backed chair.

'Have you remembered to take your vitamins?' Helen smiled at her mother. 'I've bought you a new bottle and put it in the cupboard. You'd almost run out.'

Mrs Adams' beady eyes swivelled to her daughter. 'Yes, Helen, I've seen them. I'm not as incompetent as you believe! And yes, I have taken them, like I always do! Right, so now the girl has arrived, you two can push off and leave us be!'

Teagan swallowed her growing smile. She had no idea how this assignment would go, but from what she'd seen over the last few minutes, she already liked Dulcie Adams.

FOUR

TEAGAN TAPPED the text quickly into her phone:

    Am here. Crap signal. Miss you already xx

Teagan held her phone up searching for a network signal, but receiving nothing, she knelt on the window seat, wincing as the hard wood pressed into her knees.

Come on, send! She muttered, tilting her phone. She'd promised Joe she'd text as soon as she could, but it was proving easier said than done. Spotting a waver on the network bar, Teagan angled her phone a little more.

    Message sent...

Finally! Whether she'd receive a response was uncertain. Putting her phone down, Teagan leant against the wall, her back pressing against dated 1960s floral curtains and looked down into the garden below. From a rear-facing room on the top storey, she was afforded a decent view, although she couldn't see all of it as it was sectioned by borders of tall hedges and trees. A crazy-paved path ran higgledy-piggledy through well-stocked beds crammed full of different shrubs and bright flowers, bringing a cottage-garden feel to the overall look. Although overgrown, it had a magical feel to it.

Teagan smiled, not thinking she'd ever seen such a fascinating garden. Her mother's idea of gardening had been to pay some bloke a few quid to pour concrete over the small patch of grass of the rear of *their* house. *'Low maintenance',* she'd said.

Teagan scowled. She was here to look after Mrs Adams, not enjoy the garden. After Helen and Robert had left, Mrs Adams had briskly told her to take her things up to her room and then to come back downstairs in half an hour so they could 'talk'.

Teagan glanced at her watch. She still had fifteen minutes, but she'd better organise her things. Getting up, she walked over to the iron-framed single bed covered with a heavy damask bedspread and unzipped her wheeled case. Sitting on the bed, she winced as it sagged worryingly with a loud groaning of springs.

Taking out her neatly folded clothes, Teagan yanked open one of the stiff drawers on a small chest, smiling to see it lined with flowered paper and a stitched sachet of lavender sitting in the bottom. The high-ceilinged room was old-fashioned, but somehow comforting. Placing some of her clothes in the drawer, she hung more clothes in the wooden single wardrobe.

Jumping as her phone suddenly pinged, Teagan rushed to grab her mobile from the window seat.

Sounds nightmarish. Off out now. X

Feeling a small pang of envy, Teagan wondered where Joe was off to. Was he missing her as much as she was already missing him? Every time she wasn't with Joe there was very rarely more than a minute that passed without thoughts of him overtaking her mind.

Glancing at the clock again, she realised she didn't have the time to mull over the endless possibilities of what her boyfriend was doing. It was time to go and speak to Mrs Adams.

Taking a deep breath to calm her increasing nerves, Teagan glanced in the mirror, smoothed her hair down and left her new bedroom, shutting the door behind her.

. . . .

LENA TAYLOR stalked along the corridor of Feathers like she owned the joint. She flicked her blonde hair extensions over her shoulder flamboyantly, unable to help the smile that weaved across her face, resembling a cherry-red gash every time she thought about the massive possibilities which were now opening up to her.

Oh, she was clever. Very clever. Those snotty bunch of teachers in their stupid tweed suits complete with elbow patches; the ones who'd loved telling her on a regular basis that she'd never amount to anything. Well, they'd been wrong, hadn't they? *So fucking wrong.*

Half the people she'd ever come into contact with treated her like shit; all because of her name, but eleven years on, she had more collateral underneath one fingernail than the lot of them put together. She'd love to see their grumpy faces if they found out just how successful she had been in her mission to land on her feet.

And she was nearly there. *Almost.*

Her family were the same – well, they hadn't been; not until she'd decided to move to London several years ago. They believed she was purposefully going against what they wanted, thinking it completely unacceptable after what had happened. They believed she was insulting them. Insulting the family name.

But she wasn't. That was the furthest thing from her mind and they would soon realise that.

Lena couldn't say she wasn't upset when, after she'd gone ahead and stuck to her plans, her entire family had ostracised her and washed their hands of her, because she was. She was *deeply* upset.

But what they didn't realise was that she was doing it for them. And for herself, of course, but mainly for them. She could have told them why, she supposed, rather than in their eyes, betray them, but they'd have tried to stop her and she couldn't allow that.

Her eyes narrowed and her painted mouth curled into a sneer. Soon they'd all be grateful. Soon they'd understand why she'd left and once they knew she'd engineered an alliance that would have to be honoured they would welcome her back with open arms. When she pulled this off it would set both her and her family up for life based on reputation alone and then they'd be queuing up to fucking thank her.

And to top it all, she would have achieved vengeance for them in the best possible way.

Lena repositioned her Gucci bag on her forearm, making sure to have a quick glance in the reflection of a dressing room window as she passed, confirming she looked as damn gorgeous as ever. She'd always looked bloody cracking, otherwise she'd have never landed a job dancing at The Feathers in the first place, but thanks to Jonah kindly funding the procedures she'd requested, she now looked even better - if that were at all possible?

Lena unconsciously pushed her over-inflated cleavage out as she strutted along the corridor, making no effort to acknowledge a girl who had come out of a dressing room. *One of the girls she used to dance alongside.*

She sneered to herself. She didn't need to be friendly to them anymore. Besides, they were all far too busy falling over themselves keeping in her good books, thanks to her cleverly engineering an intimate involvement with Jonah to need to make the effort. As long as she could pull off the last segment of her mission, she'd have no worries ever again.

Lena grinned. In all truth, even though there had been an ulterior motive, it had been quite a bit of fun working here. There had been good banter with the other girls and apart from the odd bit of rivalry, they'd got on pretty well. She hadn't even minded donning nipple tassels on the stage and playing up for the punters. It wasn't much different to what she did for free on a regular basis anyway, so it was hardly a big deal. Of course, there had been the occasional perv, but those sorts were soon ejected. The club wasn't one of those seedy strip joints like most of the Soho places – this one was far too high-class to put up with tossers.

Lena's plumped up lips morphed into a sneer. High-class punters meant high-class tips. Still, she was done with all that lark. No need to be pleasant to any fucker. Not now she was officially Jonah Powell's missus. And soon – *very* soon, assuming things went to plan – and she would make damn sure they did, she would be Jonah Powell's *wife*.

Opening one of the dressing room doors, Lena was relieved to see it was empty. Fishing in her handbag she pulled out a half bottle of vodka and unscrewing the top, gulped from it greedily.

That was better. She needed something to take the edge off all this. She couldn't completely relax until her future was assured. *Shouldn't be long to wait now though.*

Lena inspected her over-painted brows in a mirrored compact case, then quickly cut a line of coke on the dressing room table, expertly snorting it through a rolled up fiver. Inhaling deeply, she savoured the burn at the back of her nostrils. Something else she'd have to hide from Jonah until this farce was done and dusted. And not a moment too soon. And now was the time to start putting the wheels in motion.

Lena scrolled through her contacts list on her mobile until she found the name she was looking for. Although things were not completely in place, it was time to make contact. It had been a long time – a very long time, but Uncle Ron was her best bet and the one who would most likely be able to offer her some insurance, should she need it.

Tapping out a text, she pressed the send button and leaning back in the leather swivel chair, smiled to herself.

• • • •

GWEN VELLA WATCHED LENA enter the dressing room and waited patiently for her to leave, but she hadn't.

Her forehead creased into a frown as she made her way down the corridor. Lena was a shit. She'd never liked the woman from the off - long before the tart had got her claws into Jonah. Lena had been a pain in the arse from day dot. There was something about her and Gwen had enough experience to know when a girl was trouble.

Gwen had run the girls at the Feathers for thirty-two years. Since 1973 in fact. She'd been a dancer herself back in the day, but with such a knack for organisation, Jacky Powell had spotted her potential and handed her the reins, meaning by the tender age of twenty-three she'd been managing both the girls *and* the show.

And she'd been doing it ever since.

Although when Jonah had taken over from his father she'd been worried for a short amount of time that she might be replaced, it would spoil their friendship or that he might be difficult to work with, but she'd had nothing to worry about. It would have been a different story had the reins gone to Saul, but blessings came in strange disguises and although it had been upsetting for Jacky when his eldest son got imprisoned, it was the best thing that could have happened, otherwise his beloved club and firm would be history by now.

Jonah, however, was a different kettle of fish. That boy was as loyal to his staff and the club as his father had been and Gwen respected him a lot, but she'd always had a different sort of relationship with him compared to the others.

She'd known him since he was a young boy. After the death of his wife, Carole, Jacky had regularly brought his young son to work with him. Not at night of course, but sometimes during the day when there were no punters around, Jonah was allowed to mess about on the stage or play hide and seek in the maze of corridors behind the scenes.

Gwen swallowed the lump forming in her throat. That business with Jacky losing his wife had been a horrible time.

Horrible. And the less she thought about that, the better.

All the dancing girls had loved mothering Jonah, but out of all of them, it was always *her* he'd come to when tumbling off the stage or thirsty.

Only a couple of years after that, the then adolescent Jonah developed more of an interest in watching the dancing girls and before she knew it, he was old enough to be brought into the firm for real. Despite him being one of the best and most vicious enforcers his father had, they'd always maintained their unlikely friendship.

Gwen smiled to herself. She would probably describe their relationship as a pseudo mother/big sister, but when push came to shove, Jonah was now her boss and she never overstepped the mark with her opinion – unless he outright asked her to.

She respected Jonah immensely, but she didn't respect Lena.

What he saw in the conceited jumped-up loudmouth, short of her over-inflated tits, was a mystery. But regardless of her personal opinion, she wouldn't put up with the scrawny bitch running amok over her girls just because she believed she now had the right to do so.

Gwen scowled. Girlfriend or not, Jonah wouldn't let anyone balls up the business, so now Lena had taken it upon herself to fire two of the dancers, leaving them all in the shit for tonight's show, she had no choice but to let him know the woman was making waves.

Peering through the small glass window of the dressing room door, Gwen watched Lena swigging from a vodka bottle then do a line of coke. Jonah wouldn't much like *that* either. Despite the firm dealing in cocaine, amongst other things, Gwen knew Jonah was one of the few who didn't partake personally in the white stuff. It was a hard and fast rule that *no one* on his payroll took gear under the company roof and she didn't expect his live-in tart to be exempt from that rule.

Gwen's hazel eyes fixed on Lena still swigging from the vodka whilst tapping out a message on her jewel-encrusted iPhone with those hideous talons of hers. Losing her patience, she pushed open the door, forcing Lena to hastily scoop her drug paraphernalia from the table into her oversized bag.

'Oh!' she exclaimed. 'I didn't realise you were in here, Lena! Are you looking for Jonah?' Gwen enjoyed the uncomfortable look on Lena's plastic face.

Lena stared at Gwen contemptuously. 'I don't think I have to explain that, but if you must know, I'm planning on surprising him.'

Gwen shook her head, her eyes cold. Lena was only *ever* here when she wanted to stir shit.

• • • •

TEAGAN MADE HER WAY carefully down the wide staircase, careful not to trip on the threadbare carpet runner. Keeping hold of the sticky banister, the thought flashed through her mind as to why none of the previous home helps hadn't done more to keep the place in, for want of a better word, *cleaner* or in a better state of repair. She shrugged. It was none of her business, but she'd make a start with some decent cleaning as one of the first things she undertook.

Reaching the bottom of the staircase, Teagan glanced down the hallway, realising she had no way of knowing where Mrs Adams may have gone and a flash of unease stirred.

Was the lady a danger to herself or have a habit of wandering off unannounced? She'd taken on a huge amount of responsibility being here 24/7 with no background knowledge of the situation. It was now *her* responsibility to look after the woman, ensuring no harm came to her, but how could she do that if she didn't know what she was up against? She'd have to get in contact with the daughter to get a proper low down on what her mother was like and find out exactly how severe her dementia was.

She pulled Helen's business card from her pocket:

Helen Shepherd BSB MNAEA

Shepherd, Percival and Proctor Estate Agents

Tel: 01628 673244
Email: hshepherd@sppestateagents.co.uk

She'd call first thing in the morning and see if they could have a quick chat.

'Mrs Adams?' Teagan called, shoving the business card back in her pocket. She stuck her head around the sitting room door, but to her dismay found it empty. 'Mrs Adams?' she called again, this time louder as she apprehensively made her way down the hallway, conscious that she felt to be trespassing. She'd previously noticed a lot of the rooms upstairs were closed; the doors tightly shut. She hadn't attempted to open any of them, even though she'd been tempted.

Detecting music, Teagan followed the sound. Moving through a door into another cluttered room, she continued through more double doors, the music getting louder and with relief, spotted Mrs Adams thumbing through records in a large case next to an old bulky stereo system.

She glanced around this room also jam-packed with knick knacks and photographs, trying to deduce what music was playing. She'd heard it before – a long time ago at her nan's house - some funny sounding stuff from the 50s or 60s. *Was it Fats Domino or something like that?*

'Mrs Adams?' Teagan shouted, hoping to be heard over the music.

The old lady swung around, surprisingly supple, her wide blue eyes holding an expression of hopeful anticipation and then on seeing Teagan, disappointment.

'Sorry,' Teagan said, seeing Mrs Adams' confused expression. 'I didn't mean to startle you. I…'

With a teeth curling screech, Mrs Adams scraped the needle from the record and the room fell into silence, leaving only the sound of birds drifting through the double doors from the garden.

'I said, I'm sorry to have startled you,' Teagan repeated. 'I didn't know where you were.' She could still see confusion in the older lady's eyes. 'You said to come back down in half an hour? I'm Teagan, you booked me fr...'

Mrs Adams flapped her hand dismissively. 'I know who you are, young lady. Despite what my children want you to believe, I'm not barking mad!' She beckoned Teagan over. 'I get caught up with the music, that's all. It transports me back into another world.' Her eyes tracked over to the window wistfully. 'A better world...'

'Lovely garden.' Teagan watched Mrs Adams shaking her head slightly, perhaps to dismiss the train of thought in her mind.

'Never mind that. Come and sit down.' Mrs Adams patted the seat next to the chair she lowered herself into. She gestured to a small table complete with a small lamp with hanging jewels dripping from its shade and jug of something with sliced lemons floating in it. 'I've made us some fresh lemonade. You can tell me all about yourself.'

Teagan made her way to the proffered chair. 'I'm sure I should be the one making the lemonade for you, Mrs Adams. You're paying me to come and I...'

'Nonsense!' Mrs Adams scoffed. 'I'm not derelict! Neither am I dead! I'm more than capable, so come!' Her eyes narrowed. 'And call me Dulcie. I *hate* being called Mrs Adams. It's the wrong name.'

Teagan frowned. 'The wrong name? I...'

Mrs Adams laughed, a tinkling musical sound. 'Oh, take no notice of me. It's an old joke. But *please*, I insist you call me Dulcie.'

Teagan picked up a glass. 'Ok, thank you, Mrs Ad... Dulcie.'

Dulcie nodded in approval. 'Much better!' she grinned. 'Now, tell me about yourself.'

'Me? Well, erm... I'm twenty five and erm... Oh, I don't know, there's not a lot to tell really...'

Dulcie frowned. 'Not a lot to tell? What a load of claptrap! A pretty young thing like you with nothing to say about your life? I doubt that! I like to know a bit about who is in my house.'

Teagan suddenly felt embarrassed as Mrs Adams scrutinised her with those sharp, all-seeing blue eyes.

'No young man on the scene? You young things have so much freedom.' She swept her arms around theatrically. 'The whole world to explore at the touch of a button! Hopping on planes; jetting off here, there and everywhere.'

Teagan stumbled over what to say. 'I… erm… I do have a boyfriend, his name's Joe Singleton.'

Dulcie's eyebrows raised high on her lined forehead and for the first time, Teagan noticed the eyebrows were pencilled on. 'Well, he's not a singleton anymore, is he? Not now he's got you. Handsome, is he?'

Teagan's eyes lit up. 'We're saving up to rent a flat. We've been together for three years and he's, well… he's *everything* to me.'

Dulcie raised her hands to her mouth in an extravagant gesture. 'Oh, you poor soul! Instead of being with your handsome beau, you're having to waste the best years of your life with only the company of old duffers like me!'

Teagan couldn't help but giggle. 'You're not an old duffer!'

Dulcie pulled a face. 'Oh, shut up! I am!' She raised a pencilled eyebrow. 'But I wasn't always so old...' Pushing herself out of the chair, she picked up one of the many photographs from the sideboard. Wiping dust from the edge of the frame, she glanced at the picture fondly, then passed it to Teagan. 'That's me!'

Teagan stared at the black and white photograph of a stunningly beautiful young woman wearing a sequinned leotard; one seamed stockinged shapely leg cocked behind the other, leaning side on against a gold-tipped cane. A small top hat perched jauntily and ringlets of blonde hair spilled out underneath whilst one eye stared inquisitively at the lens, the other forming a coquettish wink, framed by heavy false lashes.

The pencilled-on eyebrows were very much the same ones that the lady in front of her sported, although on the photo they were heavier and more defined.

'Wow! You look amazing!' Teagan exclaimed.

Dulcie grinned happily. 'Bit of a looker, wasn't I? And to think I was convinced I could be thinner or prettier or, I don't know... You mention it, I thought it! I wish I could have seen what age would do to me because I'd have shut up bloody moaning and been grateful!'

Teagan laughed, liking Dulcie Adams more and more by the minute. 'You look like a film star. When was it taken?'

Dulcie reached for the photo and studied it again. 'With that costume it must have been the Pegasus show at The Feathers, so 1962 or thereabouts. Possibly the start of 1963. It wasn't long after I'd had Helen, my daughter.'

Teagan faltered. She'd noticed a lot of the photos and paraphernalia, especially in this room, centred around showbiz. *Had Dulcie Adams been some kind of celebrity? How could she ask without being nosy?*

'The Feathers? Was that... Was that a theatre or...'

'A club,' Dulcie said. 'Or rather it *was*. I presume it's no longer there. It...'

Teagan blinked as Dulcie's voice trailed off, her expression wistful once again. 'So you were an actress?'

Snapping back to the here and now, Dulcie laughed. 'No! Well, sort of... The Feathers is, *was* a club in Soho. I used to dance... Cabaret... Sing a bit... Other stuff. Lots of things... There were lots of people in the clubs in those days. Famous musicians, celebrities, gangsters...' she continued, her gaze fixed through the double doors into the greenery of the garden.

'Wow! How exciting!' Teagan cried. 'Was that where you met your husband?'

Dulcie slapped the picture face down. 'Enough of that, I think. Drink your lemonade and let's get on to what I expect during your time here, shall we?'

FIVE

MIKE POINTER SLAMMED his mouse on the desk, his face reddening with rage. He was past all this crap. Far too bloody old to learn new tricks.

Not the most patient man, he had little time for things that wasted his time. It had taken him years to get to grips with putting together an email for God's sake, and as for sending them, that had taken even longer to get his head around.

He'd never fully understood or accepted this computer malarkey. In the early 90s when computers started becoming all the rage, he'd steered well clear. Paper was just fine, thank you. Everyone had managed perfectly well for hundreds of years without needing an oversized lump of whirring plastic to do anything, so he'd never understood how it could ever have become so popular. But it hadn't just become popular, it had overtaken the bloody world.

He seethed silently. These days there was little that could be achieved unless it was done via computer; shopping, paying bills, booking appointments. *Blah, blah, blah.*

He was surprised the human race wasn't extinct. And this social media garbage was even worse! People sitting in the same room with no one talking because they were all stuck in their own virtual worlds. Absolutely ridiculous, that's what it was. And it was even more ridiculous because he didn't understand it. And for once in his life, he needed to. He hated feeling incompetent, but that's exactly how he felt. And that feeling didn't sit well. *Ever.* His mother had done a good enough job of making him feeling inferior for pretty much as long as he could remember, so he didn't need anything or anyone else doing that.

Guilt prickled. Almost at the end after a heart attack and then a bout of pneumonia, he knew it wouldn't be long now for his mother. He'd visited her in hospital a few times – of course he had, but she still had the ability to make him feel utterly worthless.

Knowing that he would feel a lot better once she'd shuffled off this mortal coil, even without the apology he'd waited so long for, only intensified his guilt. But then she'd *always* made him feel guilty.

Mike's eyes tracked back to the computer sitting on his desk like a gargoyle. Everything had been so much simpler when it had just been a case of putting adverts in Auto Trader, the local papers or every so often, a nice glossy double page in one of the top end motor magazines.

He'd had some cracking sales from those, but by God, they'd cost a bloody fortune! However, the well-off fell over themselves getting their hands on some of the motors he supplied and he was never unhappy to relieve them of their cash and cash was what he was short of right now.

Mike glanced around his large office decked out in fashionable contemporary furniture with the predictable potted plants for 'ambience'. That's what the interior designer had said as part of her over-priced upgrade to the overall look and feel of his showroom. He looked through the huge glass window spanning the width of his office out into the cavernous area of the showroom beyond and just had to hope that forking out for this place paid off because until it did, he was lumbered with another big debt to juggle.

Mike pushed his finger into the neck of his collar, loosening it a little. This money situation was getting to him. He'd been doing ok – not brilliantly, but ok. But the sinking realisation that the gamble he'd taken by taking on this new showroom had placed him well and truly out of his depth and he was sinking faster than he cared to admit. But he had to face facts – if something didn't change, like a *big* something, he was fucked hence why it was vital to keep up with the times. And that meant *computers*.

He glared at the black screen, unwilling to nudge the mouse because that would mean the computer coming to life and taunting him.

Mike glanced back into the showroom to see Heath turning on the charm with a middle-aged lady eyeing a top of the range BMW. As well as being good with the punters, his son was a dab hand at computers. Good job, otherwise his adverts would still be confined to the defunct paper editions. But did he really want to relay to his son what a mess the business was really in?

He hadn't even told Tammy, for Christ's sake. His wife knew he'd been landed with a hefty tax bill back in April, but she didn't know about the other mass of debts he'd accrued whilst attempting to up his game.

Mike raked his fingers through his hair, ignoring the sweat building at the base of his neck. Tammy was a good woman; she'd stuck with him from the start. She'd *believed* in him and he wanted to give her the life and house she deserved, but now it looked like he would even fail to keep the poxy house which he *had* managed to provide.

Mike stared at the gilt-framed clock on the wall. Only another hour until close. Snatching up his mobile, he resisted the usual urge to smash it to smithereens every time it told him his screen passcode was wrong. Something else he hated. Mobile phones... His passcode wasn't bloody incorrect. He knew what it was, thank you. His fingers were just too big for the piddly little thing to cope with.

Stabbing his finger on the phone screen, it finally unlocked and he clumsily tapped out a text:

```
Hi Tams, gong for drink with heave after wank.
Put dinnr in oven. Wont be be b late. M
```

Scowling at the half-illiterate message, Mike pressed send. Thanks to the super-helpful predictive text, or whatever they called it, it would take longer to correct the damn thing. Tammy would know what he meant. *Probably.*

Almost jumping out of his skin as his mobile started ringing, Mike tried to remember what he needed to press to answer the call.

'Hello?' he barked, expecting it to be yet another double glazing salesman.

Bloody mobiles gave everyone the ability to stalk him 24/7. No escape. Being tracked by Google and GPS and mobile mast locations. Beeping all the time and never any peace. He rued the day he'd ever bought one, but again, to keep in the game, what choice did he have?

It didn't mean he had to *like* them though, did it?

'Yes, this is Michael Pointer,' he said. 'Right... ok...' His heart began to race. 'Should I come now? Ok... Thank you.'

Ending the call, Mike stared at the black screen before shoving the phone deep into his pocket. So, there it was - the call he'd been half-expecting to come any day, just had. But what he *hadn't* expected when the hospital rang, telling him it was time to say goodbye to his mother, was that she had specifically asked to talk to him.

• • • •

JONAH SMILED AT LENA as they ate dinner. She'd barely said two words all evening - not that this was particularly unusual. There wasn't much about her, short of looking damn gorgeous, but there were worse things in life after all.

She may not be the most well-educated or well-mannered woman, but that wasn't an issue. In all honesty, she was as common as muck, but she had a cracking figure and was great between the sheets, but lately she'd started to take liberties.

Some fellas' missuses and wives nagged like harridans. Some blokes on his payroll; blokes who grown men were terrified to argue with or put a foot wrong around, their wives ruled them with a rod of iron. But he hadn't had that problem with Lena. *Until recently.*

Jonah shovelled another forkful of chicken into his mouth, happy for the silence and watched Lena push her food around her plate as if the extra effort of using cutlery properly would damage her nail extensions. The nail extensions *he* paid for. And not just *any* old nail extensions – oh no – nail extensions from the top of the range beauticians in Liberty's. No cheap shit for Lena.

It was also a bit like her hair extensions, lip-plumping injections and botox – even though she was only twenty-seven. Oh yes, and the countless amounts of designer clothes which rivalled the fucking ladieswear floor at Harrods.

But that was ok – that wasn't the problem.

She was his bird – one of many – nothing serious. An easy, familiar and no hassle lay. He'd happily treat her to whatever she wanted – that was part and parcel of how a woman should be treated. And being as she was the one he was seen with most regularly, he didn't want her looking less than her best, did he? That wouldn't do anything for his reputation. Anyway, it wasn't like he had any intention of marrying the girl.

He wouldn't pretend he didn't enjoy bedding her, along with many others, as an added bonus of inheriting the club in Soho as part of his father's empire. He'd never disguised loving that added perk of his prominent position within the firm, but she had begun to be a bit of a pain in the arse where the club was concerned. No one had actually come out and said anything to him about it, but he'd heard the whispers and he'd have been blind and deaf not to have picked up on the atmosphere anytime she was around. And *that* was the problem.

Jonah slugged the beer straight from the bottle.

Admittedly, he'd been so wrapped up with the club and firm he hadn't even noticed half the things Lena had been doing - like moving herself into his house six months ago. She used to stay over on a regular basis, but then she was there permanently. Most of the time it was good having the sex on tap, but he didn't like how she'd started encroaching on all aspects of his life. Now she was getting people's backs up at the club wasn't a good sign and one which he'd have to keep a very close eye on.

'Grab us another beer will you, babe?' Jonah said, winking at Lena, watching her immediately get up and move towards the fridge. He needed a good few beers to take his mind off all the latest goings on.

This business with Dulcie Adams was playing on his mind something chronic and Saul's attitude today to what should be done about it hadn't helped.

During his visit earlier, his brother had made it very clear that he expected Dulcie Adams to be taken out and the firm's property returned immediately. No ifs or buts. But Jonah didn't work like that. For a start, Dulcie was a woman and he didn't condone that sort of shit being laid on a female. He wanted *answers*.

Sure, he wanted the diamonds back and would get them, but he also, and probably more importantly, wanted to know what had possessed her to help rip off the man who had made her career.

Jonah knew all about Dulcie Adams' popularity at the club in the 60s – she was a Soho sensation, thanks to The Feathers and then, at the height of her heyday, she'd decided to leave – citing her husband's unfortunate death as the reason. But it *wasn't* the reason was it? Dulcie Adams had known what her lover, Pointer, was planning and Jonah wanted the woman to know just how much her actions had hurt.

Jonah knew Saul wouldn't understand his take on this, he never had. Jonah had no problem meting out violence, under the right circumstances, and sometimes not. Plus, he was extremely good at it. His ability had helped the firm remain in the position it was, but other things were important too.

He frowned. Saul was pure violence – always had been. The man had no 'on/off' switch, but he wasn't here and he could ladle on as much shit as he wanted, but Jonah was doing things *his* way. *He* ran the firm, not Saul.

He looked up as Lena sashayed back across the room his eyes fixed on her pert backside encased in skin-tight jeans.

'Can we get some extra help around the house, Jonah,' Lena said, widening her heavily made up eyes. 'I just don't have the time to get the food preparation done these days, I seem to be constantly exhausted.'

Jonah bit back his retort. *It wasn't like she was rushed off her bloody feet.* 'What are you thinking of?'

'Oh, I don't know… Perhaps a cook? Someone to prepare the meals? Only part time though.' Lena batted her false lashes. 'We don't want someone else here all the time now do we?'

Jonah took another swig of his beer, rather than laugh in Lena's face. *Cook the dinner?* All she'd done was turn the fucking oven on. Was even that too difficult? She certainly hadn't prepared anything because the food they were eating now was courtesy of Marks and Spencer's pre-prepared meals range. He knew this because it was listed on his credit card - one of the many she maxed out on a regular basis. But he wouldn't lose his temper. Women should have what they wanted. That's what his father always said. *Treat your women like gold, Jonah.*

But Lena was demanding and it was starting to grate on his tits. 'I'll think about it, ok?'

Lena smiled, exposing her brilliant white veneers. 'Thanks, babe.'

She placed Jonah's fresh bottle of beer down onto the table and wrapped her arms around his thick neck from behind. When her fingers traced down his chest, he felt his groin twitch in anticipation.

'What's this?' Lena's hand rested on the papers in the chest pocket of Jonah's shirt.

'What's what?' Jonah mumbled, pushing his chair back and pulling Lena onto his lap.

Lena's lips trailed across Jonah's earlobe. 'That wodge of paper in your pocket.'

'Never you mind...' Jonah undid the button of Lena's jeans, his mind only intent on sating his growing arousal.

Lena pulled away, arching her eyebrows. 'It had better not be something to do with another woman!'

Jonah tensed, irritation flashing. 'If you must know, it's a list of things I need to do,' he lied. 'Not that it's any of your fucking business!' He wasn't discussing the notes Nero had given him about Helen Shepherd with Lena. He wouldn't discuss *anything* about the Dulcie Adams business with her.

And since when had she been bothered about other women? Jonah felt a growl forming at the back of his throat. Maybe it was time to seriously rethink the situation where Lena was concerned. He would not take any hassle from a woman.

'Sorry, babe,' Lena purred, readjusting herself in Jonah's lap. 'I think I must be a bit hormonal today.'

As Lena straddled him, wiggling slightly, despite his annoyance, Jonah felt himself spring back into action. And when she set about slowly undoing the buttons of his shirt, followed by unzipping his trousers, he offered no resistance.

Standing up and lifting Lena with him, Jonah deposited her on the dining table. Unceremoniously pulling her jeans clean off the ends of her legs, he wrapped his hand in her thick hair extensions. Tugging her head back, his teeth nipped at her throat as he pushed into her with pent up frustration.

Six

THE REMAINDER OF THE DAY passed surprisingly quickly and without event. Teagan had made good inroads with a thorough clean of the kitchen whilst preparing the dinner. It had taken longer than expected because she'd wasted nearly an hour locating where everything was in the large kitchen, pantry and scullery, but having now reorganised everything in sensible locations, it would prove a lot easier from now on.

Dulcie had insisted they ate dinner together and so they'd engaged in some general chit chat - nothing more about the old days, which Teagan admitted she'd hoped Dulcie would return to, but she hadn't dared bring up the subject, what with the earlier reaction over the husband.

She realised her question may have been horribly insensitive. What if the husband had only recently died? What she'd said could have opened the wound. It may also explain Robert's attitude if he'd recently lost his father.

Having now finished the washing up, Teagan decided to ask if there was anything Dulcie wanted. She was unsure what the etiquette was as she'd never had a live-in job before. Was she expected to keep Dulcie company in the evenings?

Making her way to the sitting room, Teagan heard the music

again, the record player loud and found Dulcie staring out of the window into the darkness of the evening singing along to the music. Even with age her voice was beautiful and Teagan stood transfixed, unable to drag herself away from the melody and Dulcie's voice. For a moment she envisaged the woman on stage in her heyday, dressed in the outfit from the photograph surrounded by a rapt audience.

She cautiously stepped from the doorway into the room and as the record drew to a close, the only sound was the clicking of the stylus as it stuck at the end of the now silent record.

Teagan was about to speak but without turning away from the window Dulcie beat her to it. 'I love that song.'

Teagan moved closer. 'You have a beautiful voice.'

Turning around, Dulcie smiled. 'Thank you, my dear. It's a bit crackly these days.'

'Is there anything I can get you? Anything you need?'

Dulcie shuffled to a seat, picking up a strand of beads from the table. Sitting down, she let the beads fall through her fingers from one hand to the other. 'You don't have to babysit me.'

'I… I guess I'm not sure what's expected.' Teagan looked down at her hands uncomfortably. 'I've only previously done day care.'

Dulcie smiled, her blue eyes twinkling. 'I'm well aware of that. I asked that woman – whatever she's called, at your agency for someone who *hadn't* done live-in work. That was my one and only demand.'

Teagan smiled, imagining Sheila's horror to be referred to as a 'whatever she's called'. 'I can assure you I've had plenty of experience wi…'

'Yes, I know. I spoke to some of the other oldies you've looked after,' Dulcie grinned. 'You'll be pleased to learn they all spoke highly of you.' A knowing smile spread across Dulcie's face. 'If you're wondering why I don't want anyone with previous live-in experience, then I'll tell you.' She leaned forward conspiringly. 'It's because they're set in their bloody ways, that's why. They'd make me go to bed at 8 o'clock and drink hot chocolate.'

Getting up, Dulcie pulled down the front of a tall cabinet, exposing an array of different bottles. 'And I don't like hot chocolate!' Looking over her shoulder, she grinned and raised a painted eyebrow. 'But I *do* like gin!' Holding up a bottle of Gordons, Dulcie laughed. 'Lighten up, young lady! You're too young to be so old. Care to join me?'

Teagan moved towards the drinks cabinet. 'Only if you let *me* pour whilst you sit down?'

'Done!' Dulcie winked.

Pouring two measures of gin and topping the drinks up with a generous helping of tonic water, Teagan couldn't help but think Helen and Robert would not be impressed if they discovered she was encouraging their mother to drink, but this lady fascinated her. She hadn't been here a day, yet was already enthralled by Dulcie Adams. There was something about her; so full of life and aside from the couple of times that she'd drifted off into some kind of trance, she didn't seem to be suffering from dementia. But she could hardly have an opinion of the woman's mental state after a matter of hours? Neither was she in any way medically qualified, so it was best not to draw any conclusions.

Taking the drinks to the table, Teagan found Dulcie lighting a long, thin cigarette.

'Another thing my children disapprove of. But this is *my* house, so I'll do what I like!' Dulcie quipped. 'They're only menthol and besides, if they were going to kill me, they'd have done so by now!'

'Have you taken your vitamins? Helen asked me to remind you,' Teagan said.

Dulcie rolled her eyes. 'Bloody vitamins! Helen's obsessed with them. Of course I have! I'd only get moaned at otherwise!' She took the tall glass from Teagan's hand. 'Now, getting back to why you came in looking for me in the first place.'

Teagan sipped at her drink. 'Ok, so do you prefer being left on your own of an evening or would you like me to keep you company? Also, tomorrow I thought I'd make a start cleaning things up? Robert said th...'

'Take absolutely *no* notice of what Robert said,' Dulcie snapped, her eyes bright. 'That boy believes anything Helen says. I want nothing cleared or 'tidied'. Do you understand? If you've come here to box my life up and throw it away then you can pack your bags right now, young lady.'

Teagan blinked, taken aback and fought to remain collected. 'I...'

'Look,' Dulcie continued, her eyes softening. 'I just need you to understand something very important. It's a huge gamble, but I've got to give you a try. There's something about you... something I can see...'

She pointed to her own eyes, a pink-nailed bony finger tapping precariously closely to her eyeball. 'I get the feeling that you're alright.' She slowly put her glass down on the table. 'My instincts are telling me that I like you and I hope I'm not wrong.'

Teagan swallowed a large gulp of gin. She didn't for one minute know where this was going or why.

Dulcie picked up her glass again, sipped from it and blew a ring of minty-scented smoke towards the ceiling. 'I hired you because I need someone on my side.'

Teagan frowned. 'Your *side*?'

'They won't admit it, but I know my children are trying to get me shipped out of here,' Dulcie frowned. 'Helen especially. She's slowly convincing everyone that I'm crazy.' She raised an eyebrow, her piercing eyes drilling into Teagan's. 'I bet she's already said something to you along those lines, has she not?'

Teagan shuffled uncomfortably. 'Well, I... er...'

'Just as I thought,' Dulcie sighed. 'It's always the same. She won't be happy until I get carted off. She's even convinced Robert and that is worrying, considering he's very much like his father.'

Teagan frowned. From what she'd deduced so far, Helen was the rational one; the caring one – unlike Robert.

Dulcie stared into the empty hearth. 'Don't let *anyone* fool you with this rubbish about me being madder than a box of frogs.'

Teagan nodded, her teeth playing with the inside of her cheek. She liked this lady and wanted to make her happy, but on the flip side, it was her job to make sure she was safe and well looked after, wasn't it?

Although Dulcie had seemed very much clear headed, now Teagan was beginning to wonder because this was the first time that what Helen had said rang true.

• • • •

TEAGAN LAY IN BED WIDE AWAKE. It was impossible to sleep. Ages she'd been lying here and was no closer to dropping off than she had been in the first place.

As well as the strange conversation this evening, being in a different house wasn't helping. A big, old echoey house with its unique set of noises; every pipe clank, floorboard creak or crack as the receding heat of the day caused the wood to contract; every shuffle from above from nesting birds or squirrels in the eaves, played on her mind.

She'd get used to it she didn't doubt, but tonight – this first night under this big old roof was playing havoc with her ability to switch off.

Teagan glanced at the small travel clock she'd brought with her. 2 am. *Would Joe still be up?*

Throwing back the heavy bedspread, Teagan grabbed her phone from the bedside table and moved to the window seat where she'd previously managed to get a signal of sorts. Opening her text messages she was disappointed to see nothing from Joe.

Oh well, she'd text and if he was up, she'd give him a call.

Are you still up? Can I call? Love you xx

Pressing send, Teagan waited to see if Joe would reply and

willed the shaky one bar on the network indicator to hold, but several minutes later, with still no reply, she sighed. Joe must be asleep, out or otherwise engaged.

Pushing away the slight hurt that he hadn't texted her to say goodnight, Teagan reminded herself that she'd promised not to allow festering incriminations to form. She was doing this so they could be together. It was what they both wanted.

A sudden crash from downstairs shook Teagan from her thoughts. *What the hell was that?* That certainly wasn't like any other noise she'd heard so far. Holding her breath, she listened intently to see if it happened again.

Nothing. Just silence.

What if Dulcie had got up to use the toilet and fallen? Or what if there was an intruder?

Heart beating frantically, Teagan jumped up from the window seat and pulled her dressing-gown over her pyjamas. She'd have to go and look. She couldn't ignore that crash.

Opening her bedroom door, she peered cautiously down the landing of the top storey into the darkness. Feeling around for the light switch, she was glad when the creepy, seemingly endless corridor became illuminated. *Get a grip of yourself, girl*, she thought, padding along the landing to the staircase.

Dulcie's bedroom was on the first floor, so she'd got another staircase to go down yet.

Reaching the bottom of the staircase, unable to find a light switch, she fumbled along that landing. As she neared the end of the corridor, she saw an open door which had been closed when she'd come to bed. Fear prickled. She stopped and listened, hearing nothing, but could see a faint illumination from inside the room. 'Dulcie?' Teagan said, her voice barely more than a whisper. 'Mrs Adams?'

Teagan inched forward, peering around the edge of the doorway and adjusted her eyes to the dim light within the huge bedroom. Her focus was directed to the small figure by the large bay window looking through the open curtains.

'Dulcie?' Teagan said softly, unwilling to make the old lady jump. Getting no response, she stepped into the room. 'Mrs Adams?'

Turning around suddenly, Dulcie stared at Teagan, her eyes unfocused. 'I am *not* Mrs Adams!'

Taken aback, Teagan faltered. 'Are you alright? I heard a crash... I...'

'How did you get into my house?' Dulcie cried. 'Get out! Do you hear me?' She picked up a shoe; an old shoe with a high kitten heel and a strap across the front and raised it.

Teagan froze. 'I'm Teagan. I'm from the agency you...'

'Where is he?' Dulcie yelled.

Teagan inched closer. 'Dulcie, you ne...'

'I said, where is he?' Dulcie screamed, her eyes wide. 'He promised me! Why are you in my house?'

For the first time, Teagan felt unnerved. Was Dulcie sleepwalking or dreaming? 'I heard a crash. I wanted to make sure you were ok.'

Dulcie's whole countenance, along with her aggressive posturing slumped like the wind had fallen from her sails. She peered at Teagan. 'Oh God...' She glanced across the other side of the room. 'The cabinet. It fell... I...'

Teagan followed Dulcie's gaze, spotting a tall, thin cabinet lying face down on the polished floorboards. 'This cabinet didn't land on you, did it?'

Dulcie shook her head. 'I was trying to move the rug. It just... it just toppled...'

Slowly approaching, Teagan dared to reach out. 'Don't worry, I'll sort this out tomorrow. As long as you're not hurt.' Having made contact with Dulcie's bony arm, she steered her towards a chair in front of the large dressing table. 'Come and sit down here for a moment an...'

'Get off that!' Dulcie screeched. 'That's *his* chair. That's where he puts his things.'

Teagan quickly dropped her arm and kept her voice calm and neutral. 'Let's get you back to bed.'

'I *am* in my bedroom, you silly girl! Can't you see?' Dulcie waved her arms around the room. 'Where are my cigarettes? I want a cigarette.'

Teagan risked taking hold of Dulcie's arm once more. She had to get her back to bed. Although this was a beautiful room, this was not the one Dulcie used. 'Let's get you out of here and I'll fetch your cigarettes.'

Dulcie resisted for a few seconds before being steered out of the room. She stared up at Teagan pleadingly. 'If he comes back whilst I'm gone, you'll tell him where to find me, won't you? He won't know where to look if I'm not in here.'

Teagan smiled convincingly, although she felt anything but. 'Of course. Now, let's go and find your cigarettes.'

'Can you get me some more tomorrow?'

'Absolutely.' She'd get Dulcie back to her room and stay while she smoked a cigarette. There was no way she could leave in case she burnt the place down. Hopefully then she'd go back to sleep.

Whatever happened, she now knew she had no choice but to get into contact with Helen.

SEVEN

'THAT'S A GOOD IDEA. I'LL SEE YOU THERE AT 10.'
Teagan ended the call, glad Helen had suggested to meet at the
newsagents down the end of the road, rather than at the house.

Teagan still felt like she was going behind Dulcie's back,
but she desperately needed some background information, but
wanted to get it without Dulcie feeling she was betraying her
confidence.

Teagan glanced at the clock. She'd better get moving – it
was almost 8. Opening her text messages her finger hovered
over the 'Compose text' button and, despite her misgivings,
gave into the urge to text Joe again.

```
Morning gorgeous xx Miss you xx
```

Finding she'd got the knack of holding the phone at just the
angle needed to squeeze enough network signal, the text to Joe
sent without delay. Leaving the phone on the windowsill, she
hurried downstairs to prepare Dulcie's breakfast.

'Good morning,' Dulcie said brightly as Teagan walked
into the sitting room.

'Oh!' Teagan exclaimed, looking at Dulcie; dressed, hair

coiffed and full make-up - her lack of sleep hadn't seemed to have affected her at all. 'I didn't expect you to be up. I'm so sorry. I'll make sure I get up earlier tomorrow, I...'

'No need,' Dulcie smiled. 'I've made a pot of tea. Come and sit down.'

Teagan poured herself a cup of tea from the beautifully hand-painted teapot, then sat down. She should be the one to do all of this.

'It took me a while to find where you'd put the tea tin,' Dulcie said, an eyebrow arched.

'I'm sorry. I should have checked with you before I moved the kitchen around.'

'Don't apologise,' Dulcie said. 'The last woman – ghastly she was, moved things to the most illogical places. I'm sure she did it on purpose! Did you sleep well?'

Teagan paused. Did Dulcie not remember what had happened last night? If she had no recollection, she must have been sleepwalking. Should she say something?

No. At least not yet. She didn't want to embarrass the poor woman. 'Erm, yes... fine...'

Dulcie nodded approvingly. 'Good, that's good... So, when will I meet this young man of yours?'

'Joe?' Teagan said, surprised. 'Oh, I don't know... I...' Her face fell slightly as the knowledge that he hadn't contacted her pushed sharply into her mind.

'Why don't you invite him round one afternoon?' Dulcie said, frowning at the expression on Teagan's face. 'Whatever's the matter?'

Teagan shrugged. 'Oh, it's just... I texted him yesterday and... and he didn't get back to me. I...'

'Don't let that worry you, my dear. He's probably beside himself imagining being without you for the next six months,' Dulcie laughed.

Teagan smiled weakly, guilt forming that she had no intention of remaining here for anywhere near that length of time.

'Hasn't he asked to marry you yet? Is that it?' Dulcie cried. 'Pah, that means nothing. If you love him, then you'll wait. Wait for as long as it takes...' Her voice drifted off and her gaze reverted to staring through the large double doors into the garden. The silence weighed heavily as her fingers played with her cigarette packet.

'I'll go and get some more cigarettes for you in a little while,' Teagan said breezily in an attempt to bring the lady out of the trance-like state she'd drifted back off into.

Dulcie's attention returned. 'My cigarettes? Oh, how good of you to notice I'm running low.'

Teagan moved to clear the china away. If Dulcie had forgotten she'd asked her to get more cigarettes, then she really didn't have any memory of last night.

· · · ·

JONAH NODDED TO JIM as he opened the wide entrance door to the club, moving his massive frame to one side. Despite his increasing foul mood and the remnants of a particularly bad hangover, Jonah wanted to retain his reputation of being respectful to his hard-working staff.

As he proceeded through the foyer, his black shoes sinking into the deep pile burgundy carpet, Jonah glanced at the large gold plume of feathers emblem on the wall behind the reception desk, pleased to see it gleamed impressively under the illumination of the heavy chandeliers suspended by thick gold chains from the high ceiling.

He liked to ensure the club gave off the impression he wanted – high class. And it did. Maintaining that would ensure the high-paying clientele would keep returning and the waiting list for VIP membership remained at an all-time high.

Things were ticking over very nicely in this part of the business as well as most of the other parts of the firm. Jonah knew he had a good, trusted and reliable staff – many of whom he'd inherited or previously worked alongside. Others had been drafted in at his request. All in all, things couldn't be going any better. The Feathers reputation for being one of the best, if not *the* best club in Soho, had stood for many years – all through the period his father had run it and he was pleased that he had maintained the excellent standards.

Although Soho was widely known for its Gentlemen's clubs, The Feathers offered a lot more than that. Admittedly, the shows were risqué, but more burlesque cabaret, rather than a classic strip show and with The Feathers sumptuous and lavish surroundings and rich and powerful clientele, it attracted a mix of both male and female customers – the place to be for anyone who was *anyone*.

Yes, everything was going well. Apart from Saul insisting Jonah take the heavy handed approach. That and what was going on at home right now.

Jonah's handsome face hardened as he clenched his jaw in irritation, thinking of Lena. What Gwen had told him this morning had irritated him profusely and something he would have to do something about.

Jonah had inherited Gwen from his father's days of running The Feathers. His father had always very much trusted Gwen's judgement and left her to take charge of the girls and run the shows in the way she saw fit. She'd always done a great job and so there had been no reason whatsoever why he should have altered that when he'd taken the reins.

His father's judgment, as always, had proved right. Gwen would have been his choice for the position anyway.

In fact, there was more to it than that.

After his mother's death, Gwen had been the one out of everyone who had helped him the most and he would never forget that. As a scared and lost young lad, she'd been the one who'd given him the time and the confidence – making him realise that he could go to her with anything. She was a little diamond and he trusted her implicitly and so when she'd taken him to one side, awkwardly voicing her concerns about how Lena had taken it upon herself to elbow her way into what had been meticulously arranged, he wasn't pleased. Even worse was learning Lena had gone even further and sacked two of the girls.

Lena had overstepped the mark. Her leaving the stage show was something he'd agreed with at the time. She'd been right when she'd said it wasn't fitting, being as now she belonged to him. That was one thing, but nowhere had he given her the right to swan in and order the girls about, changing their dance slots or who they staged with. He would not put up with her coming in here and pissing off the rest of the girls and certainly not upsetting Gwen.

Jonah clenched his teeth, surprised they hadn't worn down to stumps the way he'd been grinding them lately. He may not be able to change some things, but he could sort *this*.

As much as he didn't like to admit it, he'd been slack where Lena was concerned. As well as her ever increasing demands, she'd even started changing things around in his house. He'd been so wrapped up with putting his all into the firm he'd ignored all of the warning signs where she was concerned and he shouldn't have done.

Pushing open the door from the foyer into the staff only corridor, Jonah winked at one of his showgirls scuttling down the corridor to one of the many dressing rooms.

The blonde dressed in a skimpy leotard and sky-high stilettoes beamed at him. 'Hello Mr Powell,' she said, her face tilting up coquettishly, before hurrying off.

Despite his mood, Jonah grinned, his handsome face relaxing. He couldn't remember that girl's name, she'd be an ideal candidate to take his mind off what was weighing heavily.

Bursting into his office, he walked to his desk and sat down heavily in his chair. Glancing at his Rolex, he waited for Nero and Keith to arrive so he could instruct them with what he wanted to happen next regarding Dulcie Adams.

Unlike the problems Lena was bringing to the table, locating Dulcie Adams would bring long awaited benefits, including the end to an issue that had haunted him, his family and their firm for far too long.

EIGHT

HELEN DIDN'T HAVE MUCH TIME TO SPARE before
meeting her next client and couldn't afford to be late, so drove
rapidly towards where she'd arranged to meet Teagan. The
prospect of being pleasant to the pointless girl was irritating
beyond belief, but it would pay to keep her on side. She didn't
want to go to Footlights and discuss her mother where there was
a possibility of her being within hearing distance. She did not
want to give any reason, however small, for suspicion.

Overtaking a car crawling along at a leisurely rate, her brain
fizzed with irritation. James had been on at her again this
morning; pressing for her to take a few days off to sort medical
tests out for her mother.

Helen scowled. Her mother didn't need medical tests – she
just needed to be removed as far away as possible as quickly as
possible. But she could hardly expect James to understand that.
As far as he was concerned, she was being 'uncharitable' over
her mother's diminishing mental health.

If that's the way James saw it, then that was absolutely fine.
He didn't have a clue.

Helen gnawed at her lip, mindful that she mustn't get
lipstick on her teeth.

As for Robert - he was another problem. There had always been something amiss where she, Robert and their mother were concerned, but she'd never been able to put her finger on it. He'd always been her mother's favourite and she'd always felt she'd been treated slightly differently to him.

Rounding the corner and spotting Teagan nearing the shop, Helen drew her sleek silver Mercedes up to the kerb alongside. Lowering the tinted passenger window, she leant across and beckoned towards the empty passenger seat.

Teagan opened the door, hit with the smell of leather combined with freshly valeted car and clambered into the sumptuous seat. Helen stepped on the accelerator and continued down the road without saying another word.

'Thanks for making the time to meet me,' Teagan spluttered, eyeing Helen's navy blue tailored suit and her immaculately styled hair. 'I don't want to be a nuisance.'

Helen turned to Teagan. *Yes, she was a bloody nuisance, but she must remember she needed the girl on side however aggravating it was.* 'You're not a nuisance. Like I said before, any issues - call me.' She pulled into the small car park of a children's play area, killed the engine and smiled. 'Now what's bothering you?'

Teagan faltered. 'I could do with an insight on what you touched on before. I would have asked more at the time, but... well, it seemed it was upsetting your brother and then Dulcie came in and...'

'Dulcie?' Helen's eyebrows raised. 'Acting like your best friend already is she? I'm sorry about that, she does like to get very familiar.'

Personally, Teagan liked that Dulcie was so pleasant and approachable; not what she would class as 'overfamiliar' and certainly nothing to apologise for. 'Erm, you mentioned dementia and I just wondered how it tends to affect her? As in I...'

'What's she done now?' Helen sighed, worry bubbling. *If her mother had pulled another stunt like that TV interview, then perhaps she needed to adjust the dosage of her special medication?*

'Nothing particularly.' Teagan didn't want to mention the trance-like states and the sleepwalking just yet. 'I just need to know if she wanders off or leaves the house at all? Could she be a danger to herself? Any medication I need to make sure she takes?'

Helen shook her head. 'No. Well, not as yet, although I can only presume things will get worse as time goes on.' *That was the plan, at least.* 'And there's no medication other than the vitamins. They're very important because it's all I can do at the moment to keep her healthy.' *The vitamins were more than important – they were what would get her out of this mess.*

Helen sighed. 'Mother told us wonderful stories when we were children.' She pretended to smile fondly at the memories. 'Both myself and Robert were enthralled by her fantastical tales of mythical creatures, fairies, dragons, handsome princes… She had a way with words… she still does.'

Teagan studied Helen, the serious and professional expression replaced with a childlike wonder.

Helen smiled sadly. 'Oh, how I loved her stories. They were so good and realistic. The type of story to transport you to another world, but her life has now become one of these stories… It's got so very much worse recently…' She looked down at her perfectly manicured nails. 'I've suspected dementia for a while, but Robert wouldn't hear a word of it. He's only recently begun to accept that I'm right. But like you've quite rightly noticed, he isn't happy about it.'

Teagan smiled kindly. 'It must be hard fo…'

'Robert finds it embarrassing,' Helen interrupted. 'Our mother has been telling anyone who will listen a whole load of made up nonsense. It's like she's written a story in her own head of what she'd wanted her life to be like, rather than what it actually was. It's very sad.'

Teagan frowned. 'What do you mean?'

Helen rolled her eyes. 'Oh, lots of things. Mainly, she goes on like she was some kind of red carpet celebrity. She makes out that she was friendly with celebrities...'

'She did say that she worked at a pl...'

'See!' Helen raised her hands. 'By the sounds of it she's already given you clap-trap. What has she said?'

Teagan hadn't planned on recounting any of the conversations she'd had with Dulcie, but seeing the despair on Helen's face, she felt obliged to tell her at least *part* of it. 'Not much really. Just about the dancer bits and something about a club. She showed me a photograph...'

Helen stared up at the car roof, her head pressed against the padded leather headrest. 'Oh God, I knew it. That's why Robert wants rid of all that ridiculous paraphernalia she hoards. I have to say I agree with him. It only encourages her delusions.' She turned back to Teagan. 'My mother did work at a club. That's where she met our father. He worked behind the bar and she... well... You should have heard the kind of stuff she was coming out with when I was stupid enough to take her to one of my business functions. Never again.'

Teagan made murmuring noises in the hope that it would sound comforting. So, their father had worked at the club Dulcie had mentioned?

Helen shook her head sadly. 'Our father died when I was about five years old when my mother was pregnant with Robert.'

Teagan's mouth fell open. *That's why Dulcie had closed up about her husband.* 'Oh, how awful! I'm so sorry.'

'I think that's why Robert hates all the things mother's been saying. He hates anything to do with talk of the clubs. I guess he associates that with what killed our father.'

'W-What happened? I mean, if you don't mind me asking? You don't have to say if it's going to upset y...'

'Mother rarely talked about it – a car accident, apparently, but I'm afraid there's no point in asking her now. Very little she talks about is real. I guess losing a husband with a young child and one on the way must have been hard. It was probably that which triggered all of this, although it's only been recently that it has become a real problem.'

Helen sighed once again. *Yes, this was good. The girl was swallowing it. Well, why wouldn't she?* 'I feel terrible that I haven't spent more time with her or kept on top of things in the house - it's far too big and unmanageable. I'm so busy with work it's difficult to get enough time to organise everything. Robert and I need to get her into a proper care home setting.' She glanced at Teagan apologetically. 'No offence to you, of course. I'm sure you'll do a wonderful job of looking after her, but it's important not to fall for her ramblings. She can be very convincing, but for God's sake don't take any of it seriously. And *please* don't encourage her.'

Teagan nodded. 'I understand. I really appreciate you telling me this. It makes things easier to know the background and I'll do whatever you need to help with what's best for her. Your mother is a lovely lady.'

Helen patted Teagan's hand. *No, she's not. My mother is in the way.* 'Thank you and yes, she is. It's so sad that her mind is going. Now, unless there's anything else, I must get on. I've got a client that I need to show around an exclusive property.'

Teagan shook her head 'No, there's nothing else,' she lied. Poor Helen. This must be so difficult for her and Robert and she didn't want to worry her further by bringing up the sleepwalking or other things Dulcie had said.

. . . .

'WHY DON'T WE GO in there and buy a house?' Keith said, grinning widely. 'You're always saying we need more places to offload cash and what's better than property? That way we could work on Helen Shepherd or tempt her to spill the beans.' His eyes gleamed, already imagining how he would enjoy torturing the information out of the fit bird.

Jonah stared at Keith. He was spot on with the strong arm of things, but wasn't blessed with the equivalent brains as he was brawn. And he had that manic glint in his eyes that was always visible when the possibility of violence was on the cards.

Keith Grogan hadn't initially been Jonah's choice for his main team. He'd filtered into it via legacy more than anything else and had been inherited once Saul had got locked up. Keith was Saul's right hand man, when he'd headed up the enforcement section, and to be fair, they had done a cracking job running that side of the business. There was a reason for that; Keith's persona and attitude were so similar to Saul's it was worrying, but perfect for what they dealt with.

Jonah eyed Keith's massive frame, his savage looking expression and his half-ear – sliced off a few years back during a particularly nasty set-to with a bunch of Russians. There was also that long scar running the length of his left cheek - that was from a separate incident, although he couldn't remember which there had been so many. Apart from looking very much like a contender for the latest WWE Smackdown match, Keith didn't look the sort who would be wandering into an upmarket estate agent in Maidenhead without causing at least *some* suspicion. He didn't want anything to set the cat amongst the pigeons, neither did he want violence coming into it. Not at this point. That could wait until later – and only if needs be.

Keith was extremely useful when it came to certain things; mainly involving unparalleled violence, but Jonah couldn't risk anything alerting the Old Bill. The catch from the heist was his and his alone and he would not stand by whilst it got lifted by the cops because Keith had his violent head on. *No fucking way*.

Shaking his head, he pushed the bottle of whisky across the desk towards his best two wing men. 'I want *no* violence or anything like that at this stage.' He glanced at Nero, entrusting him to keep Keith in line. 'And regarding a house, we haven't got things in place right now to purchase a property without leaving a paper trail for the Old Bill, not to mention our friends, The Inland Revenue.'

Nero raised his eyebrows. 'Could we not get it set up? We did it for the gear coming in.'

Jonah nodded, watching Keith pour himself a liberal helping of whisky, almost filling the crystal tumbler to the top. 'We could, but that takes time we haven't got. We can't use the same accounts as for the gear - too much cross over. I'm not faffing about with all that anyway.' His eyes narrowed. 'I just want a definite on where Dulcie Adams is. Once we know that we should be able to move relatively quickly. The main problem here is we're moving into civilian territory, so we'll have to amend our usual tactics.' He gave Keith a hard stare.

Nero eyed Jonah. 'At this precise moment, all we've got is the daughter. We know where she works and where she went for a drink.'

Jonah pulled his cuffs down, inspecting them to check the right length was showing under the sleeves of his suit jacket, then fixed his gaze on the two men. 'Then we'll concentrate on this Helen bitch. Continue keeping tabs on her. It will only be a matter of time before she gives us something of use or visits her mother. Once we know for definite where the sly old thief is, then we can work out how we're going to infiltrate it to get my stuff back.'

· · · ·

'ALRIGHT, MIKE. How's it going?'

Mike smiled at Jilly, the buxom barmaid who'd worked at the Crown for as long as he could remember. 'As always, every day of mine is successful,' he lied. *If only, but now that might be about to change. If what his mother had told him was true, then he'd be bloody laughing.*

Jilly picked up a fresh pint glass. 'The usual?' She eyed Mike closely. 'Are you *really* alright?' she pressed. 'I heard about your ma and I'm really sorry. You must be right cut up about it? I wasn't sure whether to mention anything.'

'Happens to us all in the end, doesn't it?' Mike shrugged. 'It's not like I wasn't expecting it.' He frowned inwardly. He wasn't particularly bothered about his mother's death shortly after he'd reached the hospital last night. That alone made him feel guilty like he'd suspected it would. She'd never been nice to him, but she hadn't always been that way. He'd felt loved and cherished once, but that had changed after his father died. Becoming cold and bitter, his mother had treated him like it was his fault, but now the reason for this abrupt change made more sense.

Looking back at Jilly, Mike smiled. *Act normal.* 'Getting on with things helps, hence why I've been at work today. No point moping around.'

'You going to treat me to that nice Roller you've been promising me for years then or what? I know you've got one in stock cos I've seen it in the adverts,' Jilly bantered, getting the hint to change the subject.

Mike laughed. 'Why not. In fact, if you'd prefer a different colour to the delectable baby blue one in my showroom, then I've got another due in that may be more to your liking.'

'Actually, you don't have the blue one any longer,' Heath said, appearing behind his father and slapping him on the back. 'I've just sold it. Sorry I couldn't get away before. I had to tie it up.'

Mike grinned widely. 'Well done, son. On this occasion I'll forgive your lateness,' he winked. 'Make that two pints please, Jilly.' *See, things were looking up already.*

Jilly pulled a face. 'Now that's no longer available I'll just have to set my sights on another one.' Placing the first pint on a beer towel, she put her finger to her mouth thoughtfully. 'Hmm, what should I go for? A Lamborghini, perhaps?'

Laughing, Mike took the pint and handed it to Heath. 'Go and sit yourself down, son. Grab that cubicle over the back.' *The further away from everyone, the better.*

Handing over a tenner, Mike grinned at Jilly. 'Here you go, love. Keep the change and get yourself one.'

'Thanks,' Jilly winked, wasting no time in shooting a double gin into a glass for herself.

Mike pushed through the crowded pub, nodding acknowledgments to people as they muttered their condolences, glad Heath had sat in the partitioned off cubby hole seat. A lot of people avoided it, feeling it excluded them from the pub's atmosphere and on a normal occasion, Mike would agree, but today it was the perfect location.

Casually loosening his tie, Heath took a drink from his pint and wasted no time getting straight to the point, 'Ok Dad, so what's with the secrecy booth? Why are we hiding in the corner?'

'No flies on you, is there?' Mike shrugged off his suit jacket, glad to be free of it after wearing it for the best part of ten hours.

Heath's frown deepened. 'Is it Nan?' He glanced down at his pint, already half empty and hoped this wouldn't take long. He'd got a curry and beers planned with the lads tonight and, if his luck was in, pull a tasty bit of totty too.

Heath placed his hand on his father's arm. 'I know I didn't see much of her, but I've just been so busy an…'

'She didn't exactly make visits pleasant.' Mike frowned. He'd taken Heath to visit when he was younger, but he didn't know why he'd bothered. His mother had never had anything nice to say and subsequently none of them had had much to do with her. 'But it seems my father may have been to blame for that…'

Heath stared. He'd never heard his father ever say anything less than positive about Michael Senior. 'What do you mean?'

Mike took a deep breath. 'Before she died last night, my mother told me something. I have no reason to suspect it's not true and so I'm going to need your help.'

Heath's concentration sharpened. 'Tell me more.'

Mike glanced around to make sure no one was within earshot and lowered his voice. 'My mother dropped a bombshell,' he began. *Bombshell wasn't the word.* What had been disclosed was something he hadn't expected in a million years. 'It appears my father was involved in more things than I was aware of.'

Heath smiled. 'I knew your side of the family had a kind of

history – you told me a bit about my Grandfather's shady deals.'

Mike took a swig from his pint. Although he had patchy memories of his father, he had clear recollections of the rest of his younger years. 'I knew my father was shot by a group of men he'd done a job with. I don't remember much about him. He wasn't there very often and then he just wasn't there at all.'

He turned his pint around and around on the beer mat. 'My father was involved with a big firm and did some heavy duty jobs for them. One job – the last one he did went pear-shaped and that's why he got taken out. After he died, with no money and no one to make sure we were looked after, like was the done thing in those days, things quickly went to pot. Unable to afford the upkeep for the house, my mother was forced to sell and we moved away. After what happened I think she wanted to get away from the area. From there, she took a string of dead end jobs to keep our heads above water. The remainder of my childhood was not good, but what I didn't know was before we moved, my mum received a visit.'

Heath frowned, still trying to digest this information. 'What kind of visit?'

Mike shrugged. 'Not sure, but these men weren't happy. They were convinced my mother was hiding something. Something of *theirs*.'

Heath opened his mouth to speak, but Mike silenced him by holding his hand up. 'One guy demanded the bag and started getting quite rough.'

Mike's mind replayed the conversation with his mother as she'd laid in her hospital bed. There had been many more questions he'd wanted to ask, but he'd never got the chance...

He couldn't say he'd been happy to hear that his father had pulled an underhand stunt. He'd always held the romanticised idea of his father being the strong, silent and respectable, albeit shady provider, yet it seemed that wasn't quite the case.

'She told me this man kept demanding a bag.' Mike's voice was barely audible. 'He said my father had taken something worth thousands for his part in this big job he'd done.'

Heath blew threw his teeth. 'Heavy shit!'

Mike smiled grimly. 'Something like that, yes, but anyway, he'd lifted this stash as payment and the firm wasn't best pleased. Before he got shot, my father allegedly let it slip that the girl had the bag.'

'So Nan *did* have hold of this stuff?' Heath exclaimed, his estimation of his sour-faced grandmother suddenly going up a thousand fold.

'No, she genuinely knew nothing about it and the men turning over the house eventually realised she didn't have a clue. She was lucky she didn't get finished off there and then, but even so, after that she was never quite the same. I think that was the final straw which made her move away. Trouble was, she had to take me with her and she *hated* me.'

'Hated *you*?' Heath exclaimed. 'Why?'

Mike shrugged. 'I guess I reminded her of my father. I've been told I look a lot like him, as do you. But it gets worse… Last night I also learnt he'd been having a long-standing affair with a woman who worked at the club he frequented.'

'What club?'

'A place called Feathers in Soho.'

'Soho? This bird was a stripper?'

'Perhaps. Some kind of dancer, but my mum said she'd known about the affair. In those days that sort of thing was brushed under the carpet, but during a bitchy argument with the wife of another of the firm's members, it came out that Michael was planning on divorce. Having an affair was one thing, but *divorce*, another. My mother had put up with his philandering ways; she'd been threatened, had her house turned over, been left destitute and all along he'd been planning on leaving her.'

'But was it true?'

'I don't know, but it looked like he'd pinched this stuff and left it – whatever it was, with this other woman of his. Who, I might add was pregnant…'

'So, you have a brother or sister somewhere?'

'It looks like it. My mother also finally apologised for

taking things out on me. I'd been waiting to hear her say that for years.' Mike's voice trailed off and looked at his son, his eyes gleaming. 'She wants me to have what should have been mine. And *yours*. Whatever it is, it could be worth a good amount of money. Like, I mean, a *lot*.'

Anticipation pounded in Heath's veins. 'This stash... How do we know if this woman still has it? That firm could have caught up with her ages ago.'

'My mother said she did some detective work just before we moved. She went to the club where this other woman worked only to find she'd disappeared a few months before my father got shot.' Mike fell silent for a moment before continuing. 'My mother's last words were, *'Get back what's rightfully yours'*, and that is what we're going to do.'

Heath ran his hands through his dark hair. 'Christ! But where do we start?'

'That's where I was hoping you'd come in. I've been told records and stuff are online now, so with your knowledge of computers perhaps we can locate this woman or her child. The child must be around the same age as me...'

Heath frowned, his mind whirring ten to the dozen. 'I'd need some info. I could start looking at records from Soho clubs. No point looking on Ancestry.'

'An... what?'

'Ancestry – family tree search software. Don't worry about it.'

'What about that new Facebook thing I keep hearing about?'

'I doubt whether anyone would list themselves as, *'illegitimate child of gangster whose mother stashed stolen goods'* - I'd need names. The woman's for a start. Any ideas? Is she even alive?'

Mike frowned. 'My mother said the 'scarlet woman', as she put it, was known as Faye. No idea if that's her real name, a stage name, or even if she's alive.'

'I need another drink.' Heath stood up. *Sod the curry and*

beers. This was way more important. If this stuff was worth thousands forty years ago, imagine how much it would be worth now? Holy fuck! And his dad was right. It was legitimately theirs, not this tart's or her kid's. Having that for himself would come in handy. *Very handy indeed.*

• • • •

JONAH WAS PLEASED with the way things were going with the instructions he'd given Nero and Keith. The best way of dealing with Dulcie Adams was in a way that would not raise suspicions.

Relieving some much needed frustration courtesy of the charms of that pretty little dancer had also helped.

Pulling up through the gates to his large detached house, Jonah turned off the engine of his top spec Range Rover and jogged up the steps to his front door. It was late – almost midnight and he was knackered, but he was determined to pull Lena up about her interference at the club. He may have to tread lightly with this Dulcie Adams lark, but he didn't need to take things at a snail's pace in his personal life. Lena was one thing he could put the kybosh on. He should never have let things go this far with her in the first place. Moving into his house and his life? *Not anymore.*

Nah, he was knocking it all on the head. *Right fucking now.*

Entering the sitting room, he glared at Lena lounging on the huge corner sofa – the one she'd ordered last month to replace the chesterfield. Another thing she'd taken upon herself to do. *Why the fuck hadn't he noticed any of these things before?*

Jonah slung his suit jacket over one of the matching armchairs. The sort that were as big as a Waltzer and revolved in whichever direction you wanted to face. He hated the bloody things. It was like being at the fucking fair and he wasn't at the fair, this was his *house.*

'Where have you been?' Lena's eyes scrutinised Jonah whilst she sipped at her wine.

Jonah stared back at Lena. Judging by the amount of

lipstick plastered around the rim of the extortionately expense wine glass, she'd had plenty before the one she was busy downing.

'Where the fuck do you think I've been?' he snapped. 'At the club of course.'

Lena got to her feet and moved unsteadily towards him, draping herself around his neck like a cheap suit. She ran one of her talons along his square jaw. 'Being as you're back, shall we have an early night?'

Jonah stepped away and moved to the drinks cabinet. 'Why have you been interfering at the club, Lena?' he asked bluntly, pouring himself a large whisky.

'Interfering?' Lena tried not to let her eyes narrow in rage. This was that fucking old bag, Gwen. She'd half-expected her to go running to Jonah about something sooner or later. 'I-I didn't int…'

'You sacked two of the girls. That's not your call and I won't have it.'

Lena sidled up behind Jonah and wrapped her arms around his waist. 'You need someone who knows what they're doing running that place, Jonah. I…'

'Don't tell me what I need at my own club!' Jonah unwrapped Lena's arms and turned to face her. 'Things aren't working out for me. I think we should knock whatever we've got together on the head now.'

Lena's mouth dropped open. *What the fuck?* 'You're dumping me because of something that I happened to do at the club. Something I thought would be helpful?' she wailed, willing the tears to flow on tap. *He couldn't dump her. No, no, NO! She wasn't having this. Not now. Not now she was so close. Far too close for this to happen.*

She rushed over to Jonah, clinging on to his shirt, her lips searching for his. 'Please don't say that. I'm sorry. I didn't realise it would upset you. I…'

Jonah untangled himself once more from Lena's grasp. He didn't want this. *Any* of it. 'It's not just that,' he said, his eyes cold. 'It's you. I want my house back to myself. I want my *life* back to myself too. I'm not ready for this kind of relationship.'

Lena blinked rapidly, desperately trying to work out how to play this. She had to do something quick.

Melodramatically throwing herself face down on the sofa, ignoring her bright pink lipstick had smeared all over one of the matching cream cushions, she let out a howl of what she hoped sounded genuine anguish.

Jonah raked his fingers through his hair, irritation rising rapidly. 'Oh, stop the histrionics. This is what I mean. *This* sort of shit – I don't want it. You're fun, Lena – a good shag and all and we've had a good crack, but things are going in the wrong direction now - a direction I don't want to go.'

Missing her stolen glance as he walked past to refill his whisky, Lena knew she had to use the trump card. Although part of the plan at some stage, she'd been planning to pull it out of the hat under less extenuating circumstances.

'Don't worry about cash. I'll sort it so you get a nice flat of your own,' Jonah continued, the weight off his shoulders already considerably lightened. 'As a temporary measure, take one of my flats in town until you can find one you really want. You can even have your job back on the stage if you wish.'

'I don't want to go back on the stage. I *can't*! Oh God...' Lena cried, her sobbing becoming louder.

Jonah's nerves jangled from the high-pitched wailing. *He could only be nice for so long.* 'Shut up!' he barked. 'Just get out of my life, will you? I've had enough.'

Lena sat up slowly. She'd been acting most of her life and wouldn't let herself down now. Not when the catch of the century was within her grasp.

'I don't want to get out of your life,' Lena sobbed in her best bereft voice, the tears now coming nicely on cue.

Jonah sighed. He'd throw her out with his bare hands in a minute if she kept on. She wouldn't get a flat now either. He'd had enough. 'I want you out of my life, Lena. I'm done.'

'It's not that simple,' Lena whimpered.

'Yes it is.' Jonah pointed to Lena and then to the door. 'See? It's not difficult. Now, off you fuck.'

'I-I'm pregnant…' Lena whispered. *Not exactly how she'd planned to deliver this whammy, but needs must.*

Ringing clamoured inside Jonah's ears, along with a high-pitched buzzing sound. Whisky slopped from his glass down the front of his trousers. 'You're *what*?' he managed to force from his throat.

'I-I'm pregnant,' she repeated. 'I only found out myself for definite this afternoon.' She stared up at him beseechingly. *She'd got him – she could see it clear as day.* 'I've suspected for a few weeks now… That's why I've been so tired…'

A big fat tear rolled down Lena's face, making another track of black mascara to match the others. 'I wanted to surprise you when you got home… I waited up… I had no idea you were planning to dump me…'

'Pregnant?' Jonah repeated again, the death knell tolling loudly in the back of his mind.

Lena began sobbing louder, her body scrunched into a ball, visibly shaking. With legs like concrete, Jonah forced himself to perch on the edge of the sofa and pull her into his arms.

He'd been stupid. *Really* stupid.

And now he was completely trapped. *Fuck*.

NINE

'FOR FUCK'S SAKE, THIS IS RIDICULOUS!' Nero muttered, his temper frayed. Eighteen miles they'd tailed Helen Shepherd since leaving the office, but where on earth was she going? Siberia?

'I think we can safely say she isn't going to her mother's. The old dear wouldn't live this far out in the bloody sticks, would she?' Keith said, opening his third Mars bar since they'd left Maidenhead. 'Where the hell are we?'

'Fuck knows,' Nero spat, frowning as a van pulled out of a side road in front of them, blocking the Mercedes from sight. There were temporary traffic lights up ahead and if Helen Shepherd got through those and then they changed to red because of this fucking van, he'd personally throttle the fat bastard driving it. Furthermore, he wished Keith would shut up – his bloody gob constantly going on wasn't helping. He had no clue where they were either, but it certainly did seem unlikely the mother would live *this* far out of town. Although it wasn't impossible being as she'd spent the last four decades in hiding. Not that *they'd* caught up with her. She may as well have lived next door to one of them.

His jaw clenched. If he'd trailed this silly tart all this way purely to see her daintily sipping from a glass of wine with some pin-striped mincers again he'd go bloody mad.

Glad to get through the temporary traffic lights, Nero was relieved to see the Mercedes at the brow of the hill five motors ahead. At least he hadn't lost her – that would have been the icing on the cake.

'Maybe she lives out this way herself?' Keith craned his neck as they passed a partly hidden road sign pointing to a village. 'That said, 'Little Freith'.'

Nero scowled. He didn't care *what* it said. He was getting sick of this. Suddenly seeing the Mercedes indicate to turn left, he pulled back and waved the car behind him past. 'She's turning in somewhere.'

Slowly moving up to the entrance the Mercedes had taken, Nero saw a large, almost stately building set back up a long driveway behind the hedge.

'Jesus wept! Don't tell me she lives here?' Keith gasped. 'The place is fucking massive!'

Nero squinted at a plaque partially obscured by surrounding bushes. 'I doubt it. It's one of those private old-folks' homes by the looks of that sign. Maybe the mother lives here after all.' *And if that was the case then they stood absolutely zilch chance of getting the stuff back.*

'Bloody hell,' Keith said. 'It's right posh. All the old folks' homes round our neck of the woods look like derelict prisons, not National Trust gaffs.'

Nero slowly steered the car up the driveway. There were enough other cars parked outside the large building not to draw attention to them. He pulled into a space far enough away from the building so that Helen Shepherd would not notice them, but close enough for them to see her walking towards a man standing in the car park.

'Who's that?' Keith asked as Helen approached the man, kissed him on the cheek and then walked through the ornate entrance of the building. 'That her husband?'

Nero shot Keith daggers, hating people asking questions

that they knew full well no one knew the answers to. Husband or not, they'd wait here until Helen Shepherd came out. At least they'd got a good eyeball on the man. He might be someone they could use. And there was a good chance Dulcie Adams was a resident here, so in the interim he'd be using this waiting time to find out.

· · · ·

HELEN SMILED WIDELY at Ken Manning, knowing he had been eyeing her backside for the last hour whilst she'd inspected the apartment. Inheriting her mother's build and physique meant by maintaining short, but regular sessions at the gym everything was as firm and toned as it could be and she knew she still looked good.

Ken was the perfect choice regarding this proposition. Knowing him since college, she knew he'd be open to the proposal and also that he'd fall for her acting skills. There was no way she was telling him the dire position Shepherd, Percival and Proctor was in. Or rather, *she* was in.

'What do you think?' Ken said, pleased to see that Helen Adams or should he say, *Shepherd*, seemed impressed.

Helen turned to give Ken her full attention. 'I think it's perfect!' She glanced around once more, making sure her expression was appraising. 'It's in a great location and has all the support facilities required.'

Her gaze remained on Ken for just that little bit too long which she knew would work in her favour. 'I really do appreciate you giving me the chance of first refusal of this.' She lowered her eyes and sniffed sadly. 'It's been difficult reaching this decision, but it will be the best thing for mother.' *Yeah, yeah.*

Ken felt he knew Helen well enough to offer a comforting touch of her arm. The poor woman was heartbroken – anyone could see that. 'You know I'll always be there for you, Helen,' he said, his hand lingering. 'We go back a long way, remember?'

Helen smiled sweetly. She could barely remember the couple of times they'd ended up in bed together all those years ago. It had hardly been anything to write home about, but she knew he'd always held a torch for her.

She patted down her hair. 'Oh Ken, things have been so difficult. I really am distraught. This place will be ideal though, so that's something.' Turning away, she made a point of dabbing at her bone-dry eyes.

'I'm just sorry this particular site isn't closer to where you live.'

'Oh, but that's where you're wrong,' Helen exclaimed. *She wasn't sorry it was so far away. The further away, the better.* 'Mother's state of mind has deteriorated so much she doesn't want to be anywhere near the house anymore. She can't bear the memories, yet acts like my father's death was yesterday... and oh...' She turned away once more. 'The worst thing is she's begun making things up about her life. She's so deluded in what actually happened, but believes her own stories. And Robert, well, Robert hasn't taken it well at all. He... he gets angry and I think he blames me for wanting to do something to help her.'

'What?' Ken cried, anger forming. 'Why would he do that?'

Helen squeezed her eyes shut in the hope that she could possibly force a tear out. 'He doesn't want to accept that this is happening. I... I only want what's best for our mother and then we've, or rather, *I* have got all the worries with the house to deal with.' She paused dramatically. 'I shouldn't really be telling you this, but I found out that Robert... he's been taking advantage.'

Ken frowned. 'Advantage?'

Helen looked at Ken, her eyes soulful. 'Unbeknown to me, Robert persuaded mother to cash in the equity on the house.' She lowered her voice even though there was no one else around. 'He's got a gambling problem.' *Oh, all of this made things sound so tragic. She'd done well thinking up this particular vein of the story.*

'I had no idea! I'm so sorry,' Ken exclaimed.

Helen shook her head sadly. 'I've bailed him out several times myself over the last ten years. The whole thing with my brother's finances has put a dreadful amount of pressure on my marriage over the years and this latest thing… well, I'm not sure if my marriage will survive. I need to sell mother's house at the best possible price to cover all the debts, whilst leaving enough left over to buy this place, plus money for her care, of course.'

Ken's eyebrows knitted together. 'Now, don't you worry about that. I'm sure I can secure you a knock down price on this place.' He ran his hand through his thinning hair. 'Robert has a lot to answer for. I feel like giving him a piece of my mind!'

'Oh no, you mustn't!' Helen grabbed Ken's arm, knowing that would bolster him further. 'He's still my brother.'

'You're a good woman, Helen. You leave this to me. I'll speak to the developer and get this sorted for you. He owes me a favour anyway.'

Helen stared at Ken wide-eyed. 'You'd really do that for *me*? I don't want to put you out.' *Ken, you're as much of a sucker as I always remembered you were.*

'What are friends for? You also know I'm happy to broker the sale of your mother's house,' Ken winked. 'I'll personally make sure you get the best price. It goes without saying I won't take any commission.'

Helen smiled gratefully, placing her hand just that little bit too long on Ken's suit jacket lapel. 'I don't know how I'll ever be able to thank you.'

Ken puffed his chest out proudly. 'Just leave everything to me.'

Helen walked down the manicured path to her Mercedes. It had gone promisingly well with Ken, apart from having to act overly bloody nice. That alone left a bad taste. Still, that was a trifling inconvenience compared to what it would bring when this pulled off.

Her usually unlined forehead creased. The one thing risking throwing her plans into disarray was that idiotic Teagan girl. Damn and blast her mother for taking it upon herself to arrange a bloody live-in home help. The worst timing *ever*. Still, the girl wasn't the brightest and she'd swallowed everything so far, which was something and if she was as pliable as she seemed, then her presence might even work favourably.

But now she'd have to pop and see her mother on the way back, just to maintain the public belief that she was a caring and loving daughter.

And then she'd go home and sort her stuff in the garage before James got back.

TEN

JONAH AWOKE GRADUALLY, his consciousness slowly seeping to the 'on' setting, helped by the feel of a hand sliding down his stomach. The fingers brushed tantalisingly over his rigid erection, then moved down to cup his balls.

The extent of his arousal was almost painful in its intensity and desire all but overtook the banging headache in his temples. God, he must have had sunk far too many last night for a headache like this - he very rarely got plastered.

As the hand began working him mercilessly, he groaned with need.

Wait... Shit!

Freezing as the rapid recall of the previous night hit him, Jonah's eyes flashed open, daylight searing the back of his eyeballs.

'Glad to see you still find me as attractive as ever,' Lena purred, her face perfectly made up – a massive contrast to last night.

'What's the time?' Jonah mumbled for want of nothing else to say, dread sitting like a lead weight at the base of his stomach.

'Almost 11,' Lena smiled, her body naked, her large breasts resplendent. Her hand wrapped back around Jonah's quickly deflating length. 'I thought I'd let you sleep. You seemed to need it.'

'Eleven o'clock?' Jonah jumped out of bed, his head pounding. 'Christ! I should be at the club! Fuck!'

Lena watched Jonah pull fresh underwear from the chest of drawers. 'You remember what you said last night, don't you? You haven't changed your mind?'

Jonah glanced at her, his tongue threatening to choke him rather than utter what he knew he must. 'No, I haven't. Now, I need to get showered and out. I'll see you later.'

Shutting the door of the en-suite bathroom and flicking the light on, Jonah for once in his life, locked the door and leant up against it, breathing heavily.

He staggered over to the sink and stared at his reflection in the mirror. His bleary eyes stared back at him accusingly. Grabbing his toothbrush, he began brushing his teeth, scrubbing hard to rid his mouth of the rancid taste of stale whisky.

Yep, Lena was pregnant; he remembered all of it. No wonder he'd got drunk. But maybe if he hadn't got quite so drunk he could have talked some sense into himself before he'd made things even worse.

Even through his alcohol-hazed memory, he could still picture Lena's red, tear-stained face, her eyes wide with panic. *'You are going to marry me now, aren't you, Jonah?'*, she'd sobbed.

And what could he say, apart from agree.

Jonah gagged in the sink, the toothpaste burning his mouth. *What had he done? What the fuck had he done?*

Opening the shower cubicle he stepped inside, closing his eyes as the powerful jets of hot water covered him. *If only he could wash all of this away.*

Oh he'd been so close to getting his house and life back, but he could hardly do that now. Despite being a hard and violent man, he hadn't been brought up to mistreat a woman. His father had instilled in him since day dot the importance of family values and would turn in his grave if his son were to chuck out a pregnant woman. The woman he had now agreed to marry… The woman he would now *have* to marry because he wouldn't have any child of *his* being born a bastard.

Jonah sighed with resignation as he grabbed the shower gel. He'd just have to get on with it and make the best of it. *Somehow.*

But the rest of the world didn't stop turning and right now he needed to get his arse up to the club. Nero and Keith were out on a reccy and he wanted to be there the minute they had an update. He hoped to fuck it would be good news because he sure as hell needed some.

· · · ·

WHILST THEY'D BEEN WAITING, Nero called up the number on the sign outside the posh old folk's gaff.

Putting on his best voice he thought he'd done a stunning job of impersonating Dulcie Adams' doctor, even though Keith had been a prick by laughing in the background.

Most insistent, Nero had demanded to speak to the on-duty nurse, going to great pains insisting it was *imperative* to give an update about test results requiring an alteration to medication dosage. He'd impressed himself using 'imperative' in the correct way.

He'd been winging it of course. He didn't have the first clue whether the old bat was even on medication, never mind what sort, but regardless of that, it had got him what he wanted. Well, not what he *wanted*, but what he wanted to know. And that was that Dulcie Adams was not a resident at Oak Apple Residential Home.

Spluttering apologies about how he must have got his patients' notes mixed up, Nero had hung up quick sharp. But they were still none the wiser where Dulcie Adams was and when Helen Shepherd had walked out through the doorway, he was so frustrated with the whole thing that he felt like taking a leaf out of Keith's book and smashing her face into the nicely gravelled driveway until she told them where the fuck her mother was.

The bloke Helen had met earlier was nowhere to be seen either. They were getting nowhere fast and Nero had just about had enough. He certainly hadn't wanted to go with Keith's idea of following Helen *again* just in case, but with a face like a slapped arse, he sulkily tailed the Mercedes back into Maidenhead, this time to a rather upmarket residential area the other side of town.

'I reckon we're on to something here,' Keith muttered, twitching in his seat as they turned into yet another road full of big houses.

'Probably *her* place,' Nero spat. 'We've been just about everywhere else that she goes to, so why not there? Wherever she's heading is bound to be anywhere apart from where we want it to fucking be.'

Seeing Helen pull up outside a large, but decrepit-looking gaff, a flutter of hope stirred and Nero's pulse accelerated. *Could it be? An upmarket estate agent was unlikely to live in a place with peeling paint...* He grinned. For fuck's sake. He didn't know about Dulcie Adams - this gaff looked more like Morticia Adams lived there.

Both men watched with bated breath as Helen walked up the steps to the front door. Seeing the geriatric opening it was the same one featured in that stupid dance clip, Nero grinned.

Bingo. Dulcie Adams.

'Thank fuck for that,' Nero muttered, now glad he'd gone along with Keith's idea. He puffed his chest out, feeling weirdly proud that he, out of everyone in the Powell firm, was the *first* person to lay eyes on Dulcie Adams – the woman that had given everyone the slip for the last forty years.

He grinned. Jonah would be pleased with this – that's if he could get hold of him. Unusually for Jonah, he hadn't answered his mobile when he'd called first thing this morning.

Nero shrugged. He'd be around by the time they got back to Soho and once he found out about this, with any luck it would mean he'd get an early one and sink a few beers down the boozer.

• • • •

HEATH'S BACKSIDE WAS STIFFER than the proverbial board, but this was the best chance he'd had in a while, correction – *ever*, to get ahead. He glanced at his watch. Gone midnight already. He'd been at this all evening and his eyes felt like they were falling out, but he'd stay up all night if it brought answers.

His aching fingers fumbled to open a can of coke. If, and it was a big *if*, what he'd discovered so far was anything to do with what his father had been going on about, then it would set him up for life.

Opening the Google link in a new tab, he could barely hide his impatience for the page to load. He needed a couple more accounts to back up his findings and if they did, and he was right, that would make him very happy. *Very happy indeed.*

He glanced at his notebook. He hadn't got much to work with, but he knew more than yesterday so that was a start. The main problem – at least, the one most important to him, was what had been swiped? What had this mistress of his grandfather got?

Heath had shelled out for an Ancestry account and, finding himself on there, along with his parents, he'd drilled down, locating his grandfather, Michael Pointer Senior and downloaded his death certificate, showing the date as 18th May 1965.

The robbery had obviously taken place at some point beforehand and scouring Google brought reports of several robberies preceding that date. Further searching narrowed it down, but there were a couple fitting the bill large enough to have made the nationals. And if it was one of *those*...

Heath stared at his notes: a bank robbery netting thirty grand, a safe deposit box containing six gold bullion, two post office jobs and a burglary on a house in Chelsea. All of these occurred in the six months prior to May 1965. The spoils from *any* of those would be appreciated, but if the job in question wasn't any of these, it meant scouring through past records of the local London papers. It would be a case of wading through microfilm in a local library like he'd seen someone doing once in an 80s film and he realised with a sinking heart a robbery not making the nationals would be worth a hell of a lot less than his Nan had given the impression of.

Further digging ruled out the bank robbery and the post office jobs. Clicking on several links relating to the bullion job made Heath's heart plummet further. The goods were recovered a month after the robbery and the perpetrators jailed, which only left one...

Heath's pulse gained pace as he scanned the article dated 12th May 1965:

> *'...A large amount of money, silverware and jewels were stolen from a house belonging to a known figure in the London underworld in Chelsea on Tuesday night. Police have linked this robbery to a vendetta between members of rival gangs.*
>
> *Jewellers are to remain alert to anyone approaching them with unusual and rare gemstones...'*

Reading on, Heath focused. *It couldn't be this one could it? If it was this one...?* Opening another tab digging for more accounts, his eyes flicked feverishly over the text:

> *'...items stolen from the exclusive Chelsea townhouse included extremely valuable pieces...'*

His fingers trembled as his mouse scrolled down the page. Aside from 19th century silverware and money, it looked like the biggest part of the haul were rare gemstones:

'...it is estimated that at least fifteen gemstones were taken - four of which were white diamonds, the rest pink...'

Heath frowned. The word 'diamonds' interested him enough, but *pink* diamonds, he'd never heard of. Frantically opening another tab, he blinked rapidly. It was an American site, the article written last year, but that didn't matter.

Heath gulped at his can of coke, wishing he had something stronger to hand. *Fuck me! If this was true.... If this was what his grandfather had lifted...?*

'...since 1979 the price of pink diamonds has skyrocketed,' Heath muttered, his eyes scanning the screen. 'Light pink diamonds used to fetch around $10,000 per carat... now around $220,000 per carat...'

He gulped at more coke, partially missing his mouth, the fizzy brown liquid sloshing down his shirt. 'Vivid pink diamonds, a rare colour... are now worth in excess of $600,000 per carat...'

Almost choking in his rush for further detail and aware he was talking to himself like a lunatic, Heath flicked between the tabs. 'Owner of the stolen gemstones listed items missing as several small pink diamonds of less than 0.4ct... 3 pink diamonds between 1 and 2ct and 2 at over 12ct each... Diamonds had previously been bought as investments... substantial reward for information as to their whereabouts...'

Grabbing his calculator, Heath stabbed at the numbers. 'Worst case scenario, forget the smaller ones, let's see... call it three at one carat – maybe bigger... it said between one and two, but we'll say one...' He tapped in the figures. 'Hang on, what's this? Pink diamonds can be various shades which alters the price... Light pink... vivid...'

He scribbled in his notebook. 'And the big ones... two at twelve carats...' Heath stared at the calculation in shock.

'Depending on what sort of pink they are, then three of at

least one carat would fetch… for the least valuable pinks, 1.8 million dollars…' Nausea bubbled. 'And the two big ones – the twelve carats - worst case scenario, over \$2.6 mil each, top of the range ones, over \$7.2 mil each.

Wait! So that was at least… Jesus Christ! 'That's at least \$600,000 for the three one carat diamonds, best case \$1.8 mil. And the bigger ones… \$5.2 million or best, \$14.4 mil.' Sweat formed on the back of Heath's neck. 'So, in total around twenty million dollars, whatever that is in sterling. Let me think, erm… about fifteen million quid!'

Fuck!

Heath blinked once, twice and then blinked again. *Fuck, fuck, fuck!* And these should be *his*? His eyes narrowed. They *would* be his come hell or high water. That was unless whoever was behind the shooting of his grandfather had got them back?

A further frantic Google search found no results mentioning the Chelsea haul had ever been recovered, but then it wouldn't. If whoever owned these things had got them back it was likely to have been by less than salubrious means and they'd hardly be advertising that in the paper. But if these *hadn't* been reclaimed, it meant they were still out there - either in the possession of some crusty old bag or her family. The family, who were also related to *him*.

Related or not, as the legal offspring of Michael Pointer Senior, his father was the legitimate beneficiary, but being as spoils from a robbery hardly stood as a legitimate source, that didn't count for much.

Heath slammed the lid of his laptop closed. He needed a proper drink and a large one at that. There was no way he was letting this one go. He had to find the woman who had stolen his inheritance and get back what was rightfully his.

• • • •

'WHAT ARE YOU DOING?' the voice screeched, making Teagan bash her head on the dressing table that she'd been under on her hands and knees.

Scrambling to her feet, she spotted the tiny figure of Dulcie in the doorway of the second floor bedroom, her face crimson with rage. 'Dulcie! I…'

'You have no right to be in here!' Dulcie screamed. 'No right at all! This room is *private*. If I wished you to enter any of the closed rooms, then I would have asked you to.' Her cheeks trembled. 'Did you hear me? You are *not* to go anywhere that is not open. This is not your house to do with as you please, it is *mine*.'

Cheeks scarlet from being scolded like a naughty child, Teagan held her hands up to reason, her left hand holding the little silver box that she'd been retrieving from the floor. 'Dulcie, I came in here to tidy up after y…'

Dulcie's eyes narrowed as she focused on Teagan's hands. 'Think you can steal from me, do you?' She marched over to Teagan and snatched the trinket box. 'One of you girls before tried a stunt like this. Trying to steal my silverware she was, but even *she* didn't have the audacity to snoop around private rooms and…'

'I wasn't stealing!' Teagan protested. 'I came in to…'

'I'm calling your agency to lodge a formal complaint. Go and pack your things straight away, young lady. I'm very disappointed.'

Feeling the burn of tears at the unprovoked attack, Teagan moved towards the door, 'I was righting the cabinet you knocked over last night. It must have hit your dressing table and knocked things off. I promised you I'd clear this up today.'

Teagan was almost at the doorway when Dulcie spoke again. 'Wait!' Her voice was now quiet. 'Last night? I was in here last night?'

Turning, Teagan nodded. 'I heard a crash so came downstairs to see if you'd fallen. The door was open, so I looked in and you were in here.'

Dulcie visibly shrank. 'I… I was in here? I…'

'You must have been sleepwalking,' Teagan said quietly. 'You weren't yourself.'

Dulcie staggered slightly as if Teagan's words had pushed her off balance and she rushed forward to steady the lady. 'I wasn't stealing, Dulcie. I'd never d...'

Dulcie flapped her hand for quiet and tentatively lowered herself on to the bed.

'Are you alright? You've gone very pale? I didn't mean to upset you. I thought I was helping by putting the furniture back.'

'I upset myself, dear,' Dulcie said, her blue eyes meeting Teagan's. 'I should have known you weren't the type to snoop. I-I didn't think I'd... I don't remember coming in here... I...'

Teagan patted Dulcie's hand. 'Don't get upset. As I said, I think you were sleepwalking.'

'I wasn't sleepwalking,' Dulcie snapped. 'I do come in here sometimes, just not very often. I-I don't remember doing it last night. Oh, this is so frustrating.'

Teagan smiled. 'Come on, let's go and have a cup of tea.'

Dulcie gripped Teagan's hand. 'I know what they say about me, you know. I might be old but I'm not deaf.' She studied Teagan's face. 'They think I'm crazy, don't they? My children?'

Teagan bit her bottom lip. 'I'm sure they don't think that.'

'Yes they do! I know they do. Well, Helen does. She's always saying it. She was always such a lovely girl, but now she just wants to get rid of me and convince everyone I've lost my mind. What do they call it? Dementia? And now even Robert believes it. I might be forgetful, but I'm not mad.'

Teagan got to her feet. Dulcie's children did think she had dementia and now, if she was honest, she was finding it more and more difficult not to agree, but Dulcie was wrong about one thing. Helen wasn't horrible - the opposite if anything. Anyone could see the woman was worried sick over the state of her mother's mental health. 'I'm sure Helen and Robert don't think you're mad.' *A little white lie never hurt anyone, did it?*

Seeing a brooch on the floor, Teagan stooped to pick it up. Admiring it, she held it up to the light. 'What a beautiful brooch! It's a good job neither of us trod on it.'

Dulcie's eyes clouded over. 'Yes... the brooch... It's one of my favourites.'

'Shall I put it back in your trinket box?' Teagan asked, stepping towards the bedside table.

Dulcie reached out for the brooch. 'No! I'd like to wear that today.' Holding it in her hands, she smiled. 'It's beautiful, isn't it? I remember the day he gave me this. Can you pin it on my blouse?'

Fiddling with the dainty clasp, Teagan passed the pin through Dulcie's blouse and fastened it carefully. 'There, that looks lovely,' she smiled. 'Your husband had very good taste!'

Dulcie scowled. 'Peter didn't buy it. He never bought me *anything*! Michael... Michael bought it for me.' She stared through the window to somewhere far beyond. 'These last few months things have been getting confusing and I'm not sure where I am sometimes. I can't explain it.'

Teagan faltered. Would she worsen Dulcie's delusions if she asked questions, or would it help? Perhaps if she finished telling her story – the one in her head, then she'd realise it wasn't real. She might realise it was just *that* – a story. The blur between fantasy and reality?

She swallowed nervously. 'Do you think it might be a good idea to speak to a doctor. If you're not happy with how you're feeling, th...'

'Now you sound like Helen!' Dulcie snapped. 'She keeps going on and on about that. Why do you think I haven't mentioned this to her or Robert? They'd have me in the loony bin, like *that*!' She snapped her fingers together.

'Perhaps you just need a bit more sleep,' Teagan suggested, even though she knew that to be pointless. Poor Dulcie. It really did look like she had dementia and being aware of it must be even more terrifying.

'I'm sorry for shouting at you and for what I said about stealing,' Dulcie said, her voice small.

'Already forgotten.' Teagan patted Dulcie's hand again.

'Come on, let's go downstairs and put some music on. I'll get your vitamins. They'll perk you up.'

'I don't want those pills,' Dulcie pouted. 'Helen and her new-fangled ideas. I have no idea what she thinks they will do! All of this has only been happening since I started taking them.'

'They're good for you! Even I take vitamins and I'm only twenty five!' Teagan grinned. 'Helen just wants to make sure you're healthy.'

Dulcie got to her feet. 'No she doesn't. She's trying to poison me.'

Swallowing uncomfortably Teagan led Dulcie out of the bedroom. *Poisoning her? This was worse than she thought.*

• • • •

LENA PERCHED on the velvet stool she'd bought to go with the new dressing table for their bedroom. Yes, *their* bedroom. Jonah could hardly have an issue with her wanting to put her own personal touch on the house anymore now she was officially his fiancée.

Her stomach did a flip. *She'd done it. She'd only gone and done it.*

A wide smile slid across her face and she stared at her reflection in the tri-fold mirror. 'Cracking job, Lena. Cracking job!' she said out loud.

Blowing on the third coat of bright pink polish she'd applied to her nails, Lena glanced at her phone. Still no reply to that text she'd sent? She'd send another one - an update. If *that* didn't spur things into action, then she didn't know what would.

At least she'd succeeded in getting the next part of the plan rolling. She glanced at her bag. The trip to the registry office this morning was worth putting up with the godforsaken twenty minutes stuck with a cab driver sporting horrendous body odour.

The marriage was pencilled in for a date nine weeks from now. She'd been hoping to get a slot sooner, but it would have to do. All she needed now was to get Jonah to countersign these forms.

Happily sipping at her wine, she glanced at the glass. *That* was a huge downside. Having to lay off the booze wasn't anything that she was much relishing, but she couldn't risk openly drinking too much in front of Jonah. At least she could have a few on the sly, being as no one knew about the baby yet.

Not that there was one and there bloody wouldn't be either.

Lena's overpainted brows arched. She wasn't ruining her figure for a bleeding kid, but as long as Jonah believed her to be pregnant, then she was home and dry. The minute the signed and sealed wedding certificate was in her hand, not only would she be entitled to half of everything he owned by law, but she'd break the news to him that the baby was no more.

It went without saying that she'd keep it to herself there had never been one. Jonah didn't need to know that bit. People lost babies all the time, didn't they? Especially early on.

Lena grinned. She'd also booked out the VIP suite at The Feathers for their engagement party. She hadn't mentioned this to Jonah yet either. She'd surprise him with that once she'd picked up the invitations she'd ordered from the printers. She couldn't wait to see the ravenously jealous faces of all the slags at the club once it was announced.

A very productive morning. *Very* productive. Things were now more on track than ever.

All there was left to do was to get her feet under the table at The Feathers so she had some proper clout.

ELEVEN

'I THINK I MAY have found who this woman is. Or *was*.' Heath leant back in a leather chair in his father's office, pleased to have got this far so quickly.

Mike placed his pen down. 'Really? How on earth have you managed that?'

Heath grinned. 'I have my ways…' He pulled out a couple of pieces of paper from his suit jacket's inside pocket. 'I think this…' Unfolding one of the pieces of paper, he flattened it out on his father's desk. '…is the woman we're looking for…'

Mike stared at a printout of a newspaper article dated from June 1964. It was an article on a new cabaret show opening that week at The Feathers club in Soho. A photo accompanying the article showed a line of women dressed in, from what he could tell from the bad reproduction of the article, feathered leotards and headdresses, posed in a fan-shaped line on the stage.

He frowned. 'Where did you get this? Which one's supposed to be her?'

'An archive website. It took a lot of digging, but there's a lot out there if you know where to look,' Heath said proudly, pointing to the caption underneath the picture. 'I presume, from what you said, she's the one in the middle.'

Mike squinted at the tiny print:

Jubilation as new show, Pegasus, launches this Friday, headlined by everyone's favourite - Faye.

'If you read the rest of the article, you'll see that it only mentions Faye in passing and only ever by that name, but...' Heath unfolded the second piece of paper and laid it over the top of the other article. 'If you look at *this* one...'

Mike peered at another article from back in the day. This time January 1965:

Josene Takes Top Billing at The Feathers

Clients of the famous Feathers nightclub in Soho have welcomed a new leading lady of the club's famous cabaret.

The Feathers was broken hearted to lose Dulcie Adams, affectionally known as Faye, but understood remaining in the club after her husband tragically lost his life was difficult. Now Josene will keep up Faye's great work which helped to make The Feathers Club into such a star attraction...

'Dulcie Adams...' Mike whispered. 'Are you sure?'

Heath shrugged. 'As sure as I can be, based on the snippets we've got.'

Mike grinned. 'This is amazing. Well done! I think if the internet was around in the 1960s, then this woman wouldn't have got away with it for so long!'

Heath grinned. 'But that's not all...' He pulled out more paper from his pocket.

'Remember I told you about that Ancestry website? I started looking for Dulcie Adams on there.' Heath glanced up expecting to see amazement on his father's face, but instead just saw impatience. Unperturbed, he continued, 'Based on what you said, I looked for births of someone who became Dulcie Adams from between 1940 to 1950 in London. I picked London as I thought that most likely. I found twenty-six of them and looked into each and every one, but none had children born at the right time.'

Mike poured both himself and Heath a whisky and listened intently.

'So, I looked further afield.' Heath took a sip of the whisky and smacked his lips together in appreciation.

'Can you just cut to the chase?' Mike barked. 'You really don't have to tell me the entire story. If you have a point to get to, could you just please get to it?'

Slightly hurt, Heath looked back at his notes. 'The Dulcie Adams we want was born in Margate in 1940 to Richard and Lucy Girding. Ancestry shows Dulcie Girding was christened in 1941 – again in Margate. She was present on the 1951 census, living at an address in Margate with her parents and a brother. She was 11 at the time. The next census was in 1961 and she wasn't on that one, so I continued looking. A Dulcie Girling, aged 20, married a Peter Adams in 1960 in Dalston, Hackney. So, somewhere between 1951 and 1960 she moved to London.'

Mike sat forward in his chair. 'Go on...'

'There's a birth certificate for a Helen Adams – Mother Dulcie, Father – Peter, born 1961 in Dalston and then... wait for it... a death entry for Peter Adams in 1964.' Heath laid all of the pieces of paper on the desk in front of Mike.

'And this is her?'

Heath nodded. 'It must be. This Dulcie Adams went on to have a *second* child – a Robert Adams, born June 1965 – with the birth registered in *Maidenhead*.'

Mike frowned. 'Maidenhead?'

'Nan said this woman disappeared several months before your father's death in May 1965 and was pregnant, didn't she? She must have moved *here*.' Heath stabbed his finger at the word 'Maidenhead'. 'But,' he continued, 'Robert's birth certificate lists Dulcie as mother but the father is blank.'

Mike frowned. 'It would be if the father was dead.'

'This *is* the Dulcie Adams we're interested in. It all adds up. This has to be the woman involved with your father and this Robert bloke must be your brother.'

Mike sat back in the chair. *Heath had found this all out from a computer?* He glanced at the hated plastic monstrosity on the desk, suddenly feeling a newfound respect for it.

'There's more...' Heath beamed, placing another piece of paper in front of his father. 'The Electoral role shows Dulcie Adams (Widower) at this address.'

'Footlights, Frogmore Road, Maidenhead? And she still lives there?' Mike asked.

Heath shrugged. 'According to the latest electoral role, yes. Unless she's died very recently.'

'What about the children? Helen, did you say? What about her? And this... this Robert?' Mike could barely bring himself to utter the name. *Robert Adams, who it looked like was his brother... Shit the bed! This was real.*

Heath puffed his chest out proudly. 'Helen is married to a James Shepherd. No kids as far as I can see. There's loads to do, but a Google search on 'Helen Shepherd' brings up an estate agent in Maidenhead where she's a partner.'

Mike frowned. 'And Robert? What have you found on him?'

Heath fiddled with the notebook in his lap. 'Nothing as yet, which is a bit odd. Nothing on the electoral role or Ancestry, apart from his birth and christening.'

'Could be dead?' Mike suggested, still unable to get his head around the likely conclusion that he'd randomly gained a brother.

Heath shrugged. 'I can't find a death notice, but that doesn't mean anything. He could have emigrated. I've barely touched the sides yet, but where do we go from here? I mean, I could spend months or even *years* digging around the family tree, but unless I'm mistaken, we want to move on this sooner rather than later, don't we?'

Finishing the rest of his drink, Mike nodded. 'That we do, so being as we've got something to work with on the daughter, let's concentrate on her. She should lead us to the brother if he's around and ultimately to the mother, Dulcie Adams. I just need to think about how we're going to go about it.'

· · · ·

TEAGAN POTTERED AROUND as quietly as possible. She'd been supposed to take Dulcie to her weekly indoor bowls match that she went to once a week, but today she was adamant that she wasn't going.

Complaining of a headache, Dulcie had gone for a lie down after lunch, so Teagan had taken the opportunity to do some dusting and cleaning. She'd done all the bannisters so far – well almost… Just this last one on the first floor and then all the bannisters in the house would be freshly dusted and polished.

Sitting down on the top step, Teagan fished her phone from her pocket. She'd promised herself she wouldn't have it on her during the day, especially when she was working, but she couldn't resist the temptation.

She opened the text messages, seeing one from Joe and eagerly opened it:

    Sorry. Been really busy.

Teagan frowned. Was that it? Not even a kiss?
She quickly tapped in her reply.

    Is everything alright? Missing you like crazy!
    Love you xx

Pressing send, Teagan found she'd discovered the top step of the first floor staircase was another place with a pocket of network coverage. She stared at the phone and within seconds came a reply:

Any chance you can get out for half an hour?

Teagan's heart skipped a beat. She so missed Joe and longed to feel his arms around her. Perhaps she could sneak out later for a few minutes?

Not right now but will try later. Love you xx

Teagan waited for a response but there was nothing further. Shoving the phone back in her pocket, she pulled herself to her feet. Walking past Dulcie's room, she listened at the door, hearing the faint sound of muffled snoring and smiled to herself. Dulcie was tired after all, bless her.

For want of what to do next, Teagan decided she'd make a start on dusting the sitting room, although the prospect of carefully moving, dusting and replacing the countless ornaments and assorted objects on every level surface didn't fill her with eagerness, but it needed doing, so do it she must.

Making her way downstairs she froze hearing noise from below. Heart racing, she reached the ground floor and tentatively crept along the hallway, pausing at each doorway to gauge where the sound was coming from. It was very distinct and definitive.

A rush of cold flooded over her. *It wouldn't be a burglar in the middle of the day, would it?*

Straining her ears, she pinpointed the noise to be coming from the kitchen. Creeping forwards, she edged towards the half-open door and pressing herself flat against the wall, peered through the gap.

It was a man! Heart pounding, she remained paralysed against the wall hardly daring to breathe. The man had his back turned as he rifled through a drawer. Indignation flared as she witnessed this person going through Dulcie's things.

Wait. Was that Robert? She peered closer. *It was Robert!*

What on earth was he doing?

Teagan watched Robert move to a cupboard, yank the door open and peer inside. Slamming that door, he moved to another drawer, pulling things out haphazardly and then shoved them back.

Opening another cupboard, Robert pulled out some paperwork and squinting, ran his eyes over the documents in his hand. Teagan frowned. She had to make her presence known. She couldn't just stand and watch him, he was Dulcie's son, for God's sake.

Robert swung around as Teagan cleared her throat slightly, his face a mask of surprise, but on seeing Teagan, changed to that of anger. 'What the hell are you doing?' he barked, shoving the paperwork back in the cupboard.

Swallowing the urge to ask Robert the same, Teagan smiled, despite the hostile expression on his face. 'I heard a noise,' she said. 'I was worried someone had broken in. Dulcie didn't mention you were coming round today.'

'Why isn't she at bowls?' Robert barked. 'She always goes to bowls.'

'Dulcie had a headache and didn't want to go.' She eyed Robert shutting the cupboard he'd been sifting through. 'Were you looking for something? I rearranged the kitchen yesterday, so if I know what you're looking for, then I might be able to help?'

'It's none of your damn business!' Robert snarled, stepping forward. 'This is my house or rather, my mother's. It's not up to you to tell me what I can or can't do.'

For the first time Teagan noticed just quite how physically unnerving the man was. Sporting a large well-built frame and defined, angry features, Robert was quite intimidating. If she was honest, he scared her a little. She instinctively stepped back. 'I wasn't... I mean, I didn't mean to insinuate that you were...'

'I know what you were doing! Stop making excuses!' Robert yelled. 'You shouldn't be here anyway!'

Teagan gasped. This man may be Dulcie's son, but it didn't mean he had the right to sneak about and insult her. 'I thought you were a burglar!'

'Burglar? Don't be absurd! Is Helen here?'

'Helen? No, I'm not expecting her to…'

'*You* don't have to be expecting anything! We don't have to run anything past you. I asked you a simple question.'

Teagan bit the inside of her cheek to stop herself from giving this man a piece of her mind. 'No, she's not here.'

'She hasn't dropped anything off for my mother?' Robert pushed.

Teagan shook her head. 'Not as far as I know, no.'

Robert made that harrumphing sound again as he scowled at her, then stalked past without another word.

Staring in confusion, Teagan watched Robert stride down the long hallway and leave the house, slamming the door behind him.

TWELVE

NERO SCREWED UP HIS EYES and inhaled deeply. They'd been here almost half an hour and he was already bored shitless. This was the *third* time they'd trekked up to Maidenhead, but at least now they knew this was the correct house; the old dear was still on this mortal coil and Helen Shepherd was in regular contact with her mother.

He glanced at Keith and then at the mounting piles of sandwich packets, empty crisp and chocolate bar wrappers in his usually pristine footwell and scowled. Keith's gargantuan appetite and the amount of stuff he'd gnawed his way through today had beaten his previous record and had made the car resemble an overflowing rubbish bin which did nothing to help his OCD of tidy motors. It made him twitchy.

Having to come up and down to Maidenhead also wasn't doing anything to help the rest of his side of the business either. Keith had already been forced to arrange for some of the other lads to double up with the collection work. Running behind with anything made him uncomfortable.

Nero glanced at the house. It still looked just as much of a dump as yesterday; the gleaming exterior of the adjacent houses only accentuating what a state it was in.

Nero wasn't sure what they were now supposed to be watching for. The instructions had been a tad vague.

'Watch to see if anyone else comes and goes,' Jonah had barked. *'We need to see who we can use, aside from Helen Shepherd, to get in the place without resorting to force.'*

Nero sighed. Neither did it help that when they arrived he'd glimpsed the back of a bloke walking near the house – a big, miserable fucker, but he hadn't seen where the man had come from. It was Keith's fault. If they hadn't stopped for more sandwiches they'd have seen where he'd come from.

It *looked* like he'd come from the ramshackle place, but he couldn't be sure. And Nero didn't like not being sure. Not where Jonah was concerned. And certainly not on this subject. Reporting back with anything that wasn't one hundred percent certain, in the frame of mind Jonah was in, wasn't a good idea. People had died for less and he wasn't going to be one of them. There was too much riding on getting the business with this old bat spot on and they couldn't afford to fuck it up.

Jonah had been in a particularly bad mood, considering he was supposed to be getting married. That had been a bit of a shock too.

Nero shrugged. Although he knew Jonah was shacked up with that Lena bird, he hadn't thought it to be *that* serious. That sort of stuff had never been mentioned, which was a bit of surprise, as he'd thought Jonah regarded him as a little more than an employee, considering their long history since teens together. In all honesty, he felt slightly hurt. Why hadn't this engagement thing been mentioned during one of their chats if it was on the cards, rather than an impersonal invite left at the club reception for him?

Nero decided to sit tight a while longer and see what else, if anything, happened. His forehead creased. It wasn't the sort of neighbourhood likely to have any sudden all-night raves, gun fights or spontaneous drug deals and suspected it wasn't going to be particularly scintillating viewing.

Fucking boring in other words.

But Jonah had made it clear, in no uncertain terms, that they needed to wait for the right opportunity to present itself. An opportunity to enable them to get in the house and take the haul back. The sooner that opportunity presented itself, the better.

'Hey up! Who's this?' Keith said suddenly.

Nero looked up, seeing a crappy old Vauxhall making its way up the road, his attention sharpening when it drew to a halt outside the house in question.

Leaning forwards slightly in their seats to give them a clearer view, Nero and Keith waited and watched.

• • • •

TEAGAN HAD SPENT the last twenty five minutes peering through the heavy velvet drapes of the front reception room. With Dulcie still having made no move to come downstairs, she'd taken the opportunity to ask Joe if he could pop around now. It wasn't her afternoon off, but being as Dulcie was still asleep and she was more than a little shaken and confused over Robert's sudden appearance and then abrupt departure, she could do with a slice of normality, even if just for ten minutes. And, more to the point, she wanted to see Joe. *Really* wanted to see him.

She leant against the velvet curtain, her nose twitching from the dust and seeing Joe's familiar blue Vauxhall pull up at the bottom of the steps, Teagan ran to the over mantle mirror, hastily checking her hair and makeup. Not anywhere near her absolute best, but she didn't look bad.

Quickly moving into the hallway, she pulled open the old heavy door, put the catch on and slipped outside, pulling the door to behind her.

Her heart fluttered as Joe strode up the steps, still looking as attractive as ever, his wavy blond hair reaching the collar of a checked shirt thrown casually over a tight T-shirt outlining his well-defined physique.

Beaming, Teagan rushed into his arms. 'Oh, am I glad to see you!' She wrapped her arms around Joe's neck and stretched to kiss him.

Joe pulled away. 'I can't stay long, I...'

'Oh my God, Joe.' Teagan gestured to the imposing house looming over them. 'You should see it in there. It's massive!' she gabbled. 'It's just me and Dulcie in there – the lady I'm looking after, but she's a sweetheart. She's got two children – Helen, who's really nice and Robert. Robert's scary – rude too and...'

'Teagan, I...' Joe shifted from one foot to the other.

'I'd invite you in, but I'd have to ask Dulcie first. Actually, she wants to meet you and suggested you come around on my afternoon off!' She smiled widely. 'You'll like her. She's ever so nice. Drinks gin too and...'

'*Teagan!*' Joe's face was serious. 'I wanted to see you because I didn't want to do this over text.'

Teagan froze, for the first time noticing Joe's expression. 'What's happened?' She clutched at his arm. 'Are you alright? Oh no, please don't tell me you've lost your job?'

Joe gently removed Teagan's hand from his sleeve. 'No, I haven't lost my job. It's...'

'Thank God! We'd be going backwards with the money for the flat if that had happened and...'

'Teagan!' Joe hissed. 'You're not making this easy.'

Falling silent, Teagan blanched. 'Easy? What's going on?'

Joe sucked his bottom lip and looked at the floor sheepishly. 'This isn't working.'

Teagan blinked and frowned. 'What isn't working?'

'Us,' Joe said. '*We're* not working.'

'What do you mean?' Teagan cried. *Joe wasn't saying what she thought he was saying, was he? Surely he wasn't saying...?*

'This isn't going to work out,' Joe repeated.

Relieved, Teagan grabbed back hold of his arm. 'I had a feeling being away like this would be too much. I know it's only been a few days, but I've missed you like crazy too.' She wrapped her arms around his waist. 'Don't worry, I'll leave. I'm sure Dulcie will understand, but I might have to stay to the end of the week. We'll find another way to save up the money for the flat.'

Joe dragged his hand through his floppy hair. 'It's nothing to do with you being away. I meant it's not working between *us* anymore.'

'B-But you said... This was *your* idea. You...'

'I guess I wanted a few days to myself to prove myself right. And I did.'

Teagan's eyebrows knitted together. 'You sent me on a six month assignment to get money to move in together and then *three* days into it you decide we're done?' she cried, her eyes filling with tears.

'Oh, come on Teag. You know as well as I do that we've been going through the motions for ages!' Joe said. 'There hasn't been anything between us for a long time.'

Teagan felt like she'd been punched in the stomach. *She* hadn't been going through the motions. She thought she'd marry Joe, when he eventually got round to asking her, that was. Nothing between them? There was *everything* between them. Joe was her world and the most important thing in it. 'You wanted to get a flat. It was your idea. *You* said th...'

'No, Teag. *You* said. *You* wanted us to move in together. You've been bleating on about it for ages! All the lads dig me about it. You're like a fucking stuck record! I should have stopped this ages ago, but it was less hassle not to.'

'Is that all I am? Hassle?' Teagan sobbed, tears trickling down her cheeks.

Joe shrugged. 'Look, I just don't want to be with you anymore. I'm sorry, alright?'

Teagan's eyes narrowed and she eyed Joe suspiciously. 'There someone else, isn't there?'

Joe laughed. 'There's been a few actually, but no – this isn't because of anyone else. I just don't want to settle down and you do. It's not working. Simples.'

Teagan dropped her hand from Joe's arm and resisted the burning urge to slap the lopsided grin she'd always loved so much off his smug face. 'Who are they?' she whispered. 'Who were these others? These other girls?'

'It doesn't matter, they're unimportant,' Joe said.

'It matters to *me*!' Teagan wailed.

'You're embarrassing yourself,' Joe snapped. 'Listen, I could have let things drag on and let you think we'd got a future, but I didn't. You've been texting and texting and driving me mad. I've done the decent thing and yet you're still bloody moaning!'

'Decent thing?' Teagan screamed. 'This is decent? Years we've been together and now you're telling me it's over? Just like that?'

Joe nodded. 'That's about the extent of it, yes!'

'Interrupting your time with other women, was I?' Teagan spat, her whole body shaking.

Joe rolled his eyes. 'You always have to be melodramatic and over the top. You're a goddamn bunny boiler!'

'That's quite enough!' Dulcie's voice spoke clearly and loudly.

Teagan swung around, mortified to find Dulcie behind her. 'Dulcie... I....'

Dulcie looked through Teagan, her sharp blue eyes fixed on Joe. 'You've said what you came to say young man, so now I suggest you scuttle back to where you crawled from!'

Joe stared at the elderly lady. 'You what? Who are...?'

'This is *my* property and you're on it. *Uninvited*!' Dulcie countered. 'Make yourself scarce and when or rather *if*, you ever grow up you'll realise your mistake in treating this young lady in such a fashion!'

Teagan's mouth hung open at Dulcie's words, taking a small amount of pleasure as Joe's face turned an uncomfortable shade of red.

'Did you not hear me, you imbecile?' Dulcie roared. 'Get off my property! That's the *last* time I will tell you!'

Joe scowled at Dulcie, then at Teagan before turning and stomping down the steps. 'Fucking mad old bag!' he muttered.

As Joe got in his car, slammed the door and fired the engine, Dulcie stepped towards Teagan. 'Come on, dear. Let's go back inside. You can't stand here all day.'

No one noticed the engine of a second car starting slightly afterwards and following Joe's car down the road as he drove away.

. . . .

'I WANTED IT TO BE A SURPRISE,' Lena whined, realising she'd possibly overdone the doe-eyed look when Jonah shook her hand from her arm.

'It was that alright,' Jonah scowled. Agreeing to marry Lena was one thing, but he could have done with longer than forty-eight hours to get his head around everything before she'd taken it upon herself to organise a full-on fuck off engagement bash at his own club – inviting just about anyone and everyone. Including the goddamn press.

The first he'd known about it was when people started congratulating him this morning. Bloody embarrassing it was. He hadn't even had the chance to mention anything to Gwen or Nero. Actually, it was *very* embarrassing. And there was only one way to look at it: his impending nuptials were now official.

'I'm sorry babe,' Lena slithered her arm around Jonah's neck as he flopped into a chair.

Jonah forced himself to smile. He'd have to swallow it – put it down to her excitement. This pregnancy thing had been a shock to them both, but that didn't make it any better. For a nanosecond, he felt guilty being as he'd never had any genuine plans to marry the woman – far from it. But at least he was doing the right thing - the *only* thing under the circumstances.

Jonah stared at the plate of food Lena put in front of him and forced himself to pick up the cutlery. He wasn't in the slightest bit hungry.

'I hope you'll make the effort to spend more time with me now.' Lena eyed Jonah carefully. *It was time to up the ante.* She placed her hand on her washboard stomach. 'I know how things work, but now I'm pregnant with *your* child, the least you can do is stay faithful. I don't want my baby infected with an STD because you can't keep your dick in your pants.'

Jonah slammed his fork down, his eyes blazing. 'Don't you dare start dictating shit. I've never had no STD, nor will I!'

Quickly changing tack, Lena forced tears into her eyes. 'I'm sorry... I-It's just... I'm feeling unattractive at the moment.' She looked sadly at her plate. 'I-I've never been fat...'

Jonah contained the urge to punch her in the face. The silly cow was as thin as she had always been. 'You said you're only five weeks pregnant, Lena. You're hardly fat. You look the same as always.'

'But I won't *soon*,' Lena whined, her heavily-made up eyes scrutinising Jonah. 'I'll be all fat and pregnant and you won't want me. You'll go off with other women, I know you will.'

'No I won't,' Jonah said through gritted teeth, wishing she'd shut up.

Lena sighed heavily. 'And I'm so exhausted with these baby hormones. I could really do with a housekeeper or at least a cook and a second cleaner. You said you'd sort it the other day and it's the least you could do being as you got me pregnant.'

Jonah bit back his retort. She spoke as if he'd planned to somehow purposefully override the chemical contraceptive. *Hardly!*

He'd have to try and do what she wanted. His father would expect that of him now she was carrying his child, but it didn't mean he had to like it. 'I said I'd look into it and I will.'

'Thanks, babe. My tits don't half hurt too. I think they've got bigger already. What do you think?'

Jonah shrugged as she shoved her more than ample cleavage in his general direction. Personally, he couldn't see how they could get any bigger with the amount of implants she'd had put in.

'What if they go saggy? I'll have to have them done again,' she gasped, her taloned fingers clutching Jonah's hand over the table. 'You'll still love me though, won't you?'

Jonah moved his hand away from Lena's grasp in the pretence of picking up his beer. 'Yeah, course.' Well, he might have done if he'd ever loved her in the fucking first place, which he hadn't. Not even slightly. And now he was struggling to even *like* her. *Christ, what a mess...*

'Jonah, you haven't mentioned the baby to anyone, have you?' Lena batted her false eyelashes. 'I don't want anyone to know our exciting news until after we're married. Plus, it's bad luck to say anything until after the twelve-week mark. Promise me you won't.'

Jonah shook his head. 'I've already said I wouldn't the other day and I haven't.' *She didn't need to worry about that.* If people hadn't already guessed the reason for their marriage, he'd drag out having to publicly announce he'd been so bloody stupid to get her pregnant too for as long as possible.

'I've also got a date for our wedding pencilled in too.' Smiling, Lena reached for her bag and fished out the registry office paperwork. 'Nine weeks' time.' She pouted her lips. 'I wanted something sooner because we need to get married before I start to show. I don't want to look like a heifer walking down the aisle. Maybe they'll get a cancellation? Perhaps you can have a word?'

Jonah nodded numbly, supressed rage pushing its way to the surface. Whether he liked it or not, he was stuck with Lena Taylor and found himself hating her more and more every fucking minute.

So engrossed with trying to keep his impotent rage under wraps, Jonah didn't notice Lena's hand leaning on the paperwork and partially obscuring what, if he had seen it, he wouldn't have taken the pen and scrawled his signature. If he'd have seen what was there in black and white, he'd have thrown her out of his life and the house there and then.

THIRTEEN

COLLAPSING ON TOP OF THE BLONDE, Joe rolled onto his back, sated.

'Joe?' the woman whined, her fingers trailing down Joe's sweaty chest. 'Aren't you going to finish me off?'

Stretching across to the bedside cabinet, brushing the woman's fingers away, Joe grabbed his packet of cigarettes and lit one, inhaling deeply. 'Greedy, aren't you? I think you were pleasured more than enough last night. I'm surprised you haven't seized up!'

'But I'm still well horny,' she continued. 'You can't leave me half done.'

'Fraid you'll have to put up with it, babe. I've got lots on today, so you'd best make tracks.' Joe smiled, but he really wanted to just tell this woman to shut up and sling her hook.

The woman propped herself up on her elbows, her eyes caked with last night's makeup. 'What? You want me to leave?'

'No, of course not,' Joe lied. 'It's just that I...' Hearing his phone beep, he swung out of the bed and grabbed his phone, betting that was *her* texting again. *It usually was.*

But then he remembered. Teagan was no more. His face split into a wide grin and just to prove the point, he opened the text messages, breathing a sigh of relief to find a spammy text about upgrades from Vodafone. *Voila. No Teagan.*

He grinned. Even if it *had* been her, he could now happily ignore her. Yesterday afternoon's visit had lifted a massive weight from his shoulders and he should have done it a long time back. In fact, he should have never got involved in what would be classed as a 'proper' relationship with Teagan Fraser from the off. He wasn't the type.

Joe hid the smile creeping back across his face. At least his housemates couldn't take the piss anymore. Oh yeah, he'd seen them pressing their thumbs onto their foreheads when Teagan was mentioned. Now there would be no more of that, or no more digs about getting married either. Their faces last night when he'd announced he and Teagan were over had been a picture and they'd gone for a decent night on the town to celebrate his newfound freedom. Not that being with Teagan had ever stopped him from taking what he fancied where the ladies were concerned.

Hastily pulling on his jeans, Joe glanced at the woman that he'd brought back last night and grinned to himself, realising that at last he didn't have to constantly think of excuses to answer the never ending rounds of Teagan's questions.

Shoving his phone in his pocket, he yanked a T-shirt over his head, one eye on the large exposed breasts of the girl in his bed. He wouldn't mind a bit more with her, but being as she'd already started demanding things it was best he got rid of her quick smart before she started stalking him too.

Picking up a bundle of hastily discarded clothes from the floor, Joe chucked them at the blonde. 'Here's your stuff. Sling anything of mine back on the floor and I'll sort it later.'

Turning his back, he walked from the room, desperate for a drink. It was almost lunchtime and hoped the others would be up for grabbing a beer at the pub. He needed to offload his hangover, plus he wanted to get away from this chick before she decided she wanted to move in.

Joe moved into the kitchen, shutting the door behind him

and stumbled to the fridge. Yanking it open, he saw it was empty, apart from a rather wizened tomato embedded to the back wall and a carton of milk.

Pulling out the milk, he unscrewed the top, sniffing at the contents. 'Jesus Christ! That fucking stinks!' he muttered.

'We'd have bought some fresh with us had we known,' a voice snarled.

Spinning around, Joe dropped the carton of milk, the curdled contents spreading in a lumpy pool around his bare feet. He stared at the rabid strangers in his kitchen, then his eyes quickly found his housemates, Alan and Dave, bound to kitchen chairs, their mouths covered with gaffer tape.

'What the fuck?' Joe gasped, his usual bolshie confidence evaporating at a rate of knots. 'Who…?'

'Who are we?' the man growled, a ghost of a smile on his face. 'That doesn't matter. I'm here to ask questions and my friend here is making sure everyone obliges, nothing more.'

Joe dared a quick look at the monster in the other corner of the room and shivered internally at the thick scar down his face. *And what the fuck was that? Half an ear? Oh, Jesus…*

He shook his head slightly to double check he wasn't seeing things. He'd been a tad heavy on both the weed and the beer last night, so it was feasible he was hallucinating. Unfortunately, he wasn't. He focused back on the man talking – at least six foot six, with a thick neck and hands like shovels. They both looked pretty damn real to him and fear pooled in his feet, spreading rapidly up his legs into his spine.

This man didn't look any more friendly than the other one; slightly less physically repulsive, but that was about it. Joe next looked across to Dave and Alan, their eyes pleading with him to do whatever these people wanted. This was typical of them. The first day as a free man away from the clutches of a bunny-boiler and his bloody housemates involved him in weird shit?

He took a deep breath and smiled at the vicious-looking pair. 'Listen guys, I don't know what's going on here, but we don't want any trouble. If my mates owe you money for gear, then let's not stress. I'm sure we can sort it o…'

'Do we look like lackeys collecting drug money from a bunch of wasters?' the less ugly man spat, his eyes narrowing.

'Erm, no… I meant…' Joe hesitated, feeling even more uncomfortable. *If it wasn't to do with them, then…?*

Before he could think of anything more suitable to say a meaty hand grabbed a handful of his wayward hair, the other wrapped tightly around his throat and forced his head down on the small kitchen table.

Joe concentrated on a cluster of congealed baked beans encrusted on the tabletop in an attempt to control his rapidly escalating panic.

'Being as we're nice, we decided to let you finish whatever you were doing in your bedroom.' The man jutted his bull head towards the closed door. 'And I used that time to talk to your *friends…*'

Joe blinked rapidly, pointlessly fumbling over the man's thick fingers in the hope that he could loosen the grip around his windpipe. His eyes flicked back to Dave and Alan who looked just as terrified as he felt, possibly more, finding with mounting unease that they both averted their gaze. *What had they said? Oh shit! Was the woman in his bed this guy's wife or something? Please no…*

His eyes flicked towards the closed kitchen door, hoping to God the woman didn't wander in, only to find her seething husband, boyfriend, or whoever the hell this geezer was.

'The house you went to? Yesterday?' the man's growling voice interrupted Joe from the unpleasant scenarios washing around his head.

'H-House?' Joe spluttered. 'What house?'

Alan's eyes darted towards Joe. 'Joe, you…'

Joe watched in horror as the second man – the one with the mangled ear, lurched forward at record speed to give Alan a swift kick in the side of his face.

Alan yelped in pain, whilst the man reverted to his statue-like position to the side of them.

Pulling Joe up from his enforced close-up view of the kitchen table, the first man slammed him down into the one remaining kitchen chair. 'Don't fuck about, otherwise you and your mates will see me lose my temper. Do you understand?'

Joe nodded feverishly, sweat running down the back of his neck. *This was not good. He had no idea what any of them were supposed to have done.*

'Now tell me about the house. Your girlfriend lives there, right?'

Joe's fuddled brain desperately tried to work out what on earth this man was talking about. *House?* Then it suddenly fell into place. The guy was talking about the place he'd gone to dump Teagan? *What the hell?*

Seeing recollection on Joe's face, the man grinned, his maniacal smile making him look even more ferocious. 'Coming back to you, is it? Your mates here informed me your girlfriend is called Teagan. Nice looking bird she is too.'

Joe glanced at Dave and Alan once more, both still avoiding his gaze by staring at the floor. *What the fuck had they told this bruiser and why?* 'S-She's not my girlfriend. We split up yesterday and...'

'Look, dickhead,' the man growled. 'It's not like I'm going to tell her you've got some slag in your bedroom. That's your call. I don't give a flying fuck, so don't talk shit.'

Joe swallowed uncomfortably, his throat still half-crushed. 'She really isn't my girlfriend anymore. I...'

'Who owns the house?'

'The house?' Joe repeated. 'I...'

'That's what I fucking said, wasn't it?' the man snarled, grabbing Joe's hair again and pulling his head backwards, forced him to look into cold reptilian eyes. 'Who. Owns. The. Fucking. House?'

'I-I don't know. My girlfriend... my *ex*-girlfriend started working there for an old woman,' he muttered.

'This old woman – what's her name?'

'I-I don't... I don't know,' Joe spluttered.

Joe found himself being dragged out of the kitchen by his hair. His nails scraped futilely against the scuffed walls attempting to slow his journey, but within seconds the man kicked open the door to the downstairs toilet and pulled him inside.

'No! NO! Wait!' Joe wailed, his voice promptly cut off when his head was forced into the toilet bowl. He screwed up his eyes as the stench of at least two weeks' worth of leftovers from the uncleaned bog assaulted his nostrils, panic thundering as his head was held down.

He didn't even have the chance to wish he'd bothered flushing the loo after using it earlier, when piss mixed with God knows what else pushed into his mouth and up his nose.

'Fucking state of it in here,' the man muttered, pulling the chain, unloading an avalanche of water onto Joe's head. 'Have you thought of her name yet?' he growled. He'd shove this prick's head into the U-bend if he didn't hurry up and start talking sensibly.

Think, Think! Joe panicked, his scalp burning. He flailed his arms around frantically and was relieved when the grip on his head was released.

Coughing and sputtering, he fell back against the wall, gagging at the taste in his mouth. He looked up through his dripping hair at the giant of the man crammed into the small cloakroom with him. 'I-I think it's Dulcie. Yeah, that's it. Dulcie. Don't know her surname.'

The man smiled menacingly. 'Dulcie? Ok, that wasn't so hard, was it? Right, so now we've got that sorted let's talk about the bit of work you'll be doing for me. Your girlfriend will be helping too.'

'But she not m...'

'If she's your ex, like you say, then make it so she's not.' The man's mouth formed a sinister grin. 'Now, pin your lugholes back and listen to what you're going to do.'

• • • •

'YOU DON'T NEED TO BE SORRY,' Dulcie said as Teagan apologised for the third time. She crossed her legs daintily in the chair opposite. 'You said that enough times yesterday, so don't waste one more tear on that buffoon!'

Teagan laughed sadly amid the tears still coursing down her cheeks.

'It's no laughing matter, girl!' Dulcie continued. 'The boy's an idiot! You may not think that now, but you will, believe me. I've had a few of those in my time and they're a waste of space. You'll know when you meet the real one.'

Teagan sniffed miserably. 'I thought I had...'

'Poppycock! No way was that creature right for you. I only had true love once myself.'

Teagan nodded. 'Your husband?'

'Christ, no!' Dulcie exclaimed. Getting up from the chair she strolled over to the cabinet. 'Let's have a gin. I've never cared whether it's too early.' She turned to Teagan. 'Oh, don't look so startled. My husband was an idiot and a selfish one at that! I only married him because, oh I don't know... because I was stupid as well, I guess.'

Dulcie poured two large gins and shoved a glass into Teagan's hand. Sipping it, Teagan almost choked on the burn of the neat spirit and watched astounded whilst Dulcie drank hers like water.

'Peter was a moron. Very much like that one of yours. He had lots of women on the side too - the difference was I didn't care.'

'W-What happened?' Teagan asked tentatively.

'He was a barman and worked at The Feathers with me but fancied himself as going up in the world. He resented I was on the stage and partying with all the celebs whilst he was stuck behind the bar.' Dulcie laughed. 'And of course, that was what got him killed. He annoyed the wrong people and then he was no more...'

'But that left you and the children and...'

'I was *glad* to be rid of him!' Dulcie spat. 'It meant I could be with the man I *really* loved.'

Teagan sipped at her drink, waiting for Dulcie to continue, unsure whether she was making everything worse by humouring these vivid stories. She watched her refill her glass, then walk over to the French doors. *Was this another one of her stories too?*

Dulcie shook her head and then glared at Teagan. 'I spent *years* waiting for Michael... How I loved him!' She rose from her chair and fished around in a tiny drawer inside the walnut bureau. 'I know it's in here somewhere...' She frowned. 'Oh, I can't seem to find it.'

Teagan smiled kindly. 'Never mind. I'm sure whatever it is will turn up eventually.' This was so sad. Dulcie really believed all of this. She really did need help – a lot more help that she had the capacity to give. She knew Helen was aware that Dulcie had got worse, but was she aware of *just* how much worse? Unlikely, because Dulcie acted normal quite a lot of the time.

Teagan sighed inwardly. She would have to tell Helen. It was only right she was made aware. Helen would be so distressed though and Dulcie, well, Dulcie would be devastated to have to go into one of those homes, but there wasn't a lot longer she could let this continue. It wasn't right. There was also the persistent worry that sooner or later Dulcie would injure herself whilst wandering around. What was in her head was so real, it was heart-breaking.

Seeing the sadness on Teagan's face, Dulcie smiled. 'You're thinking about that boy again, aren't you?' she said suddenly. 'Well, don't! I mean it, Teagan. You still have lots of time to meet the *real* one. I met mine and lost him, but *you* haven't.'

Teagan nodded, smiling weakly. She hadn't been thinking about that, but she'd let Dulcie believe so. It was a lot easier than having to explain to her that she was planning on betraying her confidence and speaking to Helen.

The question was, when would be right time to do that?

. . . .

JOE, DAVE AND ALAN sat around the table for a good five minutes before anyone spoke.

Once the men had left, it had taken Joe some time to free his housemates from the chairs they'd been bound to and several more minutes to painfully rip the gaffer tape off their mouths. Unsurprisingly, they were not happy. *He* was not happy. He stank like a public urinal and didn't think he'd ever get the foul taste out of his mouth. Neither would he analyse where the suspect hair going round his mouth had come from… But aside from that, fear had taken priority.

Joe didn't need to check to see if the girl in his bed was still there because he'd heard the front door slam for the second time shortly after the men had left. She'd clearly taken the first available opportunity to make a sharp exit and he could hardly blame her - he'd have done the same if it were possible. And to say he was confused, not to mention, terrified, was an understatement.

He didn't do shit like this. He was into free love and a good time, not dealing with thugs manacling his mates to chairs in his kitchen and trying to drown him in the fucking bog.

'Are you going to tell us what the fuck all of that was about?' Dave said, rubbing the red raw wheals around his wrists.

'How the hell do I know? You heard what I said to that bloke. I don't have a clue what he was talking about,' Joe replied, glancing at Alan who was also eyeing him suspiciously. '*Seriously*, I don't. I don't know anything about it!'

Dave shook his head. 'Whatever's going on, I don't want to be involved. I don't know who they were and I don't want to either!'

'But now, thanks to them following Joe back from that house, they know where we live. Cheers for that,' Alan added, gingerly touching the red skin around his mouth, courtesy of the gaffer tape and the already darkening, swelling bruise across his cheekbone.

Dave folded his arms across his chest. 'We need to go to the police.'

'Are you serious?' Joe gasped. 'You heard what he said would happen if we made the 'mistake' of bringing the police into it.' If Dave had missed that bit, he certainly hadn't. There was no way on God's earth he was going to the Police. Those people were the sort you didn't mess with. The sort you saw in films. And he knew what happened to people who spoke to the police in situations such as this…

'Could this be Teagan's way of getting her own back on you for dumping her?' Alan suggested. 'I mean, she's always been a bit full on and it's a bit weird that you haven't heard from her, don't you think?'

Joe frowned. He'd been surprised too. He'd have presumed he'd have had at least fifty text messages and a thousand missed calls by now, but he hadn't had one. But Teagan wouldn't know where to start to arrange for two psychos to intimidate him. He shook his head. 'It's not her. She's too dippy for that.'

'What are you going to do then?' Alan asked. 'If you don't sort it, you can fuck off. I'm not having that again, I can tell you that much!'

'You can't kick me out! We're the Three Musketeers!' Joe smiled, attempting to make light of the situation.

'This isn't fucking funny,' Dave barked. 'If you won't let us go to the cops, then you'll have to do as he said and I hope for everyone's sakes that this shit doesn't get complicated.'

'But I've dumped Teagan. I told you that last night. How am I supposed to do th…'

'Undump her, then,' Alan cried. 'Just bloody sort it!' He stood up, still rubbing at his wrists. 'Screw this. I need a drink and a smoke. You coming, Dave?'

'Damn right,' Dave glanced at Joe nastily. 'Don't even think about joining us. You've got things to sort out, remember?'

Joe watched Alan and Dave walk from the kitchen and

straight out of the front door. He put his head in his hands and stared at the congealed beans again. *Fuck.* They were right. He'd have to do what was asked. But how could he wheedle his way into some old dear's house off the back of Teagan? And furthermore, *why* did these blokes want him to? Just that she'd got something of theirs? *Like what?*

He hadn't felt it wise to further question the gorilla who had a steady grip of his neck whilst forcing his nose into the U-bend. If they wanted him to get keys for the place, then that's what he'd do. Then perhaps he could get on with his life Teagan-free, like he had been happily planning, until this had happened.

The only problem was, he was in no way sure how he would do it.

FOURTEEN

HEATH HOVERED IN FRONT of the large expanse of glass, taking occasional glances through the window, hoping he wasn't being obvious.

It had taken a good hour and a half to get here, thanks to being stupid enough to set off during the rush hour, but once he'd reached Maidenhead, finding the place was easy enough. Shepherd, Percival and Proctor occupied a prominent position on the High Street of the affluent market town and the gentile atmosphere of the place was a stark contrast to where he lived.

A ripple of unease ran up Heath's spine. Judging by what he was seeing, Helen Shepherd had done alright for herself. What if this Dulcie woman had cashed in the spoils a long time ago? If the benefits had been already festooned on her children, then it would be too late for *him*. But if the benefits had been given to Dulcie's children, they couldn't have lasted long.

Although looking pristine on the outside, according to the research he'd done on Shepherd, Percival and Proctor on the Companies House website, it had traded at a loss for the past three consecutive years, with the last financial years' turnover being the worst yet.

Whatever façade Helen Shepherd liked to portray about her

company, it was not doing well at all. And in that case, the chances were that Helen Shepherd wouldn't be either – which could leave the way open for some very useful negotiation.

Heath focused harder on who was behind the large shop front. From what he could see there were three women and two men in there – all of whom looked like they worked there. But which of the women, if any, was Helen Shepherd?

When one of the women noticed him staring, Heath hastily made a show of perusing the colour printouts of featured houses for sale in the window, each positioned behind columns of Perspex. He feigned extra interest in a farmhouse-style property, wincing at the £2.1 million price tag. Although smart in his work suit, would a twenty-six year old enquiring about a £2.1 million gaff be taken seriously?

Heath clenched his jaw. Why not? If he had anything to do with it, he *would* have a hell of a lot more than that soon.

Taking a deep breath, he strolled inside only to be faced with an over-thin middle-aged woman with a botoxed face. He watched as she forced her frozen muscles into something partly resembling a smile.

'Good morning,' the woman said. 'Can I help you?'

'I hope so.' Heath smiled, noticing the woman's eyes travelling over him, making no secret she was assessing him for worth. He moved towards the desk, quietly wondering whether this botoxed creature was Helen Shepherd. His charm worked like a dream with car sales, but would it fare equally as well with middle-class women of Berkshire, even the ones hiding behind a posh frontage covering financial ruin.

'I'm interested in one of your properties.' Heath motioned to the window. 'I saw it the other day and was going to call, but being as I was coming to the area, I thought I'd pop along in person.'

Heath looked to see if Ms Botox had a name badge to give him a clue if she was the one he was after, but there was nothing. He could hardly peer at her chest too long without it being taken the wrong way. Not that by the looks of it there was much to see.

Ms Botox shuffled paperwork and glanced at him with disinterest. 'Which property is it that you're interested in... *Sir*?'

Heath kept his smile in place, despite not missing the emphasis placed on the word 'Sir'. *The snotty bitch.* 'The farmhouse called 'The Gables'? It's in the window and...'

'The *Gables*?' Ms Botox repeated, glancing at her colleague.

Seeing his chance to locate Helen Shepherd slip further away, Heath decided he'd better up the game. 'Excuse me one moment.' He pulled his mobile from his suit jacket.

Stepping away from the desk he pretended to answer a call and listened for a couple of seconds, hoping his phone wouldn't start ringing for real. *Now that would be embarrassing.*

'It needs to happen today!' Heath barked in an authoritative voice. 'It has *got* to get sign off. One more take and then that's it!' Making a flourish of ending the non-existent call, Heath turned his attention back to Ms Botox. 'I'm very sorry about that. Business is hectic at the moment. Now, where were we?'

A blonde woman suddenly appeared from a separate office at the back of the room. 'Thank you, Joanne. I'll look after Mr...?'

'Harding,' Heath blurted, stepping forward and extending his hand. 'Darren Harding.'

'I hear you're interested in knowing more about The Gables? I'm Helen Shepherd, partner of Shepherd, Percival and Proctor. Please come and sit down and I'll tell you about the property and you can let me know your current situation.'

Heath smiled widely. Probably too widely. *Bingo. This was her?* She wasn't too bad for an old bird, this aunt of sorts. Was she an aunt? Half-aunt perhaps? Was there even such a thing?

Confidently following Helen Shepherd into the swish-looking office at the back of the estate agents, he was unable to help from giving Ms Botox a smug smirk as he passed. Now she'd be kicking herself about not giving him her full attention and working out just how much commission she'd just lost. Well, she would be if he had any intention of buying the place, which he didn't, but that wasn't the point. Either way, the woman needed a refresher course in customer service.

But it looked like his initial theory about Helen Shepherd may have been correct. He'd always had a bit of a gift for being able to read between the lines and he could see that despite the deliberate dignified and controlled poise the woman in front of him held, he was fairly certain that flickering below the surface was stress and worry – all pointing to deep personal troubles. This woman distinctly had things on her mind which bothered her.

Heath took the proffered chair, whilst Helen seated herself in a plush leather desk chair, her elbows resting on the glass-topped desk. She pulled a leather-covered notebook towards her and opened it to a clean page, gold Parker pen in hand.

'Ok, Mr Harding. If you'd like to tell me about your situation? Do you have a property to sell?'

Suddenly, Heath realised he hadn't given this situation much thought. *Oh well, he'd have to rely on his trusty gift of the gab.* 'Property? No. I'm, well... *we're...* myself and my business partner, are looking for something more of an investment, rather than a straightforward home move.'

Helen frowned. 'Business investment? In that case you might be more interested in our developer opportunities...' She opened a desk drawer. 'Let me see if I can find the particulars for...'

'I'm not interested in property development,' Heath interrupted. 'I need a property to suit *my* business. I'm a music producer and need somewhere large, offering spacious accommodation, but also something that contains more than enough room for a recording studio – preferably several.'

If Helen's eyes could have displayed pound signs, Heath was sure they would have been huge. He really did have to take his hat off to himself in his ad-libbing ability being second to none.

'Music producer? How fascinating,' Helen gushed. 'In that case The Gables will be ideal. It's in a lovely semi-rural location between here and Marlow and...'

'I'd like to view it,' Heath said.

'When did you have in mind?'

Heath smiled apologetically. 'I know it's short notice, but as I'm in the area I was hoping to see it this afternoon?'

'Today?' Helen exclaimed.

'I've got a meeting I must dash to shortly before returning to London, but if you could make some time free after 12, that would be perfect.'

'Gosh,' Helen said. 'Let me see... I've got a lot of viewings and meetings today myself, but I'll just check my diary.'

Heath watched Helen pull a red A4 hardback from another drawer and make a big show of flicking through the pages. It was all complete bullshit. He did crap like this to make himself look important in front of clients too. Helen had every intention of showing him the property today and he knew it. He could see a mile off that she was desperate for his commission. *Don't bullshit a bullshitter.*

'I suppose if I can juggle my schedule I could try and return next week. It just seemed too good of an opportunity not to see if there was a chance of a viewing whilst I was here,' he pushed.

'I'm sure I can delegate some of my appointments for this afternoon,' Helen smiled, tapping her manicured nails on the diary. 'Give me one moment.'

Not breaking eye contact with Heath, Helen picked up her desk phone and stabbed in numbers. 'Joanne? Yes, could you take my 2 and 3 o'clock appointments?' She covered the mouthpiece. 'Would 2 be convenient?'

'That would be fine,' Heath replied. *Gotcha.*

Smiling, Helen turned back to the phone. 'Yes, today... the 2 and 3 o'clocks? Great. Thank you.' Replacing the handset, she looked at Heath. '2 o'clock it is. Now, can I get you a drink? Coffee? Tea? I can tell you a bit more about th...'

Heath stood up. 'Thank you, but no. I must get to my

meeting. A new artist's signing today,' he lied.

Helen handed Heath a sheaf of glossy paperwork. 'Take a copy of the particulars with you in case you get chance to have a read through before the viewing.'

'Wonderful. Great to meet you, Ms Shepherd.' Heath shook Helen's hand once again.

'Call me Helen. I'll look forward to seeing you later on today.'

Heath left the estate agents, knowing that everyone was watching him get into the pristine Lexus borrowed from his father's forecourt that he'd purposefully parked outside.

Now he'd got a couple of hours to work out what would be the best way to go about this.

Firing the engine, he drove away, desperate to have a pint or three, but decided against it. It stood a good chance that he'd end up getting involved and have more than a couple. He couldn't afford to bugger up his chance to do some digging whilst feigning interest in an overpriced bunch of stables, or whatever the hell it was he was allegedly interested in buying.

Getting some time with the woman in the first place had been surprisingly easy and down to pure luck more than anything else. His appointment could easily have ended up being with that sour-faced Botox woman and as well as not being particularly pleasant to look at, spending his time with her was totally pointless.

But what now?

His forehead furrowed. Opening the window to let a little more air into the confined space.

Short of luring Helen Shepherd to a secluded place, then when she least expected it, threaten her and/or rough her up until she'd given him the details of where this valuable stuff was stashed, there was only two real ways to do this: either suss her out a bit longer or go in headfirst, explain the situation and give her an in?

FIFTEEN

TEAGAN BUSIED HERSELF cleaning the kitchen. She wiped her hand across her forehead, removing suds which had splashed from the washing up bowl. Having had little sleep, her head pounded and she wished she had some paracetamol to take the edge off it.

Filling a glass with water she gulped at the liquid, grateful for the coolness. This morning, like last night, she'd resisted the urge to text Joe. She'd written plenty, her fingers alternating between accusations to begging. Each one she'd deleted.

Dulcie's words about Joe not being the one stuck in her mind and was the only thing stopping her from acting on the uncontrollable need to contact him. But that was all they'd been. *Words*. And they certainly didn't stop any of it from hurting more than a blunt knife sawing against an open wound.

Thankfully, she'd been too busy to have spare time to think about Joe too much today, but every so often he forced his way into her brain regardless of how much she kept herself occupied. Tiredness wasn't helping. Last night Dulcie had had another one of her walkabouts and Teagan had found herself having to coax Dulcie out of that room again. It had taken an age to get her stable enough to return to her proper bedroom.

Dulcie definitely had spates of confusing the past from the present and the more she learnt the more it seemed likely that all her tales were fabricated.

Suddenly hearing voices, Teagan quickly dried her hands on a tea towel and hurried along the hallway. Her heart sank. She couldn't hear very well, but the brusque tone sounded like it may be Robert. She paused halfway, unwilling to interrupt a conversation between mother and son. There was something she found uncomfortable about that man and found herself mistrusting him being left alone with the lady that she was growing more fond of by the day, so she had no choice for her own peace of mind to make sure Dulcie was ok.

Taking a deep breath, Teagan entered the room. 'Is everything alr...' Stopping stock still, she blinked in surprise. 'Joe? What are you doing here?'

• • • •

'THIS REALLY IS A SUPERB PLACE.' Heath smiled brightly at Helen as he walked from the huge open plan lounge into the state of the art refitted kitchen.

'Indeed it is,' Helen agreed, but despite her best efforts, her voice sounded decidedly flat, even to her own ears. Two more phone calls she'd received today from clients informing her that they'd decided not to proceed with Shepherd, Percival and Proctor for their upcoming sales. *That was now eight this week...*

Her lips formed a tight line. None of the clients had *directly* said it was anything to do with those clips of her mother doing the rounds, but it was obvious. At least to her. She really couldn't wait much longer. Her mother needed to go before she ruined anything else. Wrecking her reputation was not part of the side-effects of her plan. And it certainly did the opposite of getting the business thriving again.

Part of her regretted delegating her other appointments to Joanne. She could have easily put off those two until tomorrow, but she couldn't put *this* one off. Mr Harding was the type – one of those pretentious young things with too much money for their own good, to do anything other than purchase something like a property on a whim and she strongly suspected he'd put an offer in for The Gables off the back of the viewing. There was no way she would pass up that amount of easily-earned commission for minimal work.

Heath kept his smile fixed in place, but it hadn't escaped his notice that in the space between leaving the estate agents this morning and meeting her again this afternoon, something had occurred to knock Helen Shepherd off kilter. He hoped it wasn't anything to do with him. Had she been digging around and discovered Darren Harding, Music Producer, did not actually exist? But if she had, surely she wouldn't be here?

Heath dismissed the idea as quickly as it had formed. It wasn't anything to do with him, but *something* had irked her and this could be his opportunity to do some digging. 'Are you alright, Mrs Shepherd?'

'What? Oh yes. Yes, I'm fine. Let's move through to the second reception room, shall we? As you may have seen from the particulars, there's actually four reception rooms. Along with its location and the land accompanying this property, I'm certain you would have no issue obtaining planning permission to build additional extensions to the main dwelling, or even a detached building if you wished. I was thinking of a separate studio complex?' Helen looked around pointedly as if outlining the vast size of the rooms.

Heath nodded, making positive noises like he was considering the potential and the scope it offered. Realistically he was pissed off that he could fit his entire flat into one corner of any of the rooms he'd seen so far, but that would change. Oh, that would so change once he's got his mitts on this money and the woman standing in front of him was the key to getting his hands on it.

When Helen's mobile rang, Heath watched her snatch the phone from her shoulder bag and eye it irritably. She turned to him briefly. 'I'm so sorry, I'm going to have to take this call.'

Heath held his hand up. 'Not a problem. You carry on. I'll wander through here.' Walking through a door into what seemed to be a combined utility and pantry area, yet still twice the size of his lounge, he hovered out of sight of Helen, yet remained within hearing distance.

'What is it, Robert? Is it important? I'm with a client at the moment.' Helen's voice was spiky, strained. 'Well, I'm not sure what to suggest. It's mother's choice and there's not a lot we can do about that. If she wants Teagan there, then we'll have to put up with it. Look, I really have to go… I'll pop over after work tonight if I can.'

Heath's ears pricked up and he strained his hearing further. *Robert? Was that his father's brother? And she said mother? That would be Dulcie Adams…*

Hearing Helen end the call, Heath dashed across the other side of the massive utility room into the next room - a large square back hallway and pretended to admire the landscaped garden through the double doors.

'Sorry about that.' Helen joined Heath in the back hall. 'I don't usually take calls when I'm with clients.' She waved her hand dismissively. 'My mother is suffering with dementia and she does the most ridiculous things. She's hired a home help that my brother doesn't like and… Oh, what am I saying? I'm sure you don't want to know about any of this.'

Heath smiled. 'Don't worry. I can imagine how stressful, not to mention upsetting it must be for you.' *Yep, things were far from rosy.* As well as Helen's financial issues, the old dear was going loony? And she was going round her mother's tonight, was she? And the carer was called Teagan?

He wondered if the girl was local. Teagan was a fairly unusual name, so there couldn't be too many people with that name in Maidenhead. If he could follow Helen to the mother's house and perhaps spot a glimpse of this Teagan person, then not only would he have Dulcie Adams' address, but would also be able to narrow down the age range of Teagan, whoever she was, for when he did a Facebook search.

Heath smiled. His dad would have to wait a bit longer than planned for that beer on his way back. It looked like he may be later than planned leaving Maidenhead tonight.

SIXTEEN

JAMES HADN'T PURPOSEFULLY been digging around his wife's things. As far he was aware Helen didn't have anything in the garage. It had been his domain for years purely to house his collection of tools and odds and sods. That was why he'd noticed the box the second he'd seen it. He wouldn't have noticed it at all had he not moved the workbench and three toolboxes out of the way whilst looking for a box of heads for his sander.

James frowned. He could see that the box he'd uncovered was too big to be his sandpaper, but he did have a habit of buying additional things that he didn't need and then storing them in here, only to forget about them. He'd presumed this was what had happened here because he couldn't for the life of him remember what he'd bought that could have come in that box. That was the only reason he'd looked and how he wished he hadn't.

He stared at the folder he'd pulled from the box – the one he'd flicked through which held the documents regarding the remortgage of their house. It was dated last year and this was the first thing he knew of it.

Helen dealt with all the finances – she always had. She'd

always earnt the lion's share of the money and knew what she was doing where that sort of stuff was concerned, but surely remortgaging the house should have been discussed with him?

He was well aware the mortgage had all but been paid off three years ago and now it was back up to the hilt, plus more!

But what had really hurt was the additional paperwork in the folder showing the whole remortgage amount had been transferred into the bank account of Shepherd, Percival and Proctor and Helen had never said a word?

Although she hadn't come out and said it, James knew the company hadn't been doing so well the last few years, but *this*? This in itself was bad enough, but nowhere near as bad as the rest...

James stared into the box once more, his eyebrows furrowing. These definitely were nothing to do with him, so they *had* to be Helen's.

Sorrow washed over him. Why had she felt the need to hide this from him? If she was struggling so much, surely she could have come to him about it? He knew their marriage hadn't been the best the last few years, but he hadn't realised she thought so little of him; mistrusted him *quite* so much to not tell him she couldn't cope.

James picked up two of the empty bottles and stared at them miserably. Helen had never been one to allow anyone to know of her emotions, but *these*? It looked like he'd underestimated just how much the worry over her mother's health was getting to her. Every single bottle of these were empty. Exactly how many pills was his wife taking?

Crushing guilt overwhelmed him. All this time he'd been convinced Helen was cold and unemotional, when really she was crumbling inside so badly that she had to take all this medication to hide it?

But why was she buying these over the internet? Was that even safe? Could she be that embarrassed over her inability to cope that she felt unable to seek help from her doctor?

James pursed his lips. In retrospect it was the sort of thing

Helen would do. So headstrong that she would feel unable to admit to anyone that she was struggling? There was no shame in it, he knew that, but knew Helen well enough to know that she wouldn't see it that way. Oh, she'd die a death rather than admit any perceived weakness. *Anyone* would struggle with what she'd got on her plate and that wasn't including the undeniable pressure she must be under as a partner at work - a company in financial jeopardy that *she* was holding up.

James sighed. He must make a concerted effort to help her more or try and get her to open up. The chances of that were slimmer than an anorexic, but he'd got to do *something*.

He stared at the bottles in his hands. This was heavy duty medication. Although nowhere near an expert on prescribed drugs, he'd heard of Fluoxetine. His colleague's wife had been prescribed that a while ago for depression and they'd had a conversation about it. Prozac, they called it. Apparently, it was quite the rage.

And this one... Temazepam. He knew that to be an anti-anxiety medication. *Anti-depressants and anti-anxiety drugs?*

He felt a lump forming in his throat. What a crap husband he must be for failing to spot just how distressed his wife was and her distrusting him so much that she felt the need to *hide* the evidence. Hide it so much that she hadn't even put the empty bottles in the bin. Not that he made a habit of going through the dustbin, but being as he was the one who put the bins out every Tuesday, Helen must be convinced he *could* have spotted them.

Chucking the bottles back in the box, James rummaged around more of the empties. *What was this?* This one's labelling was different from the ones he'd seen so far.

Benztropine? His forehead furrowed. Another anti-depressant? He'd have to find out. Perhaps he could have a word with one of the chemists next time he went into town?

But how could he raise what he'd found with Helen? She'd go berserk to find he'd discovered her secret. She might pull away from him even more than she already had. But he couldn't leave her to deal with these demons alone. Regardless of anything, Helen was his wife - for better, for worse – and he loved her.

Placing the empty bottles and the folder back in the box, James put it back exactly where he'd found it and duly moved all of the kit back in front of it.

What was important was that she didn't feel he'd been spying on her. He'd find out exactly what he was dealing with here so he'd have a better idea on how to approach the problem.

• • • •

TEAGAN WAS CONFUSED. After her initial mix of surprise and elation to find Joe in Dulcie's sitting room, she'd become uncomfortable with the rapid realisation that Dulcie was anything but happy.

She looked at Joe, his hands trembling. He never trembled. He was never nervous, always being far too laid back for that. What had happened? Regardless of his previous behaviour, she cared for him very much. 'Joe? Is everything alright?'

'This young man thinks that after the way he treated you, he can walk back into your life, snap his fingers and you'll accept him back with open arms.' Dulcie snapped as she glared at Joe with unbridled venom.

Teagan's heart lurched. *Joe didn't want her out of his life after all?* Relief coursed through her, but she refrained from rushing over. He didn't look himself. He looked... different...

'I've already told him he must have rocks in his head if he thinks you'd be so gullible,' Dulcie continued. She swung around to face Joe. 'I think you made your feelings quite clear the other day, boy.'

Teagan's initial flood of elation subsided rapidly. Dulcie was right. Joe had cut her to the quick and broken her heart. Furthermore, he shouldn't be coming to her place of work and inviting himself in – stressing Dulcie out.

What should she do? How should she react? Oh God, this was dreadful.

Joe looked up, caught Teagan's eye and looked away

quickly. *This was a nightmare. The ultimate bloody nightmare.* Here he was, getting shit off an old crone and having to take it up the arse. Why? Because he only had until tonight to get this done.

Cold sweat gathered in his hair. The thought of dealing with those two blokes again made him feel sick. He hadn't slept a wink all night and was completely shattered. And now – now he'd *finally* got rid of Teagan, here he was, having to *beg* for her back. *For fuck's sake. It was the last bloody thing he wanted.*

He took a deep breath and pulled his brain into a less scrambled mess, but it was difficult. He was all over the shop and could barely think, let alone form anything coherent to say which might possibly explain his U-turn. But he had to think of something and he had to do it fast.

His eyes flicked around, searching for Teagan's handbag. *She'd keep her keys in there, wouldn't she? Where was it? In her room?*

Joe turned his head to look at Teagan who was still frozen to the spot just inside the doorway, wearing that stupid wide-eyed expression that he'd always hated. He cleared his throat noisily and pushed his shaking hands under his thighs so the craggy old bag giving him the evils from the opposite chair couldn't see how much everything was terrifying him. What was so special about what she'd got for those two psychos to want access so badly?

Joe moved his focus to the older woman, hoping her death stare wasn't destroying his brain cells and wished more than anything that he'd smoked a joint before coming here. At least it would have chilled him out.

'I realise I behaved badly and it wasn't the best first impression,' Joe said, keeping his eyes connected with the older woman before turning to Teagan. 'I've fu... screwed up. I didn't know what I was saying the other day. I didn't mean it... I...'

'You seemed pretty sure from where I was standing,'

Dulcie barked.

Joe's eyes flashed with annoyance. *Shut the fuck up,* he thought. This was bad enough without her sticking her hooter in. He'd never get the keys unless he could get back with Teagan. Forcing himself to keep going, he smiled weakly. 'I panicked... Things have been getting on top of me... Please forgive me Teagan.'

He stared at Teagan, his expression pleading. 'I want things to go back to the way they were,' Joe continued. 'I-I want to be with you... More than anything...' *No, I don't. I don't. I. Do. NOT.*

'You can't want to be with her that much otherwise why would you be swanning around like a bachelor after three years? Sleeping with other women?' Dulcie interrupted, her eyes fiery. 'Mr *Singleton*... fitting name...'

Joe looked up in surprise. What exactly had Teagan said to this old cow? Had she given her his life story? Told her what colour his underpants tend to be? The length of his penis?

'I do want to be with her,' Joe countered, the words grating. 'And... and the women... they... I... Oh, tell me we can sort this out, Teagan? Please? Perhaps we could talk about this somewhere else? Could we talk in your room?' If he could just get into her room – the keys would have to be in there, wouldn't they? He hadn't seen them in the hall. *Christ.*

Dulcie laughed loudly. 'If you think I'd allow *you* to talk anyone into allowing you go up to this young lady's room, you have a screw loose!'

Joe looked at Teagan beseechingly. 'Teagan? Please?'

Tears formed in Teagan's eyes. This was what she'd wanted to happen. Her throat constricted tightly. All she had to say was that she'd give Joe one more chance and her life could be back to normal. Her eyes flicked involuntarily to Dulcie, but Dulcie wasn't even looking in her direction. She was staring at Joe, shaking her head. Teagan bit down on her bottom lip. Why wasn't she jumping at the chance to accept Joe's apology and get her life back?

Because she didn't believe him. Something was wrong, but she didn't know what.

She folded her arms across her chest and took a deep breath. 'I think you should leave,' Teagan whispered.

Joe's head snapped up, shock evident on his face. Teagan wanted him to leave? She wasn't running into his arms? What the fuck? *No, no no.* This couldn't happen. He *had* to get her back on side. Those blokes... they'd... 'Teag?' he muttered. 'Please... you've got to...'

Dulcie's slow clapping interrupted Joe. 'That's a very sensible decision, dear,' she said, her mouth smiling at Teagan, but her cold eyes were fixed on Joe. She got to her feet. 'Off you go then, young man. My children won't take kindly to hear someone refused to leave my home.'

Joe rose from his chair. *Fuck.* What the hell was he supposed to do now? He hadn't expected getting Teagan back would be anything less than plain sailing. *Shit.* 'Just think about it?' he asked, forcing himself to smile at her.

Teagan looked away. *This felt the right thing to do, but why did it hurt so very much?*

SEVENTEEN

JAMES SHEPHERD WALKED into Boots the Chemist, his heart sinking seeing two elderly people at the pharmacist counter. He'd been hoping by nipping in here mid-morning between appointments there would be no one else about.

Standing a polite distance away, James prayed they wouldn't be too long or start rambling on about the weather in a bid to help fill their day. His thoughts were hardly charitable, but he couldn't afford to be. He hadn't much time to find out the information he needed.

He hadn't broached the subject with Helen. He'd tried dropping a few hints – asking how the business was going or how she *really* felt about this or that, but it had got him nowhere. Every time he'd tried to get an inkling into anything, Helen looked at him like he'd dropped out of the nearest tree, dismissing his questions with thinly-veiled irritation.

James fidgeted uncomfortably, his arms hanging by his sides. For want of not knowing what else to do while he waited, he stared at the nearest display stand vacantly, stopping after getting a rather strange look from a woman and realising he'd been feigning avid interest in a rack of female incontinence pants.

Flustered, he looked away, grateful when the pharmacist beckoned him forward.

'Good Morning, Sir. How can I help?'

James smiled awkwardly. 'I, erm… I need to ask a question about some medication.'

'Of course. Is this medication yours, Sir?'

James quickly shook his head. 'No. It's erm… it's been prescribed for a friend of mine…' He smiled, ignoring the pharmacist's suspicious expression. Reddening slightly, he continued. 'It's Benztropine. Could you tell me what it is please?'

The pharmacist frowned. 'What is the issue exactly? Have there been adverse reactions? Anything worrying?'

'Not as far as I know. I just want to know what it is.'

'Benztropine is an anticholinergic, Sir,' the pharmacist answered, then seeing the look of confusion on James' face, attempted to explain. 'It's used to block the effects of acetylcholine and dopamine – a chemical in the brain - a neurotransmitter.'

James must have still looked completely blank because the pharmacist smiled at him kindly. 'Does your friend have Parkinson's disease, Sir?'

'Parkinson's Disease?' James spluttered. 'I-Is this what these are usually prescribed for?'

The pharmacist frowned. 'Well, usually, yes. They are used to help reduce the involuntary movements Parkinson's causes. Are you sure the medication is definitely Benztropine? Could it be Benadryl, the antihistamine? The names are quite similar and it would be easily d…'

'No, it was definitely Benztropine,' James muttered, his mind reeling.

'If you bring the bottle in for me, I can certainly double check it for you. Do you know if it was dispensed from here?'

James forced his attention back to the pharmacist. 'Oh, erm… I don't know… Maybe I got the name wrong. I'll double check. Thanks for your help.'

Turning, James hastily left the store before the pharmacist asked anything else and before he could not hold back the tears that were desperately trying to escape from his eyes.

Did his wife have Parkinson's? Was that what was happening? Oh, this was dreadful.

• • • •

JOE SWEATED like a beast as he frantically stabbed another text message out to Teagan. Pressing send, he scraped his hand across his brow, before slamming the phone down on the bedside table.

Why wasn't the stupid cow responding? He'd sent her about fifty bloody texts so far since she'd turned him down, not to mention the voicemails. In fact, he'd left so many there was no longer any room to leave one.

'Pick up your messages and respond, you fucking bitch,' Joe muttered, his fingers fumbling for his Rizla papers. He shakily put together a joint – he needed *something*.

Teagan had always banged on that he never bothered to text or phone and now he was, she was playing hard to get!

Pulling a lighter from his jeans pocket, Joe's hand shook as he lit the joint. Christ, look at the state of him! Teagan had best get in contact soon. *She had to.* Because of her and whatever she was involved in, Alan and Dave weren't speaking to him. When they'd got back from the pub last night they'd blanked him and they'd done the same again all bloody day so far, apart from Alan reiterating that if this business wasn't sorted out and if those nutters kept turning up then he'd be out by the end of the week.

Joe scowled. He wasn't losing his place and his best mates because of Teagan. Plus, he had nowhere else to go. He couldn't afford to rent anywhere else even if he wanted to. For fuck's sake, he couldn't even afford a hotel for a night at the moment, let alone anything else being as he'd blown all of his cash on this last wad of grass.

Inhaling deeply on the joint, he held the pungent smoke in

his lungs for as long as possible before slowly breathing it out towards the ceiling. Good job he'd bought it. He needed something to calm him down.

His face screwed into a grimace. He'd been certain Teagan would have had him back. No, he'd been *counting* on it. He'd have even bet his weed stash on it and that he'd never do unless he was certain he was right. There hadn't been a smidgen of doubt that she wouldn't come running into his arms, but she hadn't. And that meant he was screwed.

Why had she not jumped at the chance to take him back? The girl was crazy for him – everyone knew that. That's why she bordered on the obsessive where he was concerned. But now she suddenly wasn't interested? It wasn't possible. It must be something to do with that crusty old boot putting ideas in her head. If he'd had a bit more time, he'd have been able to talk Teagan round, He still could. She just had to answer the phone.

Joe's eyes narrowed. He had to find a way of getting her to listen otherwise he was fucked. Those nutters were due back tonight and they'd expect him to have results. How could he get the fuck into that house and get what they wanted if Teagan, the stupid cow, was ignoring him?

Joe lay back on his bed and took another deep drag of the joint. Was it not bad enough that he'd had to *beg* for another chance? All that grovelling and it had achieved nothing.

Feeling the effect of the cannabis, Joe began to relax. What time were those gorillas coming back tonight? Had they even mentioned a time?

He mentally shrugged, feeling his confidence return. Sod them, they'd have to wait. He couldn't give them something he hadn't got and he was not sitting here waiting for them to come and drown him in the shower or whatever they were planning.

Puffing out thick smoke rings, Joe's brain buzzed nicely. Fuck it. He was done with stressing out and being dictated to. Teagan would return his calls soon enough. She was too hung up wanting to play happy families not to take him up on his offer. Not that it would last. No fucking way. He'd get what these blokes wanted so they were off his case and then he'd crack on with his life. *Without Teagan.*

One thing was for certain – he wouldn't be hanging around tonight waiting for those nutjobs to turn up. Alan and Dave had already arranged to go on the piss without him, so they wouldn't be here. He knew this because he'd heard them planning their jolly earlier. How long would *that* go on for? It was already getting on his tits. The three of them had been mates for donkey's years and just because of this they thought it gave them the right to sideswipe him?

Well, he could play at that game too. He'd go somewhere himself, get smashed and find a decent bit of skirt. He'd kip at her place and by the time he got back tomorrow morning Teagan would have had a predicted change of tune, he'd get in that house and copy the keys as requested. Job done.

After that, Dave and Alan could eat shit and apologise for having so little faith in his ability to rectify things.

Pushing himself off the bed before he got too zoned out on this extremely decent batch of sensimilla, Joe shoved a few bits into a rucksack and ambled out of the flat with a smile on his face.

· · · ·

JONAH KNITTED HIS FINGERS TOGETHER. He'd listened intently whilst Nero had brought him up to speed, but nothing was helping the tension headache he'd woken up with this morning.

His plan of speaking to Lena over dinner last night about more whispers he'd heard from the girls about her bitchy comments and threats hadn't happened. Arriving home later than planned, he'd found her holed up in the spare bedroom. And not only was she in the spare bedroom - she'd locked the fucking door.

No one locked the door on him.

Jonah's jaw clenched. In any other given scenario he'd have kicked the door in, dragged Lena out by the hair, pointed out that no one locked him out and then put her bang to rights, but he was in unfamiliar and unchartered waters. She was pregnant with his child and therefore he couldn't do half of what he wanted to do.

Correction. He couldn't do *any* of what he wanted to do.

What he would do though was anything to make sure his son or daughter arrived into this world safely and so, despite it being nowhere near what he'd had in mind for Lena Taylor to be the mother of his child, she was and that was all there was to it.

By the time Lena had surfaced this morning he was halfway out of the door. He'd felt almost guilty for wanting to rip her to pieces last night when she'd apologised for squirreling herself away. The morning sickness had begun to last most of the day, as well as into the evening, she'd explained. She had looked bloody dreadful too.

Jonah massaged his temples and then stared at his left hand – the one which would very shortly be sporting a wedding band on one of the fingers. His head pounded and nausea rose. *What a fucking mess.*

'How do you want us to move forward from here?'

Nero's voice jolted Jonah from his thoughts. Jesus he'd forgotten they were even here. That showed how much all this shit with Lena was playing with his mind. He had to concentrate.

Jonah's dark eyebrows knitted together. 'You say this stoner is giving you a key to the Adams' house – Footlights? And you're getting this tonight? Is that correct?'

'That's the plan, but being as stoners are hardly the most reliable of people, I have the distinct feeling that we'll need to up the ante before he delivers,' Nero said, ignoring the buzzing electric he sensed radiating from Keith when the slight prospect of violence was on the cards.

Jonah felt unable to hide his escalating irritation over how Lena's behaviour was distracting him from the thing he held above everything – taking revenge on the person who had ripped the firm off all that time ago. 'Just do whatever needs to be done. If the thick fuck needs it spelling out, rather than being asked nicely, then so be it.'

He'd had enough of people pissing around. If Keith wanted to rip this dickhead's arms off in return for getting into Dulcie Adams' house, then he didn't give a rat's arse. He had to move on this and wouldn't hang around any longer. 'Just make sure you clean anything up.'

Nero looked between Jonah and Keith and inwardly sighed. Keith *always* made a bloody mess - his beatings were never tidy.

'Oh, and that bloke – the one you saw at that old folk's home?' Jonah continued.

Nero frowned. 'The bloke who met Shepherd?'

Jonah nodded, his eyes cold. 'Yeah, him. I want gen on him. Locate him. Is he her lover? Who is he?'

'Dunno, but by the looks of what we saw I wouldn't have said that. He had a clipboard,' Keith said, itching to get out of the meeting so he could go and mess that stoner kid up.

'Clipboard?' Jonah poured himself a whisky. He wouldn't offer these two a drink. He wanted them back on the road. 'A doctor then? Someone working at the old fogey's place?'

Nero eyed Jonah's tumbler of whisky longingly. 'More likely an estate agent. I saw a noticeboard saying there were two apartments available for sale. It's her industry and she clearly knew him.'

Jonah nodded. 'Look into it. Find which estate agents are marketing them and check the guy out. There may be more to it – he could be her bit on the side, but either way, he'll be our next port of call.'

Jonah topped up his glass, noticing both Keith and Nero staring in his direction. 'What are you waiting for?' he barked.

As his two best men left, Jonah scowled. He must get a handle on himself. Taking his personal issues out on them wasn't his style and he was edging precariously near to doing just that. And that was not a road he wanted to go down.

He ran his hand through his dark hair and willed his jagged pulse rate to settle. Only the tapping at the office door made him remember that he'd also got a catch-up meeting with Gwen.

EIGHTEEN

GWEN COULD READ MORE than ever that something was eating at Jonah and she'd hazard a guess what it was regarding. She had no right to intrude on his personal life, but she'd been more surprised than anyone to receive an invitation to his engagement bash.

Jonah hadn't mentioned anything and that hurt more than she cared to admit, but even that didn't bother her anywhere near as much as the nagging doubt where that woman was concerned.

Lena Taylor was poison and would ruin Jonah's life. She didn't know how, but knew it all the same. She had to make him see that this was not a good idea – she owed that to his mother at the very least. But how could she get Jonah to see sense? It was his personal business, after all.

Gwen nibbled at the inside of her cheek. Whatever happened, she had to make sure she was around for him when the conniving little cow showed her true colours. She'd then pick up the pieces of his broken heart like his mother would have done.

If only Jonah had fallen in love with a girl worthy of him, rather than Lena. The woman was a gold-digger if she'd ever seen one.

Sitting in silence in Jonah's plush office, Gwen couldn't help but notice the fresh worry lines on his ruggedly handsome face. She was loathe to add to his problems, but she had to press for Lena's repeat interference at the club to be dealt with.

Gwen had also seen Nero and Keith faces as they'd left the office. Nero's expression was thunderous and Keith's – well, Keith looked the same, just slightly more deranged than usual. Something was afoot and although she didn't quite know how to broach it, she knew she must.

The question was, how did she do it without insulting the man, or upset the apple cart even more than it already seemed to be?

Either way, she had no choice but to attempt it in the best way she saw fit. Deciding she may as well cut straight to the chase, Gwen placed her hands on the table to draw Jonah's attention. 'She's at it again.'

Jonah's piercing blue eyes focused on Gwen, suddenly coming fully to the moment. 'Who?' Even though he knew immediately who she was referring to, he hoped he was wrong.

Gwen sighed. 'Lena. She's upset the girls I reinstated again. She won't stop interfering, Jonah. She told them you'd said they needed to lose weight otherwise they were out.'

Jonah sighed loudly to mask his teeth grinding. *Christ, this was all so... all so difficult.*

He cracked his knuckles. For the first time in his life he felt impotent, plus things were running far too slowly where Dulcie Adams was concerned.

Jonah's brow furrowed deeper and wondered whether the rest of the firm believed the whole Dulcie Adams thing should have been written off by now and that too much time had passed to warrant the manpower. But not for him. He'd *never* let it go. He'd seen what it had done to his father and for that reason and that reason alone, he'd see it through. He wouldn't let what Pointer had done drop until he had retrieved what had been taken back to where it belonged. With the *Powell* family.

That's probably where his own issue of trust came from – he trusted *no one*. As his father had proved, even the ones you thought you could trust betrayed you in the end. It wasn't about the worth. It had never been about that. It was the principle. Principles were important.

Putting an end to this was, for the first time in decades, within his grasp, yet with each minute that passed he felt the chance was slipping through his fingertips like sand.

'Are you alright?' Gwen asked. She'd sat waiting for Jonah's response for several minutes, yet he'd remained silent, his eyes glazed and his mind clearly elsewhere. In all truth she was worried. He was acting out of sorts – something she'd never seen him do before. Whatever was bothering him was a lot more complicated than whatever Lena Taylor was doing with the club staff and dancing rota.

She studied Jonah's face; his chiselled jaw set like stone, a nerve in his neck twitching. Reaching over the desk, Gwen lightly touched his hand. 'Jonah?'

Jerking forward, Jonah blinked. Out of all of the people around him, Gwen was the one he trusted most. 'I'll speak with Lena again tonight, ok?' he muttered.

'I'm sorry to load more pressure on you, love. I can see you've got lots on your mind,' Gwen said softly. 'I'm happy to speak to Lena myself, but I didn't want to do that without speaking to you first. I mean she's your fiancée... and it's awkward what with that connection and...'

'Regardless of whatever Lena is to me, you know you have my backing to do whatever's needed to ensure the club remains running well,' Jonah said, his anger growing.

Fiancé. The word made Jonah feel ill. Just the thought of being stuck with Lena for the rest of time put him in the worst mood ever. But what could he do about it? Fuck all, that's what.

He could sort drug shipments, gun running and dole out violence to match no other, but he couldn't sling out the mother of his unborn child, no matter how much he wanted to.

Even with what had happened to his mother, he'd always

wanted a family of his own, but Lena wasn't wife material – she was a good time girl and lately she didn't even warrant being a decent shag. Now, because of his stupidity, she was about to become his bloody wife.

Jonah forced a smile. 'Lena is not to use that we're... that we're getting married as an excuse to throw her weight around. You have my full authority to pull her up if she steps out of line, but like I said, I'll speak to her again tonight.'

Gwen nodded. 'I don't think she'll appreciate me saying anything to her ab...'

'I don't give a fuck what she appreciates!' Jonah snarled. How he wished he could tell Gwen how he really felt about Lena, but he couldn't. It wouldn't be right. She'd think badly of him for wanting out, especially when she found out that Lena was carrying his child. Out of all the people he was surrounded by, Gwen Vella was the only one whom it would bother him if she thought badly of him.

'Is everything ok? I mean, *really*?' Gwen could see Jonah was holding back.

Jonah refilled his whisky and held the bottle out to Gwen, replacing it on his desk when she shook her head. 'Everything's fine,' he lied, his expression neutral. 'Just hectic.'

Gwen inclined her head slightly. She recognised that expression – his father did exactly the same when he didn't want to discuss something. 'I saw Nero and Keith on the way down. They looked stressed.'

Jonah studied Gwen. 'Do you remember the Pointer incident?'

Gwen nodded. 'Who doesn't?' Jacky had told her all about it more than once. She could clearly picture his face – the way it turned crimson with rage each time he spoke about the subject.

'We've located Pointer's mistress...' Jonah decided he might as well fill Gwen in with these details at least. She wouldn't speak of it to anyone else, he knew that much.

Gwen raised her eyebrows. 'What? How?'

'Long story and I might add, a total fluke. I've put tabs out to see if she has the stash, but it's easier said than done and it's running too slowly for my liking.'

'Hmm, not feasible to use the standard methods, I don't expect?' Gwen mused. She may be only the floor manager for the show, but she knew a damn sight more of what really went on in his firm than she ever got credit for. 'Civilian territory, right?'

Seeing Jonah's surprise, Gwen laughed. 'Your father used to offload his tricky situations on to me for another take on things. We used to brainstorm ideas.'

Jonah grinned. 'He never said.'

Gwen shrugged. 'Why would he? I just want you to know that as it was with your father, the same applies to you - nothing you say will ever go any further.'

Jonah squeezed Gwen's hand. 'Good to know. And it underlines why my father always spoke so highly of you.'

Gwen coloured, then her face turned serious. 'I presume you've filled Saul in about this?' She raised her eyebrows. She would hazard a guess how Saul would deal with it, given half a chance. He'd deal with it in such a way that there would be nothing left of anyone. There was no nice way to say it, but that man was a bloody nasty piece of work.

Jonah jutted out his chin. 'Yeah, he knows.' And he hadn't even been slightly impressed by his not agreeing to barge into the old woman's place, smash her up along with the house and rip every floorboard up until the haul was located. 'He doesn't agree with how I'm handling it, as you can probably guess.'

Gwen smiled and patted Jonah's hand. 'Listen, you know as well as I do that you're doing things the right way.'

Jonah nodded, his gaze fixed on paperwork on his desk.

Gwen lowered her head so Jonah was forced to look into her eyes. 'And Lena? Are you happy?' There. She was overstepping the mark but now he had the option to either tell her to sling her hook or tell her anything else that was bothering him.

Jonah necked his whisky and placed the glass down just that little bit heavily. 'I'm getting married, aren't I?' A nerve in his jaw twitched. 'Everything's fine. Or it will be once I get this business with the shit Pointer caused finally finished.'

Gwen smiled, but she knew Jonah was lying. She'd always been able to tell when he was lying. The problem was, she didn't know how to help him.

. . . .

'I'M FINE, MUM,' Heath kissed Tammy on the cheek. 'Just thought I'd pop round on my way out with the lads to drop some stuff off for Dad and ask how Nan's funeral went. I thought I should have gone myself, but Dad said Nan wouldn't want us to close the showroom for the day on her account.'

Tammy pursed her lips. 'You didn't miss much. It went ok – as funerals go, that is. Your Dad's a bit on edge, but I suppose that's to be expected.' She handed Heath an order of service. 'You can have this. Not sure why your Dad had so many printed. There was only six of us.'

'Thanks,' Heath took the folded paper from his mother's hand and looked at the photograph of his Nan taken in her younger days, surrounded by the words:

In remembrance of Sophie Pointer
Beloved mother, wife and grandmother

Frowning, he was unsure exactly how true the gold embossed words were, but what did it matter?

Tammy eyed her son suspiciously. 'You say you're going out? That's your work suit isn't it? Have you only just finished?' She frowned. 'Your father's working you too hard. I keep telling him th...'

'It's fine Mum, honestly. Listen, is Dad around?' Heath knew he should have just phoned. His mum was always giving him the Spanish inquisition, but he needed to fill his father in with the updates and didn't want to talk over the mobile. Not when he was trying to retrieve millions of pounds worth of stolen diamonds, that was.

A frisson of excitement travelled up Heath's spine like it always did when he thought about what could be within his reach. Now he'd got another bit of the jigsaw the prospect was getting nearer.

'Your dad's in the study,' Tammy nodded up the hallway. 'Can I get you some dinner?'

Heath shook his head. 'No, I'm not stopping long.'

'Ah, Heath!' Mike stuck his head around the door. 'Thought I heard you. Come in.'

Heath moved into the tiny study which had once been a utility room and, by the looks of it, still doubled up as one. Shutting the door, he squashed himself onto the only other chair in the small room – the one wedged between a tumble drier and a pile of neatly folded clothes. 'Mum said the funeral went ok?'

Mike nodded. 'Yeah, but don't worry about that. Tell me how it went from your side.'

'I met Helen Shepherd,' Heath gabbled, barely able to wait to tell his father what he knew. 'She's a bit snooty, but on the whole, she's ok. I viewed this posh house. I tell you, when we get this money we should buy somewhere like that – you should have seen it! Massive! You could have a proper home office - not like this set up.' He waved his arm around the tiny space, inadvertently knocking off a packet of washing powder from the side.

'For fuck's sake, Heath,' Mike grumbled, stooping to pick the packet up, balancing it back on the side. He'd love a big place too. A lot better than this stupid house. He'd move out of Shepherd's Bush too – that was a certainty and buy somewhere nice – somewhere upmarket, but that was presuming he got his hands on the stash.

To be honest, Heath rambling on about big country piles wasn't getting them any closer to achieving it in real life. All it did was underline how far they actually were away from getting anywhere. 'Have you made headway with anything or are you purely dreaming of what you *could* get if we ever got our hands on the stuff. By the looks of it, it's a big 'if'.'

This was all starting to feel pointless. Despair crept over Mike. He'd been on a downer since opening a statement from one of the loan companies he owed that was waiting for him when he'd got back from the funeral. It had done nothing to help his mood. Yet another piece of threatening correspondence he'd had to make sure Tammy didn't see.

Unperturbed by his father's despondent attitude, Heath remained optimistic. 'Well, I can certainly arrange another viewing – make Helen believe I'm really interested and...'

'But what will that achieve? I mean, really achieve? It won't get us anywhere, will it?'

Heath frowned. Where had his father's excitement emigrated to? 'It might. I learnt quite a bit about Helen Shepherd's family today.'

Mike sat forward. 'Like what?' He scowled as he knocked a hole punch off, what was marketed as a 'computer desk', but should realistically have been described as an extra small table for kids under twelve or a dressing table for dwarves. He might sue Argos for misinformation.

'It looks like my assumptions about the company finances were correct. Although it looks very swish from the outside, she's definitely got stuff on her mind. Far too much in a rush to take over anyone showing interest for the expensive properties. Plus, I overheard her talking on the phone to Robert – you know, your brother? He doesn't sound a very happy chappy and things are far from rosy in Dulcie Adams' camp by the sound of it. They reckon she's got dementia and losing the plot big time. And to top it all off, in case you're interested, Robert hates the home help.'

'How fascinating... And that's supposed to be useful?

Heath grinned. 'It could be... I heard Helen say 'Teagan' – that's the name of the girl looking after Dulcie. But it's better than that... I followed Helen back as she said he was visiting her mother and I saw this Teagan person when she answered the door.'

Mike scowled. *Did Heath think this was some kind of fucking adventure game?* 'Forgive me, but I don't get why I'm supposed to be impressed. What has this Teabag, Teagan or whatever she's called, got to do with anything?'

Heath smiled widely. 'Unusual name, right? I saw her – a nice looking bird. Early twenties and...'

'Oh my God. Is this about getting your leg over? For fuck's sake, Heath. If you...'

'I wouldn't say no!' Heath winked, 'but that's not what I mean. When I got back, I searched Facebook.' He tapped the side of his nose. 'I suspected there wouldn't be many Teagans in that age bracket in the Maidenhead area and I thought if she was on Facebook then...' Fishing his mobile from his pocket, he opened the app, placing the screen to face his father. 'This is her, so I've sent her a friends request.'

Mike raked his fingers through his hair. 'Friends request? What's that supposed to mean? Whatever it is, I'm very pleased for you! Christ, boy – are you winding me up? What are y...'

'No!' Heath cried. 'You're missing the point! This Teagan – her profile is public, so I looked and after a bit of digging, I found where she went to school, so along with the friends request, I sent a message acting like I knew her – an old classmate.'

Seeing his father was still confused, Heath sighed. 'Don't you see? Most people will automatically assume they must know someone, but just can't remember them, yes? Come on, we've all done it. She hasn't yet accepted my friends request, but I'm guessing she will.' He grinned. 'And when she does, I'll suggest meeting for a catch up. If I can get in with her, then I can pick her brains for info on Dulcie Adams. You never know, I might even be able to get into the house.'

A flicker of a smile formed on Mike's face as it dawned on him what Heath was doing. It was a good job his son understood all of this computer stuff. He wouldn't have had the first clue to think of doing something like that, or that it was even possible.

'That's bloody good, that is. I see what you're saying.'

Maybe things weren't quite so bleak as he'd been thinking after all.

NINETEEN

TEAGAN WAS BUSY keeping out of the way like she had been ever since Robert arrived an hour ago. Pushing straight past her without so much as a word in greeting, short of an unpleasant glare in her general direction, he'd made his way up the hall, making a point of loudly shutting the door behind him to the room Dulcie was in.

There really was something distinctly unpleasant about that man that made Teagan wary, but she could hardly lurk around eavesdropping; her nerves were already in tatters. She placed the vacuum cleaner against the scullery wall and leant against the door, inhaling deeply.

Reading all of those text messages from Joe that had come through in one go when her phone had picked up the inconsistent network signal did very little to help her already fried brain. Ever since he'd begged to have her back she'd wavered between standing her ground and changing her mind, but digging her heels in, she'd refused to reply to his messages. If she did, then he might worm his way back under her skin.

Oh, who was she trying to kid. He'd been under her skin for a very long time, hence why his betrayal had hurt so much.

The voicemails were worse. They made things even *harder*.

Hearing Joe's voice was a lot harder to ignore than reading words on a tiny screen. Voices were *real*. As he'd begged over and over for her to reconsider her decision and give him one more chance she could hear the pleading in his voice.

Teagan would be lying if she said she wasn't tempted, but something had shifted. There was *something* that didn't pan out and the clanging instinct not to believe what Joe said was loud and clear. No matter how much her heart ached, she had to face the fact: Joe Singleton was not who she thought he was and the sooner she remembered that the better.

But there was something else too - something that had piqued her interest, probably more than it should have. It also made her question whether she too had a problem with her memory.

The friends request from Darren Harding puzzled her no end. They'd been at school together, but for the life of her she had absolutely no recollection of him at all.

Teagan frowned. She didn't doubt that she *must* know him – why else would he make the effort to contact her otherwise? But she couldn't remember him. She'd wracked her brains, but had come up with a blank. It wasn't altogether surprising. That period in her life was almost ten years ago and it wasn't like she'd been one of the popular girls. Painfully shy, she'd had very few friends – and no *male* ones. Most of her school years had been spent keeping her head down, avoiding getting involved or noticed by anyone.

It didn't matter now. Teagan bit her lip, still unsure whether she'd done the right thing. She'd studied Darren's profile; there was *something* about him that rang a bell, but she couldn't place him. Nevertheless, she'd thrown caution to the wind and accepted his friend request, tapping out a short reply to his message.

Obviously, she'd omitted the embarrassing part of being unable to recall him and just asked how he was – the normal sort of thing and had been quietly chuffed when he'd replied within seconds, saying how great it was to hear from her and how he'd love to catch up on the old days if she ever had a spare afternoon.

Darren's messages were friendly – the sort expected from an old classmate or colleague, but it was empowering that he was glad to be back in contact with her. Having an old friend on the scene – and a nice-looking one at that, was just what she needed. Something to concentrate on other than how worthless Joe had made her feel. It was a refreshing change for someone to be interested in her life and what she was up to.

Joe, in all the years of their relationship, had not *once* asked how her day had been. In fact, it was doubtful he'd ever been aware of what she liked/disliked. That spoke *volumes* and only fuelled her reserve to leave Joe where he belonged. *In the past.*

Teagan's face broke into a cheeky grin. Accepting Darren's request may have been out of character, but why the hell not? She'd agreed to meet up with him for a coffee on her upcoming afternoon off and as luck would have it, he was coming up to Maidenhead on business the very day she was free.

He'd even asked where and what she'd like to do and she'd ended the online messaging, promising to message him again soon to arrange it.

Teagan had a long overdue spring in her step after that. That was until Robert had arrived and made her feel like a piece of shit; an usurper in the house - the viper in the nest.

From what she could see, it was *Robert* who was the problem around here, not anyone else.

· · · ·

NERO STARED AT KEITH whilst he rapped loudly at Joe Singleton's door, seeing the man was almost salivating with the need to torture some sense into the stoner. 'Remember we're finding out if he's got what we want before we go in guns blazing.'

Keith nodded, his meaty fingers itching to close around someone's throat. This wasn't how he worked. When he was on a job, he sorted it whatever the cost. He so missed Saul's way of working. There would have been none of this egg-shell treading, fannying around business if Saul had been directing this.

The door opened and panic registered straight away on the face of one of the men who had been unceremoniously tied to a kitchen chair the other day. Pre-empting the situation as the man went to shut the door in his face, Nero's steel toe cap took the brunt when the door slammed painlessly on his boot.

Without giving the guy a second to react, Nero pushed through the door, followed by Keith, who effortlessly crushed the panicked man into the wall. 'Alright, mate,' he grinned. 'Joe in?'

Alan shook his head so frantically it looked like it might fall off. 'No. No, he's not here. I-I haven't seen him.'

'Mind if we come in?' Keith growled. Not that there was any point asking being as they were already inside and he'd kicked the door shut behind him, but he liked to at least pretend to have manners.

Alan's eyes darted between the two big men. 'Seriously, Joe's not here. I don't know where he is. We… we sort of fell out after… after…'

'I hope *we* didn't cause any problems between you and your bum-pals,' Nero said, a sickly smile forming across his face. Despite his reticence to let Keith loose, the pathetic lies drivelling out of the gobs of this type always had the immediate effect of making him want to smash their faces in himself. Bunch of pointless fucking toe rags, the lot of them.

'You won't mind if we have a look around, then?' Keith squeezed past and went to check the rooms, leaving Alan attempting to embed himself into the wallpaper of the damp-looking hallway.

'On our last visit, your mate assured us he'd be here with what we asked for.' Nero glanced around. 'And if he's not, then we'd presume he'd have the sense to leave *you* to hand us what's required, yes?'

'J-Joe hasn't given me anything!' Alan gibbered. 'I-I

176

haven't seen him... I...'

'What about the other guy? The ugly, lanky fucker?' Nero spat. 'Where's he? Oh, don't tell me... he's out too?'

'H-He's only popped out to get some grub.' Alan nearly choked. He shouldn't have said that. Now they knew he was here on his own. *Shit. Fuck.*

'Hmm... that's the problem with the old green stuff, ain't it?' Keith returned to the hallway, his eyes gleaming with a refreshed lust for violence. 'Gives you the munchies.' He glanced at Nero. 'There's no one else here.'

Nero snarled inwardly. So, Joe whateverhisname, the dickhead, thought it a good idea to mess with them? That was stupid – *very* stupid. And he hadn't got time for stupid. Jonah would not be happy hearing another day had passed without progress.

The way things were going they'd be better off doing things the usual way - dealing with the old bat directly, but like Jonah said, that ran the risk of the shit hitting the fan and bringing the attention of the boys in blue back to the unsolved robbery from the 60s, landing it straight on the firm's doorstep. *That* none of them wanted.

That risk was the whole reason of getting a dweeb to arrange their entry into the old bird's gaff rather than smashing their way in, but it looked like the prick they'd picked was leading them on a merry dance.

Nero's eyebrows knitted together so tightly they almost became a monobrow. He was fucked off with this. He glared at the shaking man still pressed to the wall. They'd send a message loud and clear to this Joe twat – wherever he'd gone. A message that would give him the impetus to review his situation and make a better choice to deliver what they asked. *And fast.*

'What shall we do with this pathetic cunt?' Keith snarled, his bulging eyes drilling into Alan's.

'When are you expecting Joe back?' Nero glanced at his watch. *Time was ticking on.*

'I-I don't know. He hasn't anywhere else to go as far as I

know, so he can't stay away for long, but…'

'But your other pal has only popped out for food, yeah? I'm hungry, so I hope he'll have some left over to share with us,' Keith rasped, smiling widely enough to expose the one gold tooth shining like a beacon amidst all the yellowing ones.

'I-I don't know if Dave's coming back either,' Alan lied, visibly cringing. He had to get these two to leave. If they believed he didn't know anything, then surely they'd go? They wouldn't hang around waiting for Joe to come back, would they? *Please don't let them do that.*

The thought of these two as temporary housemates made Alan want to pass out. How had he become tangled up in this mess?

Besides, it wasn't like he was lying. He genuinely didn't know where Joe was or when he'd be back, but he'd best get back soon and sort this shit out. If he didn't, then this time he would be going to the Police, regardless of what Joe wanted.

Alan smiled through his fear. 'I swear that when Joe returns, I'll tell him you came and to get a move on,' he blathered. 'That's probably where is right now! He might be at that house and…'

'Bullshit!' Nero roared, easily able to tell this dipshit was stringing them along. 'Don't talk wet. You know as well as I do that your bendy-spined mate has done a runner.'

'No! He hasn't,' Alan cried. *Joe wouldn't do that to him and Dave, he just wouldn't.* 'Look, he promised us yesterday that he would sort this. I said if he didn't, then I'd go to the p…' He quickly trailed off, realising what he'd just nearly said.

'Otherwise you'd go *where*?' Keith growled, stepping closer to Alan's trembling body. 'The Police? Was that what you were about to say?'

'No, No… I wasn't going to say that…' Alan squeaked, panic gripping his bowels. 'I…'

'Fuck this!' Nero muttered. Turning his back, he paced three steps which covered the entire length of the hallway, then swinging around, he smiled nastily. 'You're coming for a little ride with us, mate.' He nodded to Keith. 'Get him into the boot.'

Alan blinked. *The boot? What the fuck?* 'No, wait! I…'

Keith rapidly silenced Alan with one hefty punch to the side of his head and began trussing him up.

· · · ·

ALTHOUGH HELEN WASN'T in the mood to attend this business dinner and had relished the prospect of bringing her husband even less, she'd forced herself to make the effort because Ken Manning was attending. It was astute to see if he'd made any headway on securing a knockdown price for one of those apartments at the Oak Apple Residential home for mummy dearest.

She glanced at James two places along on the opposite side of the table and hoped her inner strength was enough to keep the resentment that she felt towards him hidden.

There! He'd done it again – that sideways glance – like he was analysing her.

Whatever James was doing, she didn't like it. Although he'd been studying her covertly out of the corner of his eye for several days, tonight had been by far the worst yet and it was fast getting on her nerves.

He was the sort of man who wouldn't come out and say what he wanted to ask. Neither would he speak about what was needling him, preferring to beat around the bush or pose leading questions in the hope of getting information without making it obvious.

Helen bit back her scowl. Well, he *was* obvious. She knew him too well. James was far too predictable for his own good and she could see him coming a mile off. But he didn't have a clue that she was planning on buying a flat for her mother and shifting her out of their lives, did he? And even if he did, he'd never have the balls to question her about it.

What had she been thinking to marry such a mealy-mouthed washout?

Unconsciously nodding and smiling at a man next to her

wearing a toupee as he regaled her with how property was booming in the Buckingham area, Helen pretended to be interested.

Well, she *was* interested, in as much that it paid to be up to date and alert to what was going on in her industry, but Buckingham properties were of little use to her. That area was out of her catchment. Bob Proctor's latest idea of having networking dinners was all very well, but pointless if half the attendees dealt in out of range areas. This sort of gathering was only beneficial if it provided leads to areas of development that Shepherd, Percival and Proctor could take advantage of. She knew more than anyone they needed that, but the man she'd been placed next to was not in any way at all useful.

Helen picked up her wine glass to help quell the urge to flip her empty plate in the man's face. At least the sit down part of the dinner was drawing to a close, meaning shortly she'd be able to get up and mingle. Ken Manning was seated at the other end of the long table and having caught his eye several times during the meal she hoped that was enough to signify she wanted to talk. Hopefully he'd have good news.

Helen's lips pursed in irritation. It was a disappointment the young entrepreneur, Darren Harding, hadn't yet put in an offer for The Gables. From the way he'd reacted to the property during the viewing she'd been confident that was all but guaranteed, but it looked like she'd been wrong. The commission up for grabs on that place was immense – still, it wasn't over yet.

Seeing several people leave the table, Helen got up, making a mental note to put in a courtesy call to Darren Harding in the morning to see if she could read anything into what he was thinking and what his plans were going forward.

• • • •

JAMES KEPT HIS EYE ON HELEN as she worked her way through the room, stopping to chat with various people as she went.

He didn't like these networking dinners at the best of times, but this one was the worst yet. Not because it was particularly any more boring than the previous ones, but because it was impossible to concentrate on anything going on around him.

It was even more obvious that he was sticking out like a sore thumb because everyone else was chatting in couples or groups, whilst he stood limply on the outskirts like a lemon. But he could do nothing to propel himself forward and go through the rigmarole of false socialising tonight – not when all he could focus on was what he'd learnt from the chemists.

His eyes tracked back to Helen, deep in conversation with a man. James focused intently, looking for any sign, any sign at all – no matter how small, of her making jerky movements or twitches. He'd watched her like a hawk since she'd stepped into the house tonight but so far seen nothing to suggest there was anything wrong.

In fact, she appeared no different than usual. So much so that he'd looked up those tablets on the internet himself in the hope that the pharmacist had got it wrong and the drugs Helen was taking weren't anything to do with Parkinson's at all.

No such luck. The pharmacist hadn't been wrong. Benztropine was indeed a drug commonly prescribed to treat the associated tremors of Parkinson's. And Benztropine was definitely one of the drugs Helen was hiding in the garage.

James felt sticky perspiration under the armpits of his shirt and hoped it hadn't seeped though. He looked around for his jacket just in case he needed to cover up. The horror he felt about being up to the hilt with their mortgage was bad enough, but knowing his wife might be suffering with that dreadful disease didn't bear thinking about, but think about it he must. If that's what she had then he'd better get used to it because from what he'd heard, it only got worse.

But there was another worry too. As Helen had bought those pills from the internet, she could have ordered them mistakenly, thinking they were another type of anti-depressant? Clearly, judging by all the other pills she was taking, depression was definitely a big problem for her.

James' pulse raced. If Helen had ordered the wrong medication, then she wouldn't know if the pills were safe to take alongside the other ones. He'd been worried enough in the first place over their source, but now this new development made things even worse.

It was no use. He'd have to speak to her about this. There was no putting it off. She could be putting herself at risk.

Suddenly seeing Helen making her way over, James averted his eyes and instead became very interested in his watch.

'James,' Helen hissed, grabbing his arm and pulling him away from the centre of the room. 'What on earth are you doing?'

James blinked. *Did she just twitch or had he imagined it?* 'What do you mean? I was just standing here and...'

'You're making a fool out of yourself. You're standing there with your bloody mouth hanging open like the village idiot! Are you trying to embarrass me now as well?'

Despite trying to keep her voice level, the volume of Helen's voice increased as her irritation grew. 'It is not bad enough that my mother's lost me clients because of her need to prance around like a geriatric Barbie doll for the benefit of online news channels? Now *you're* standing there in front of all of my colleagues – my *husband*, acting like you've had a lobotomy!'

'Don't get worked up,' James pleaded. 'I'm not trying to embarrass you. I was just standing here an...'

'And *then* you start blatantly staring at your watch! For Christ's sake, James! How many times do you come with me to these work functions? Not often – yet you still can't help yourself from making it completely bloody obvious to everyone that you're bored shitless!' Helen raged.

God, how she despised him. Ken had been in the middle of telling her that he'd spoken to the developer and had got her an exceptional deal on the flat, providing she acted fast. He was about to give her further details when his attention had been diverted by the sight of James standing in the centre of the room like a basket case.

Helen seethed. How embarrassing. It was *her* who was supposed to be the victim as far as Ken was concerned. She'd told him how much of a mess her marriage was in because of James' controlling nature and there he was making out he was a few brain cells short. She was sure James must be doing this on purpose.

James' mouth flapped up and down as he tried to think of something to say, his cheeks burning at being dressed down in public. People must have heard what Helen had said. Was this how it was would be? Was her illness making her aggressive? How much worse would it get?

Helen linked her arm through his. 'Come on,' she hissed through her false smile. 'I can't stay here with you like this.'

Almost pulling James from the room, Helen marched forward, leaving James to mutter an embarrassed apology to the two large men he bumped into standing against the bar.

TWENTY

JOE HADN'T EXPECTED DAVE TO BE IN, but then he hadn't expected to be back tonight himself either.

He'd avoided his usual drinking holes because he couldn't face the insult of being publicly ignored by Alan and Dave in their crusade to continue their silent treatment over this Teagan business. He knew the usual pubs they drank in would have been where they'd headed on tonight's jolly, so he'd had no choice but to go somewhere else.

He scowled. The only other place within walking distance was an upmarket gaff. Wine bars and that sort of shindig weren't his cup of tea, but he'd given it a go. Not that there had been any point because he hadn't even got one foot over the threshold. *Literally.*

The silverback bouncer had obviously made his decision watching him come along the road, but had waited until he'd reached the door before, much to Joe's utter humiliation, barring the way with his log-like arm.

'No trainers in here, mate', the guy had said, or rather shouted – just in case the group of gorgeous birds not far behind him hadn't heard.

Unable to sway the bouncer's decision, Joe had no choice

but to slope off rapidly, his cheeks redder than a hooker's lipstick. Fucking poncey wine bars. Oh well, he hadn't wanted to go in there anyway.

Despite this setback, Joe dismissed the idea of the usual pubs for the second time and instead, grabbed some crisps and a four-pack of supermarket own lager from Tescos and sat on a bench to consume them. He'd done a good job of pretending he was having a good time and didn't miss Alan and Dave's friendship at all. That was until it started to bucket down and then he'd thrown the towel in and come home.

Rolling a joint on the kitchen table, Joe swigged at another can of lager, ignoring his socks were soaked through. He'd probably end up with trench foot because of this, but at least Dave wasn't ignoring him. *So far.*

'Where's Al?' Joe asked. 'Thought you two were out on the piss tonight?' He kept the bitterness about his lack of invitation, along with the irritation that being as they hadn't ended up going out, he could have gone to the usual boozers after all. If Dave was speaking to him right now, he didn't want to rock the boat.

Dave shrugged. 'We were supposed to be going out. I went to grab some chips for us first, but when I got back, Alan wasn't here. I must have only been gone about twenty minutes.'

Joe frowned. 'What time was this?'

'Dunno. About eight?'

A glimmer of fear hovered in Joe's brain. 'Erm, any calls or anything for me?'

Dave shook his head. 'Nope and I've been here all night, apart from the chips thing. Weren't those nutters supposed to be returning tonight? I thought I saw them on the way back from the chippy, but it couldn't have been because they were heading the opposite way.'

Joe's fear grew. 'You saw them?'

Dave accepted the joint Joe held out and took a deep drag. 'Yeah, a few streets away in a car. It looked like them, anyway.'

'Was anyone else with them?'

'No, just the two of them, but it wasn't them otherwise they'd be round here by now.'

Relaxing, Joe lit his joint. *Thank fuck for that.* 'It wasn't tonight they were due back anyway,' he lied.

Getting up from the table, Dave ambled towards the fridge for another can. 'I still can't think where Alan's got to.'

'He's probably with that Hairy Mary bird he pulled the other week. Perhaps she's finished shaving her fucking beard and wanted to see him again,' Joe winked and hearing Dave laugh, felt he'd now been forgiven.

As the joint took effect, the beginnings of laughter bubbled at the back of Joe's throat. Dave was cool with him, so it was a shame Alan was missing them getting on again. It just proved that Alan was the one being a big girl's blouse about the situation. Dave wasn't flapping around like an old woman, treating him like he'd got leprosy anymore, so when Alan returned from chucking his teddy out of the pram, he'd just have to accept he'd overreacted. If he still found everything so unpalatable, then maybe *Alan* should be the one to look for somewhere else to live?

Forcing himself to his feet, Joe was about to suggest putting on some chillout music when there was an almighty bang from the direction of the front door.

'What the fuck was that?' Dave cried. 'It sounded like someone just booted the door!'

Joe froze. *It wasn't those blokes again, was it?* He couldn't take that right now. He still hadn't heard from Teagan and didn't know what he could possibly say to fob those men off this time.

Dave fidgeted. 'What shall we do? What if it's th…'

'It's won't be them,' Joe groaned. 'If it was, they'd still be banging on the door. There was only one thump, so it's probably the wheely bin falling over. You know what it's been like since one of the wheels fell off.'

Dave nodded, but didn't look convinced. 'We'd best go and look though, don't you think?'

Joe hesitated. He didn't want to look. He was knackered and if he was honest, the small possibility that it was those gorillas lurking about outside was filtering, albeit slowly, into his half-stoned brain.

'Come on,' Dave insisted, pulling at Joe's T-shirt. 'I'm not going on my own just in case.'

Joe begrudgingly got to his feet and followed Dave into the hallway. If it *was* those blokes, then it was irrelevant if both him and Dave fronted up to the door because neither of those brick shithouses would have any trouble getting past.

At the front door, Dave hovered with his hand over the latch whilst Joe's ears strained for movement or obvious sign of two six foot six bruisers standing on the other side, but all was silent.

Joe turned on his heels, shaking his head in exasperation. 'There's no one there. For God's sake, Dave, stop worrying!' He wanted to finish his joint in peace. He'd left it propped in the ashtray and the last thing he wanted was it falling out and then having Alan on his back again when he returned to find there was a burn mark in his fair trade ethnic rug he'd bought from the market a couple of weeks ago.

As Joe made his way back to the kitchen, horror froze him in his tracks hearing Dave make a strangulated screaming noise.

• • • •

'MAKE SURE YOU only have the one, Lena,' Jonah said, as Lena swigged from a glass of white wine.

Anger flickered behind Lena's eyes before concealing it with a well-timed flutter of her false lashes. 'It's fine to have the occasional glass, babe,' she purred. 'The doctor said it's beneficial to drink small amounts. Does me good and it won't do the baby any harm.' *Especially being as there isn't one.*

She'd had no choice but to have a glass on the go when Jonah had got back otherwise he'd smell the vodka she'd been drinking the best part of the afternoon. She'd snorted enough coke to liven her up so no traces of the spirit were visible behind her eyes, but she had to make sure the smell was masked. He'd go ape otherwise.

'The doctor said that?' Jonah's eyes narrowed suspiciously. 'When did you go to the doctors?'

Lena flapped his question away. 'Oh, sometime last week... I don't remember exactly...' *Shit. She needed to be more careful with what she said.*

'You didn't mention anything.'

Lena paused pensively. 'Didn't I? I thought I had. I went to arrange my first scan. Oh well, I must have forgotten to tell you.'

Walking over to Jonah she made a big show of forcing her fingers into the waistband of the extra tight skirt she'd put on in readiness of his arrival. 'God, my clothes are getting tight now, don't you think?'

Jonah glanced at Lena's still perfectly flat stomach and shrugged. 'If you say so.'

'You could act interested! This is *your* baby, you know?' Lena huffed.

Jonah forced a smile and pulled Lena towards him, brushing a lock of her hair extension off her face. 'I am, course I'm interested. It's been a difficult day.'

Lena pouted up at Jonah and pressed her breasts up against his chest. 'I don't expect it's crossed your mind that I'll need a new dress for our party next week? There's only four days to go and I want to look my best. Especially with the press being there.'

Jonah kept his smile fixed, even though it was becoming increasingly difficult. Yes, the engagement party. How could he forget? All he knew was that he wished he could bloody forget. Forget all of it. Sadly, that was no longer an option.

'I'll need to get my hair done too,' she pushed, her fingers interlacing behind Jonah's collar.

Pulling out his wallet, Jonah peeled a wad of fifty pound notes out and tucked them down Lena's cleavage. 'There's a couple of grand there. That should do you,' he muttered, wondering how long it would take to untangle her from his neck.

'A couple of grand? What about the shoes and handbag? I'll need those too. You don't want me to look like a tramp, do you babe?'

Jonah felt like he was drowning. This engagement rubbish and the added stress Lena was causing at the club on top of this Dulcie Adams business was driving him up the wall. Plus, he was on edge waiting for a call from Nero. Two things were happening tonight: one – they were meeting with that guy to arrange access to Dulcie Adams' house and two, putting a tail on that bloke that the Shepherd woman had been seen with.

He'd already received one call to tell him they'd located the estate agents involved in the sale of the retirement home apartments and as all of the staff were due at a function later on this evening, Nero and Keith were going along after seeing the stoner lad. But both of these things should have all but finished by now and he wanted an update and all Lena could bang on about was poxy dresses?

Pressing closer against Jonah, Lena palmed her taloned hand over his crotch hoping to elicit a response, but scowled as he gently moved her aside and walked over to the drinks cabinet.

Her mouth twitched as he poured a large measure of whisky. 'It's alright for you to drink then? Just not me?' Lena snapped sulkily.

Jonah peered through hooded eyes, his irritation festering. 'I'm not the one who's pregnant.'

Swallowing her retort, Lena sat in the big round armchair and crossed her long legs. *She'd tap him for more cash later.* 'Being as I'm not allowed to enjoy myself anymore, why don't you tell me what's been so difficult about your day?'

Not that she wanted to know. He never told her anything anyway and she didn't much care, providing he kept the money flowing and treated her like a princess. 'You're not the only one that has to deal with stress at that club of yours.'

She uncrossed her legs and inspected her long bright pink

fingernails. 'The people there have a real problem. They get uppity with everything I say and you need to do something about it now beca...'

'I want to talk to you about that,' Jonah interrupted. *Now she'd raised it, this was a good a time as any.*

'Ah, so you've noticed it too? I knew you would. Those tarts have no right to think they can do what they like. I know more about how the club works than them and if they aren't go...'

'I don't want you interfering with the club anymore. I've already had to tell you once, yet you've gone and done it again,' Jonah said. Shrugging off his suit jacket, he chucked it across the back of the leather sofa and unbuttoning his collar, he pulled his tie loose.

Lena blinked in confusion, sure she hadn't heard correctly.

'Did you hear what I said?' Jonah asked, his tone neutral. He wouldn't go at her aggressively. He'd be rational however much he wanted to shout. 'I said, I don't want you interfering with the club.'

Lena's eyes hardened. 'What do you mean, you don't want me interfering with the club?' she screeched. 'I'm about to become your wife and now you're saying that for some reason I'm suddenly fucking banned from my husband-to-be's club?'

Jonah inwardly sighed at the immediate rise in the pitch of Lena's voice. She wasn't dealing with this well, just like he'd suspected. 'If you'd listened, I said, I didn't want you interfering at the club, not that you're banned.'

Lena jumped to her feet, hands on her hips. 'And why's that?'

Jonah pursed his lips. 'There's no point getting over dramatic. You said yourself that you're exhausted and getting involved with a gentlemen's club isn't the best thing for someone in your condition.'

'In *my* condition?' Lena screamed. 'What, so pregnant women aren't allowed, is that it? Or does that only apply to me? Am I even allowed to come to my own fucking engagement party?'

'Be sensible!' Jonah barked, getting irritated. He knew Lena would rile him and hey presto, she had.

'You're the one who needs to be sensible! It's not me you should be worried about. People don't want to watch fat birds on stage. I only told those two thick bitches that they were getting too lardy. Christ, they must be a size twelve! You shouldn't have girls bigger than a size eight; ten, tops - and even that's pushing it!' Lena couldn't help but rant. Those ugly dykes should have been long gone by now. At least one of them had shagged Jonah in the past and she was having *no one* hanging around who had history with him. She wasn't having his attention diverted anywhere else but one hundred percent on *her* and her alone. Not now she was almost where she wanted to be.

She stomped to the cabinet, ignoring Jonah's glare as she poured herself another wine. 'I've already got rid of those two once and somehow they've been reinstated,' she raged. 'I can't imagine you'd be so stupid to do that, so I can only presume that old has-been, Gwen, took it upon herself to override us both.'

Anger bristled and Jonah snatched the wine glass from Lena's hand. 'You've already had a drink!' He slammed the glass down on the side. '*I* told Gwen to reinstate those girls. You had no right to sack them. It isn't your call to interfere. Even if I hadn't reinstated them, Gwen has the right to. She's got the right to run the show as she sees fit. Unlike *you*.'

Jonah paced around the other side of the room. 'You're pissing people off and I won't have it. Not in my club. Do you understand?'

'But I'm your fiancée,' Lena whined, changing tactics. She couldn't believe this. He was putting what that old bat thought before *her*? She'd been about to suggest that *she* take over from Gwen. That way she'd have plenty of time to weed out all of the girls who had ever pissed her off whilst also having plenty of opportunity to sneak drinks for as long as this baby crap continued.

'Being my fiancée is irrelevant.' *The word 'fiancée' jammed in Jonah's throat.* 'It's purely business and you're not good for it.'

Lena almost choked. 'You're saying what we've got together is business?' she screamed, forcing tears from her eyes. 'I'm having your baby! We're getting married in a few weeks and all of that is purely *business*?'

Jonah felt sick. He didn't want Lena getting upset and stressed out – that wasn't good for the baby, but he couldn't back down. The Feathers was his club and she would not ruin it. 'I didn't say that, did I? I said the decisions I make over the *club* are purely business, not you.'

Unplaced, Lena glared at Jonah. 'So, what is it with you fighting Gwen's corner? You've always sided with that old witch. I'd do a much better job than her, not to mention looking a damn sight fucking better!'

She fronted up to Jonah, her finger pointing into his face. 'Or is there more to it? Is that what you're trying to say? Are you fucking that savage old bitch? Is that why she hates me so much?'

Jonah felt like slapping the taste out of Lena's mouth. 'You need to watch what you're fucking saying, Lena. I will not have you insulting Gwen.'

'See? You're doing it again!' Lena spat, incandescent with rage and jealousy.

When Jonah's mobile rang, he stared at Lena with cold hard eyes before snatching up his phone. 'I need to take this call. We'll discuss this later,' he spat, marching from the room.

Launching the half-empty bottle of wine at the wall as the door closed behind Jonah, Lena slumped into the chair, shaking with rage. *No, we won't discuss this later, Jonah*, she thought.

He didn't want her involved at the club? Well, she would see about that. This was all down to Gwen and her band of tarts. Being side-tracked in favour of *them* was not something she would put up with.

Grabbing her phone, she smiled seeing a new text message

had arrived.

TWENTY ONE

JOE'S BRAIN SPAN both from worry and fear, as well as the remnants of the joint he'd smoked. Courtesy of the weed, his mouth was as dry as the bottom of a bird cage and his tongue felt glued to the roof of his mouth.

He was sure it was stuck so tightly that he wouldn't be able to speak. Not that he wanted to. He was scared that if he opened his mouth, he'd utter something to cause even more problems than he'd already got - if that were possible. Although it didn't seem feasible things could get any worse, he had the sinking suspicion that they could.

If those men's intention was getting a message through to him, then they'd succeeded. Although neither he, nor Dave had spoken out loud that what had happened to Alan was anything to do with those two men, they both knew it *had* to be. And Joe was more than shitting himself about that. He didn't want what had happened to Alan, happening to *him*. Nor did he want to think what had happened to Alan was *his* fault.

Guilt burnt behind Joe's eyeballs. He should have done more to get what those blokes wanted. He hadn't realised… hadn't thought that they… that they'd do something like *this*.

As well as having drug induced dry mouth, the weed was

also not helping Joe's mental state. He studiously avoided meeting the eyes of anyone in the hospital waiting room, sure they were all staring at him. He could feel it. He could feel their eyes boring holes into his brain. They knew. They all knew what he'd done. Or rather, what he *hadn't* done.

Joe forced his eyes to focus on Dave sitting next to him in an identical plastic chairs and refused to let his mind speculate why hospital chairs were attached to the floor. *Who would want to nick uncomfortable plastic chairs?*

Dave's head was in his hands, his face a dismal shade of grey; he was shaking and although his sobs had died down, there was an occasional hiccup as he fought to control himself.

Joe swallowed uncomfortably. He didn't feel too clever either. In fact, he felt distinctly green around the gills and it would be a long time before he got the image of Alan's battered and broken body crumpled on the doorstep out of his mind. That's if he ever did, which at this precise moment, felt unlikely.

Panic gained momentum once more. He had to do what those guys wanted. But how? This was all Teagan's fault. If she'd called him back in the first place, he could have sorted it and this wouldn't have happened.

Snatching his phone from his pocket, he frantically stabbed out another text message:

> Please call me. It's an emergency. Not joking.
> I need to speak to you. PLEASE.

'What the fuck are you doing?' Dave snapped.

'Messaging Teagan,' Joe replied. *She'd better answer this one. If she didn't answer this one, then he'd...*

'And you're doing that while our mate's life is hanging in the fucking balance?' Dave cried, aghast. 'What the hell's wrong with you?'

'I'm trying to get her to answer my messages,' Joe hissed through gritted teeth. 'I need to get around there and do what they want.'

'You must be joking? This is something for the police to deal with now. They'll want to speak to us soon. The doctor said th...'

'Keep your fucking voice down,' Joe mumbled, aware several heads had turned in their direction. He wasn't being paranoid - they *were* all looking at them. 'We can't involve the police! You heard what those blokes said and I think th...'

'No, Joe. After what's happened, I'm telling the police everything that went on. Those men should be held accountable.'

'Don't you see?' Joe gripped Dave's arm. 'If you go to the police, then what happened to Alan will be the tip of the iceberg! It will be me or you or *both* of us next time. And I suspect we won't end up in hospital like Alan - that was merely a warning. Hospitals don't tend to corpses, which is what we'll be!'

Dave visibly paled, his skin turning even more grey, but this time tinged with a hue of sickly green.

'Yes, that's right. We'll be fucking dead if we open our gobs,' Joe insisted, nausea rising. He was right on that one, no doubt.

For the moment, the only one he didn't have to worry about opening his trap and signing all of their death warrants, was Alan. And that was only because the poor bastard was in a coma.

• • • •

KEN MANNING PRESSED HIS KEY FOB, setting the central locking on his Audi. He glanced back at the shiny black car gleaming in the moonlight and smiled to himself as he walked up the drive.

It had gone well tonight. Helen had seemed pleased to hear the news that he'd got a massive chunk knocked off the price for that apartment. In reality, that wasn't how it happened at all - all he'd done was blag the developer to drop the price by ten grand, but it had been *him* who'd taken the main knock.

Ken was commanding a huge commission from the sale of the apartments, so he'd cut his commission to a measly 5k, rather than 30. Ok, so he was personally losing out on 25k, but Helen was getting the apartment at a massive reduction of 35k in total, which was a *big* drop. And he'd do anything to make her life easier.

From what she'd said about all this business with her husband, mother and brother, she was having a really hard time and he'd do whatever he could to ease that for her. With any luck she'd realise after this and after he'd set up the seamless sale of her mother's home – again with a distinct financial benefit to her pocket, that she'd be better off with him than with her husband.

Ken shrugged as he walked up the three steps to his front door, fumbling with his keys. It looked like Helen's marriage had just about run its course, but he had to admit he'd been surprised to see the state of James Shepherd tonight.

From what she'd said, the control freak gave her grief left, right and centre – determining what she could do with their finances, despite her being the one who'd undoubtedly brought in the lion's share of the money during their marriage, if not all of it. He wasn't even sure what the man did for a job – if anything, but by the looks of it, he was on the sick. James Shepherd looked far from stable – but not in an aggressive way – in a nervous wreck way - like he'd got the weight of the world on his shoulders – certainly not what he'd imagined the man to look or behave like.

Ken frowned as he shoved his key in the lock. Appearances could be deceptive and if Helen said he was unsupportive and made her life a misery, then it was true. She wasn't the type to make things up, that's why he was more than happy to take a knock financially to help her out.

He glanced up at his nice four-bedroomed house. It wasn't like he couldn't afford to help out a friend. Plus, he thought with a slight smile, there was the added incentive that helping Helen should also convince her to look at him in a way other than someone from college. And perhaps make her realise the handful of one night stands they'd had back in the day meant a lot more to him than she'd realised.

That was pretty much all he was missing from his near-on perfect life – a good woman. And Helen was that woman.

Opening the door, Ken flicked on the light, but had little time to react before a hand was clamped over his mouth and he was forcibly dragged backwards down the hallway.

• • • •

'I'VE NEVER HEARD OF HER!' Ken spluttered after the grip of the massive gnarled hand eased from around his throat.

He scrabbled around on the floor, the elbows of his charcoal grey pin-striped suit coated with dust as he pulled himself up to a sitting position against the radiator. His eyes darted to the window, dismayed to see the curtains closed scuppering the remote chance that a neighbour might see what was happening in his rear-facing sitting room. Number 34 might just have been able to see in if they happened to be in their bedroom, but not with the curtains closed. *Who'd closed the curtains because it wasn't him?*

Panic hammered in Ken's chest along with his heart.

'Don't wind us up, squire,' Keith rasped, squatting on his haunches. 'You can't expect us to believe that bullshit, being as we watched you – yes, *you* having a cosy chat with Mrs Shepherd at your poncey function earlier.' He smiled. 'Shame you were too busy eyeing her up to notice us, wasn't it?'

Ken coughed hard, the salmon canapes he'd eaten earlier threatening to come back up on him. Had these two really been there? He swallowed hard. They must have been if they knew he'd been taking to Helen.

'What is it with you and her then, eh?' Keith grinned. 'You her bit on the side? Giving her a break from that wet lettuce of a husband of hers?' Bet she can't wait to wrap her legs around your neck after being boned by that piece of piss. Bet she's a real goer between the sheets.'

Ken's cheeks flushed crimson with a combination of indignation and embarrassment. In his own mind, what the man said wasn't too far from the truth. 'Don't talk about Helen like that.'

His mind raced. Were these men here because of James Shepherd? Did James suspect something was going on between them? If he'd organised this, then the man was nowhere near as fragile as he looked. No wonder he'd been so jumpy. 'Look, Helen's a colleague and an old friend.'

Keith pulled Ken up with one hand, the lapel of his suit straining as it took his weight. 'I don't give a fuck if you're screwing her. We're here for information, nothing else.'

'I-Information?' Ken stuttered. 'What kind of information?'

Nero, who had been leaning against the wall casually watching the proceedings, stepped forward. 'Helen Shepherd, her mother or someone else in her family is in possession of something that doesn't belong to them.' He moved closer. 'It's worth a lot of money and the owners want it back.'

'W-Want it back?' Ken cried. What on earth were these men talking about? What could Helen Shepherd possibly have to do with people such as this? She didn't have vast amounts of hidden money otherwise she wouldn't be in such a financial mess to need favours on the apartment and the house. It was preposterous.

'They fucking stole it, mate,' Keith growled. 'That's what they did, so they need to give it back before one of them gets hurt.' He grinned, exposing his gold tooth. 'And being as you're so pally with your *friend*, Helen, we thought you'd like to ensure that nothing – shall we say, *unfortunate* befalls her or her dear mother.'

Anger he wasn't aware he possessed washed over Ken and he shook Keith's hand from the front of his suit. 'Helen and her family are nice people!' he cried. 'They wouldn't steal anything. How dare you break into my house and threaten that if I don't d…'

'You what?' Grabbing Ken by the shoulders, Keith slammed him hard into the radiator. 'Not wise to be so unhelpful.'

Winded, Ken dropped to his knees, gasping for breath.

Nero could feel his own rage building and gave Keith the signal to hold fire. First of all, they'd been jerked around by that moron stoner and had to give that mate of his a bit of a kicking. Now this besuited muppet was getting holier than thou?

He nudged Ken with his foot. 'You're going to get us access to Helen's house, Ken. That way we can retrieve what is ours. That's all we want you to do.' *Being as the stoner was dragging his feet, this tosser could get on with it.*

Trying to get his breath back, Ken moved to a sitting position. Shaking from fear, he wondered whether it was feasible for Helen or any of her family to have done something such as this? Something to warrant the ire of these… these *people.*

No, it wasn't possible. Helen didn't have a dishonest bone in her body. But wait! What about her brother? She said he had a gambling problem. Was he responsible for this? 'Is it Robert you're after?' Ken rasped, his lungs the size of peanuts. 'Does he owe you money?'

Keith glanced at Nero, whose frown appeared even deeper across his forehead.

Mistaking the silence for a positive, Ken continued. He didn't like the position Robert had put Helen in, so regardless of her oath not to go against him, he wouldn't stand by and have the man bring trouble to Helen and her mother's door. Robert had done enough damage as it was, so whatever he'd done he'd have to take it on the chin, not drag everyone into his problems.

'Robert owes everyone money! Helen told me only recently about her brother's gambling problem. It's *his* problem, so leave Helen and mother out of it!' Ken's voice sounded braver than he felt, but he would not stand by whilst these brutes had the audacity to threaten the woman he loved. *Yes, loved. He loved Helen and always had.*

He had no idea how he would broach this awkward situation with her, but he'd have to. He'd have to warn her that these lunatics were sniffing around. She'd be mortified to find out that these thugs had broken into his house and had the cheek to threaten him, but he wasn't bothered about that. The only important thing was that Helen and her mother came to no harm because of that idiot, Robert.

Keith pulled out his cigarettes and slowly lit one. Squatting back down, he blew the smoke into Ken's face. 'Well, thanks for that,' he chortled. 'Except we don't give a damn who Robert is or what he's done. If he owes people brass, then I agree with you – it's his problem, but that's not why we're here.'

Putting his hand back round Ken's throat, he pulled him off the floor. 'Now,' he spat, 'your friend's mother is harbouring stolen goods and you, via the lovely Helen will make sure we get them back before Helen isn't quite as attractive as she is at the moment. Keith's smile widened. 'That would be an awful thing to happen because you're not thinking straight, wouldn't it?'

Rage flooded through Ken at the slightest thought of anyone touching a hair on Helen's head. 'She would know nothing about this and neither would her mother. I've had enough. Get out of my house! I have CCTV and I'll go to the police. You've broken in, threatened me and for what? Helen's mother has dementia, you stupid fool! She'd never dream of do…'

Keith's fist slammed into Ken's face with the use of the words 'stupid' and 'fool'. *No one spoke to him like that.* 'Going to the police, are you?' He watched Ken clutch at his smashed nose, blood spewing down his shirt and over his suit, forming a puddle on the polished wooden floor.

Nero calmly watched Keith lose his rag. They would get nowhere with this pompous prick. As for the CCTV, they'd already fixed that, there was no record of anything, but he didn't doubt that this man was indeed foolish enough to go to the police. He sighed. *It really wasn't their day today.*

This time when Keith wrapped both hands around Ken Manning's neck and applied pressure, Nero didn't bother calling him off. It had to be done and at least for once it wouldn't be too messy.

• • • •

'ATTACKED?' TEAGAN CRIED. 'What do you mean?'

Teagan had been glad to finally get up to her room and get ready for bed. Robert's visit had put Dulcie in not one of her better moods and she had the sneaking suspicion there would be another walkabout tonight. It was already after midnight, so if that happened the chances of getting more than a couple of hours sleep were slim and she was already exhausted.

Checking her phone as usual before she got into bed, Teagan was dismayed to see a text message notification. Seeing it was off Joe again, she'd very nearly ignored it, but curiosity got the better of her and she'd looked. Now she very much wished she hadn't.

Joe's text begging her to ring and that it was an emergency hadn't resounded at first. Putting her phone back, she'd got into bed, but after five minutes of lying in the dark, thinking, she'd wondered if there really *was* an emergency. How would she feel if something *had* happened and she'd ignored it.

Against her better judgement, Teagan found herself getting back out of bed and before she could stop herself, dialled Joe's number. But she was still none the wiser. He was blabbing and nothing he said made sense.

'Joe?' she repeated. 'Can you hear me? I said, what do you mean, attacked?' Her heart raced. *Was Joe hurt? Or was it a cheap attempt to get her to ring?*

'I can hear you, I can hear you,' Joe babbled. 'It's Alan… Oh Christ, I don't know what to do… I…'

'Alan? Alan your housemate?' *Another fight in the pub over a woman, no doubt? Probably something to do with Joe.*

'I-I'm at the hospital with him… Dave too,' Joe said.

'Dave's ok - it's just Alan. Oh shit... I...'

'What's gone on?' Teagan asked, her heart hardening. *Had Joe taken some funny kind of drugs?* She'd never liked his penchant for dabbling with that sort of stuff at the best of times and if he'd lost his mind because of the crap he took, then it was his own fault.

'I don't know what to do,' Joe muttered. 'Shit!'

Teagan frowned. 'Joe, you're not making sense. Look, I'm really tired. I'm sure Alan will be fine. Don't worry and...'

'You don't understand!' Joe wailed. 'Alan's in a coma. They beat him so badly, they think he's got brain damage. Fucking *brain damage*, Teagan! He... he may not survive and...'

'Brain damage?' Teagan went cold. If this was a windup, then she'd never speak to Joe ever again. But if it wasn't, what kind of beating must Alan have had?

'It's my fault. It's all my fault,' Joe repeated. 'I've got to see you. I...'

'How did this happen? Where were y...'

'I daren't say much over the phone. I... Look, please... I'm in the shit. I need to see you. I've got to talk to you ab...'

'No,' Teagan said firmly. 'I'm sorry about Alan, I really am, but seeing each other won't change anything with wh...'

'You don't get it,' Joe screeched. 'Please, Teagan. I'm begging you. It will make more sense when I explain. This is because... because of you... It's beca...'

'Because of *me*?' Teagan cried. 'Don't you dare blame me because you went out and Alan got into a fight! You ditched *me*, Joe – not the other way around. It was your decision to sleep with other girls behind my back and...'

Hearing Joe openly sobbing, Teagan stopped. *What was going on?*

'Christ, Teag,' Joe sniffed, 'I can't explain over the phone, that's why I need to see you. But please, you've *got* to believe me on this one. I'm fucking dead if I don't sort this out. I need your help. *Please* meet me. I won't hassle you, I just need to speak to you.'

Teagan remained silent. *Torn*. Worry rattled through her.

'Teagan, *please…*' Joe begged. 'Please meet me. As soon as possible?'

Teagan hesitated. It went against everything she'd decided on where Joe was concerned. On top of that, she'd arranged to go for a coffee with Darren Harding tomorrow.

'Teagan?' Joe paused. 'I need…'

'It's my half day tomorrow, but I've already arranged something,' Teagan said, begrudgingly. She wasn't cancelling Darren. He was the first positive thing to happen in ages and she wasn't giving that up only for Joe to rip her confidence to shreds again and remind her what a doormat she'd been.

Joe's voice became even more pleading. 'Can we not meet up before or after? I won't take up much of your time. Shit is at stake here and whether you believe me or not, you're the only one who can help.'

'Ok,' Teagan said, immediately regretting it. 'I'll meet you tomorrow, but it can't be for long. And don't get in the habit of running to me when things aren't going well. This will be the one and only time.'

'I won't,' Joe promised. In fact, he more than promised. The last thing he'd wanted was to get back in touch with Teagan. After she'd sorted this, he'd never have to speak to her again – which was what he'd been angling for all along, but at least now he'd formulated a plan as to how to pull this off.

TWENTY TWO

HELEN PUT HER COFFEE MUG down on her desk and flicked through the pages of her red A4 planner. No meetings or appointments this morning, thankfully.

She glanced through the window to the main part of the estate agents, seeing Joanne with a customer – a customer who she'd felt the need to point out, was there to complete on a property. *So, Joanne had made a sale. Whoopee-doo!*

Well, *she* needed a sale. She needed more than bloody one to sort this mess. To top it all, the interest had gone up on her mortgage for the second time in six months and what with the lack of commission lately, things were anything but flush. She was dreading Bob Proctor suggesting they made another joint financial injection into company funds. It was only a matter of time.

Bob was out today following 'successful leads' from the networking dinner. It seemed that everyone was doing well. *Except for her.*

Helen had always excelled in her ability to sell and broker deals, but this last few weeks things had ground to a halt and she wasn't happy about that. She was also still smarting over James' toe-curlingly embarrassing behaviour last night. No one had mentioned it, but she knew they must have noticed. *Everyone* must have noticed.

Picking up her mug again, Helen took a sip of the now tepid sour-tasting coffee and glanced at the clock on the wall. It was almost 10, so why had she been unable to get hold of anyone? She'd called Ken's mobile first thing, but it had gone straight through to voicemail. She'd tried a further three times since, but the same thing had happened. By the time it had reached 9.30, she'd even called him at the office, not that she'd wanted to. She'd have preferred to catch him before he'd got to work. It was always difficult to talk with everyone hanging around, but she was desperate to know the rest of the details about the apartment.

Last night he'd said she needed to move at double quick speed to secure the offer the developer was prepared to give. She had to admit he'd wangled a bloody good offer. A 35k reduction was not to be sniffed at, but Ken hadn't had chance to let her know what the proposed time frame was before James' stellar performance of acting like a loon had diverted his attention. Plus, she needed to confirm how fast he could get the contracts drawn up so she could have everything down in writing before the developer changed his mind.

Another reason why she needed Darren Harding to buy the Gables and for her sales to pick up.

Helen's teeth dug into her bottom lip. There was no way she had anywhere near all of the money required for the apartment to guarantee a fast transaction. There was no way she could swing another mortgage at the bank – not with her own remortgage and the state of the company finances hanging round her neck. Perhaps Robert would loan her some until the next few commissions came in? But then he'd want to know why. *Oh, God, what a mess.*

Her eyebrows knitted together, an idea forming. Perhaps if her mother's 'illness' took a drastic turn for the worse, Robert would be more pliable with stepping up for the money?

Helen picked up the phone again, feeling a lot happier in

her mind now she'd thought of a way forward. She'd try Ken one last time - he couldn't be out all day. The idiot had probably left his phone somewhere. Then she'd call Darren Harding and give him a nudge in the right direction.

She'd got halfway through dialling Ken's number when she glanced up to see two police enter the estate agents. Seeing Joanne turn to look in the direction of her office, Helen replaced the handset and got to her feet.

• • • •

DULCIE SANG LOUDLY to a tune blaring from the record player whilst Teagan hovered in the doorway.

Maybe she should reconsider having the afternoon off? Last night was the worst so far for Dulcie's sleep confusion. The woman had been totally out of it when Teagan had rushed from her bed after hearing the shouting. It had been almost 3am, but unable to sleep in anything more than fits and starts, her mind running on overtime since the frantic and strange phone call with Joe, it had literally felt like she'd only had seconds of sleep before the noise from the floor below had woken her with a jolt.

As expected, Dulcie was back in the pink bedroom, but this time she'd been having a heated argument with someone invisible. Despite entering the room and making herself known, she'd been unable to get through to Dulcie. Even physically interacting with the woman hadn't been enough to break the world Dulcie was visiting last night.

Despite appearing fully awake and coherent, moving around as she would do usually, Dulcie's eyes were glazed, looking straight through Teagan during the many attempts she'd tried to get her attention. Wherever Dulcie had been, it was real to her. The heated and loud argument she'd been having, judging by the names used, was with Michael – the man she'd said had never returned.

The anger and resentment in Dulcie's voice as she'd spewed forth a host of profanities had unnerved Teagan. Although she'd seen Dulcie behave erratically before and act quite aggressively when she was in one of her confused states, last night was, without a doubt, the most unnerving and unpleasant one yet. So much so that she was now really concerned about the lady's well-being.

Teagan faltered as she moved further into the room. Helen said dementia only got worse, but this was *so* much worse and it had escalated so very quickly.

Watching as Dulcie picked the needle off the record, Teagan could see as plain as day that her hands were shaking. Shaking a lot. As the room fell silent she stepped forward. 'Dulcie? Would you like a cup of tea? Or a coffee, perhaps?'

Dulcie swung around, her eyes flashing with fury, her mouth cracked into a sneer. 'I know what you're doing. I know you're in on it with her.'

Teagan frowned. *Act normal, Teagan. Pretend she isn't saying weird things. She'll snap out of it – she usually does.* 'You must be tired,' she smiled. 'You had a rather disturbed night.'

Dulcie shook her head, her beady blue eyes pinpointed on Teagan. 'Trying that again are you? All that tosh about me saying things?' She slammed her gnarled hand down on the top of the stereo cabinet, making Teagan jump. 'Well, it won't work!'

'W-What? I...'

'Shut up, you stupid girl. Don't come in here telling me this, that and whatever. You know as well as I do that I didn't have a disturbed night at all.' Something suddenly changed behind Dulcie's eyes and she raised her hands in the air and looked at the ceiling dramatically. 'What am I even doing attempting to justify myself to you? Tell me that?'

Teagan blinked. *She was still on one then?* 'Dulcie, I'm not...'

'Be quiet!' Dulcie barked. 'Don't you *dare* make excuses. *I'm* top billing at this club and you know it!' Her lips flattened into an unflattering smirk.

Teagan remained motionless, not knowing what to do or

say and perspiration beaded at the back of her neck. Should she call Helen? Maybe she should call the doctor?

'What are you planning now? Come on! Out with it! What are you thinking you could possibly do?' Dulcie laughed nastily as she shook her head. 'Well, I tell you this, lady. There's *nothing* you can do. Nothing at all.'

She moved quickly across the room, her bony finger pointing towards Teagan, her face slowly twisting.

Teagan stepped backwards. Even though she knew Dulcie wasn't speaking to her personally, the woman's expression and tone was vicious and, dare she say it, it was scaring her.

Moving closer, Dulcie pushed herself into Teagan's face; close enough to be able to smell the mint tea on her breath. 'Now piss off out of this room before I drag you out myself.'

Dulcie's eyes flashed with unbridled rage and despite thinking herself ridiculous for doing so, Teagan found herself running from the room in fright.

• • • •

JONAH SCROLLED THROUGH the local news feed on the internet, his forehead furrowing. This wasn't what he'd been hoping to see.

He always had his eyes and ears open for anything that may concern his club, along with developments and possible openings for any part of the business, not to mention whispers of criminal activity which might shout up handy leads to what rival firms were up to; hints of possible opportunities on the horizon, trouble coming his way or anyone who looked like they were edging towards infringing on his territory.

Not that he'd ever had many problems with the latter. Any firm worth their salt respected each other's boundaries and didn't go looking for trouble, himself included. Every now or then there would be the odd one pushing their luck – invariably foreigners, but on the whole there was usually little point of concern on that angle. Most trouble came from within, as his father's own experience with Michael Fucking Pointer had proven.

That alone made him more edgy than most over loyalty and trust. But today was different. The local headlines were *definitely* centred on him.

Well, not *him*, per se, but courtesy of what he'd sanctioned - both the hospitalised kid and the concern surrounding the missing estate agent were solely on his back.

Sure, he'd instructed Nero and Keith to get things moving by doing whatever necessary to move things forward, but they'd drawn attention with these two and the worst thing of all was that he was still no nearer to getting what he wanted. At least there was no connection between him, his business or anyone to do with him and the two latest newsworthy articles. *Yet…*

Jonah ran his fingers through his hair. This was the age-old problem when business ran into civilian territory. Civilians were missed and things got noticed.

From what Nero had said when filling him in first thing with more details then he'd been able to give over the blower last night, he hadn't been too happy that Keith had gone in at the deep end. The lad in the coma was one thing. The kid most likely had a glass jaw to start with – those type always did, but finishing off the suit because of an insult was another.

Keith was a loose cannon in situations such as these – more diplomacy and control was needed where the great unwashed public were concerned, so perhaps Keith hadn't been the best choice to work alongside Nero on this particular case after all. But then, he understood the reasoning too. From what had been said, the suit wasn't ever going to talk and if they'd let him walk, it was almost a dead cert he'd have run to the Old Bill, so there hadn't been too much choice in the outcome.

Jonah frowned. He'd just have to rely that a decent enough job had been undertaken on the clean-up operation. Nero had called in their best guys who frequently dealt with situations such as this and he had every faith in their ability to leave no traces. All should be good, but it was still a risk and one that he'd been hoping to avoid.

Jonah's eyes wandered to the envelope containing the Visiting Order he'd received in the post this morning. He knew Saul wanted an update on how the retrieval of the goods was progressing, but the last thing he wanted to do was go and see his brother. He would want to know why it hadn't happened yet and furthermore, want to know why valuable time was being 'wasted' on civilians, rather than going straight for the prize.

Jonah's lips flattened into a thin line. He didn't need Saul's lectures and he certainly didn't need any more pressure being lumped on him. Saul was in nick, not him and *he* was dealing with this, not his bloody brother.

The fact that, due to his own impatience and losing his temper, giving Nero and Keith the go-ahead to be a bit more heavy handed had cost one bloke his life – possibly two, didn't sit well. Jonah scowled, not liking the concept that perhaps he was sometimes more like his brother than he wanted to be.

Picking up the envelope, he stuffed it in the bottom drawer of his desk. He wouldn't be going to see Saul – not this time. He'd wait until this was done before he did that.

Jonah picked up his glass of whisky and absentmindedly sipped at it, his eyes once again straying to the finger on his left hand and scowled.

She hadn't shown her face this morning either. *Lena.*

When he'd returned to the sitting room last night after taking Nero's call, she'd disappeared off to bed – to bed in the spare room again, but for once, he hadn't bothered pulling her out of there. He had no wish to continue the conversation. He'd made his point loud and clear and she'd just have to put up with it.

• • • •

HEATH WALKED CONFIDENTLY down the street towards the café that Teagan suggested they meet in, glancing at his reflection in a shop window as he passed.

Having put on a pair of smart jeans and a decent shirt, he

looked good – not overdressed, but not too casual either. His hair was smart and the pair of leather loafers he wore completed the look.

Borrowing the Lexus again, he'd hoped to park it in range of the café so she'd have a good view, but unfortunately, this particular place didn't have a car park and all the spaces outside on the road were taken, so he'd settled with parking further down the road. It wasn't a problem. If he played his cards right, she'd have plenty of chance to see the car later.

Heath grinned. He'd done enough digging on Facebook to get enough gen on the school he'd allegedly attended with Teagan to make a conversation plausible. He'd come across a Facebook group of ex-pupils, which luckily, Teagan wasn't a member of and by working out the years she would have attended, he'd pinpointed a handful of people who would have been in her year. Names he could casually drop into the conversation, knowing she should remember them, even though she couldn't remember him. He just had to hope the names he was planning on using weren't girls she'd hated or boys who'd dumped her. Still, whatever – dropping in these peoples' names would confirm his authenticity if she had any lurking doubts.

Pushing open the door of the Piccolo Café, Heath glanced around, hoping to spot her, but he couldn't see anyone fitting the bill. Walking up to the counter, he smiled easily at the woman standing behind it. 'Sit anywhere?' he asked.

'Being as this isn't the Ritz, yes love,' the woman replied. 'Whatever takes your fancy. I'll come and take your order in a moment.'

Supressing a shudder as the woman with her greying, scraped-back hair winked at him, he smiled. *She* didn't take his fancy, that was for sure, but it never hurt to be pleasant.

Heath moved to a table in the window, partially steamed up from condensation. This way he could get a view who was coming up the road. He'd studied Teagan's profile picture and reckoned he'd spot her easily enough. From what he'd seen during the quick glimpse he'd had when she'd opened the door to Helen Shepherd the other night, she looked the same in real life as she did on her profile. He'd lost count of the amount of times he'd heard of people sticking old photos up, sometimes even photos of a completely different person. Or worse, a picture of a flower or a cat.

If he was into trying to find a bird via the internet then he dreaded to think what he'd end up with. Probably some sixty-year-old woman, based on a profile picture of thirty years prior, not to mention twelve stone lighter!

Glancing at his mobile, Heath was glad to see there were no texts or missed calls from Teagan. He'd be gutted if she cried off at this late stage. It would balls up his plans – however loose they were. There was another missed call from Helen Shepherd though. Probably chasing up about that house. He'd have to call her, but he wasn't quite sure how to play that one now. His father thought pursuing that route was a waste of time and he had to admit, he agreed.

Suddenly spotting a young woman walking down the road, Heath sat forward. *Was this Teagan?*

His heart raced as his mind played out various scenarios of what he would say. *Calm, Heath. Treat this as a potential car sale, play it by ear and you'll be fine.*

He watched the woman near the café. She looked flustered and nervous – not a great sign.

Unconsciously smoothing down his hair, Heath adopted a relaxed expression, even though he felt anything but. Pulling his mobile back out of his pocket, he flicked through his contacts. It always looked better not to appear on edge and fiddling with a mobile was the perfect and commonly used distraction.

'Ok then, love. What can I get you?'

Heath's head jerked up, only to see the woman from behind the counter leaning disturbingly close to him, notepad in hand. 'Oh, erm… could you just give me a moment? I'm waiting for a friend before I order.' *Fuck off. I can't see Teagan come in if you stand there.*

The waitress nodded and moved away, revealing Teagan standing by the counter looking around uncomfortably.

'Teagan?' Heath jumped to his feet a little too hastily, knocking a vinegar bottle over in the process. 'Bollocks!' he muttered, the liquid splashing over the table as well as his jeans, the noise making all of the other customer crane their necks to stare at him.

'Don't worry, love. I'll sort this out.' The waitress shoved herself between the tables, mopping at the spilt vinegar with a cloth.

Heath pushed through the remaining gap and rushed over to Teagan, trying to stop his eyes running over her nice figure inside the well-fitted black trousers and top. 'Teagan? Great to see you again!'

Teagan returned a shy smile. 'Darren?'

'It is indeed.' For want of thinking it the right and usual thing to do if she really had been an old schoolmate, Heath pulled Teagan towards him, enveloping her into a hug and then kissed her on the cheek.

Heath smiled bashfully. 'I knocked the vinegar over…'

'I heard,' Teagan smiled, relaxing a little.

Heath pulled out a chair for Teagan, seeing her hesitate for a moment before sitting down. 'What would you like to drink?'

'Just tea please,' Teagan said, placing her handbag on the chair nearest to her.

Taking the hint, Heath sat opposite and grinned at the waitress. 'Two teas, please.' He then turned his attention back to Teagan. 'Wow! It's been ages. It's so great to see you, you look fantastic!' He hoped that didn't come across as slimy. He didn't want to put her off or make her any more uncomfortable than she already was. 'I can't believe it's been so long since I last saw you. How have you been?'

Teagan smiled nervously. 'It must be nearly ten years.' She looked down at the table awkwardly. 'It sounds awful, but I can't place you. I'm ever so embarrassed. I know I should be able to and it makes me feel very rude.'

Heath laughed. 'It's fine - we weren't in loads of classes together... Hey, do you remember when Tom Bunting accidentally set fire to his tie with a Bunsen burner in chemistry?'

Teagan's eyes widened. 'Oh my God, I'd completely forgotten about that!' She relaxed tenfold. *She must know Darren Harding if he remembered that.*

Heath grinned, knowing from her expression alone that Teagan now believed he wasn't a random stranger. Not that he was who he said he was, but at least it wasn't in a creepy way. It was all in aid of the greater good.

'Here's your teas.' The waitress deposited two mugs of tea on the chipped tabletop and indicated to the stained sachets of sugar in a bowl next to the salt and pepper.

Nodding his thanks, Heath turned back to Teagan, catching her studying him before quickly averting her eyes. 'Right, you'd best start filling me in with what you've been doing for the last ten years.'

TWENTY THREE

TEAGAN COULDN'T BELIEVE two hours had passed. She hadn't expected to be more than half an hour, presuming that there wouldn't be much to talk about once they'd covered the school days. Darren had mentioned a couple more funny things she'd forgotten about and a handful of people she remembered, but he hadn't just gone on about school – he was interested in *her* life too – what she'd been doing and how she was.

Chatting easily, time had flown by and she caught herself taking another surreptitious glance at Darren. He was a nice-looking man, no doubt about that and the more she looked at him, the more she noticed something familiar about him. Maybe she was starting to remember him after all?

He had manners too. So, *so* much different to what she'd been used to.

Just thinking of Joe caused Teagan's spirits to plummet like a brick and the prospect of seeing him later wasn't something she was looking forward to.

'Was it something I said?' Heath said, giving Teagan a cheeky wink. 'I must be boring you rigid! I keep forgetting people aren't generally interested in the ins and outs of music production.' *Yes, he'd used that one again.*

Teagan looked flustered. 'Sorry, I was just thinking, that's all.'

'Anything I can help with?'

Teagan shook her head and sighed loudly. 'It's my ex. I've got to meet him later.'

Heath laughed. 'There's easier ways of getting away from me without the ex story!'

Teagan was horrified. *Oh God, now she'd insulted him.* 'I didn't mean it like that, honestly. I'm really enjoying our chat and the thought of having to leave is a bit of a downer, that's all.'

'Hey, I was only pulling your leg,' Heath smiled. 'Talk about your ex as much as you want - as long as he's not giving you a hard time because then I won't be happy.'

Teagan blushed. *Did that mean Darren liked her?*

When Teagan didn't elaborate about the ex, Heath changed direction. 'Working as a carer must be stressful.'

'Probably nowhere near as stressful as music production,' Teagan said. *He'd got such a high-flying career, whereas she… well…*

'But *your* job makes a difference.' Heath said. 'Yes, producing music is great and I love my work, but you… you make a *real* difference to peoples' lives which is so important.'

Teagan's cheeks burned from the complement. No one ever said anything she did was important. 'It can be difficult sometimes.' She looked into Darren's face. 'The lady I'm working for at the moment has some… erm… health issues unfortunately, which can make her a bit difficult at times, but the rest of the time she's a joy to be around.'

Heath kept the caring expression on his face. 'She sounds lovely.' *She was talking about Dulcie Adams. Wonderful. Carry on, Teagan.*

'Oh, she is,' Teagan said animatedly. 'Fascinating too. I'd love to go and see some of the places she talks about.' She knew she shouldn't discuss clients, but it wasn't like Darren knew Dulcie. It wasn't like she was talking about anything personal.

'Like where?' Heath said, keeping up his feigned interest.

'She used to work at a place called The Feathers – a club. It sounds wonderful, but I don't know whether it even still exists, or if it ever did.' Teagan looked down shyly. 'Sometimes what Dulcie says isn't true, but if it is still there, I'd love to see what it's like.'

Heath frowned. 'The Feathers? Where is it?' He knew *exactly* where it was and that it was still going - owned by the family responsible for murdering his grandfather...

'Oh, it's in London somewhere. Soho, I think,' Teagan continued. 'I keep meaning to look it up, but the internet is so flaky back at the house, it's difficult.'

Heath smiled. *Yep, this girl was definitely working for the woman they wanted. This was good.* 'It sounds amazing! Now, can I get you another drink?'

• • • •

LENA ALLOWED THE MEANINGLESS CHATTER of Nina drift over her head whilst she deftly made the monthly adjustments to tighten her hair extensions. The girl could talk for England, but it was no skin off her nose. All she had to do was 'um' and 'ah' in the right places and it was plain sailing.

Lena scrolled through the recent text messages on her phone – staring at the last one from her Uncle Ron.

She'd been more than happy with what he'd told her when she'd filled him in with the news of where she was at with her life. *More* than happy. She'd heard nothing since, but now he knew what her news meant for the rest of her family, she strongly suspected that it wouldn't be long before they all came out of the woodwork.

Lena's overly made-up face morphed into a scowl. The nugget of information from trusty old Uncle Ron would help immensely in securing her position. She'd let Jonah think he'd succeeded in relegating her to the bottom of the pile and heeding what he'd said about interfering at the club. She'd keep a low profile for a bit and *then* she'd use it.

Lena smiled widely, not doubting for a moment that within a day or two of letting this bombshell slip, Jonah would be convinced that not giving her reins to do what she wished where the club was concerned was an ill-informed oversight. He'd soon be convinced that *she* was perfect for the job over that sour-faced old bat after all and Gwen herself would be the one to convince him of that – she just didn't know it yet. But she would. *Soon.*

'I didn't think it was *that* funny!' Nina's voice pulled Lena from her plans.

'What?' Lena snapped, glancing at Nina rummaging around in her roots in the mirror.

'All I said was that I'd lost a stone on that new diet that's all the rage and you're grinning like a Cheshire cat! It's ok for you – it's not like you need to lose any weight,' Nina moaned.

Lena laughed and proudly smoothed her hand over her toned denim-clad thighs. 'No, I suppose not, but you look great,' she lied, then stared at the empty wine glass on the marble counter in front of her. 'What really *would* make me smile though is if you'd top up my wine. Another large one if you wouldn't mind?'

Nina grinned. Putting the long-tailed comb down, she picked up Lena's glass. 'How I'd love to spend afternoons drinking wine. That would be my idea of a perfect day!'

Lena smiled serenely as Nina wandered off to refill her glass, only letting it drop the minute she was out of sight.

That girl had no chance of spending her afternoons sipping wine and getting her hair done. Neither did she have the chance of getting hitched to the most eligible bachelor this side of Watford Gap, looking the way she did. For a start, the woman was not *her* and secondly, with a bin man for a husband, she didn't have a hope in hell of achieving it either.

Seeing Nina return, Lena slid her smile back in place and picked up the fresh glass of wine. 'Cheers! Oh, it's all go – it really is. I've got to go and find my outfit for the party after I've finished here.'

She raised her eyebrows slightly, waiting for Nina to ask either a question about what she would be wearing or about the party itself. Thanks to Jonah's stinginess, it put the dress she'd had her eye on out of the equation. Fancy only giving her two grand to spend! What heap of shit was that supposed to buy? A bloody bag of crap from Primark? No fucking thanks.

Luckily, she still had a couple of his credit cards in her purse, one of which had 25k still available on it which should suffice. She wouldn't be looking anything but perfect at such an important event.

'I still can't believe you're going to be Mrs Jonah Powell,' gushed Nina. 'It's so exciting.'

'I know,' Lena said smugly, silently wondering why anyone should think it such an unbelievable prospect. Jonah was getting his money's worth out of her, wasn't he? 'It'll be a *huge* night at the club. Anybody worth anything will be there. The usual celebrities and everything.'

Nina's mouth dropped open. 'Really? Wow! And in the VIP suite too.'

Lena laughed 'There's not much of a problem bagging that when your *fiancé* owns the club.'

'I've always wanted to go in there,' Nina hinted. 'It's one of those places you always dream of being invited to…' She looked at Lena hopefully.

Lena smiled. She knew what Nina was angling at, but the woman had no chance of an invite in a million years. 'If you or your husband were members of the main club, then you might perhaps get a glimpse of the celebs as they arrive, but I don't expect you are, are you?'

Blushing, Nina shook her head in embarrassment. 'Oh, erm… no, but we were thinking about it not so long ago.'

Lena smiled patronisingly. *A years' membership to The Feathers would be more than both their salaries combined.* 'Oh well, never mind.' She turned her head from side to side, inspecting her finished locks. 'That looks much better now, doesn't it?'

Twenty Four

TEAGAN HAD BEEN RELUCTANT to leave Darren – she'd been really enjoying his company, but she'd promised Joe and she didn't like going back on promises.

Cutting through the park, she diverted towards the bench where they'd arranged to meet. In hindsight, she'd been stupid to suggest meeting there, being as that had been their special place – the one back at the start of their relationship when things had been good. At least, when *she'd* thought things had been good… But according to Joe, apparently things had *never* been good.

That didn't matter now. Her life with him was over and despite being gutted, it was slowly becoming easier. This afternoon with Darren had done wonders for that.

Spotting Joe's familiar figure as the bench came into view, Teagan's mind raced. Her afternoon with Darren now felt like it had occurred a lifetime ago and the excitement and renewed sense of confidence she'd felt when he'd asked to see her again evaporated into thin air.

Joe looked dreadful. He sat, his elbows resting on his thighs and his chin in his hands, staring into space. The over-confident cocky man she'd once fallen madly for had disappeared, replaced by a washed-out, grey-looking, terrified shell.

Teagan didn't think she'd ever seen Joe look so withdrawn and shaken. Exactly what could have gone wrong? What could have happened to Alan? Why did Joe so desperately need to see her?

'Hi,' she said awkwardly.

Joe's head jerked up and he thrust a newspaper into Teagan's hands. 'Look at this! This will prove I wasn't making up what I said.'

Sitting down, Teagan looked at the newspaper, open at a specific page:

Coma Nightmare After Horrific Attack

Local man, Alan Hardwick, 28, was found unconscious and badly beaten on the doorstep of his home by his two horrified housemates.

Mr Hardwick still remains in a critical condition in intensive care following his extensive head injuries. It is not known at this stage whether Mr Hardwick will have suffered any permanent damage if he regains consciousness.

At present, Police have been unable to find any motive for the attack and are appealing for witnesses who saw anything in the Weir Road area around 8pm on 15th June to come forward as soon as possible.

Folding the paper in two, Teagan was about to speak when Joe launched into a wild babble. Listening to what was coming out of his mouth she could barely believe what she was hearing. She'd love to believe he was making it up, or at the very least, exaggerating, but she could tell from his body language alone, that every single word he spoke was for once, the truth.

Closing her eyes in despair, she leant her head against the back of the bench, allowing the breeze to flow over her and inhaled slowly to stop herself escalating into full-blown panic. She didn't know what to say and still couldn't quite get her head around any of it.

'You think what happened to Alan was definitely these two men that you've just told me about? The two who came to your house before?'

Joe nodded, his bloodshot eyes flickering nervously. 'It's got to be. Who else would have done that? It was a message. A very clear one.'

'Then I really don't understand why you haven't told the police? These men have previously threatened you, also Dave said he'd seen them in the area around the time of the attack? You're withholding information about things that are clearly connected, Joe. You could identify these people if...'

'We can't!' Joe cried, raking his shaking fingers through his unwashed hair. 'You don't understand! If we did that it would make things a thousand times worse.'

Teagan frowned. *How could it make things worse?* 'But if yo...'

'They weren't messing around. They're not normal people, Teag,' Joe blathered. 'Those fuckers are the real deal. And I mean *proper* gangster-types.'

Teagan listened with mounting dread as Joe filled her in with what the visit to the house had been about in the first place. She felt like screaming. She didn't want to be involved in something like this, but much to her horror, apparently the only reason *she* was involved was because they'd spotted him talking to her on the doorstep the day he'd come to the house to dump her.

And what about Dulcie? There was no way Dulcie would have had anything to do with this sort of thing. Despite how she sometimes acted, she was a lovely, sweet lady and was only having periods of strange behaviour because of this bloody cruel disease.

'I can see you don't think it's feasible,' Joe said. 'And to be quite honest, nor do I - even if that lady of yours is a miserable, vicious old cow. But what I do know is, whether they're right or not, it's what they *believe*. They're not going to walk away from it.'

He grasped Teagan's hand. 'If it isn't me they come for next, Teagan, it will be you. You're the only one with access.'

Teagan pulled her hand away. Joe's very touch felt like her skin was being dipped in acid. How could he put her in this position? She shook her head with confusion. She wanted to run away as quickly as possible to a destination as far removed as time would allow.

Teagan bit back the tears threatening to spill from her eyes. Whether she liked it or not, *she* was earmarked by these… these people, whoever they were, and what Joe said was true - if she didn't help him get what they wanted, then it didn't look likely they would casually forget about all of this.

A shudder ran through her. It still could be her and *would* be if she didn't do something. But what if she did what Joe asked, then wouldn't Dulcie be in danger? *A huge amount of danger?*

Teagan rose from the bench, her legs unwilling to hold her upright.

Joe grasped the hem of Teagan's jumper. 'Where are you going? You can't leave! You've got to sort this, Teag.'

Teagan willed her brain to work. It felt stuck – *jammed.*

Joe's eyes narrowed. 'Don't forget I've only been dragged into this because of *you*!'

'I need to think about this,' Teagan interrupted. It may be true that Joe was only involved because they'd seen him at the house talking to her, but apart from working somewhere they believed a bunch of their stolen cash or whatever it was, was being hidden, *she* had nothing to do with this either.

She hadn't stolen a thing and neither would Dulcie have either. It was ridiculous. Dulcie said that Peter, her husband, had tried to get involved with shady people, but that was back in the 60s, not now. Not *recently*. But like Helen said, Dulcie spoke rubbish and didn't know what she was saying half the time.

But what about Robert? He was shifty and what about that day when he was rooting through the cupboards when he'd thought no one was in? *Could this be something to do with him?*

'There isn't time to think,' Joe wailed, his eyes wide. 'Do you not realise how serious this is?'

'Yes, I'm well aware of that, but I still need to think.' Teagan brushed her hair away from her face. 'I'll call you, ok?'

Joe stood up, pacing around in agitation. 'When? How long are you going to make me wait? Is this your way of making me fucking suffer? Because if it is, then you're doing a good job.'

Stepping back, Teagan slung her handbag over her shoulder, amazed she could still manage it, her hands were shaking so much. She handed Joe back his newspaper. 'Just give me a day or so to work out what to do.'

'You won't go to the police though, will you?' Joe spluttered, a fresh wave of panic engulfing him.

Teagan shook her head. 'I don't know, but I won't do anything without speaking to you first, ok? Now I really must go.'

As Teagan made her way back through the park, Joe's parting shot of, *'It's on your back should anything happen to anyone else'*, played on her mind.

· · · ·

TEAGAN RETURNED TO Footlights as slowly as possible. God knows what awaited her there and for the first time since arriving, the temptation to not return was strong - even stronger now with what Joe had dumped her with.

She fought her unwilling legs to move in the right direction as she trudged along the road. Maybe she should talk to Helen? Or ask Darren for his opinion?

Teagan bit down on her lip, the pain forcing her to concentrate. She couldn't speak to anyone about it. Any sane person would insist on going to the police and she couldn't say she'd blame them, but this wasn't a normal situation by any stretch of the imagination. Regardless of what was right, wrong or indifferent, she could not put Joe in any more danger. Whatever had happened between them, she still cared for him and he'd come to her for help.

And what had Joe said she needed to do? Just get a set of keys to the house? He'd get a copy made and then bring them back. No one would ever know.

But she would know.

And she would be personally responsible for allowing those men to have access to Dulcie's house. How could she give someone a free rein to do that? The whole thing was crazy. How could she pretend she was ok with that? Furthermore, how would she ever sleep again knowing these people had keys and could appear at any given time?

Reluctantly opening the front door, Teagan stared at the keys in her hand. She couldn't just hand them over. She *wouldn't*. She couldn't sell out and leave Dulcie at the mercy of nutters, she just couldn't.

What did those men think was hidden here?

Wait a minute...

Teagan suddenly felt the creeping suspicion that all of this was nothing to do with Dulcie at all, but everything to do with Joe and Joe alone.

Her eyes narrowed. This was *him*, wasn't it? Joe owed those men money for drugs. She would bet her life it was that. He was always up to his neck over that stupid stuff he smoked. He'd promised he'd stop taking it, but then he'd promised a lot of things...

Anger rose. Joe had got in over his head with some kind of nutter dealers – owed them money for a shed load of weed or something, hadn't he? She knew it, she just *knew* it!

Knowing Joe and the lies that spewed from his mouth, he'd panicked when they'd turned up at his place and told them he'd given *her* the money or something like that...

Teagan felt sick. Would Joe really do something like that to her? Would he actually have lied to those type of people and say *she'd* got what he owed them? She closed her eyes in despair.

Yes, he would. That was why he'd looked so strange when he'd unexpectedly turned up at Dulcie's the other day. And *that* was why he'd pretended he wanted her back – not because he did – he just wanted to butter her up because he'd used her as an excuse. *The bastard.*

'You're back early, dear.'

Tensing at Dulcie's voice, Teagan turned to see her walking up the hallway with a big smile on her face. All the previous aggression and anger this morning was nowhere to be seen. Breathing an inward sigh of relief, Teagan then stiffened with the stark reminder of what had happened.

She could scarcely believe that for a moment back there at the park she'd even given what Joe had asked a second of credibility. That she'd actually *considered* whether it was something she would do for him.

Teagan was incensed beyond belief at herself for taking even a millisecond to see through Joe's lies and work out what was *really* going on.

Joe would be dealing with his own bloody mess.

Teagan's nerves jangled harder, getting a horrible feeling that Alan wouldn't be the only casualty resulting from Joe's pathetic games. But she had to put her foot down. She was not going to take the rap for his bad choices and lies.

Teagan looked at Dulcie, excitedly beckoning her towards a freshly made jug of homemade lemonade and made her way over, dragging a convincing smile onto her face as she went.

Joe had better put this right and quickly. If anything happened to her or worse, Dulcie, because of his drug habit, greediness and the need to lie to those thugs to save his own neck, then she'd definitely be going to the police to drop him right in it.

TWENTY FIVE

'WHAT DO YOU THINK HAS HAPPENED TO HIM?' James asked, watching Helen aimlessly pushing her toast around her plate.

'Why does everyone assume I know?' Helen snapped, fury already steadily building and it wasn't even 7am.

By the time she'd got out of the shower she'd hoped James had already left for work, but no... here he was with more questions, just like yesterday.

The minute she'd got home last night, James had greeted her with one of those expressions – the type reserved for people who had received bad news. The sort used when a sympathetic attitude was needed. She knew when to use those because she put them into play on a frequent basis herself.

Yes, she'd known by the simpering look on his face he must have heard the local news and probably the following update that Ken Manning's close friends and colleagues had been questioned for clues as to his whereabouts and James would know that included *her*.

James presumed she was worried sick about Ken's out of character disappearance - after all, she was one of the last ones to see him and she *was* worried sick. But not about Ken.

Helen was far more on edge about what Ken's walkabout meant for her and the deal on the apartment. How could she move fast if he wasn't here to tell her what the next stage was and where he was at with the contracts? If it wasn't for James, she'd have been better informed being as Ken had been about to tell her.

'Why are you staring at me?' Helen barked.

'Because you haven't answered my question.'

'Are you insinuating that *I* know something about his disappearance?'

'W-What? No of course not! I...'

'I've already been grilled by the police and now you're doing it!' Helen snapped. 'I wish people, including *you* would remember that when we - yes, *we* left the function the other night, Ken was still there.'

She glared at her husband. 'Apparently, he left shortly afterwards and hasn't been seen since, so what are you saying? That I somehow sneaked out of bed in the middle of the night, teleported to his house, convinced him to leave his car on the drive and talked him into wandering off into outer space?'

'There's no need to be sarcastic,' James muttered, hurt plastered across his face. 'I'm just worried that you're upset, that's all.'

'Of course I'm damn well upset!' Helen screeched. 'I've known Ken for years. He's a good friend.' *No, he's not and I'm not upset – I'm angry. I couldn't give two hoots about Ken, but I'm depending on him right now. How dare he do a runner. This would slow everything up.*

'Ok, ok – don't get str...'

'Oh, shut up, James. Just shut up!' Helen slammed her plate down on the thick oak table and watched James flinch as the china broke into two pieces with a satisfying crack. She stood up and glared at him. 'Why can't you just leave me be? You make me fucking sick!'

James sat in silence as Helen stormed from the room, despair weighing heavily in the pit of his stomach. Helen needed help – much more than he was capable of offering. She was in a bad enough way before, but this stress about Ken had pushed her over the edge. Should he go and ask Dulcie for her advice?

He pursed his lips. It was pointless. Helen frequently said how much worse the state of Dulcie's mind had got, therefore expecting anything rational from the woman was slim and, in a way, he felt guilty. He'd accompanied Helen plenty of times over the years when visiting Dulcie, but she'd refused point blank to let him come with her these past few months – saying seeing her mother the way she now was would be too upsetting.

Admittedly, James knew he hadn't pushed the point, accepting Helen's decision a bit too readily. Mental illness freaked him out and he was ashamed to say he'd felt better not witnessing it, but now… now his choice had come back to haunt him. His own wife was now suffering with a mental illness, or worse…

• • • •

MIKE THUMBED THROUGH last weeks' sales figures. Not bad, but nowhere near what he needed to keep on top of the debts and the overheads for this bloody place.

He glanced around the massive showroom. He shouldn't have bought this place, but how was he supposed to maintain the impression of being the go-to dealer if his cars were stacked up in some crummy gaff under a bridge at the arse end of nowhere?

Mike's jaw set determinedly. It would all come good. He just needed Heath to hurry up and secure this wedge. But was he hedging all of his bets on an unreliable pipe dream?

Seeing movement outside his fishbowl of an office, he glanced up, relieved to see it was Heath, rather than the postman with another sack of overdue invoices.

'Morning,' Heath grinned, pulling out the chair opposite his father's desk. 'All ok?'

Mike forced a smile. 'Not too bad. Now, have you got any

news for me? How did it go with the girl? Did you get anywhere?'

Heath's face cracked into a wide smile. 'Teagan was nicer than I'd expected. We got on really well and I'm seeing her again.'

Mike's mouth flattened into an unimpressed line. 'That's all very well and good and I hate to spoil your fun, but we need to move on this.'

'Ok, ok, but I can't just magic up things. It'll take me a few more weeks of wining and dining her before I can get into the house. She doesn't seem the type to want a quick lay, if you get my drift, but once I've g…'

'A few weeks?' Mike cried. 'Christ! I haven't got that sort of time.'

Heath sat forward. 'What's wrong, Dad? I mean, *really*? You know as well as I do that things like this can't happen overnight, so what's the big rush?'

Mike exhaled, his whole body visibly shrinking. 'I'm in the shit, son… The finances… I'm behind with, well… just about fucking everything.' He wiped the back of his hand across his forehead. 'If I can't come up with a good chunk of cash soon then this place will go under.'

Heath slumped back in shock. He knew things were tight, what with expanding to bigger premises, but not in dire straits. 'Does Mum know?'

Mike shook his head. 'No and she's not going to either. I don't want her worrying.' His fingers fidgeted over the sheaf of paper in his hand. 'There's nowhere else I can go to get interim loans. I've outstayed my welcome pretty much everywhere and now my credit is fucked, no one will touch me with a bargepole.'

'How much to do you need to buy a bit more time?' Heath asked. 'I've got a couple of grand put by, plus I should be able to swing a loan for, say, 5k. Would that help?'

Mike's humiliation felt absolute. 'Thanks, son, but I wouldn't take your money even if it was an option.'

'It *is* an option,' Heath said. 'It's in my interests too remember! This is my job an...'

Mike could barely bring himself to look at his son. 'Look, I need at least 40k to cover the loans, the late payments and a missed invoice that I can't drag out any longer.'

'*Forty* grand? What? For one month?' Heath's mouth hung open. 'I didn't realise it was that extreme. Shit, Dad.'

Mike shook his head dejectedly. 'No one does. Why do you think I haven't said anything. Jesus Christ, within the next couple of months, unless something drastic happens, I'm going to lose not just the business, but the house too.' He put his head in his hands. 'How can I do this to your mother?'

Heath sat back in his chair. He'd have to make sure something happened then, wouldn't he? He couldn't stand by and let everything his father had worked for go down the pan. What *he'd* worked for too. Not when there was a chance there was a fortune to be had sitting just out of their reach.

He pulled out his mobile, looking at the call log listing the missed calls from Helen Shepherd from yesterday. He'd never got around to phoning her back and she hadn't called since either. Perhaps his father's idea to abandon the Helen Shepherd route wasn't the best way to go after all. Pursuing the house tactic wasn't the greatest use of time, true, but there could be another way...

Heath ran his tongue over his teeth and leant his elbow on his father's desk – the desk that should eventually be *his*. 'I think under the circumstances we've got nothing to lose by trying Plan C on Helen Shepherd.'

'Plan C?' Mike looked at Heath quizzically. 'What's that then?'

Grinning, Heath leant back in the chair and prepared to outline his idea.

· · · ·

'AS I SAID BEFORE, we're running behind with the collections, but we're just about keeping on top of it,' Nero said, his long legs stretched out in front of him.

He hadn't been looking forward to today's daily meet with Jonah after the latest set of events had hit the papers. Although Jonah had taken his explanation well, understanding the situation was limited where Ken Manning was concerned, he knew it was attention they could do without ending up being brought to the firm's door.

Nero watched Jonah peruse the folder of debtors, wondering whether that would be the next thing in line for the chopping block. He'd previously warned against taking too much time out from the collection side of the business for the Dulcie Adams stuff, but Jonah was like a dog with a bone where that subject was concerned. And he couldn't say he blamed him, but still, he didn't want his neck in the noose for falling behind.

Everyone knew that falling behind on chasing debts gave the impression that people could get away with taking the piss. Something that would never be allowed to happen.

'There's a couple more of the boys who can be rerostered to work on those.' Nero leant over to point at a list on the page Jonah had open. 'I can't pull any more of the lads off other duties as we're a bit stretched.'

He frowned, unsure whether to broach his other idea, but figured it was worth a try. It would mean a bit more breathing space to catch up with what had fallen behind. 'Maybe it might be worth thinking about putting a couple of the other men on Dulcie Adams stuff, rather than us?' he suggested. 'I mean, it might...'

'Absolutely not!' Jonah barked, his blue eyes flashing. 'You and Keith are dealing with it - no one else. It's too important. We do, however need to pull back on putting the pressure on Joe Simpleton, or whatever his fucking name is. It's a pain in the arse, but it's only until the dust settles.' He frowned. 'Have you heard any more about how the one in hospital is?'

Nero shook his head. 'Nope. No more reports on that. He's still in a coma as far as I know.'

Jonah grinned. 'At least it's not a murder charge then as yet!'

'One of the lads on the collection team, his brother-in-law is a porter at the hospital. I could get him to put the feelers out. Discreetly, I mean.'

Jonah shook his head. 'No. We don't want anything getting back that we're interested. It wouldn't look good.'

Nero pursed his lips. He felt horribly responsible for the case being put on hold because of what had happened to the stoner's mate and Manning - annoyed that progress had been slowed courtesy of a fucking suit and a bloody stoner who had fuck all to do with it.

Keith and his bloody heavy-handed tactics. Although there hadn't been a lot of choice about finishing Manning off – that one was a bleater for definite, but the lad – that was a different story.

Nero grated his teeth, feeling he wasn't delivering for Jonah, nor his father - of whom he'd respected greatly. He didn't appreciate not being able to sort this. He was renowned for delivering and he wasn't. Far from it. The one thing that had haunted the firm for decades and the ability to sort it out was being scuppered by the likes of tossers. And this didn't sit well.

Jonah slammed the folder shut. He could see Nero was frustrated. He was too, but they had to tread carefully. Since he'd told Lena to pull her head in, he felt more able to look at this a lot more logically again.

'Nero, you're my most trusted man in this firm and as you well know, I don't say that lightly,' Jonah said. 'I can see there wasn't another way around it with Manning. And as for the other one – these things happen, so don't beat yourself up.'

Keith leant forward. 'We might have to give the Joe bloke a wide berth for a day or two, but there's another option we could consider…'

'And that is?'

'Manning was quick to sell the son out – Robert Adams? He presumed we were after Robert for monies unpaid, yes?'

Nero frowned at Keith. 'Yeah, but as he seemed to think it must have been Robert who nicked the stash, it clearly shows he knows fuck all about it.'

'But what it does show,' Keith grinned, 'is that this Robert must be strapped for cash. A gambling problem, according to Manning. Any fucker who would cash in the equity on his old mum's gaff to raise brass for his habit or debts is a prize cunt, even if his mother is that thieving old witch.'

Nero could see where this was heading and nodded. *It could work.*

Keith sat back in his chair, grinning proudly at his solution. 'We offer this Robert cunt a way out of his debts, yeah? Make a nice earner for the loan side at the same time?' he winked. 'He will spill his gob for some brass.'

'Gamblers usually do,' Jonah agreed. 'They're nearly as desperate as junkies, that lot.'

'I'll get the feelers out to see where the prick lives and then we'll give him a visit.' Keith got to his feet, excited at the prospect of more bloodshed.

Jonah raised his hand. 'Hold your horses!' He waited whilst Keith turned back to face him. 'It's a good thought, but I want to sit on that for now. We've got so far with the stoner, so I want to remain focused on him.'

Keith scowled, enraged. *More wasting fucking time. Why couldn't he go and torture the answers out of the Robert bloke? Make a few extra quid at the same time. It was a good fucking idea.* 'But you said we had to lay off the stoner until heat dies down.'

Jonah smiled. 'I know that's what I said and that's still what I want. We might be pulling back with heavy hand approach where Joe Singleton is concerned, but that doesn't mean you can't let him *see* you. Let him see you somewhere so he knows you're still watching and can reach him at any time.'

A sly smile spread across Jonah's face. 'It never hurts to remind people not to relax or have the misguided thought of involving the authorities... Only in case he's thinking of getting a bit more chilled about the situation in your absence, if you get my drift?'

Jonah smiled, ignoring Keith's snort of frustration. 'It will also give him the gentle reminder that you're still expecting him to deliver on his arrangement, even if you don't say it. I am confident this tactic will work a lot better and faster than starting from scratch with the Adams son.'

'We're on it,' Nero grinned, grabbing Keith's sleeve and nudging him out the door of Jonah's office.

Walking up the corridor, Nero glanced at Keith muttering under his breath. 'What Jonah suggested made a lot more sense than involving another person in this shit. The less people involved, the less chance of anything ever pointing back to us.'

'Whatever,' Keith muttered sourly.

Nero shrugged. Keith might not be happy about the next stage in the plan, but *he* was. He was a lot happier because it showed that Jonah was back to normal with his head in control after being out of sorts the last week or so.

TWENTY SIX

HELEN STARED BLANKLY at her personal organiser. Three appointments this afternoon? She wouldn't be going to any of those – not if she could help it. She was in nowhere near enough a decent frame of mind to sweet talk people into buying houses.

Looking up through the glass of her office she scowled at Joanne, who quickly averted her eyes. What the hell was she looking at? Ever since the police had visited there was a strange atmosphere – as if everyone at Shepherd, Percival and Proctor had something to say, but remained silent - like they suspected she *did* know something about Ken's disappearance.

Well, she didn't. If she had the slightest inkling where he was, then she wouldn't be half as stressed out.

Snatching up the receiver, Helen stabbed in the numbers for Manning Sales and Lettings. She knew the number off by heart being as she'd called it so many times over the last few days. Agitatedly picking the skin around one of her fingernails, she couldn't stop her foot from impatiently tapping on the floor as she waited for the call to be answered. *Ring, ring, bloody ring. Come on!*

'Manning Sales and Lettings,' the musical voice said, sounding akin to a jingle from a dreadful radio advert.

'This is Helen Shepherd, from Shepherd, Percival and Proctor. I'm ringing to see if you've had any updates about Ken?' Helen said, maintaining decorum when really she wanted to scream.

'Hello, Mrs Shepherd. I'm afraid there's still no news. I know you're concerned - we all are, but like I said yesterday, as soon as we hear anything, one of us will give you a ca…'

'Yes, yes, I know that,' Helen snapped, her patience thin. 'Could you then please check to see if Ken had any contracts ready for me?'

The pause from the other end of the line signified that it was bad taste to request such a thing under the circumstances. Realising her mistake, Helen attempted to backtrack. 'I'm sure Ken wouldn't want any of his sales to fall through in his absence. You know how meticulous he is.'

'I can't get into his computer without his password, Mrs Shepherd.'

Yes, you can, Helen thought. Any decent technical person would know how to easily override that, but she didn't voice her thoughts. She knew when not to push things and in retrospect, it wasn't the greatest idea to get someone to go through Ken's computer. Although he wouldn't have left a trail on the Oak Apple Apartments or preliminary information for the sale of Footlights, it could still look suspicious. She didn't want to give the police any further reason to think, due to her increased contact with him lately, that she may have had something to do with his disappearance.

'None of us want to put in a request to override Ken's machine. That would… would almost feel like we're accepted he isn't coming back… and none of us want to imagine that being a possibility.'

'No, of course not,' Helen muttered, wishing she hadn't bothered phoning. Manning Sales and Lettings had a rather high percentage of snivelling gimps in its employment.

'Oh, my other line is ringing. I must go,' Helen lied. 'Please keep me posted.'

Putting the phone down without waiting for a response, Helen tapped her fingers on the desk. She could hardly call Ken on his mobile again. The police would be monitoring it and if she kept phoning, they'd be back round to interrogate her.

Where the hell was he?

Hearing her mobile buzzing, Helen scrabbled around in her handbag. *That might be him now. Finally.* Heart racing, she snatched the phone up. 'Ken?'

'Hi, Mrs Shepherd. It's Darren Harding. Sorry it's taken me so long to return your call, I've b...'

'I'll have to call you back, Mr Harding,' Helen barked, abruptly ending the call. It wasn't best practice to bin off a client who might be calling to put an offer in on a very expensive property, but she couldn't speak to him right now. She'd call him back, but not now. *Not just yet.*

Hearing a knock on the door, Helen looked up, her eyes narrowing at Joanne's botoxed face through the glass.

Taking Helen's attention as the go ahead to enter, Joanne opened the door. 'Sorry to disturb you, Mrs Sh...'

'Not now, Joanne,' Helen barked. 'I'm up to my neck. Whatever it is will have to wait.'

Joanne's face remained predictably expressionless. 'I'm afraid it's...'

'Did you not hear me? I'm busy!' Helen snarled, pointedly looking at her list of appointments, her hand reaching for the telephone. *Couldn't the stupid cow get the hint?*

'I have a lady on the main line calling about your mother. I wouldn't have interrupted, but she said she's tried you on your mobile but couldn't get through, so...'

'My mother?' Helen repeated.

'It's a lady called Teagan Fraser. I thought I'd better let you know being as she has your personal number, I thought it must be importa...'

'Put her through, put her through,' Helen muttered. *Great. This was all she needed.* What did the stupid girl want now? Probably asking what sort of cereal her mother preferred or something equally inane.

Joanne scuttled back to her desk, quickly transferring the call and when the phone rang, Helen snatched it up, steeling herself to act pleasant.

· · · ·

'MY! AREN'T THEY JUST BEAUTIFUL!' Dulcie bent to smell the red roses in the large bouquet. 'And who are these from, may I ask? A new admirer, I hope, rather than the dolt who wanted your forgiveness. If they're from *him*, I suggest you throw them out with the potato peelings!'

Teagan blushed and fiddled with the card that had accompanied the flowers. 'They're from an old friend. I thought I'd put them where we can both see them, rather than hide them away in my bedroom,' she smiled. 'I hope it's ok to use this vase?'

'Of course it is, my dear,' Dulcie replied. 'So, are you going to tell me who they're from or forever keep me hanging? An old friend, you say?'

Teagan coloured once again. Should she class Darren as an old friend? What did it matter? He'd sent her these gorgeous roses and she didn't think she'd ever had such a nice surprise. She'd certainly never had a lovely bouquet like this.

Joe had bought her flowers once. She remembered it well – her 23rd birthday. She'd been pleased, but it had been difficult to ignore the £1.50 price tag from the local garage and the 'reduced' sticker, still stuck to the ripped cellophane. She'd even bypassed that half of the carnations in the small bouquet were dead.

It was the thought that counted, wasn't it? Not that Joe put much thought into anything, but those half-dead flowers were marginally better than the previous years' birthday presents, which had been nothing.

These flowers from Darren – well, wow! Teagan's heart fluttered.

'What's the occasion?' Dulcie asked seeing the joy on

Teagan's face. 'It's not your birthday is it? Don't tell me it is and I didn't know?'

'No, it's not my birthday. I used to go to school with Darren and we got back in touch recently. I met up with him on my afternoon off.' Teagan pulled the card from her pocket. 'It says, *'Really enjoyed our afternoon'*.'

Dulcie sat forward, her eyes dancing with mischief. 'And what *else* does it say?'

Smiling bashfully, Teagan looked back at the card. 'It also says, *'Let me know when you're next free so I can take you to dinner'*. And he's put his phone number... and a kiss...'

'Well, phone him up then!' Dulcie winked. 'Tell him you'd love to go.'

'Oh, I don't know... I don't know when I'd go,' Teagan murmured.

'Go whenever you like!' Go tonight if you want.'

'But it's not my day off!'

'Pah! Who cares about that? Life's too short. If I say it's alright, then it's alright!' Dulcie clapped her hands together. 'I hope this young man is handsome? I told you it wouldn't be long before you got snapped up. That Joe was very silly to lose you.'

Teagan's face fell. *Joe.* She still hadn't told him her decision about the keys, partly because she knew he wouldn't like it, but mainly because she knew she'd rant about what he'd done and right now, she didn't have the energy. But if she didn't call him soon, it wouldn't be long before he was on her back demanding an answer.

She glanced at the excitement on Dulcie's face, sorrow and guilt engulfing her fourfold. Dulcie had been so nice about having an extra evening off to go and have dinner with Darren, whilst she had contemplated giving two random violent strangers access to her house. It might have been only for ten seconds, but she'd thought about it all the same.

She'd also called Helen and asked for an urgent meeting and sometime this afternoon she would betray this old lady's confidence further. Once Helen was aware of how much Dulcie had deteriorated, she would move her out of her beloved house and ship her off to a home – the one thing Dulcie didn't want.

All the joy from the surprise bouquet dissolved. She might be betraying Dulcie, but only because it would keep her safe. Sadly, even knowing that didn't make her feel any better.

TWENTY SEVEN

IT HAD BEEN WORTH IT. *WELL* WORTH IT.

Helen smiled as she made her way to Robert's flat. She'd been all depressed – so much so that she very nearly hadn't bothered giving Teagan the time of day, but how glad was she now that she had?

Parking up outside the small block of flats where Robert lived, Helen pressed the central locking for her car - twice, just to make sure. She looked around, making a mental note of anyone hanging around. The area wasn't particularly bad, but then it wasn't particularly good either and she didn't want some chav wandering past, scraping a key along the side of her Mercedes just because they'd never be able to afford one.

Why Robert hadn't bought himself a nice house was beyond her. He'd always been a bit off-beat, but to remain in the flat he'd purchased twenty years ago was weird. Even for *him*. It wasn't like he hadn't got the money. Going freelance as a computer programmer had done him well. And that was exactly why she was here because until Ken showed up again she was forced to talk Robert into stumping up the money for the Oak Apple apartment.

God, it was galling. Without Ken on the scene the

apartment would lose the 35k reduction. It was such a nuisance. He had to decide to go missing, didn't he? Any other time would have been just fine, but not just *now*.

Still, after what Teagan said, this was the prime opportunity to make a move and Robert would struggle finding a valid reason to disagree with her this time.

Looking a teenager up and down in contempt as he watched through a grubby net curtain from the neighbouring flat, Helen banged on Robert's green door. He worked from home on a Thursday, so he'd better not have broken the habit of a lifetime and gone into the office.

She was about to knock for the second time when the door opened. Saying nothing, Robert turned his back and walked off down the hallway.

Screwing her face up at her brother's usual display of rudeness, Helen followed, kicking the door shut behind her. She walked past the antique grandfather clock dwarfing the height of the 1970's ceiling and took extra care not to snag her blouse on a sharp swirl of the anaglypta wall.

'Why you insist remaining in this monstrosity never ceases to amaze me,' Helen griped, moving into Robert's exquisitely furnished sitting room – completely at odds with the whole place.

Without even looking up from his computer screen, Robert gestured for Helen to sit down. 'I presume you haven't graced me with your presence purely to make catty remarks about my home?'

Helen bit back the retort itching to escape from between her lips. How she hated her brother.

Although she wanted to fire back a suitable venomous comment, she refrained. Whether she liked it or not, she needed Robert to fulfil her plan. She would not lose her business. She'd worked too hard.

Helen watched her brother tap away at his computer like she wasn't even in the room. 'Aren't you even going to ask why I'm here?'

Robert continued tapping away, his eyes firmly glued to the screen. 'I'm presuming you'll get to that at some point? You don't usually have an issue saying what you want and rarely need prompting.'

Feeling her irritation rise further, Helen fought to keep it under wraps. *It was imperative she got Robert on board.* 'I had a call from Teagan this morning.'

Receiving a grunt in response, she wasn't altogether surprised. Robert made no secret of not liking the girl, thinking her presence 'pointless', but as over-protective about their mother as he was, Helen knew, when push came to shove, he'd insist on doing the best thing for mummy dearest. And it was *her* job to make sure he believed this was the best thing. If she pulled this off correctly, then he would insist they did everything she'd already planned.

Biting back a smile from the delicious irony, Helen pulled from her large reserve of on-tap expressions, settling on a concerned look to begin with. 'I wouldn't be here if it wasn't important, Robert,' she said. 'I felt it only right to discuss this with you, especially as you're under the impression I make decisions without your input and behind your back where Mother is concerned.'

She looked down at her hands. 'I probably am guilty of doing that sometimes, but I really need your opinion on this,' she said, steadily resenting having to adopt a grovelling approach, but if it got her where she wanted, she'd live with it. *For now.*

Helen's words piqued Robert's interest enough to give her some attention. Pulling himself away from his screen he turned his cold blue eyes on her. 'What has that girl done? She had better not have done anything to upset Mother. I told you that she all but treated me like a burglar not that long ago and if she's…'

'It's Mother.' Helen morphed her concerned look into a distressed one. She brushed her hair behind her ear, then put her hands in her lap, wringing them together. 'Oh, I know we haven't seen eye to eye about it for a long time and I can't blame your reticence to accept she's losing her mind, but… oh…'

Looking away, she half-covered her face, hoping that she hadn't lost the ability of forcing a few tears out on demand.

'What is it? What's happened?' Robert sat upright, his body tense. 'Is Mother alright? Helen, what's going on?'

Pulling a tissue from her bag, Helen dabbed at her eyes and sniffed sadly. 'Mother's a lot worse than we realised. Than *I* realised… Lots of things have happened and regardless of your dislike of the Teagan girl, without her being there it wouldn't have been brought to my attention. We'd never have known until something really dreadful happened.'

'Go on,' Robert said, switching his computer to standby as Helen recounted the whole worrying story of what Teagan had said.

· · · ·

PULLING ON TO THE DRIVE, glad to see James' car was nowhere to be seen, Helen made her way towards the garage.

The visit to Robert had gone so much better than she'd anticipated. He'd been horrified as she'd told him what Teagan said happened some nights – where their mother was awake and conscious, but with her mind in a different place and time. How she hallucinated - believing people were in her house and that Teagan was somebody else. Not to mention being confused over what her own surname was. Their mother had also been physically aggressive on more than one occasion too.

Helen left the bit about what Teagan had said about their mother being convinced she was being poisoned out – that wouldn't have achieved anything.

By the end of the conversation the outcome surpassed Helen's best case scenario. Robert had gone through a cycle of disbelief and anger, before ending with pure unbridled worry, but *he'd* been the one to say it. He'd been the one to say, *'you were right. There's no other way for it. We need to get her into a specialist home. A specialist facility.'* And from there it had been plain sailing.

Oh, she'd had no problem turning on the tears in the right places. She'd also done a good job mentioning Ken had been talking about a retirement complex only the other night – the night he'd disappeared and she'd buy it right now only she couldn't afford it, with the shortfall in her commission from the business over the last few months.

Even though Ken had disappeared, the apartments would still be available and they did deal specifically with people who had dementia? What did he think about something like that?

She made sure she'd omitted she'd already seen the apartments, but for once Robert hadn't nit-picked over the details. His face set, he'd told her not to waste time waiting for commission – *he'd* fund the purchase and they'd sort things out at a later date rather than risk their mother's well-being.

She'd acted suitably thankful, which had stuck in her throat, but it didn't matter. Despite the recent setbacks, things were now back on track. *More* than back on track. Things were finally moving forward in her favour.

Entering the garage with a spring in her step, Helen put her large handbag on the floor and moved the usual toolboxes in order to get to her things. Her mother would be having another one of her 'episodes' – that much was a certainty – just to make sure that Robert had no doubts on his conscience about uprooting and institutionalising her.

Kneeling on the floor, Helen took three bottles from her bag. These higher strength tablets would give mummy dearest that last little push required. The combination of the pills had already had the desired effect and her research had been spot on. Although it had taken some time to fully kick in at a high enough level to cause adverse effects, it stood to reason that increasing the dosage would also increase the side effects.

Helen smiled. *One more episode of being on a different planet would be all it took.*

Unscrewing the top of the Benztropine, she emptied a new bottle of multivitamins into a clear sandwich bag, replacing them with the anticholinergics.

Ok, so how she'd go about making a fast sale of Footlights was yet to be decided, but she'd worry about that another time. Getting her mother to have a final screwy turn was the most pressing thing and with Robert now on side, there was absolutely nothing to stand in her way.

Helen carefully moved the toolboxes and other items back in front of her secret hiding place, happy in the knowledge that regardless of what Ken had done to scupper her plans, she was still well on the way to achieving her goal.

Almost there, in fact.

If she hadn't been so distracted with how well things were turning out, she might have noticed or at the very least, *sensed* James silently watching through the connecting door to the house the entire time.

TWENTY EIGHT

LENA SMILED SERENELY at the doorman as she walked through the reception at The Feathers. She'd seen him glance at that muppet on the cloakroom desk which could only mean one of two things: One, they were admiring her sheer beauty and acknowledging what a lucky man Jonah was, or two – that busybody, Gwen, who'd never made any effort to hide her dislike, had tried her utmost to turn everyone against her.

Gwen had already dropped her in it with Jonah, but none of that would be an issue for much longer. Whether Gwen liked it or not, she'd soon be making her welcome. Lena smiled, knowing she would relish every single bloody minute of it.

Lena struggled to heft all of her bags into one hand so that she could open the VIP entrance, glad when one of the dancers rushed to open it. She splayed her hand on the now open door, making sure the girl got a good look at the massive diamond on her ring finger - a fine choice of the biggest and most expensive ring she'd been able to find in Hatton Garden. *What a rock!*

Smugly walking through without even so much as a thank you, Lena continued up the stairs, her four inch stilettoes clacking loudly on the gilt-edged steps.

Four days to go until her engagement to Jonah was official

and the preparations for getting the room just as she wanted it had better be well underway, otherwise someone's head would roll. Hopefully Gwen's – but then that would spoil all of her fun.

Walking into the plush maroon and gold VIP suite, Lena looked around, pleased to see that as instructed, the twelve foot high photograph of her and Jonah taken four months ago during another function was pride of place behind the raised stage at the back of the room.

The tables, all at varying levels separated by illuminated glass, housed strips of neon lighting underneath and were all prepared exactly to her specifications. The specially ordered silver and gold table decorations from Harrods looked the business.

She plonked her bags down on a crescent shaped velvet bench surrounding one of the many tables, glad to get the weight from her hands. The last thing she wanted was to snap one of her nails because she didn't want to waste time organising getting that fixed.

At least she'd got her clobber sorted. Several days she'd traipsed around all of her favourite boutiques and stores in Oxford Street searching for the perfect outfit. After much procrastination, she'd purchased two. They'd set her back an absolute fortune, well – set *Jonah* back an absolute fortune, but she'd made an extra special effort with him since their row the other night, so he'd be ok about the extra expense. She'd acted like the dutiful wife-to-be and accepted she'd made an error by ramping up the heat so quickly. She must keep things at a steady pace and not allow her impatience to scupper everything she'd worked for.

Faithfully apologising to Jonah for overstepping the mark and interfering in 'his' business, her suitably contrite attitude and promises of never doing it again had cooled the situation down. He was still in the foulest of moods, but it couldn't *all* be to do with her. Making the occasional reference to the baby helped too.

But even the baby wasn't a fool proof guarantee of success. Despite Jonah's desire for children of his own, Lena realised if she overstepped the mark too much he could well go through with chucking her out, regardless of whether he believed her to be pregnant or not. It was never obvious which way men like him would turn. She was on thin ice and she knew it.

Lena glanced at one of the bags she'd placed on the seat. In that one there was a beautiful 24-carat gold tie pin she'd bought as an engagement present. It had three inset diamonds and Jonah's initials engraved on it. He'd like that. Good job, being as he'd paid for that too.

She wondered what he'd bought for her? Presuming he had? Ok, so he'd got her this stunning ring, but that wasn't exactly a *present*. She'd better check he'd got something for her, otherwise it would be embarrassing on the night and she wasn't having that.

'Hello, Lena. I thought I saw you heading this way.'

Immediately recognising Gwen's voice, Lena turned and smiled graciously, even though she wanted to smash Gwen's two-faced head through one of the glass tables. *Play it nice, remember*, she reminded herself as Gwen eyed her many bags from the top London shops.

'I've been busy getting my outfit for the weekend. I hope you and your partner can make it?' Lena asked sweetly. 'Oh, I'm sorry. I didn't mean to embarrass you. I forgot you've never had a partner or husband.'

Gwen smiled, ignoring the barb. 'I wouldn't miss it. I must say, those decorations you've arranged look wonderful.'

Lena grinned once again, her face hurting from the effort. She picked up a handful of the faceted glass piled in a silver bowl and let them run through her fingers. 'It does look great, doesn't it? Jonah will love this theme.'

'I take it he hasn't seen it?' Gwen raised an eyebrow.

'No, I didn't want to bother him with details. Men aren't any good with this sort of stuff, but he'll love it. I could think of nothing more fitting than a diamonds theme. It encompasses our sparkle perfectly, don't you think? I'm having the same theme for our wedding too. I know exactly what I want.'

I bet you do, Gwen thought caustically, watching Lena tip the handful of pretend diamonds back into the silver centrepiece. Yes, Jonah would really *love* the theme of diamonds… She bit back a smile. Lena's choice underlined just how little she knew about the man she was marrying.

And why was she being so nice? Jonah had mentioned they'd had a blazing row the other night about her sticking her nose into things at the club and Lena must have guessed it had come from her, but acting like butter wouldn't melt didn't wash. The scheming little bitch was not on the level and Gwen was determined to find out what she had planned – apart from rinsing everything from Jonah - that one was obvious. *There was more… but what was it?*

'Miss Taylor?'

Both Lena and Gwen turned to find a woman standing in the doorway.

'Yes? That's me. But not for much longer…' Lena threw Gwen a smug look. 'Can I help?'

The woman shuffled uncomfortably. 'I'm sorry to bother you, but the man downstairs said I should come up. I'm from Fancy Fondants and have the cake you ordered. Can I ask you to look at it just to make sure you're happy?'

Lena clasped her hands together and squealed excitedly. 'Is it downstairs? I'll come now.' Without a second's hesitation, she hurried towards the stairs.

As the double doors closed behind Lena and the woman from the cake shop, Gwen glanced at the pile of bags around the table, her eyes focusing on the handbag amongst them.

Hurrying over, Gwen pulled Lena's phone from the bag. She had one chance to find some incriminating evidence against the little gold-digging cow and this was it.

• • • •

JAMES TRIED ROBERT'S number once again. *Voicemail*. He

couldn't leave a message – not on such a delicate subject. Did Robert ever answer his phone or just not bother if it was him who was ringing?

Robert had never given James the impression of ever liking him, but then again, he'd never given *anyone* the impression that he liked them, because he didn't. Robert seemed to dislike *everybody*. Surly and rude, the man was unapproachable and had the social finesse of a brick – but then James could hardly talk. It wasn't like he was much better when it came to being sociable, but that was because he was shy, nothing else.

James ran his hand across his forehead and stared at his call log. Four calls he'd made to Robert so far. Was it even the right number? He didn't think he'd ever called him before in all the years he and Helen had been married. He did know though that he hadn't quite worked out what to say in the event Robert did answer. He'd sat up all night to work it out and was still none the wiser.

Helen had slept soundly beside him, not a care visible on her face, whilst he'd been going round in circles manufacturing one single possibility that would explain what he'd seen, other than the one he didn't want. And he hadn't been able to think of one, apart from that he'd imagined or dreamt the whole thing. The fundamental problem with that theory was that he knew he hadn't. He didn't know anything else for definite apart from that. And he wished more than anything that he could say otherwise.

James looked back down at his phone on the off chance that Robert had returned his call and he'd somehow missed it or become deaf to it ringing, but unsurprisingly, that hadn't happened either.

He was trying his utmost to be rational. Trying to think of any marginally believable excuse for it, but he knew what he'd seen and also knew that what he'd seen pointed towards something so horribly unpalatable he didn't quite know how to deal with it.

Correction – he had *no clue* how to deal with it.

On one hand he should be overjoyed that it meant his wife wasn't mentally ill, depressed or lumbered with a dreadful condition such as Parkinson's. That should make him happy, shouldn't it? And that did make him happy, but the rest didn't. *Not even slightly.*

James' fingers fumbled as he pressed his phone again. Still no missed calls? Did he even have a signal? He peered at the network work. *Yes he did. Of course he did.*

It was a possibility, no – *likely*, that Helen – his very own wife would actually do something like this. But deep down he knew the truth. Those pills weren't for Helen. They never had been. They were for *Dulcie.*

He'd seen Helen putting them into a bottle of Seven Seas Multivitamins. He'd watched her. She'd tipped all of the vitamins out and replaced them with those Benz... benzo things. And the others too. The Fluoxetine and the Temazepam. She was always rattling on about getting new vitamins for her mother to try, but they hadn't been vitamins at all. They'd been those drugs.

Since coming to this conclusion halfway through the night, James had been ravaged with nausea and deep-seated panic that would not lift. Two hours he'd spent on Google when he could bear lying next to Helen no longer, his mind spinning like a roundabout.

By 5am he'd found enough information to answer his questions and it sickened him to the core.

The drugs contraindications he'd found on two drug databases: *'...can cause dementia-like symptoms... irritability... confusion... memory loss...'*

Helen was manufacturing her own mother's dementia. But why?

Then it had struck him. For the money. Helen was doing all of this for the money. But how long had she been doing it for? She'd been going on about the dementia for *months*, so it stood to reason that she'd been feeding those pills to Dulcie for months too. This would make everyone believe and see it with their own eyes about Dulcie's worsening erratic behaviour.

Helen wanted the money from Footlights. She'd sell it. He'd seen her loan statements.

For the first time ever, James felt an intense dislike for his wife. *Jesus Christ.*

Picking up his phone again, James hit redial. If nothing else, then he'd leave Robert a message asking him to call back.

TWENTY NINE

JOE FOUND IT NIGH ON IMPOSSIBLE TO SIT STILL.
He'd waited what seemed like *years* at Alan's bedside and the
doctors still hadn't come round so far today.

He glanced at his phone for the ten thousandth time and his
heart lurched seeing a text from Teagan. Barely able to open the
message quickly enough, he stared at the text:

```
I can't do what you asked. It's not right.
```

Joe blinked and read the message again in the hope that it
had somehow changed, but it hadn't. *For fuck's sake.*

A wave of fear slid along his spine. Slightly worse than not
hearing anything from the doctor or Teagan refusing to help
was not hearing anything further from those two nutters. Taking
it in turns with Dave, they'd spent last night in alternate shifts
– one awake, whilst the other got some kip – just in case they
returned.

Having no idea when the men might show up again –
because they *would*, was decidedly worse than knowing when
to expect another visit. Not that there was much point in
remaining 'on guard', as Dave put it. Dave didn't realise that

whatever they did, when those men wanted to speak to them again – or do whatever it was they were going to do, and the less he thought about that, the better, they'd be doing it anyway.

However, even a futile plan was better than nothing.

Hearing footsteps, Joe glanced up but the doctor coming down the corridor flanked by a pair of nurses, walked straight past.

Joe's instinct was to leg it and disappear from the area completely. It wasn't him they were after anyway, was it? Despite his urge to exit stage left, he couldn't leave Dave on his tod to deal with this – although it was an extremely tempting thought.

Joe's eyes moved to the figure lying motionless in the bed. Apart from the noises from the machines surrounding him, there didn't seem to be any sign of life in Alan, but he refused to dwell on that. If he thought there was no point and Alan wouldn't come through this, then they might as well all throw themselves out of the window right now. Alan would get through this. He *had* to.

Joe's nerves were frayed; completely and utterly splintered. His eyes tracked to Dave sitting motionless in a chair against the wall. He hadn't moved for hours either. They were both on tenterhooks, knowing that the doctors were due to give them an update at some point today. Just when that update would be, no one knew. And sometimes it was better not knowing.

Dave's silent treatment had returned too. Apart from there not being much to say, the general atmosphere hadn't been helped by another visit from the police investigating Alan's attack. First thing this morning the banging on the door had sent both Joe and Dave into a frenzy, initially presuming it was those men again.

He didn't know which was worse – the police or the nutters? Ok, so obviously the nutters were worse, but the two detectives awkwardly sitting at their kitchen table staring at both of them in turn, waiting to hear whether they'd remembered anything further to 'help with their enquiries' had only made a bad situation worse.

Joe would be lying if he said Teagan's words about telling the police hadn't tormented him on more than one occasion. And he'd also be lying if he'd said what was going to come out of Dave's mouth hadn't been terrifying him either.

Although his vocal cords felt severed, Joe realised that if he hadn't spoken up, Dave would have blurted out something– probably *everything*. He'd seen the tell-tale twitch over Dave's left eyebrow – the one that occurred without fail when the bloke was under pressure. From this alone, he knew the man was very close to folding, so he'd had to say something.

Blathering that neither of them could think of any situation or person who would want to do this to Alan, Joe imagined sweat forming deep puddles around his socks as both detectives silently scrutinised him, knowing without any doubt that he was hiding something. His theory was compounded when one of them felt the need to mention that withholding information or 'perverting the course of justice', was a criminal offence in itself and they should both 'think back very carefully' if they wanted to help their friend.

Well, Joe *did* want to help Alan. He wanted him to be back to normal. He also wanted to help Dave and more importantly, himself. Opening his gob would not achieve any of that and the threat of going to jail was nowhere near as much of a deterrent compared to the threat of what those nutters would do.

Unfortunately, Dave didn't agree and the minute the police left, he'd let him have it both barrels. But he must have had some reticence to speak to the police, otherwise if he'd felt *that* strongly about it, he'd have just told them. But he hadn't.

Thank God.

The door opening made Joe look up from the spot on the floor he'd fixated on. He got up from the chair quickly. 'Any news?'

After the two accompanying nurses had entered the room behind him, the doctor shut the door and looked between Dave and Joe. 'Am I right in understanding that you are Mr

Hardwick's next of kin?'

Joe looked at Dave wearing a panicked expression he suspected mirrored his own.

'Alan's mother is dead and he lost contact with his father many years ago. We wouldn't have any idea where to find him, that's if he's still alive,' Joe explained.

'We've been Alan's next of kin since we moved in together.' Dave added. The first words he'd spoken since the police had left.

Joe felt sickness rise. Asking about next of kin wasn't a good sign. No, actually, that was the done thing in hospitals - no need to panic. Doctors couldn't discuss personal details with random people – it didn't necessarily mean anything dreadful. *It was just the results, that's all.*

Forcing a smile, Joe sat back down. 'How did the tests go? How long do you think it will be before Alan can ge…'

'We have the test results,' the doctor interrupted, not returning Joe's smile. 'I'm afraid the news isn't good.'

'N-Not good?' Dave glanced at Joe. 'Does that mean Alan will be in coma for a bit longer? How much longer do you think it will be?'

The doctor leafed through the sheets attached to the clipboard in his hand. 'As you know we took Mr Hardwick for scans first thing this morning. He's also undergone extensive tests with our neurological team.'

Joe and Dave glanced at each other again. *Yes, they knew this - they said yesterday. Was he going to get to the point?*

'We discussed the findings at length in our MDT this afternoon and we all reached the same conclusion.'

Joe felt his feet twitching inside his shoes. This wasn't good. If it was good, then the doctor wouldn't be dragging it out. 'Ok and what is…'

'Unfortunately, Mr Hardwick's tests show there is no brain activity and…'

'What do you mean, no brain activity?' Joe spluttered. *What did that mean?* 'How long will it be before it comes back?' He looked at Dave, disturbed to see his head in his hands. Dave knew more about this sort of stuff than he did. 'What does it mean? Wh...'

'It means,' the doctor said patiently, 'that I'm afraid Mr Hardwick is brain dead. It isn't a case of this rectifying itself or resuming unfortunately and...'

'What he's saying is that they want to switch the life support system off,' Dave muttered, his voice hoarse.

Joe blinked, stared at Dave and then back at the doctor. *What? Switch the life support off? Did that mean...?* 'T-That's not what you're saying, is it? Tell him that's not what you're saying,' he cried, his voice lost even in the small room. 'Look, he's breathing. His brain must be doing *something*. It can't be completely fu...'

'The ventilators and other machines are doing the work, I'm afraid. Unfortunately, Mr Hardwick will never regain consciousness.'

Joe swallowed hard. 'But if you switch the machines off, then... then he'll die, won't he?' he cried. 'That's not what you're saying? That can't be what you're saying?'

The doctor glanced at the nurse awkwardly. 'I'm very sorry.'

'In layman's terms, Alan is already dead,' Dave rasped. 'And the doctor is saying the best decision is to let him go.'

Joe let out a sob. *This couldn't be happening.*

• • • •

EVEN THOUGH SHE'D GOT the rest of the day to get through, Teagan could barely contain her excitement about tonight's date with Darren.

That's if it was a date? Her heart pounded. *What if she was reading too much into this?*

Looking in the mirror, Teagan patted her hair, making sure she looked presentable before she went back downstairs. Having splashed bleach on her trousers whilst cleaning the bathroom, she'd have no clothes left at this rate. Nerves were making her all fingers and thumbs.

She smiled at her reflection. She wasn't reading too much into dinner with Darren. It *had* to be a date. You didn't send a massive bunch of roses to a woman and ask them to dinner if it wasn't a date.

Teagan was so happy about this realisation, she'd almost been able to put the decision about Joe's request out of her mind. *Almost – but not quite.* It still niggled that just because she'd refused to hand over the keys didn't mean it was over. What if those men broke in regardless?

She needed to tell him that she knew the real reason the men wanted to look here – and that was because he'd *lied.* She needed to tell him to sort it and take the rap himself.

It was strange that Joe hadn't harangued her though. She'd fully expected to receive countless abusive texts and calls by now, but there had been nothing. Nothing since she'd sent him that text earlier. A glimmer of worry formed. She hoped nothing had happened.

Mentally brushing the intruding worry away, Teagan left her bedroom and began the long descent down the three staircases to the ground floor. She wouldn't let anything spoil her excitement today. She couldn't remember the last time she'd looked forward to something so much.

Nearing the ground floor, Teagan was surprised to hear Helen's voice. Approaching the sitting room, she hovered in the hallway, unsure whether to interrupt.

'I really haven't got time for this, mother,' Helen snapped, her voice terse. 'I've come round between appointments especially to drop these off and you're doing nothing but making things difficult.'

'I've already told you, I don't like taking those things.'

Dulcie's voice was petulant, like a child and Teagan could just imagine the expression she wore right at this very minute. *Should she go in?* She could tell by Helen's voice that she was stressed. The poor woman had enough on her plate at the moment without this and what she'd said about Dulcie the other night probably hadn't helped.

Taking a deep breath, Teagan breezed into the sitting room, hoping Helen wouldn't let on that they'd conversed the previous day. 'Oh! Hello Helen,' she smiled, feigning surprise. 'Nice to see you. How are you?'

Looking up, irritation flashed briefly over Helen's face before it morphed into an impatient smile. 'Ah, glad you're here. Please explain to my mother that it's imperative to take these vitamins.' Snatching two bottles from the table, she held them out towards Teagan. 'I keep telling her, but she's being difficult.'

'I am here, you know!' Dulcie barked. 'I'm not a child!'

'You're acting like one!' Walking towards Teagan, Helen gave her a knowing roll of the eyes. 'She needs to take these after dinner.' She held one bottle up higher than the other. 'And *these* in the morning.'

Dulcie cut daggers at the back of her daughter's head. 'Since when do vitamins need to be taken at certain times? Maybe you'd like to tell me that?'

Helen span around. 'Because mother, these are special ones recommended by the health food shop. They're supposed to work wonders, especially for people li…'

'For people like *me*, you were going to say?' Dulcie angrily got to her feet. 'You mean, *mad* people? Is that what you meant?'

Teagan shuffled from one foot to the other awkwardly. She hadn't heard of vitamins requiring taking at specific times either, but what did she know? Helen had obviously researched it, the poor woman. She was only trying to do her best.

'Come now, Dulcie,' Teagan soothed. 'Helen didn't say that. I'm sure you'll get a whole new burst of energy with these. I could probably do with some myself!' She smiled, hoping to bring the situation down as Helen and Dulcie eyed each other in a strange kind of stand-off.

'Well, Teagan can't make sure I take them tonight because she's going out!' Dulcie said, the hint of a sneer playing on her lips.

Helen turned to Teagan. 'Out? It's not your day off?'

'*I* gave her the evening off. She's got a dinner date with a lovely young man.' Dulcie's eyes gleamed, pleased with herself.

Heat crowded Teagan's face. 'I'll cancel it. You're right, Helen. It's not my day off and this is more important. I can go another time.' She didn't want to add to the antagonistic atmosphere and neither did she want Helen getting the impression she was taking advantage of Dulcie's generosity. It was the last thing she'd do.

Besides, if these vitamins helped then that was the most important thing. Dulcie would need all the strength she could get when the news was broken that she was going to a specialist home.

'You won't do any such thing!' Dulcie cried. 'Like I said – *I* gave you the evening off, Teagan. *I* was the one who badgered you into accepting dinner with that young man and will be most put out if you don't go.'

Helen frowned. The urge to scream was overwhelming, but she needed to keep a handle on this. She couldn't afford to alienate or offend the Teagan girl by insinuating she wasn't doing her job. She needed her on side more than ever right now. She really must hold her tongue no matter how difficult it was. *It won't be for much longer.*

'Just trying to help, mother. I didn't mean to upset you.' Helen calmly placed her hand on Dulcie's shoulder, when really she wanted to dig her nails into her mother's scrawny flesh and keep them there until she stopped hindering her plans. 'Right, I really must go.' Glancing at Teagan, she left the sitting room.

'I'll just see Helen out,' Teagan said. 'I won't be a moment.'

In the hallway, Helen remained silent until she reached the front door. 'See what I mean?' she muttered.

'I didn't want to cause problems,' Teagan apologised. 'I'll cancel the dinner. That way I can make sure Dulcie takes those vitamins. I'm sure deep down she appreciates you're trying to help.'

Helen shook her head, ignoring the urge to slap this silly little thing around the face. 'No, it's fine. You go on your date. You've enough to put up with as it is. I'll come round this evening and keep mother company.' *And I'll crush the pills up and hide them in her food if I have to. Either that or shove the whole bottle down her throat.*

'Are you sure? I really don't mind. I...'

'I'm sure,' Helen said. 'I'll see you later.'

Teagan walked back down the hallway and smiled happily. She was still going out with Darren after all.

'As I said,' Dulcie said matter of factly as Teagan returned to the sitting room. 'She's trying to poison me. Surely you can see that now? I told you, didn't I?'

The smile dropped from Teagan's face. *Not this again.* Refusing to let anything put her on a downer, she grabbed a pack of playing cards from the side table. 'Come on, I challenge you to a game of knockout whist.'

Thirty

JOE WALKED DOWN THE ROAD in a daze, unsure how his legs were moving one in front of the other. Somehow they were and it was a good job because without certain parts of his body working independently of his mind, it was unlikely he'd be able to breathe right now either.

He felt numb. *Completely numb.*

Dave walked silently beside him. Both of them unable to put into words what was in their heads. What could either of them possibly say that would make any of this better?

Joe blinked away the brimming tears, still unable to comprehend what had happened. It all felt surreal and he wasn't sure how to process it in what was left of his brain.

All he wanted to do now was to get drunk. He wanted to get completely hammered in the hope that he would pass out, affording him rest that wouldn't be plagued with a persistent looping nightmare - the sort when something you really didn't want to happen, happened and no matter how many times you attempted to influence the dream, it played out in an identical way as before. Over and over. And there was nothing that could be done to stop it.

Shoving his hand in his pocket, Joe fished out a packet of

half-crushed cigarettes. He pulled out two rather sad, bent fags and handed one to Dave, who took it with shaking hands.

Lighting the cigarette, Joe inhaled, the nicotine rushing to his head. He hadn't had one for hours. After the doctor had left them alone to take in the news about Alan, he'd gone outside for a fag then, but it hadn't helped. Stalling for time wasn't going to make a difference. None whatsoever.

'Fuck!' Joe spat, kicking a can on the pavement. Nothing would make him feel better. *Nothing*.

Alan – one of his bestest buds was dead. And it was because of *him*. If he hadn't gone round to dump Teagan that day… If he hadn't been at that fucking house when those bastards were watching it… If he'd just let things with Teagan slide on for longer, like they had done for years already, then…fuck. He'd rather have put up with Teagan's bunny boiler crap for ever if it meant Alan hadn't taken the brunt of the shit.

Joe screwed his face up to stop the tears. The list was endless. If he hadn't fucked off that night… that night those bastards were due to come back, then Alan wouldn't have copped it.

But then it would have been *him* instead…

No it wouldn't. He could have explained he needed more time and that he'd sort it, but instead he'd legged it and left Alan to take the rap. *Fuck*.

Christ, he didn't think he'd ever get the image out of his head. Every time he blinked he could see it. God knows what would happen when he eventually tried to get some sleep. That's why he needed to obliterate himself tonight. He'd drink fucking meths if it meant he didn't see that image stuck in his head.

Joe almost retched, his heart racing. Dave turned out to be the one with his head screwed on this afternoon, rather than him. Joe found he'd entered into a stage of denial with what the doctors had advised. There had been no point dragging it out, he knew that, but he'd started coming out with all sorts of rubbish as to what they could do to sort it; that Alan just needed some more time; that the test results were wrong; that it happened all the time – you name it, he'd suggested it – scrabbling around in the bottom of the barrel like a tramp.

Oh, he knew deep down – he just didn't want to believe it. *Refused* to believe it.

Luckily, Dave made him to pull himself together. It was a good job as he was getting pretty close to being sedated himself. He'd been verging on hysteria. *Yep, he'd well and truly lost it.*

Dave made him see there was no other choice. To drag out Alan's state of suspended animation was for *their* benefit, not his and it wasn't helpful to anyone.

'We've got to let him go, mate,' Dave had said whilst Joe openly sobbed. He hadn't cared who had been looking at him in the hospital's café - he hadn't given a fuck. He'd just wanted this not to be happening.

Dave had read the notes the doctor handed over first. Joe couldn't see what he'd been reading when it got to his turn. He hadn't wanted to see it. Words didn't make a difference. Those notes could have said anything and however flowery they were worded, it made no difference. The short and curlies was that his mate's life was over and he knew it.

Joe chucked his fag end into the gutter. He hadn't even noticed he'd smoked it down to the filter until his lip burnt.

It hadn't taken Alan long to go once the switch had been flicked. No time at all. Joe had presumed he would have seen it happening somehow, but he hadn't. Death had nipped in quickly and silently and it was done. Alan was there and then afterwards, he was *still* there – physically, but had gone at the same time.

Afterwards, he'd sat immobile, not having a clue what he was supposed to do. Cry? Scream? No, he'd done all of that. Someone had pressed the pause button and forgotten to release it.

The nurses and the doctor had closed the curtain around Alan's bed and then that was it. They could go. And here they were...

But what happened now?

Joe didn't know. He had no bloody idea. Did they arrange a funeral? How did anyone go about doing that? Christ, he didn't know where to fucking start.

He groped in his pockets. He needed a joint. He needed *something.*

Anger burnt at the bottom of his spine, gradually creeping along it. If he saw those fuckers who had done this, then he'd kill them himself. They'd killed his mate. They had killed Alan.

Distracted by the off licence, Joe stopped. 'Let's go in here. I don't know about you, but I need to get pissed and can't face the pub,' he said, his voice gravelly like he'd forgotten how to speak properly.

'You and me both,' Dave nodded, following Joe into the shop.

It didn't take long to buy some vodka and beer, along with a shed load of fags. Armed with several carrier bags, Joe and Dave left the shop. Automatically looking ahead before he stepped into the road to be promptly mown down, Joe froze. Although it was tempting to get run over he was more concerned by who he recognised standing on the opposite side of the road.

Watching them intently was one of the men who had killed Alan – the ugly fucker with half an ear.

'Fuck!' Joe muttered, all of the previous bravado about wanting revenge on the bastards leaking out of him.

Dave nudged Joe's elbow. 'Keep walking,' he hissed.

Joe's jelly legs propelled him down the road in the opposite direction of the man. His body tensed, waiting for a bullet to embed itself into his back, but it didn't. This lunatic must have followed them, but followed them since when? All the way from the hospital? It was no coincidence he should just suddenly show up outside of the off licence they happened to go in.

'Is he following?' Joe whispered. Getting no response from Dave who stared straight ahead as they continued down the street, he glanced over his shoulder, then rapidly looked back.

The big man wasn't following, thank God, but he *was* watching; his beady, reptilian eyes burning holes into the back of Joe's head like laser points; the hasty glance he'd taken was long enough to see the man casually tapping the side of his nose as he'd stared after them.

Joe felt a cold flush spread from his feet, right up his legs and down his arms to the fingertips. It went up his torso and through the back of his eyes into his hair. *This wasn't over.*

He knew, even though it choked him to acknowledge it, the man's very presence meant they still expected him to deliver on their arrangement. He was still expected to get the keys to that old woman's house.

This time, without any shadow of a doubt, Joe realised he'd have to make sure he did it because otherwise the consequences were loud and clear.

• • • •

'HIYA!' Terri breezed cheerfully into Gwen's office. 'Just checking the rest of the weeks' rota.'

Gwen nodded towards the large black folder on the shelf and resumed chewing her bottom lip. There was only one text she'd found on Lena's phone when she'd taken the risk of scanning through it yesterday that rang any alarm bells, but even that wasn't significant enough to denote anything categoric. She didn't know what she'd expected to find, but she'd expected *something*.

Gwen picked at the skin around her fingernails. She'd already made one bleed today and it was beginning to look decidedly unpleasant. But nowhere near as unpleasant as the lurking feeling in her gut about Lena Taylor.

It wasn't a text Lena had received that bothered her, it was one she'd *sent*. Seeing nothing of interest in Lena's inbox, Gwen had looked in the Sent Messages folder and there was one to a contact called *UR*.

The text hadn't said much – but Gwen could remember ever

word:

> Brill! Yes, it's all in hand. I know, I'm
> amazing. 😊 Will update u asap. xx

It was clearly a reply, but there were no other received or sent texts to UR, meaning Lena must have deleted them. Why would she delete them unless she was hiding something?

Was Lena carrying on with another man? God help him if she was and Jonah found out.

Gwen's first reaction was to tell Jonah. With any luck he'd call off the engagement, but how could she? If Jonah had picked Lena to marry, then he wouldn't appreciate her stirring the shit – because that's what it looked like she was doing. Maybe that *was* what she was doing?

Lena was no good and she wanted to make him realise that before it was too late, but what proof did she have of anything? That was if there was anything to prove?

She wished she'd been able to make a note of the phone number for this UR person. She could do a bit more digging herself if she had that, but she hadn't had time. Lena's stilettoes making their way back up the VIP staircase had made sure of that.

'Hey, Gwen?'

Gwen looked at Terri standing in front of her, watching her curiously. 'Yes?'

'I've just been talking to you. You've been off with the fairies. Are you alright?'

Gwen smiled. 'Yes, sorry. Just got a lot on my mind.'

Terri's face broke into a wide smile. 'I was just checking to see if I'm working on Saturday night and I'm not, which means I get to go to the engagement bash!' She clapped her hands together excitedly. 'Just got to decide what to wear now.'

Gwen smiled thinly. *The engagement party. Everything was about the engagement party. There shouldn't even be an engagement party.* 'Have you seen Lena today?'

Terri frowned. 'No, should I have? Oh Christ, I bet that when she realises I'm free to be at the party she'll put the kybosh on that and swap my shifts.' She smiled conspiringly. 'I doubt whether she'd want anyone there who's previously sampled her husband-to-be. Lucky cow that she is.'

'Terri! Jonah's your boss! Don't be so disrespectful. You shouldn't be discussing him like some random lay!' Gwen cried, knowing she should act put out, but unable to hide the small smile on her face. Lena would need to ban most of the dancers at Feathers if she wanted to exile anyone with history with Jonah, but any of those girls would be better for him than the one he'd bloody chosen.

Gwen grinned at Terri. 'If you do find your shift has been mysteriously changed, you come and let me know, ok?' She watched Terri leave the office with a spring in her step.

So, what to do about Lena?

THIRTY ONE

'NO, I INSIST,' Heath grinned. 'Ladies should not pay the bill at restaurants or *anywhere* as far as I'm concerned.' He eyed Teagan cheekily and gave her a wink. 'Neither should they be paying *half*, before you suggest that!'

Despite herself, Teagan giggled, feeling like a heady teenager. This was almost too good to be true. Handsome, charming *and* good company.

'Oh no!' Heath exclaimed in a mock-worry voice. 'You're not one of those women who get offended by a man wanting to treat his date like a princess? You going to smack me around the face and tell me I've insulted and demeaned you?' His eyes sparkled. 'Because if you are, then I apologise profusely and to make up for my gross lack of judgement, I'll let you stump up for an all-expenses paid holiday for the pair of us to the Maldives. How about that?'

Teagan laughed loudly. Darren was so much fun. She wasn't offended. Some women may think it old-fashioned, yes, but she wasn't one of them. To her it was a refreshing change to be wined and dined and made to feel special. She'd had a lovely evening. As before, the conversation had flowed and she felt at ease. Despite his high-flying career and huge amount of confidence, he was down to earth and nice to be with.

She'd rarely eaten out with Joe and this exclusive restaurant was one she'd walked past many a time, wondering what it would be like inside.

Beautifully furnished, the dimmed lighting made for an ambient and tranquil backdrop, helped by the subtle music playing in the background through invisible speakers. The polished tables holding a candle in the centre of each were laid to perfection and all tucked in their own little alcoves, just the right distance away from others to ensure privacy.

The food was excellent and the wine – well, she'd drank a lot more than she should have.

Teagan squirmed, feeling another heady pull of attraction for the man opposite her, but thankfully got the distinct impression that Darren felt the attraction too. The way his eyes rested on her just that little bit too long and how his fingers lingered on hers when topping up her wine gave it away.

Feeling heat in her cheeks, she wondered whether it would be sluttish to hope that something might happen between them before the end of the evening.

Heath nodded and smiled as the waiter returned to the table with the plate holding his credit card. He breathed a silent sigh of relief to see a receipt placed under the card. He'd had a horrible creeping dread that the card would bounce, having not enough remaining credit, or worse, been stopped due to non-payment.

His father would have a fit when he learnt this meal had cost £120 and he'd got to leave a tip yet. He spent less than half of that on a month's food shopping, but this had to be done right. And his father had agreed with his idea for the revised plan.

It was a long shot going at Helen Shepherd this way, but with his father's business in so much jeopardy there was no time to do it the more preferable way. This way would either work or crash everything and it was impossible to know which way it would tip.

Wining and dining Teagan was an expensive necessity. The flowers had cost a fucking fortune too. But hey, if it worked it would all be worth it and if it didn't... well, they didn't have much to lose because they stood to lose *everything* pretty soon.

Standing up, Heath casually threw a twenty pound note he could little afford on the table, gallantly holding Teagan's jacket out for her to slip on and watched her blush for the countless time this evening. Whatever her ex-boyfriend was like he had no idea, apart from if a small helping of manners impressed her so much, then the guy must have been a complete knob. Personally, he didn't care, but he *did* need to impress this woman – at least until she got him closer to where he wanted to be.

And if he got a shag out of it, then he wouldn't complain.

Turning on his smile, Heath winked. 'Your carriage awaits, Madame.' Sticking his elbow out, he grinned inwardly as Teagan slotted her arm though his.

'Don't think I should have had that last couple of glasses of wine,' Teagan giggled as she wobbled, feeling very silly. She didn't want to embarrass herself in front of Darren. She'd never been a big drinker and it showed.

Leaving the restaurant, she watched Darren press the button on his key fob causing the lights on his Lexus to illuminate, making the car stand out like a beacon in the small car park. Getting into the Lexus, Teagan relaxed into the leather seat, the fresh air only accelerating the feeling of drunkenness.

Heath glanced sideways, sensing if he was going to make a move on Teagan, now was the time to do it. 'So,' he said softly. 'Can I see you again?'

Teagan hugged herself inwardly. She'd have done a little dance if she could. 'I've really enjoyed myself tonight, Darren. So, yes – I'd love to see you again.'

Heath leaned towards Teagan across the leather seat. Placing his lips on hers he found her surprisingly yielding, so kissed her in earnest. He didn't have to put in as much effort as he'd thought. It wasn't that Teagan wasn't beautiful – no one could say that, it was just there was no chemistry. Beautiful or not, she felt like more of a friend, or maybe it was because he knew he was doing this with a predetermined agenda that felt wrong, but being as it had been a while since he'd had any decent action between the sheets, the feel of her lips on his caused all the correct reactions.

Heath's tongue found its way into Teagan's mouth, his hand snaking its way inside her top, fuelled to feel her erect nipple under his fingertips.

'Wait!' Teagan suddenly yelled, pulling away.

Heath scowled. *For fuck's sake.* He'd been getting into that then. Now he'd gone and put himself back to square one and the 120 quid on his father's card had been for sod all. *Bollocks.* 'I'm sorry. I shouldn't ha...'

'No, it's not that,' Teagan spluttered. Flustered, she reached down into the footwell for her handbag. 'It's my bloody phone! It won't stop buzzing.'

Heath stared at Teagan in disbelief. She was binning him off in favour of a missed call or email notification? *Seriously? Was he losing his touch?*

Teagan scrabbled around in her bag. 'I would normally ignore it, but... oh, I should have told you there were problems at the house earlier. I very nearly had to cancel.' She unlocked her phone. 'I have to check just in case – just in case something's happened.'

'Don't worry, I understand,' Heath muttered, watching as Teagan dialled up her voicemail, thinking he really didn't understand at all, but at least it wasn't because of him. Even in the darkness he saw Teagan pale as she listened to the message. 'Are you ok?'

Hanging up, Teagan shook her head. 'I need to go back. I'm really sorry Darren. Something's happened.'

Grinding his teeth in frustration, Heath fired the Lexus' engine and pulled out of the car park. 'Is everything ok with the lady you look after? Mrs Adams, you said, isn't it?' This was a disaster. If the old bat had gone and died then their plans were down the swanny. Furthermore, this had thoroughly ballsed up getting a shag before the night was out.

'It's my ex,' Teagan explained. 'He's in a right state. Long story but his friend died this afternoon. I'll have to call him. There's other things too… but… oh, I just need to get back.'

With a sinking heart, completely at odds from only a few moments ago, Teagan really didn't want to hear what Joe had to say, but knew she must.

· · · ·

HELEN GLANCED AT THE CLOCK in her mother's cluttered sitting room. All this junk made her feel quite ill, but in all fairness the evening hadn't been too bad. She'd been surprised to find her mother had adopted a complete attitude change towards her compared to how she'd been this afternoon.

Teagan was right. Her mother was changing personalities like a chameleon. The tablets were really doing a good job and with the higher dose it was a certainty that she'd have a final meltdown and no one would honestly be able to say that there was a sane brain cell left in that stupid old head of hers.

Trying not to laugh out loud watching her mother do a little random dance in the corner of the room whilst singing a mish-mash of jumbled up songs in a strange voice, Helen smirked. *All was going nicely to plan.*

Hearing a clattering in the hallway, Helen jumped to her feet. 'Teagan, is that you?' Helen strode into the hall, surprised to see Teagan looking upset and the back of a man shutting the door behind them.

'I don't know what's happened, but you know you're not allowed visitors. That's part of your terms of contract,' Helen said sharply.

'I'm sorry. I-I just… I just needed to get back… I need to make a call,' Teagan spluttered.

Fastening the door, Heath took a deep breath. *He was in.* He was in the house and when he turned around, he'd see the woman herself. *Dulcie Adams.* He hadn't expected on coming

276

face to face with her tonight, but could play this to his advantage.

'I'm very sorry for intruding, Mrs Adams. I wasn't planning on staying. I'm afraid Teagan's had some bad news and I wanted to make sure she got inside.' Heath turned around wearing his best smile, hoping it pacified the woman. 'Now she's safely in, I'll...Oh!'

Standing in the hallway with an expression as surprised as his own was not Dulcie Adams, but Helen Shepherd. *Shit. How did he play this now?*

'Mr Harding?' Helen said, shocked. 'I had no idea that you knew Teagan.'

Heath smiled. 'Mrs Shepherd! I can't believe it! What a small world it is.' His mind working overtime, he beamed widely. 'I had no idea you lived here too. Teagan said she looks after a Mrs Adams.'

'Yes, yes – my mother. I was just watching her whilst Teagan went out.' Helen kept her smile in place but it was difficult. She'd babysat her mother so the hired help could go on a date with the man she wanted to sell The Gables to? A partner of Shepherd, Percival and Proctor reduced to babysitting a demented mother for the evening. *Oh, that looked good, didn't it?*

'Me and Teagan went to school together. We only recently got back in touch. Wow, I still can't believe this. Fancy you being here.' Heath's eyes subtly moved past Helen, hoping she wouldn't notice. *Where was the old woman?* Having Helen here made things a bit trickier, although this unexpected turn of events meant he might be able to move straight into the next phase of the new plan.

Teagan had rushed straight off upstairs and Heath knew there was no real need for him to be hanging around. If he was going to jump a step, then he'd better get straight on it. 'I was planning on trying to get hold of you again tomorrow.'

Helen flushed, remembering she'd all but hung the phone up on him the other day. 'Ah, yes. I'm sorry I didn't call you back.' He could want to put an offer in and she'd blanked him. She needed to right this.

She moved closer and lowered her voice, although it was unlikely her mother would overhear being as she was still warbling away to herself in the other room. 'This is very embarrassing. As you can probably tell, things are difficult with my mother's health.' Helen nodded towards the room where the singing was coming from – the singing which had morphed into a Shirley Temple sang, complete with squeaky little girl voice.

Helen failed to keep the look of contempt, disgust and utter frustration from her face. 'I'm trying to find her a place in a specialist home.' The sympathy trip might make Darren Harding up his offer for The Gables – after all, it wasn't like he was short of bloody money, was it? 'She's becoming impossible to manage and to be quite honest, it would be cheaper to pay for specialist care, rather than keeping this huge place running just for her.'

Heath made a point of looking around the hallway. 'It certainly is a big house.'

Yes and one I need to sell, Helen thought, realising frustration had spilled into her words. 'Of course, it goes without saying that it's not about the money, just that it's better for her in the long run.'

Heath nodded, despite thinking where Helen Shepherd was concerned it was very much all about the money.

'Helen?' Dulcie stepped out of the sitting room. 'Is Teagan back yet? Is…' Freezing to the spot, she paled on seeing Heath.

'Mother, this is Darren Harding. He's just dropped Teagan back and…'

'Michael?' Dulcie whispered, her mouth trembling. 'Is that you?'

Heath blinked. *Michael? Shit! Did she somehow know what he and his father were doing?* 'I'm not Michael, I'm erm… Darren.'

Helen smiled apologetically. 'I'm so sorry. She doesn't know what she's saying.' Turning to her mother she cut her a stern look. 'Like I said, mother, this is Darren. Now please go back into the sitting room - Teagan will be with you shortly.'

Dulcie stared at Heath for a good few more moments, shaking her head in confusion then unsteadily walked back into the sitting room.

Helen turned back to Heath. 'I really am very sorry, Mr Harding. This is most embarrassing, it really is. I have no idea who Michael is.'

Heath brushed the situation off, whilst his mind raced through the possible implications. His father always said they both looked very much like Michael Senior, but not *that* much, surely? And the old woman was tapped so no one would take any notice of what she said.

But as for Helen – she'd confirmed his instincts. Always adept at reading characters, he'd got the impression Helen Shepherd was on the mercenary side – after all, she was an estate agent and things he's seen and heard in the past also backed up that suspicion, but now it couldn't be clearer.

This might work after all. Despite the smile Helen turned on like a light, Heath had *always* felt it was manufactured. She was as cold as a fish – a hard-hearted woman.

'So,' Helen continued. 'I know it's late to talk business, but have you decided to put in an offer on The Gables?'

Heath hesitated. *Yep. Mercenary as fuck.* Her mother was mad, the hired help had run off in tears and all she was bothered about what whether he was going to buy that place. *Yeah, she'd do. She'd do nicely.* He strongly suspected what he would put on the table, Helen would grab with both hands. From what he'd seen of the company finances, he didn't doubt that she could use the money.

Heath swallowed nervously. *Here we go.* 'I do have an offer for you... But I think it's best to go somewhere private to discuss it.'

THIRTY TWO

WALKING ACROSS THE LANDING, Teagan frowned noticing the door to the pink bedroom ajar.

Peering in, she saw straight away that some of the furniture had moved, as well as the rug – usually placed at the end of the bed, was rolled up, exposing the polished wooden floorboards beneath.

How odd, she thought, having not heard a thing last night despite being awake most of the time worrying. She'd half expected a restless night, what with Dulcie's worsening behaviour and was surprised not to have had any disturbances at all. She hadn't heard a peep out of her all night.

Shrugging, Teagan continued down the stairs. She'd have to come up and sort it later, but needed to go and get the breakfast things out first.

By rights she should have been in a great mood after how the evening had gone with Darren, but she couldn't help but think she'd blown her chances. *What a thing to do*, she thought irritably. Was it any surprise that her relationships ended up a joke? Was it any wonder that men didn't hang around – or hang around but not take her seriously?

Fancy behaving like that at a crucial moment. Darren must

think her a complete idiot. How many other people would be on the best date they'd ever had in their lives and then, in the middle of kissing the gorgeous man, scrabble off to answer the phone to an ex?

It took all of her power not to start ripping clumps of her hair out in frustration. The only reason she was managing to refrain was because she knew Dulcie was staring at her.

And then after insisting on going home, she'd promptly burst into tears like a child and ran off upstairs leaving Darren standing in the hallway to be grilled by Helen. Helen probably thought she was in the habit of sneaking men into the house now too. *Oh, this was all becoming a nightmare. Damn Joe and his demands.*

But that was another worry. *A huge one.*

Teagan glanced at her watch. She'd have to leave shortly to go and meet Joe like she'd stupidly agreed to do last night. She sighed miserably. As angry as she was with him, she couldn't have ignored him last night, but if she'd been able to explain everything to Darren, it would have made the way she'd reacted a lot more understandable, but she could hardly tell him - she wouldn't see him for dust if he knew what she'd found herself tangled up in.

But then she'd probably never see him again anyway after acting like a weirdo.

Fancy Joe having to deal with the decision about Alan. She couldn't imagine being in such a dreadful position and was gutted that Alan had died. She'd been further horrified to hear Joe had seen one of those men again. Even though he'd been drunk when she'd spoken to him, the terror was clear in his voice through his slurred words.

Although her original reaction had been to go to the police, she could see now why Joe had been adamant not to. As much as she hated to admit it, he was right, but that didn't mean she would allow him to use her or Dulcie to buy him some time.

A shiver ran through her and she dared to glance out of the window on the first floor landing. If those men were watching

Joe, then it was likely they were also watching *her*. And Dulcie. Time was running out.

Her mind filtered back to Darren Harding. It was unlikely that she'd see him again. When she'd finally come back downstairs last night he'd gone. Hardly surprising, but Helen had disappeared too, which was a bit odd. She'd have thought Helen would have waited for her to come downstairs before leaving.

Dulcie had been acting very oddly too. She'd been staring into space and no matter what she said, Teagan had been unable to get a response. Dulcie hadn't even uttered a word when she went to bed. She'd just silently moved from the sitting room and gone upstairs, looking bewildered.

She studied Dulcie staring vacantly out of the window, that string of beads she played with in her hands. Teagan moved to pour the old lady a cup of tea, noticing her own hands were shaking. Her nerves were shot.

She lightly touched Dulcie's bony arm, hoping she wouldn't detect the tremor making its way around her whole body. 'Thank you for letting me have a night off last night. I had a really nice time and you were right. Darren's a really nice man – the perfect gentleman.' She smiled, sheepishly admitting to herself that she'd have most likely have allowed him to *not* be a gentleman at all, had it not been for Joe's bad timing.

Dulcie flinched, her blue eyes watery. 'Darren, you say?'

'Yes, Darren Harding. I told you the other day I went to school with him.'

'Darren? Darren Harding?' Dulcie repeated, almost to herself.

Teagan frowned. 'Are you alright? You seem a lit…'

'What is his father's name?' Dulcie's gaze wandered back to the French windows.

'His *father's* name?' Teagan asked. 'I-I have no idea. Why do you ask?' That reminded her. Had Dulcie taken those new tablets? She must check and make sure because she was definitely getting worse.

'He... he looks like... I thought...' Dulcie's voice trailed off.

Teagan's worry deepened. 'He looks like who? Who does he look like?'

Shaking her head quickly, Dulcie flapped her hand. 'No one. It doesn't matter. Ignore me.'

. . . .

HELEN'S ONLY CONCERN was to get to the address Darren, or should she say *Heath Pointer*, as she now knew him to be, had given to her last night.

Still unable to work out whether what he'd said was a joke, a wind up or whether he was some kind of crazed nutter. There were things he'd told her which held the glimmer of possibility of it being the truth. *And if it was...*

Her head had been going around and around all night and that was the only reason she was bothering to go to see what these people had to say today.

Yes, she was annoyed that the alleged Mr Harding wasn't in fact Mr Harding – as this meant no commission for The Gables, but her annoyance had been placated somewhat when Heath, as she now knew him to be, had informed her there was a huge amount up for grabs in what he'd got to suggest to her.

But as for this stuff about being related? She couldn't quite buy that one. Related how? He'd refused to answer any more questions, just insisted she come along today.

Normally, she'd have laughed at such a suggestion and told him where to go, but right now she would take any option to improve her finances. It was worth half an hour of her time anyway. But a car sales place in White City? There was no logic to it. Still to go to the trouble of masquerading as a completely different person and the hassle of seeking her out, not to mention spending the evening with Teagan-boring-Fraser in a mad bid to get her attention, it had to be something promising. Either that or he was a serial killer?

Even then she suspected there would be easier ways to go

about it than the way he'd done it. It certainly wasn't her money he was after. If it was, then he'd be in for a shock. Pressing down harder on the accelerator, Helen sped down the road. The quicker she got there, the quicker she'd find out what this was all about.

As the tune on her stereo was suddenly interrupted by the loud ringing of her mobile through her in-car Bluetooth system, Helen stabbed blindly at the 'answer call' button on the steering wheel.

'Yes?' she snapped.

'Helen?'

Robert's voice boomed around the car and Helen inwardly scowled. *What did he want now?* 'Hi, Robert. Is everything ok?' *Be nice, remember? Be nice.*

'I just wanted to let you know that I've put the ball in motion to purchase that apartment for mother you mentioned.'

Helen's heart skipped a beat. 'You have? Oh, that's great news! That is such a weight off my mind.' *Even better.*

'Are you sure you don't want to see it before this goes any further? I think perhaps we should go and lo…'

'No need. It's fine,' Helen said briskly. 'You saw the particulars I forwarded you by email? The ones Ken sent over before he went missing? I really don't think we need to see it. It will only slow things up and you know time is of the essence here, what with mother's health.'

Robert was being worryingly nice to her, but she wasn't complaining, even if it was slightly out of character. It would be just her luck for one of the staff there to remember her and then he'd get suspicious and she couldn't have that. *Not now.*

'Well, if you're sure?'

'I'm sure. I read up about it. The complex has everything mother needs,' Helen said confidently, suddenly swerving to take a turn she'd almost missed.

'Do we need to provide any medical assessment?'

'Medical assessment? Why would she need a medical assessment?' Helen said. *What was he trying to say now?*

Please don't say he was questioning the validity again?

'I mean, before mother is eligible for one of those apartments? We don't want to buy it only to find th...'

'No. She won't need that. But I'll double check if you'd prefer.' Helen promised - not that she had any intention of doing so.

'I was thinking of getting a private assessment done for mother not so long ago,' Robert said. 'I'll admit I was hoping to prove you wrong about her state of mind, but I guess I have to say however much it pains me, that there isn't much point now.'

Helen's skin twitched. So, he'd been trying to get one over on her? At least he'd admitted defeat. All of these people would have to admit defeat soon. 'I think it would have been difficult to get an assessment anyway being as she wouldn't see the doctor,' Helen said through gritted teeth. It was so hard being nice to Robert.

'Well, I know that she requested a copy of her medical notes from the doctors a couple of years ago. She's got them somewhere in the house, but do you think I could find them?' Robert sniffed haughtily. 'And when I was looking for them, that bloody girl all but accused me of being a burglar!'

Helen's eyes narrowed. Robert really had been sniffing around. *Well not anymore. Way too slow, Robert. Way too slow.* 'Ok, well I must go. Thanks for letting me know about the apartment. Like I said, it's a huge weight off my mind. I was so worried they'd both be snapped up before I could get the money together, but thanks to you, it's all fine.' Aaargh. It really stuck in her throat having to thank this supercilious bastard brother of hers, but being as he was playing nicely at the moment, then she'd live with it.

'That reminds me,' Robert droned. 'Tell James he needn't worry anymore.'

Helen's skin prickled. 'James?'

'Yes, James left me a message the other day. He called several times in fact. I presumed he was worrying about this.'

'This?' Helen gasped, apprehension bubbling in her throat. 'What did he say?'

'Not much. Just a short message that he needed to talk to me about something. I'm afraid I haven't got round to calling him back yet.'

'And he didn't say what?'

'No, but he sounded worried, hence why I'm presuming it was over this business over the money for the apartment. That's why I wanted to call you to put your mind and his, at rest and let you know I'd started the process. I must remember to call him back later.'

'Oh, don't worry about that,' Helen said quickly. 'I'll let him know as soon as I get home. He has been flapping about it. You know he's always been a bit of a worrier and I guess he feels uncomfortable that I've had to come to you, rather than him being in a position to fund it.'

Helen's mind churned over. James knew nothing about the apartment, so why was he calling Robert? He *never* called Robert. They'd barely said two words to each other.

Ending the call, Helen covered the last two miles to White City as quickly as the heavy traffic would allow. She'd work out what James' game was later, but first she wanted to know what Heath Pointer was talking about.

Thirty Three

'SHE'S LATE.' Mike nervously paced up and down his office. 'Are you sure she's definitely coming?'

Heath nodded. 'She'll be here.'

Mike shook his head in disbelief. 'I still can't believe you blurted it out like you did. She could have gone to the police.'

Heath laughed. 'Nah! You know I've always been pretty good at reading people and I was spot on with Helen Shepherd.' He grinned confidently, even though he'd been a lot less confident last night when he'd told Helen his real reason for being there.

It was understandable her initial reaction was disbelief, but when her face changed – physically changed as her mind digested the information, he could see her mind whirring in front of his very eyes. She knew he wouldn't be saying what he'd said unless there was truth in it. 'Yep, a mercenary bitch that one.'

'What makes you think this isn't a set up?' Mike asked, his frown lines deep as he peered through the fishbowl glass for any sign of a silver Mercedes. 'She could bring the police with her – accuse us of extortion.'

'You're far too paranoid, Dad,' Heath laughed. 'Why

would she do that? She knows I'm telling the truth, otherwise she'd have called them last night.' He shook his head. 'She wants this as much as we do. She *needs* this as much as we do.'

Mike frowned. 'Then why not tell us to sling our hook and deal with it herself?'

Heath grinned. 'Like I pointed out to her last night, she doesn't know enough yet – whereas we do. The deal is we tell her what we know and she gives us access – or locates it and we split it.'

He sat back in the chair watching his father pace around like a nervous trapped animal. 'As I bluntly said last night, you know me – she's an estate agent – she hasn't the contacts to shift stolen jewels.'

'What? And we do?' Mike raised his eyebrows. 'Because it's fucking news to me!'

Heath laughed. 'Ah, but *she* doesn't know that. It doesn't matter anyway because unlike her, we have the nous to *find* the contacts. We just need the stuff.'

'Glad you're so bloody confident,' Mike grumbled.

'I told you we'd find a way to sort out your debts and we will,' Heath reassured. 'This will work. It'll work well. We'll split the difference and everyone's happy.'

Mike clenched his jaw. As much as he loved and admired his son's optimism, he couldn't help feeling it might not be as simple as that. But maybe he was being cynical. What if Heath was correct? Even if he wasn't, things couldn't get any worse.

Seeing the reflective flash of metal outside, Mike stiffened and squinted against the morning sun. 'Is this her?'

Heath followed the direction of his father's eyes. 'Yep, that's her. Are you ready? Let's do this.'

• • • •

JOE HALF FELL DOWN THE STAIRS, his hangover grating horribly. Stumbling into the kitchen, he swallowed two paracetamol with a swig from a bottle of flat coke left on the side.

He really shouldn't have necked all that vodka last night. It was doing him no favours this morning. It was difficult to tell whether the constant nausea was courtesy of his hangover or the prospect of having to go and meet Teagan.

He glanced at the clock. At least he'd woken up in time and supposed he should be grateful he'd remembered even having the conversation with her last night at all. Christ, he'd been steaming, but nothing had changed. Alan was dead, the psychos were still on his back and he still had to get those keys off Teagan.

He would have to pull off a sterling job of distracting her, he knew that much. Although he wasn't entirely sure of the reason why she'd refused to help him with the keys, he sensed little point trying to get her to change her mind. *He'd have to do something else and do it fast.*

Joe dragged his fingers through his tangled hair in a pathetic attempt to brush it. All he wanted to do was go back to bed, but he couldn't. He took another swig of warm coke, the taste making him retch.

Spotting a small parcel on the mat at the end of the short hallway, Joe staggered to fetch it, realising with dread that it was for him. Not recognising the scrawled handwriting, he ripped at the brown paper with fumbling fingers. The minute he saw the cheap mobile phone, complete with charger, he knew what it was for. *It was from them.*

He scrabbled on the floor for the brown paper, searching it for an identifying post mark, but all that was legible or available to hint where it had been posted from was a post office stamp from 'London'. *That narrowed it down then...*

He must admit, it hadn't even crossed his mind on how to contact them once he had the keys. He presumed they'd somehow know. After all, they seemed to know everything else about his bloody life. But yeah, it made sense. This phone was from them. It was obvious.

With shaking hands he pressed the 'on' button, finding the phone fully charged as he'd expected it might be. He didn't really want it to switch on. He wanted it not to work. He wanted to go back to bed and backtrack a few weeks to when his life had been normal. When it had been simple and free from this… this abject shit.

But no…

Pressing the contacts list, Joe saw only one number listed:

```
Name: Alan
```

Joe swallowed. *They had to take the fucking piss, didn't they?*

Shoving the phone, along with his usual mobile into his pocket, he sparked up a fag and quickly left the house before he changed his mind.

• • • •

TEAGAN WAS A BAG OF NERVES and her whole body trembled. She'd told Dulcie she was nipping down the road to the shop for milk, but she'd lied. And she didn't like lying.

Dulcie had been cold towards her, almost like she sensed something was going on and the weight of the whole situation was wearing Teagan down. Maybe she should just leave? It seemed she was affecting everyone around her in a negative way and it was getting to her – around with Joe's lies – they were getting to her as well. In fact, *everyone* seemed to be lying – including *her* and the whole thing was uncomfortable.

Reaching the shop, Teagan immediately spotted Joe's blue Vauxhall parked outside and as she approached the car, Joe leaned across the passenger seat, opening the door from the inside.

'Get in,' he mumbled.

Teagan hesitated, then straight away noticing the strong smell of stale alcohol. She glanced at Joe – he looked horrific – more unkempt and terrified than ever.

'Thanks for coming,' Joe turned his bloodshot eyes towards Teagan.

Teagan nodded, unsure of what to say or furthermore, *do*. She had no idea what Joe was going to say, if anything and she bit back her anger towards him. *This felt so wrong. Everything about it was wrong.* 'I'm sorry about Alan,' she murmured, wondering whether she should reach out and touch Joe's arm.

'Yeah, me too,' Joe said, surreptitiously glancing at the handbag Teagan clutched on her lap. If she would only put it to one side he stood a chance of getting his hand in. *The keys had to be in there.*

'I can't stay long,' Teagan said, her fingers playing with the strap of her bag. 'I'm not sure... not sure what you wanted to talk to me about? I...'

'I can't believe Alan's dead,' Joe cried, remembering his plan. 'Oh, Teag, it was awful! I just don't know how I'm going to cope.'

'How much did you owe them, Joe?' Teagan asked, her promise to keep her thoughts to herself about his underhand ways, deserting her.

'W-What? How much did I owe who?' Joe gibbered, confused.

'Look, I know what you've done. I know these... these men who attacked Alan were something to do with you,' Teagan continued. 'How many times have I said that drug shit you do would eventually get you grief, but this... this time you've gone too far.'

'Wait! Me? You think this is m...'

'You dragged me into it? And you won't even admit it - even now! I can't believe what you've done, Joe. I really can't!' Teagan ranted. 'You hate me that much, you'd lay the blame at my feet for your lies and your drugs? You told those men I was something to do with the money you owe them, didn't you? Just goddamn admit it. You must have done. And to risk an old lady's well-being too? You're truly despicable!'

Joe blinked, for a moment at a loss as to what to say. She thought all of this was to do with drugs? *His* drugs? 'I...'

'And you thought by saying I'd got their money was a good

idea? Buy you more time, yes?' Teagan's voice raised to screaming pitch. 'You put me at risk and you have the cheek to ask for keys so these men can turn over a house – someone *else's* house – looking for something that doesn't even exist because *you* thought it would get you off the hook?'

Raising her hand, Teagan slapped Joe around the face. 'How could you? How the hell could you do that to me? To Dulcie?' Why? Why Joe?' Against her will, tears of frustration, anger and hurt spilt from her eyes.

Joe was about to launch at Teagan with both barrels and vehemently deny everything being as for once, this one was not on him. But then he thought better of it. What did it really matter if Teagan hated him? It didn't matter a jot – it wasn't like he cared. Although he resented taking the flack for something that wasn't down to him, it could be a way of working this to get what he needed. Galling it may be, but if it meant this was done and dusted, then it was worth the injustice. When push came to shove, Teagan was invariably soft where he was concerned and despite her lack of playing ball of late, he suspected she might relent a little in the required ways if he played his cards right.

Joe raised his hand to his stinging cheek and looked down at his lap morosely, watching out of the corner of his eye as Teagan dabbed her face with a tissue from her handbag, holding his breath as she lifted it off her lap and placed it in the footwell. *Yes! She'd put it down.*

Joe turned to Teagan. 'I'm so sorry. I didn't think this would happen. I-I thought if I gave those nutters the blag that I'd stashed a shed load of weed at that old woman's house it would work,' he lied, sniffing loudly. 'And you're right. I did it to buy some time. I-I really had no idea they would demand the keys and come after you and the lady, I really didn't.'

He dared a glimpse at Teagan to gauge her expression, but was dismayed to see her about to launch into another tirade. *Quick. Make it better. Grovel more.* 'I know we're not together any longer – again, entirely my fault, but believe me, Teag, I didn't want this to involve you. I've been really stupid. I-I still care about you,' Joe said softly, before bursting into loud sobs with shook his entire body. 'It's my fault. All of it. W-What happened to Alan... He's dead because of me...'

Teagan listened to Joe and a small pang of pity fluttered.

'I'll never *ever* forgive myself for what happened to Alan. I'm only glad nothing happened to you or your lady.' *Lady, my arse,* Joe thought. It was just a shame it hadn't happened to that vicious old bag. He hadn't forgotten the way she'd spoken to him and neither would he. More to the point, this *was* all genuinely to do with her, but Teagan would never believe that so he had to pray that this would work.

He watched Teagan cross her ankles, moving her right foot over her handbag and wondered how he could get to the bag without her seeing.

Reaching out, he touched Teagan's knee. 'I really am sorry - for everything. You've no idea how much. I should never have tried to pass them onto you. I didn't think they'd dream of coming to the house until they demanded the keys and then... well, we all know what happened when I couldn't get them the keys and...'

'Don't you *dare* blame me for what happened to Alan!' Teagan shrieked.

'No, no, sorry – I wasn't.' Joe grasped for Teagan's hand. 'I didn't mean it like that. I know all of this is down to me. At least it's all over now.'

Teagan stared at Joe's hand on hers, but didn't pull away. 'Over? How is it all over?' She eyed him suspiciously, hoping he wasn't going to try to get her to change her mind about the keys. He'd have a very long wait. 'I feel it's time I went to the police about this.'

'No!' Joe yelped. *Fuck!* 'It's all sorted now. That's what I wanted to tell you.' *Think, think, THINK.* 'I got hold of the men and admitted I lied. I told them the weed wasn't at yours and never had been.' He wiped the back of his hand across his forehead. 'To be honest, I'm lucky they didn't kill me. I've said I've got the money and they've given me a week to get it to them,' he lied.

'Oh my God! It gets worse! You're now asking me to find the money for your drugs to pay them?' Teagan cried. 'You can forget it.'

'No, Christ! I wasn't saying that. I've sorted it, like I said,' Joe blathered, fast running out of steam. 'I got a loan, so yes it's all done, but please don't go to the police… it will drop me in it with the drugs.' He looked deep into Teagan's eyes. 'I am so very sorry and I hope that one day you'll find it in your heart to forgive me.' He forced out a lone tear. 'It's going to be bad enough burying Alan without losing your friendship too.'

Teagan watched Joe tremble and her heart softened. *So, it was all done?* Yes, what he'd done was unforgiveable, but that was him all over, wasn't it? He wasn't a nasty person, he just never seemed to think things through. Pity overwhelmed her. 'It'll be alright,' she said, leaning towards him.

As Joe pulled Teagan into a hug he clung to her making sure he was shaking enough for her to feel. 'Thank you. That means so much.'

Whilst Teagan stroked Joe's tangled hair, he let his right hand drop down into the footwell and into Teagan's bag.

THIRTY FOUR

MIKE EYED HELEN NERVOUSLY as she sat opposite, her eyes running over his office décor. He couldn't make out whether she was appraising it or thought it shit – not that it mattered. She wasn't here to evaluate his interior decorating choices; neither was she here to buy a motor.

He fumbled with the cup of tea he'd fetched from his machine. *This was awkward. Was Heath driving this conversation or him?*

'So, Mr Pointer,' Helen said, saving Mike the need to start talking. 'Your son...' She raised an eyebrow, 'who, up until yesterday, I knew to be Darren Harding, tells me you have something of interest to me?'

Heath, ever the confident one, took the opportunity to step in. 'Yes, sorry about that. It was the only way we could think of to get your attention. And more importantly, to weigh you up.'

Helen frowned. 'Weigh *me* up?'

Heath's easy grin hid his internal angst. 'We needed to decide how to play this.'

Helen sighed, not in the mood for games. 'Let's not beat around the bush. Please just get to the point – presuming there is one?'

The smile refused to leave Heath's face. Helen may be playing aloof, but she wouldn't be here if she wasn't interested in what was in it for her. 'Like I touched on last night, we believe you're sitting on something very valuable. Something we think you may find handy?'

He paused, seeing no change of expression on Helen's face. *She was good, he had to give her that.* 'It seems your mother was a bit of a dark horse. She's in possession of what we want. Or rather, I should say, what we're prepared to split with you.'

Sitting back in the leather chair, Helen laughed coldly. 'My mother? If my mother has something worth anything, then please enlighten me why I would split it with you?'

Were these two after the house? It would fetch a sizable amount, but nowhere near millions. It was the only thing worth anything and even so, there was no way she would split the proceeds with them. Why on earth would she?

Heath smiled and opened a folder on the desk. 'Before I tell you what it is your mother has, presuming of course you're not already aware?' He glanced at his father. 'And I'm making the assumption that you're not, otherwise I think Shepherd, Percival and Proctor would not have been trading at a considerable loss these past few years.'

Cheeks burning, Helen cursed her body's inability to hide her embarrassment. 'That, Mr... *Pointer*, is of no consequence, or I might add, business of yours.'

'No, you're right,' Mike intervened, finally finding his voice. 'But it does show that it's unlikely you're aware of what's right under your nose. Secondly, due to, shall we say your personal shortfall where finances are concerned, you're more likely to be open to our proposition.'

Helen glanced at the printout that Heath held out to her. *Something about a robbery.* 'What has this got to do with my mother?' She sneered and laughed sarcastically. *These people were timewasters. Obviously unhinged.* 'Don't be absurd. Why would my mother have anything to do with a couple of stolen televisions or something?'

'You haven't looked properly. Your mother – Dulcie Adams, received the spoils of this robbery to look after. And those spoils weren't televisions!' Heath pointed to the small print of the newspaper cutting. 'They were pink diamonds.'

Rolling her eyes, Helen squinted at the printout. She frowned. It did say pink diamonds. She'd never heard of *pink* diamonds. She glanced at the date of the article – 3rd April 1965.

'And look at this…' Heath pushed the typed-up notes he'd made across the desk.

Helen scanned the piece of paper. *Worth £15 million? £15 million sterling?* 'Is this a joke?' She looked between Mike and Heath suspiciously. *This had to be a wind up. What were these two really playing at?*

'It's no joke,' Heath said, his smile returning. 'That's only a rough estimate, but as you can see, your mother is sitting on a fortune and these are somewhere in her house.'

Nausea, combined with a rush of excitement flowed through Helen. *Could this be correct? No, it was ludicrous. But if it wasn't…?*

Helen could feel buzzing in the base of her feet. If this was true then she'd be sorted for life, the next one and probably the one after that. Her eyes narrowed. 'Why do you believe my mother has this?' she cried. 'Do you not think, if that were the case, I'd be aware of it by now?' *Well, she would, wouldn't she? By now something would have been said, surely?* 'And furthermore, if this is true, which I very much doubt, then please explain why it means either of you believe you are owed any part of it?'

Mike glanced at Heath before meeting eyes with Helen. 'This is the awkward part…'

Helen sighed audibly. She'd almost believed all this for a moment then. Wishful thinking, most likely.

Heath saw his father's reticence and embarrassment. Personally, he felt no awkwardness towards Helen Shepherd - she had as much empathy as a manhole cover. 'Your mother was left the stolen goods by her lover…'

Helen laughed. *She'd heard it all now.* 'Her *what*?'

'Her lover – Michael Pointer. Michael Pointer was involved in the robbery and he was having an affair with Dulcie.'

'Oh come on!' Helen spat. 'You must think me insane if you beli…'

'She had a son – Michael's son – born in June 1965.' Heath glanced at Mike again. 'Making him *my* father's half-brother.' He pushed the printed out details he'd downloaded from Ancestry into Helen's hands. 'Robert Adams is my father's half-brother, so that's why we're owed the money.'

With a sickening feeling Helen scanned the sheaf of documents with shaking fingers. Remembering her mother saying loud and clear, *'Michael is that you?'*, when she'd seen Heath last night, she went cold.

She jerked her head up to look at Heath, then her eyes darted to Mike. She'd hardly even bothered looking at him since she'd arrived, and she'd never really properly looked at Heath before either. How had she missed it? The man in front of her was strikingly similar-looking to her brother. And Heath, although not so similar, did have the same cold blue eyes as Robert. Whatever it was, it was there. Definitely there.

Jesus Christ, this was true, wasn't it?

• • • •

HELEN WASN'T SURE how she'd got to the layby she found herself in. She must have driven on autopilot because she sure as hell couldn't remember physically getting there. She also hadn't a clear memory of how she'd left things with Mike and Heath Pointer, apart from remembering agreeing to something and saying she'd be in touch.

Grabbing a tissue from her handbag, Helen mopped at the perspiration on her forehead and slapped the air conditioning button up to high. Leaning back against the headrest, she breathed in slowly, the shock of the past hour starting to subside.

Helen took a swig out of the tepid water from the bottle

perched in her drinks holder. She didn't know what had made her say it or why she'd said it so quickly in response to their wish to locate Robert, which so far, they'd been unable to do.

But she knew why she'd said Robert was dead. Because he wasn't having any part of this. It was hers – it was the least her lying bitch of a mother owed her.

This afternoon had also brought back something very vividly; something she'd completely forgotten about, like a slap in the face. The truth had been out there all along, yet she'd never noticed it. Now everything fell into place.

That day – she could remember it so clearly – she'd been fifteen years old and whilst looking for something else, she'd found Robert's birth certificate.

Helen bit down on her lip. She could see it in her mind like it was yesterday. Robert's birth certificate had a blank in the place of 'father', whereas hers had clearly stated Peter Adams. She'd asked her mother about it the minute she'd got in that day and had accepted the explanation that because their father had died just before Robert's birth, he hadn't been there to be entered on the birth certificate.

God, she'd been so naïve.

Her mother had lied to both her and Robert on just about everything their whole lives.

Helen pulled the copies of the paperwork Heath had given her from her handbag and stared at Michael Pointer's death certificate, the newspaper articles and all the notes Heath had made about the robbery. There was also a newspaper article about her mother leaving The Feathers Club in Soho and on top of this she could recall almost word for word what Mike had said was relayed to him on his own mother's death bed – his father's affair… This man – Robert's father had given the spoils from the robbery to his fancy bit… *Her* mother… *Dulcie.*

Her lips pursed. Robert had always been the favourite out of the two of them and now she understood why. Because *he* was the child of that man her mother had really wanted.

Anger throbbed as the truth sank in. Her father, Peter

Adams, hadn't been killed in an accident. Her mother's lover – Robert's father, must have *arranged* it. It was obvious.

Bile rose up her throat.

Would she ever tell Robert his father was not who he'd always believed him to be?

No. *Not yet anyway*. The only time she would let Robert know that his life was even more of a lie than hers was when it benefitted her.

Yes, Robert would find out eventually and her mother would also eventually realise her stack of dirty secrets had been discovered, but by that point it would be too late because she'd be banged up in a home for nutty old folks and the money from the sale of Footlights would be *hers*.

It was the least the treacherous old cow owed her.

Now she had even more reason to shaft that lying old witch and get the woman – that bitch, who had the cheek to call herself a mother, out of her life for good.

Her eyes flickered as an image of her father flashed into her mind. She had to try hard to remember what he even looked like now. No wonder her mother hadn't any photographs of him in the house.

Helen angrily shoved the paperwork back in her handbag. Well, bollocks to Robert if he thought he would be getting a penny of his new father's spoils.

Mike and Heath had made the right choice coming to her. Well, the right choice for *her*, anyway. Regardless of what she'd agreed when leaving their poxy showroom, if they thought they'd get anything from this either, they were more stupid that they looked!

Now she knew, along with the sordid secret, what that wizened old slapper was hiding somewhere in that bloody house, then she would be the only one benefitting from it.

Helen fired the Mercedes engine into life. The urge to call Robert and scream *'your father was a murderer'*, was intense, but she'd save that. She had to. Once the purchase of the apartment at Oak Apple Residential Home had finalised, she'd get him to help her clear Footlights out, then she'd sell the place from under both their noses.

Helen sneered to herself. Not that she'd need the money once she'd located those pink diamonds, although they'd take a bit of time to sell, but she could wait.

Once all that was done and dusted, then, and only then, would she hit Robert with the truth about his parentage. Then he could fuck right off out of her life. If she never saw him again it would be too soon.

THIRTY FIVE

TEAGAN COULDN'T QUASH the nagging unrest since getting back to Footlights and realising she hadn't got her keys. Even though she usually kept them in her bag, it was possible as she'd dashed out the front door earlier she'd inadvertently left them on the table in the hall.

Luckily, when she'd been forced to ring the bell, Dulcie had answered the door. She'd explained she'd forgotten her keys, but Dulcie had just wandered back upstairs without saying a word.

Teagan had looked everywhere since. She'd emptied her handbag out twice, checked the hall table, the kitchen, the bedroom – everywhere and there was still no sign of her keys. She brushed her hand against the pocket of her trousers for the umpteenth time in the hope of feeling the outline of the keyring, but there was nothing.

Now she had little choice but to start thinking she may have lost them. They could well have dropped out of her pocket at any point whilst walking down the road to the shop. She hadn't been paying attention with what she was doing and she could have put them in her pocket rather than her bag and they might have easily fallen out.

What would that look like to Dulcie or Helen? She'd have to tell them if she couldn't find them. She'd even called Joe to see if she'd dropped them in his car, but his mobile had gone straight to voicemail.

Teagan sighed. She'd been so relieved to hear that all this business with those men was over and now she'd gone and lost the bloody keys! *How irresponsible.* She might as well have agreed to give them to Joe for all the good she'd done.

Well, she couldn't do anything about it now, so if they hadn't turned up by teatime then she'd have to arrange to get the locks changed.

Teagan wiped her clammy hands against the material of her trousers and headed up the stairs. Where had Dulcie got to? Her head was so mashed it had completely slipped her mind to ask whether Dulcie was planning to go to her weekly bowls trip this afternoon.

Walking across the landing, Teagan paused hearing movement. She poked her head around the door of the pink bedroom, seeing Dulcie perched on the edge of the ornate bed, a large wooden box in her hands. 'Dulcie? Are you planning to go to bowls today?'

Startled, Dulcie swung around, the box in her hands clattering to the floor.

'Sorry!' Teagan smiled, entering the room. She headed towards the wooden box upturned on the floor the other side of the bed. 'Here, let me get that for you.'

'Leave it!' Dulcie screeched, scrambling to her feet quicker than seemed possible. 'Do not touch that! It's personal.'

Freezing to the spot, Teagan shivered as Dulcie's cold bright blue eyes penetrated her. 'I didn't mean to infringe on y...'

'Just leave me be!' Dulcie spat, glaring at Teagan as she backed out of the room.

Back on the landing, Teagan leant against the wall, shaken. She couldn't go on like this, she really couldn't. As much as she hated to admit it, Dulcie was beginning to scare her – like *really* scare her. She'd promised herself that she was going to put that rug and furniture back that Dulcie had somehow moved during the night, but she didn't dare now.

Feeling a hand on her arm, Teagan flinched and turned quickly.

'I'm sorry, dear,' Dulcie said, her voice contrite and her eyes no longer cold. 'I-I don't know what came over me.'

Seeing the older lady wobble, Teagan reached out to steady her and reminded herself that this woman couldn't help her outbursts. *She was ill, not nasty.* 'It's ok.'

Dulcie grasped harder on Teagan's arm. 'No, it's not. I'm not usually like this, I know I'm not.' Her bottom lip wobbled. 'It's those pills - those pills Helen makes me take. They're doing this to me, I know they are.'

Teagan sighed despondently, but nodded sympathetically. 'Would you like me to speak to her about it? I could explain that you think the tablets don't suit you. Would that help?'

Dulcie shook her head. 'She won't listen. She never does. I told you before, she's trying to poison me.'

Teagan felt like screaming. She wasn't cut out for this. She didn't have the knowhow to deal with this now the illness had progressed so badly. She was out of her depth and as much as she hated to admit it, the sooner Helen could get her into somewhere with the proper resources, the better. 'Don't worry. I'll speak to her anyway.'

She had no intention of saying anything. They were only vitamins, for God's sake, but if saying that quietened Dulcie down for now, then so be it.

Seemingly placated, Dulcie happily wandered off down the landing back to the pink bedroom and Teagan shook her head in frustration. She was just about to follow, remembering she still hadn't asked about bowls, but her train of thought was interrupted hearing the doorbell ring.

. . . .

'OPEN THE DOOR PROPERLY otherwise it looks

suspicious,' Joe hissed as Teagan opened the door a crack.

He glanced over his shoulder nervously, convinced he'd been followed. It wasn't a question of being paranoid anymore. It was more than feasible – possibly guaranteed that someone was actually watching him all the time. Things were no longer a figment of his imagination, no matter how much he wished they were.

'What is it?' Teagan asked. 'I don't think it will be long before Dulcie's moved into a home, so please don't tell me there's more trouble? I-I just can't take any more.'

'Hey no, it's nothing like that.' Joe tried his best to look normal as he reached into his pocket, pulling out Teagan's keyring and glanced at it to make sure he hadn't instead pulled out the copies he'd just had made at the cobblers. 'I thought you might want these? I missed your call cos I left my phone in the car whilst I went into the undertakers to make an appointment for… you know… for Alan.'

Teagan stared at the keys in Joe's hand. 'Oh thank God for that. I thought I'd lost them. Where were they?'

'In the footwell in the car. They must have fallen out of your pocket or bag or something. I wouldn't have even noticed them had I not specially looked after getting your message.'

Teagan smiled and took the keys. 'Thanks,' she smiled, feeling guilty that the thought had crossed her mind that he'd pinched them after all. He didn't need them anyway – it was over. Besides, despite all of Joe's faults, he wasn't a thief. 'I'd better go back in, but thanks for bringing them round.'

Joe smiled sadly. 'No problem.' Turning, he made his way away from the house.

Helen pushed past Joe as she walked up the steps. 'Who's that? Another visitor?' She eyed Joe unappraisingly as he sloped off rapidly down the path. 'A different one this time? I must say I preferred the one from last night.' *No she didn't. Heath Pointer was a manipulative shit.*

Teagan was horrified. Helen was looking at her like she ran a knocking shop! 'No, no it's not like that.'

Helen frowned. 'Who was it then? Did I not see him giving you keys? He looked like a tramp!'

Teagan's cheeks burnt. Helen had seen Joe hand over the keys? *Oh God.* 'He's my ex. He... erm... he gave me his set of keys back to our flat.' *The flat they never had.*

Helen's nose wrinkled in derision. 'Ex, you say? Probably wise. The man here last night was a lot more palatable than that one.' *Had Heath been in contact with Teagan yet?* She'd told him to keep things going with her for the time being. She'd let the stupid prat think she was on his side and up for splitting things, but he'd soon find out the hard way, the stupid boy.

Teagan heard Joe's car start from somewhere down the road. She knew it was his from that screeching sound it made when the engine first turned over and she eyed Helen, hoping to God she didn't suspect anything. The woman would go crazy at her if she knew she'd almost lost the keys to Footlights whilst sneaking out this morning. And she couldn't say she'd blame her.

Helen didn't look too good either – in fact, she looked frazzled and stressed. 'I'm sorry about last night,' Teagan spluttered. 'It wasn't what it looked like.'

Helen dismissed the apology. 'As it turns out, I've met Darren Harding before. He viewed one of our properties only last week.'

'Really? I...'

'Anyway, it's neither here nor there because we've got more important things to deal with.' Helen breezed past Teagan into the hallway of Footlights and beckoned her in. 'Mother gone to bowls, I take it?'

Teagan shook her head. 'No, she's upstairs. I don't know if sh...'

'Damn,' Helen spat. Grabbing Teagan's arm, she pulled her into the sitting room. This wasn't part of the plan and made things more difficult, but she had to get on with it.

Still smarting from the revelations of earlier today, Helen knew she had to move on this fast. Her anger towards her mother was fast bubbling to a point she couldn't contain. Despite her general dislike for the woman who gave birth to her, it had surprised her to find that as well as being angrier than she thought possible, she also felt the unfamiliar pain of hurt. And that was making her more incensed than the anger.

How she would keep her ire under wraps whilst her plan came to fruition, she didn't know, but she'd have to try. What she did know though, was that she wouldn't hang around waiting to get her hands on what her mother had stashed somewhere in this dump of a house. She looked around frantically. *She'd rip the whole place apart if she had to.*

Teagan looked at Helen and felt herself begin to panic. Her head was hot and her breathing fast. She tried to calm down - going into a full-blown panic attack right now would help no one. 'I-Is there any news? You know, about a place for Dulcie?' She asked quietly, glancing towards the door, hoping that Dulcie was still far too preoccupied upstairs with whatever she was doing in the pink room to hear.

'That's why I'm here,' Helen said, also glancing around. 'I'm...'

'It's just that I'm ever so worried,' Teagan cut in. 'Dulcie's convinced those pills are poisoning her.'

Helen nearly choked. 'Is she not taking them?' *Had her whore of a mother worked it out? Had the lying, treacherous cow put two and two together?*

'Oh yes, she's taking them. I watch her and make sure of it, but she's had another turn... It's getting really bad now.'

Helen felt her racing heart stabilise. *Thank God.* If her mother had had another turn – and one so good to significantly worry this stupid girl, then the pills were definitely working well. The changed dosage must have been spot on. 'How can I be poisoning her? Vitamins don't poison people!'

'*I* know that.' Teagan mirrored Helen's exasperation. 'But she's convinced.'

'Look, I need you to help to make sure mother doesn't interfere. I'm here because I need to start getting some of her things together.' Helen's mouth formed a makeshift smile as she placed a hand on Teagan's shoulder. 'It's good news. Robert and I have found a place and we're hoping to get her settled in there within the next week or so.'

She was sure Robert's cash and her contacts in the industry could push the solicitor's habit of slow paperwork through in a matter of days, rather than the usual six weeks. There was no bloody mortgage, therefore she was not paying a solicitor money to sit on their arse and drag things out for weeks, purely to justify their extortionate fee.

'Wow, that was quick!' Teagan exclaimed, brightening somewhat. 'Shall I help you sort some of her clothes and things out? What will she need to ta...'

'No, I'll deal with that,' Helen said brusquely. 'I need to locate some paperwork first.' She fixed her scrutiny on Teagan. 'You need to keep her out of the way though. I don't want her to know I'm digging around. You know yourself how erratic she is and I can't risk her having any inkling about this until the last minute.'

Helen pulled her best distressed expression out of the bag on cue. 'This will be awful for her, but it's for the best.'

Teagan nodded. 'I completely understand. I'll try my best to keep her occupied.'

'Appreciated. If she thinks I'm going through her stuff, she'll only come up with more bizarre accusations. It's horrible to think she hates me so much...' Helen sniffed dramatically, successfully managing to hide her scathing thoughts. If only she knew... *What goes around, comes around, mother dear...*

She smiled sadly at Teagan. 'I'm sorry all of this will mean your contract coming to an end prematurely. I hope it doesn't cause too much inconvenience - you've been a wonderful help. Robert and I were discussing only yesterday that if it wasn't for you, we wouldn't know of the extent of mother's deterioration until it was much too late. And I dread to think what might have happened...'

Teagan blinked. She hadn't thought of being out of a job.

'Of course, it goes without saying that we will honour the full six months fee for your services.'

Teagan gasped. 'Really? Thank you, that's very good of you.'

Helen gave a tight-lipped smile. *Yes, it was, wasn't it? Although Robert would be the one picking up the bill. He'd like that.*

She swallowed a giggle. Robert would be livid, but tough luck. He could be bitter all he liked. He had no reason though – after all, it was *his* father who had killed *hers*, she was sure of it. He should be apologising on behalf of that bloody man, but more than anyone, her mother should be apologising. Not that she would – she was far too busy telling poisonous lies.

'Right!' Helen clasped her hands together. 'I'll make a start.' And whilst her mother was upstairs, that start would be in the cellar. No one ever went down there because it was more full of junk than the rest of the house and therefore the most likely place to stash something.

. . . .

HELEN SCREECHED TO AN ABRUPT STOP on the drive, her spinning tyres spraying gravel in all directions.

Yanking her handbag from the front seat, her neck tensed even more spotting the curtains twitch in the lounge at the front of the house. *James looking at her again. All the bloody time.*

She was in a bad enough mood already without him adding to it. Every single thing he did grated on her nerve endings and it was getting worse and worse. She'd had enough. Once all of this was done she would start divorce proceedings against him.

Helen stamped up the drive, flicking her blonde bob out of her eyes impatiently. She should never have married him in the first place – a totally pointless endeavour. And one she would be deleting as soon as time allowed.

Letting herself into the house, she put her handbag on the hall table, slipped her jacket off, hanging it neatly on the coat stand and then threw her car keys on the table.

She glanced in the mirror, her teeth clenched, waiting for it. *Just waiting...*

'You're home!' James cried, walking out of the lounge to kiss her, pretending not to notice her move swiftly out of the way.

'Yes, I'm home,' Helen snapped. 'Like you knew full well I was because you were looking out of the window when I pulled up.'

Pushing past, she walked into the large open plan lounge and through into the dining kitchen, scowling at the table laid for dinner, the smell of something herby coming from the oven.

She knew he'd pretend to be glad she was home. *She* wasn't glad she was home. She couldn't bear it. James' stupid questions, the sound of his voice, the way he looked at her with his gormless face... He was driving her crazy following her around all the time like a lost puppy.

The dislike she'd felt for her husband the past few years had now officially turned into hatred. That was right. *She hated him.* He made everything worse.

Heading straight for the glass of red wine James had thoughtfully poured for her, Helen slugged it back in one go and reached for the bottle for a top up.

'Good day?' James asked, trailing her into the kitchen.

Helen scowled. *Why did he ask that? Why did he always ask that? Did it look like she'd had a good day?*

No it didn't, so why ask? Why not say sod all?

Helen's teeth clenched so hard she was sure she'd just felt a bit come away from one of her back ones. *Be civil*, she chanted silently. 'No, the day hasn't been particularly good. I've been busy with clients,' she muttered, finishing the second glass of wine.

Seeing James' eyes linger on her empty glass, Helen knew he was itching to make a comment about it, but James being James, never would. *The pathetic pointless little worm.*

'I've made an Italian chicken and pasta for dinner,' James said brightly as he walked over to the oven, pointlessly peering through the glass. 'It shouldn't be much longer now.' He moved back to the table. 'Why don't you have a seat? I'll get you a top up o...'

'I don't want to sit down!' Helen snapped. *Why couldn't he leave her alone? Why couldn't he just bugger off. She couldn't stand it anymore.*

James smiled, silently ignoring his wife's rudeness. 'Clients today, you say? I called the office earlier – just to check to see if you were alright and they said th...'

'You're stalking me there too?' Helen slammed her glass down on the table. 'For Christ's sake, James! What's the matter with you?'

Was it not bad enough that she'd spent the afternoon and half the evening rummaging around in that dust-ridden hole of a cellar? She'd found just about everything else in the entire world, apart from what she was looking for.

Those diamonds her mother had allegedly got could be anywhere. Absolutely *anywhere*. They would only be small and could be hidden in a vast amount of places. They could even have been separated and each one put somewhere different. Her pulse raced worryingly. She might never find them and she had to. *Just had to.*

James watched Helen silently raging to herself. He couldn't go on like this and his nerves were already shot to pieces about what he'd seen her doing in the garage and the suspicions that had brought. He wanted what was really going on to be *anything* but what he suspected, but her behaviour... the things about the remortgaging of the house that she'd hidden from him...

'You're doing it again!' Helen screeched, making James physically jump. 'You're staring at me like an idiot! What the hell's wrong with you?'

James sighed. 'Helen, we need to talk.' He nodded towards a chair. Bypassing that she completely ignored him and remained standing, he sat down regardless and poured a glass of wine for himself. 'I want to know what's going on.'

Helen narrowed her eyes. 'What do you mean what's going

on?' How dare he ask that!

'You've got a bloody cheek!' she spat, her eyes burning. 'Why don't you tell me why you've been checking up on me?'

James blinked. 'Checking up on you? I haven't been ch...'

'Why are you calling my office then? What do you expect to find? Trying to catch me out are you? What for exactly?' Helen raged, her anger at fever pitch. 'Furthermore, why have you been calling my brother? Do you really think he wants to speak to you? Why do you think he hasn't called you back?'

James squirmed on the chair. The urge to have it out with Helen about the tablets and the remortgage strong. But that was a good point; why hadn't Robert called him back? Could it be that he was in all of this with Helen?

No, he couldn't be. James knew how much it irritated Helen how much Robert fought her over getting Dulcie into sheltered accommodation.

'Well?' Helen raged. 'Are you going to answer or not?'

'I-I can't remember now,' he mumbled. 'I probably couldn't get hold of you so I thought y...'

'Thought I might be at Roberts, you mean?' Helen cut in. 'Jesus Christ, James. Does it ever cross your mind that I'd rather be anywhere but here?'

So he was stalking her to her brother's now? Could she go nowhere without having him following her or trying to find out where she was? It was suffocating. *Suffocating.*

James got up from the table and looked at Helen sadly as he moved towards the door. 'I'm beginning to realise that, yes. I'm beginning to realise a lot of things...'

'Where are you going now?' Helen screamed.

'Giving you what you want. Some space.' James walked out of the dining kitchen and stood aimlessly in the hall, not knowing what to do. Whatever happened, he had to do something.

James let himself into the garage through the adjoining door and dialled Robert's number again. He had to reach him somehow.

THIRTY SIX

JONAH WAS LESS THAN IMPRESSED. Bloody Keith Grogan and his ham-fisted ways. And much to his irritation, all that business had made the top headline of Maidenhead's news, which he could do without. He didn't want it spreading further afield, or going national:

Coma Man Dies

The victim of the violent and brutal assault on 15th June, died yesterday in hospital, despite initial hope that he may recover.

Alan Hardwick, 28, never regained consciousness after the horrific head injuries he'd suffered during the attack. Extensive tests showed there was no hope of any recovery, and the unfortunate decision to withdraw life support was taken.

Police are still appealing for anyone who noticed anything suspicious in the Weir Road area on the night of the attack to come forward as a matter of urgency.

Lena watched Jonah staring at his mobile phone as she delicately nibbled at the selection of fruit in her breakfast bowl. 'Anything interesting?'

Locking his phone, Jonah placed it face down on the table. 'Just some bloke who snuffed it after an attack.'

'It wasn't anyone we knew was it?'

Jonah shook his head and slurped at his coffee. 'No, no one from around here. It was over in Maidenhead.'

Lena frowned. 'Why are you looking at Maidenhead's news? That's nowhere near here.'

Jonah shrugged dismissively. 'It just came up on my newsfeed,' he lied, wishing Lena would stop asking questions, but after their row the other night, she was making a concerted effort, so therefore he'd do the same. Focusing on Dulcie Adams was the priority and he didn't need any distractions.

He eyed Lena picking at a grape. She should eat properly for the kid's sake.

Jonah frowned. He'd also had a missed call from Saul, which he'd half-expected, having not gone to visit him yesterday. Saul would be spitting chips about that and equally angry that he'd probably queued up for some time to use the phone, only for it to go straight to voicemail.

But it was tough luck. He couldn't have distractions and Saul would distract him. His brother ranting about what needed to be done – the polar opposite of what *he* believed needing doing to properly resolve this, was not going to help.

Pushing his chair back, Jonah stood up and grabbed his suit jacket. *Saul would just have to wait.* 'I'll be off then.'

Lena put her spoon down. 'Shall I come with you? I could do with a change of scenery.'

'I don't think so. I've got a lot on today and you don't want to get in the way.' Turning on his heels, he left the kitchen before Lena noticed how clenched his jaw was.

Lena watched the door close and slammed her fist down on

the table. *In the way, was she?*

. . . .

NERO PLACED THE KEYS on Jonah's desk and grinned. 'There you go!'

Jonah picked up the small key fob, eyeing the two keys hanging from it. 'Any issues?'

Nero shook his head. 'No. The stoner called me on a burner and told me he'd got them. Shame about him, he seems to have developed a speech impediment.'

Jonah laughed. 'That's because you scare everyone to death.' His smile fell. 'Talking of which, did you hear that the one in the hospital karked it?'

Nero shrugged. 'I hadn't, but Keith said when he followed Joe and that other dopey guy the other day, they'd come from the hospital and looked fucked up, so it doesn't surprise me.'

'Nothing on the estate agent?'

'Nope. They won't find anything either. Not unless they've got a thousand years to forensically analyse all the metal blocks that were once cars at Tiny's place.'

Jonah nodded, pleased. *That was something then.*

'The stoner bloke – our friend Joe… He reckons the Adams woman is being shifted out into a nuthouse in a week or so – at least that's what the stoner thinks.' Nero raised his eyebrows and chuckled to himself.

Jonah scowled. 'How does he know that? The girl, I presume? Has he told her about you?'

Nero shook his head. 'Nah. Even he wouldn't be that stupid. He's shitting himself enough as it is. He wouldn't have said anything. She won't know anything.'

'How do you want us to tackle this now we have the keys? Hang fire until the old bat's gone? We'll have free rein of the house then?'

Jonah frowned. *He'd thought about this. Thought about it long and hard.* 'I won't be waiting until the old girl has been carted off because I want her there. I want to talk to her.'

Nero very nearly dropped his coffee down his trousers. '*Talk* to her? You want to talk to her?'

'I'll drag her in for questioning,' Keith beamed. 'Take her for a ride in the car to the warehouse? You can meet us there?'

'I don't know how much use she'll be if she's barking, but I guess one of us can turn the house over whilst you're with her,' Nero added.

Jonah placed his pen on the desk. 'And the girl?'

'The girl?' Keith frowned. 'Oh, the hired help? I'll offload her, don't you worry about that.'

'No,' Jonah said quickly. Although his instinct was to send them in to turn the house over, find the stash and then dump the old girl face down in the nearest canal for her part in the deception, he didn't kill women, no matter how tempting it was. Women were out of bounds – they always had been and he wouldn't disgrace his father by changing the code of conduct.

'That won't be happening. I'll go to the house myself. I want to look Dulcie Adams in the eye and tell the only remaining link to the fuckwit who turned my father over what she was part of.'

Nero and Keith exchanged glances. Jonah was never hands on anymore. He'd taken a back seat with that side of things the minute he'd become the gaffer. It was the way it had always worked. That probably wouldn't have applied to Saul, but then very little applied to Saul.

'I know what you're thinking, but this is different. This stuff has haunted this firm and my family for decades and I want to be the one to deal with the only person left party to it.' Jonah nodded almost to himself. 'I want to be the one she hands the stash to.'

He glanced at the framed picture on his desk of his late father. He wanted to be the one his father's rightful possessions were handed back to. He wanted to hear the apology coming directly from the horse's mouth. To *him*, not via anybody else.

Nero inhaled deeply. 'Ok, if that's how you want to do it.'

'It's the only way I'll do it,' Jonah barked. 'It's the only acceptable way under the circumstances.'

Keith stood up. 'This is nuts! We could just go straight in an...'

'Don't fucking tell me what is ludicrous or not!' Jonah roared, slamming his fist onto his desk. 'What I say, goes! Do NOT question my judgement.'

Keith raised both hands in resentful submission. 'Ok, ok! But shall we all go now? No point hanging around. I presume you'll want u...'

'I'm not doing it now,' Jonah snapped. I want you to tell me an evening when the maid, or whoever she is, will be out. When Dulcie Adams is on her own, *that's* when I'll be talking to her.' He glanced back at his father's photo again. 'Arrange it so your stoner man gets the girl out one evening this week.'

Opening one of the drawers of his desk, he pulled out a wad of notes, shoved them into an envelope and glaring coldly, handed it to Keith. 'And give him this. Only right that we should contribute to the funeral costs under the circumstances, don't you think?'

· · · ·

'DID I HEAR HELEN HERE YESTERDAY, DEAR?' Dulcie asked, pottering around the sitting room.

'Yes, she just popped over. She didn't stay long.' Teagan fidgeted awkwardly with her fingers. She couldn't say why Helen had been here. Dulcie was in a good mood today, her behaviour completely normal and she didn't want anything to set her off. Discovering Helen was preparing for her move would do just that.

Sadness engulfed Teagan once more. It was so disheartening and she wished she could do something to make this better – all of it.

'Have you heard from that young man again yet?' Dulcie said, her eyebrows raised inquisitively.

Teagan faltered. Dulcie had asked her this earlier, but she'd skirted round the subject. Dulcie's behaviour over Darren the other day had been odd to say the least. Nothing else had happened with him though, which wasn't entirely unexpected, but it was still disappointing all the same. She'd texted him a few times, apologising for the other night. He'd been fine, saying it wasn't a problem and not to worry about it, but he hadn't mentioned anything about going on another date. *And that said it all.*

'Come on, tell me,' Dulcie pushed.

Teagan shook her head. 'No, I haven't heard anything and I don't think I will either.'

Dulcie laughed, her eyes alive. 'Oh, I'm pretty sure you will.' She patted the seat next to her. 'Come and sit here, there's something I need to talk to you about.'

Teagan tentatively moved across the room and perched on the edge of the sofa.

'Do you remember yesterday when I asked you about Darren?' Dulcie asked, her eyes bright.

'Erm, yes. You asked me about his father an…'

'Don't worry about that for a moment.' Dulcie flapped her hand. 'Do you remember me mentioning about the man I wanted to be with? The man who bought me that brooch and this house?'

'This *house*?' Teagan cried. 'I didn't realise he'd bought you this house.'

Dulcie laughed again. 'I know you've started to believe I'm crazy too and I can't say I blame you, but I really do want to tell you something.' Dulcie got up from the sofa and moved to a little table. 'When we had that conversation, I was looking for something.' She pulled open a tiny inset drawer. 'And now I've found it…' Her gaze wandered to the French windows. 'He promised me he'd come back… I waited you know…'

Teagan remained silent. *She just had to let Dulcie talk, she knew that.*

'His name was Michael. He said he wouldn't be long and then we could be together properly…'

Teagan frowned, hoping Dulcie wasn't going off on a really

mad one again.

Dulcie swung around. 'I never got to be with him though. Not properly, like we'd planned, but I wanted to so badly.' She smiled slightly before flopping back down in her chair. 'He wanted to wait a bit longer before we made our relationship official, but we never got that chance.'

'He was married, you know?' Dulcie continued. 'Had a young child too, but Michael was divorcing his wife and then we were going to marry. Everyone knew we were together. It was hardly a secret - even his bloody wife knew about me. Oh and I know they all say things like 'I'll leave my wife' and never do, but Michael... Michael was different...'

Dulcie waved her arm around the room. 'He bought me this place. He was supposed to be coming back..'

Teagan saw tears brimming in Dulcie's eyes. 'But he never did?'

Angrily blinking away the forming tears, Dulcie continued, 'My instincts always told me that he must have died, but I never did find out for definite. I suppose I didn't want to know because then it would have been over.' She took a large gulp of her gin. 'I never loved anyone again. There was never another man in my life after him...'

Clearing her throat, she carefully unfolded the tissue-thin newspaper cutting she had retrieved from the tiny drawer in the table. 'I knew I had it somewhere.' She smiled at it longingly before handing it to Teagan. 'This is my Michael.'

Teagan took the aged paper carefully. An article about The Feathers with a photo of seven men sitting around a circular table.

'Michael's the one on the left,' Dulcie said proudly.

Teagan squinted at a very striking-looking powerfully built man. 'What did he do?'

Dulcie laughed. 'Oh you don't need to know about that.'

Teagan concentrated further. 'He reminds me of someone... I can't quite put my finger on it.' *Wait a minute!* She studied the man's features once again. *She had seen him before*. 'Oh my God!' She looked at Dulcie, startled.

Dulcie smiled knowingly. 'Yes, Robert looks very much like his father, doesn't he?'

Teagan sat open-mouthed. Dulcie wasn't making this up at all - at least not this part. There could be no doubt the man in the newspaper clipping had fathered Robert – the resemblance was uncanny. 'Does... does...?'

'I know what you're going to ask... No, Robert doesn't know. Neither does Helen. You're the only person I've ever told. What would be the point of ever telling them? As a child, Robert would have been ostracised for being a bastard and Helen, well, she was too young to remember Michael on the few occasions she got a glimpse of him anyway.' Dulcie looked thoughtful. 'Had Michael returned I would have told them, but... but... he never came back, so I just never mentioned it. It seemed easier somehow...'

Dulcie turned to face Teagan. 'The thing is, I'm not sure you can see the resemblance with that young man of yours, but I can. To me it's *very* clear.'

Teagan was still busy trying to get her head around the last bombshell. 'What do you mean?'

'I think,' Dulcie looked back down at the newspaper cutting, 'that your Darren is something to do with my Michael. I think his father must be Michael's first son.'

• • • •

IN THE SHOWROOM, Mike watched a well-dressed woman eyeing up one of the BMW's like a hawk. She looked pretty interested. He'd always adopted the tactic of 'no pressure' selling, rather than jumping on prospective customers the second their toe crossed the threshold of his showroom, feeling that etiquette fared better than the aggressive approach, but the minute she glanced in their direction he'd be on her like a shot. Or he'd send Heath – no matter which. There was a decent mark-up on that motor and God only knew they could do with it.

He glanced at Heath standing in the small office to the left of him, still on the phone. He'd better have some decent news from that call.

Keeping an eye on the woman by the BMW, Mike watched Heath end the call and make his way through. 'Well?'

Heath shrugged. 'Nothing as yet, but she said she'll be continuing tonight.'

Mike sighed impatiently. 'And that's it? That's all she said?' He looked up at the ceiling. 'Jeez, this just isn't going to happen is it?'

Heath grinned. 'Patience, father. Patience.'

'I haven't got any fucking patience left! It ran out the same time my bastard overdraft did!' Mike folded his arms. 'Are you sure she's not just stringing us along?'

'I'm sure. She can't afford to. She's suggested though that I take Teagan out again.'

Mike threw himself into his leather chair. 'You've got to be joking? It cost a fortune last time.'

'That's as maybe and to be honest, I had no plans to repeat it even though she's texted me a couple of times. I mean, I didn't think I'd need to. Her part is done now, but Helen says it will help.'

Mike frowned. 'How the bloody hell will it help, apart from raise the minimum payment on my Barclaycard?'

'Helen said she'll get more leeway to dig around if Teagan's not there,' Heath explained. 'She was just telling me she's only looked in the cellar so far. There was nothing there, but she thinks they're probably stashed in the bedroom.'

'But you said she'd told the girl that she's sorting stuff out, didn't you, so how will it look strange?'

Heath shrugged. 'Dunno – it's her call, I suppose. I guess she knows what she's doing. She said Teagan has a habit of wanting to help and she can hardly have her hanging around whilst she goes through everything. What would she say if she finds them when Teagan's standing next to her? It's a big gaff, Dad. Helen's got a lot of digging to do.'

Mike sighed. 'What are you going to do then?'

'Well, Helen said she'll offer to look after Dulcie one night this week – pretend she wants to spend some time with her. Wednesday, she said. Once she's told Teagan that then I'll conveniently suggest going out again.'

Mike nodded and glanced back at the woman by the BMW. 'Before you do that, get your arse out there and offload that beamer to that snotty cow, will you?'

THIRTY SEVEN

TEAGAN'S HEAD was utterly scrambled. She stared at her mobile and massaged her temples.

```
Sorry I've been quiet - got a lot on at work.
Fancy dinner or drinks sometime this week? Weds
is good for me xx
```

Flicking onto her Facebook app, Teagan willed the mobile signal to remain stable enough to load Darren's profile – the 98,000th time she'd looked at it since last night.

Clicking on his picture, she zoomed in. She still couldn't see any resemblance to Robert Adams. Admittedly, she hadn't studied Robert and certainly couldn't gauge any similarities with Michael from that newspaper cutting. The resemblance between Michael and Robert was easy because they were so uncannily similar, but as for Darren, in her opinion there was no real likeness at all, short of dark hair and light eyes, but that could be said about a lot of people. It was ridiculous to base someone being someone's son, grandson or whatever purely on those factors.

Teagan pursed her lips. Although Dulcie was clearly being

truthful about Michael being Robert's father, she got the distinct impression that she was now back down the line of fabrication and dramatic stories. But all of this opened another can of worms. There was no way she could tell Helen about this one. How could she slip in that Dulcie had happened to mention that Robert had a different father to what they'd always believed? The answer was simple – she couldn't. It would cause no end of pain and anguish, not to mention, anger and what with Dulcie's illness and imminent move, this family was fractured enough as it was and she didn't want any hand in worsening that.

She took a deep breath and decided to pretend she didn't know this volatile piece of information and strongly wished she could unhear it.

Closing the Facebook app, Teagan stared at Darren's text again. She certainly wouldn't mention it to *him*. Rushing off to phone an ex-boyfriend on their first date was bad enough, but now he wanted to take her out again, she wouldn't mess that up too by hitting him with that. She shook her head in disbelief. Darren would think her crazy.

Teagan smiled to herself. She had a good feeling about where this was going. The only trouble was, when would she next have a free evening? It looked unlikely what with everything that was going on at the moment.

> Would love to. Not sure about Weds but will
> find out xx

Hitting send, Teagan placed her phone down and decided she'd better think about making Dulcie's lunch.

. . . .

JOE SHUT THE DOOR to the undertakers and managed two paces before dragging his fags out of his pocket. With fumbling fingers he shoved one in his mouth and rushed to light it.

Inhaling deeply, he leant against the wall hoping the

cigarette would get rid of the taste of embalming fluid he was sure was in his gob purely from breathing in the air inside the funeral directors.

Glancing to the left, he caught his reflection in the window – his image resembling that of a tramp, overlaid with the display of dusty plastic white lilies against a grey backdrop and of course a polished mahogany-looking coffin. In all fairness, there was little an undertaker could put in a window display to entice people in. They could hardly prop a corpse in the window, could they?

Joe shuddered and took another drag of his fag. He could still bloody taste it. *That smell.* It lingered in the air in there – a heavy, pervading mix of death, masked with scented chemicals. It must be psychological? It wasn't like they kept bodies there or embalmed them, was it?

Joe paled. *Or did they? Maybe they did?* He didn't know. He ran his hand over his head, brushing his overgrown fringe out of his eyes. The thought that he'd just spent the last hour surrounded by stiffs stacked up the other side of the wall whilst discussing what sort of coffin Alan would like, freaked him out. He'd never been in an undertakers before, neither had he arranged a funeral and all the stuff that went with it. Personally, he didn't think Alan would care what sort of wood his coffin had, let alone the sort of handles because he shouldn't even be in one!

Joe kicked his boot against the funeral director's wall, the anger over the unjust situation rearing its ugly head once again.

Oh Christ, this was shit. Why couldn't Dave have done this? The people in there had looked at him like an alien as they'd had to slowly explain what they meant by every single thing they asked. Well, how was he supposed to know? On the other hand, he couldn't do what Dave was doing either. Out of the two of them, Dave was the only one able to get a loan to cover the funeral because there was no way the bank would lend him a penny. Not these days.

'Got a light?'

'Yeah.' Joe mechanically took his lighter from his pocket and glanced in the direction of the gruff voice. *Fuck*. His bowels made worrying moves to lose control as he saw the voice belonged to one of the nutters – the uglier one. The scar on his face looking even more offensive in the daylight.

Wasn't this all done now? Wasn't it sorted? He'd got them the keys as arranged. It was finished, wasn't it?

Joe watched the man slowly raise the lighter to his own cigarette and waited for him to say something. Either that or set fire to him. *What did he want?*

He glanced around to see if anyone was in shouting distance should this freak attempt to murder him in public. He didn't feel particularly comfortable that he was standing next to this loony outside an undertakers either, but there was obviously a reason as to why he was here.

Joe forced himself to look back at the psycho and wanted to punch him for murdering his friend, but he wasn't going to do that. To deflect from his own raging cowardice and rather than concentrating on the man's scar, he found himself unable to draw his eyes from the man's mangled ear, coming to the conclusion he wasn't sure which was worse.

'I want you to arrange for the girl to be out of the house one night this week,' Keith growled, his voice low.

Joe watched the man suck on his fag as he glanced around. To anyone looking, it would just be two men having a random chat to pass the time. *Well, it wasn't a random chat.*

'What do you mean, arrange for the g...'

'Is everything always difficult for you to understand?' Keith snapped, a tone of warning in his voice. 'Just fucking arrange it so she's not there, alright?'

'But how?' Joe flapped. 'She's a live-in carer or something and I...

'I don't know and I don't fucking care!' Keith mumbled. 'Orders from the top. The boss wants no one about apart from the old girl.' He exposed his teeth in a half-smile/half-grimace. 'Do you understand that one?'

Joe nodded, panic fluttering. 'I didn't think I'd be needed again.'

Keith made a strange snorting sound and for a moment Joe hoped the man might keel over, but unfortunately he didn't.

'So did I,' Keith muttered. 'Just sort it. Believe it or not, the sooner I don't have to trail your scrawny arse around, the better. Phone me on the burner when it's sorted.'

'Ok,' Joe mumbled, not wanting to begin thinking about how he would arrange this. There was no way Teagan would agree to leaving the old bat unattended for the evening.

Keith went to walk away, then stopped and turned back. 'Oh, I almost forgot...'

Joe tensed with dread as the man shoved his shovel-like hand in his jacket, relieved to see the only thing he pulled out was an envelope.

'What's this?' Joe asked as Keith shoved the envelope into his hand.

Keith nodded towards the undertakers. 'The boss wanted to contribute.'

Joe suddenly felt a rush of indignation. 'Probably right, considering you bastards put him in there.'

Keith's cold eyes flashed dangerously. 'Don't push your luck, cunt – otherwise you'll be joining him.' He bared his teeth for good measure. 'I'll expect your call.'

Joe was still trembling by the time Keith had disappeared around the corner at the end of the road. That was very stupid of him to react like that. *Fuck, he needed a drink.*

He glanced at the fat envelope in his hand then quickly shoved it into his jacket. Alan wouldn't mind if he borrowed a few quid to get himself a drink or two to calm his nerves, would he? Besides, he needed to clear his head to think of a way of how he could face calling Teagan again.

THIRTY EIGHT

'MRS SHEPHERD?' the voice asked. 'This is DI Marshall.'

Helen rose from her desk and stretched the phone cable so that she could reach to close her office door. 'Yes? How can I help you?'

'I just wanted to bring you up to date with where we are with the investigation into Ken Manning's disappearance.'

Helen's heart sank. She'd already told them God knows how many times that she didn't know where he'd gone and she still didn't. Nothing had changed.

'Mrs Shepherd? Are you still there?'

'Yes, I was just thinking. Have there been any new developments? Have you found him?' she asked, noticing Joanne craning her neck to see into the office. *Nosy bitch.*

'Have you had any contact with Mr Manning since we last spoke? Anything at all? Or remembered anything that might help?'

'I've already told you everything I know and no, I haven't had any further contact with Ken. I'd have told you immediately had that been the case,' Helen snapped.

Ken hadn't been in contact and if he had, she'd have been tempted to wring his neck for leaving her in the lurch about the apartment. But it didn't matter – not now Robert was dealing with it. Which reminded her to call him and see how that was going.

'I just wanted to double check, being as Mr Manning's phone logs and emails showed a lot of activity between the two of you in the week or so leading up to his disappearance. Markedly different compared to your previous level of contact, which, shall we say, wasn't very frequent…'

Helen stared at the receiver. 'I hope you're not suggesting that I had anything to do with Ken's disappearance? We may not have been in regular contact until recently – he's an old friend, but we *are* in the same industry and, if you must know, I was interested in purchasing one of the properties he was marketing.'

'I'm not suggesting anything of the sort, Mrs Shepherd.'

Helen scowled, not missing the patronising tone in the detective's voice. 'The property is for my mother. She has *dementia*.'

'I'm sorry to hear that, but the reason for my call is to let you know that I'm afraid we've moved the investigation to a possible murder, rather than a missing persons case,' DI Marshall said.

'W-What? Murder? Why?' Helen cried. *So they thought he was dead?* Well, that put paid to Ken routing the sale of Footlights through Manning Sales and Lettings. *Shit.*

'Yes, Mr Manning's bank accounts have remained static since his disappearance. His phone records and emails show a similar lack of activity and there' been no use or reissuing of his passport.'

'Who has killed him then? Why would anyone want to kill him?' Helen blathered, wanting to say the expected things and having to at least pretend to be upset about their concerns.

'We aren't saying that this is what's happened. We're just widening our investigation to include all possibilities.' There was a pause. 'Did Mr Manning have any enemies that you were aware of, Mrs Shepherd?'

'No. Not as far as I know. As you are aware, we hadn't been in contact much before recently, but he didn't mention anything like that to me,' Helen said.

'Ok, well thank you, Mrs Shepherd. We'll be in contact again should there be anything else we need to ask or if there are new developments,' DI Marshall droned. 'And if you do happen to recall anyth…'

'Yes, I'll call you. Thank you for letting me know.' Helen abruptly replaced the receiver and stared at the phone. *Ken had hacked someone off then? Oh well…*

When her mobile rang almost immediately, Helen rolled her eyes and snatched it from her handbag. 'Yes?'

'Hi, love,' said James. 'I just wanted to…'

'What? What now?' Helen barked. 'What the hell is it now?' She grabbed her mug of coffee and slurped at it irritably.

'Nothing's wrong. It's just I didn't get much chance to see you this morning at breakfast and I felt we should clear the air. Are you alright?'

'Yes, James, I'm fine. I've only been out of the house for less than an hour. And as for clearing the air, that's not something I'm prepared to discuss whilst I'm at work.' Helen didn't want to discuss it anywhere else, either. What was there to discuss? Her husband was a prick who hassled her constantly, like the needy prat he was. And furthermore, he'd even resorted to trying to run to her brother behind her back.

And no, he hadn't seen much of her at breakfast because she'd purposefully left earlier than usual for that very reason. She couldn't stand being around him.

'You need to start talking to me, Helen,' James pushed. 'I know things are difficult at the moment and also know you've had money issues which you should have spoken to me about. There's also other stuff that I…'

'What? What did you say?' Helen's volume increased, causing more necks to crane in her direction from the main office. She forced herself to lower her voice. 'You're phoning me at *work* to accuse me of having money problems?'

Had Robert said something? Had he told James he was funding the apartment because she couldn't afford it? If he had, then he was even more of a piece of shit than she'd thought. Not that he was her *real* brother – only half. A fact making her life-long dislike of his aloofness and arrogant nature a lot more understandable. Understandable, being as on the face of it, they didn't share half as many genes as she'd once thought. From looks to personality, they were as different as it was possible to get.

'I'm not accusing you of anything,' James lied. 'We just really need a conversation about things.'

Helen reined in her temper. She wasn't about to explain anything to him. None of it was any of his damn business and nor would it be.

'Can we talk tonight when you get back?' James asked.

Helen heard that pleading twang in James' voice – the one which always made her want to scream. Everything about him made her want to scream. Yeah, she'd talk to him tonight and tell him she wanted a goddamn divorce – see how he liked that? But she wouldn't be wasting all night looking at his miserable bloody face. Neither was she spending hours with him when there were 1000 other more pressing things to deal with.

'As you know, I'll be back later so we'll talk, but I won't have time to have a long conversation about whatever seems to be niggling you,' she snapped.

'You're going back out? Where are you going?'

Helen clenched her jaw. *Questions, questions, always never-ending bloody questions.* 'If you must know, I want to spend some time with my mother.' She didn't know why she'd just said that. She didn't want to spend time with that woman at all. She wanted to slap the lying bitch around the face until she apologised for being a wanton slut who had engineered the death of her own husband, *that's* what she wanted.

Helen smiled, an idea forming. Spending the evening around Footlights wasn't a bad idea. She'd give that stupid girl the evening off which would allow her all night to dig around.

She could slip the old cow some extra pills to send her to sleep. A full evening with no distractions and no interfering. With any luck she'd find those jewels or at least be a damn sight closer to doing so.

'Look, I've got to dash. I'll be late for a meeting,' Helen lied. 'We'll talk before I go to mother's.' Promptly ending the call, she changed the ring settings of her mobile to silent.

Now she'd call Teagan and let her know that tonight was her lucky night. *God, she was generous.*

• • • •

'IT GOES WITHOUT SAYING that this car comes with a full MOT and we'll throw in six months' warranty too.' Heath gave the woman standing by the Lexus a beaming smile. 'The same deal applies to that stunning Audi you like the look of.' He nodded towards the red car across the other side of the showroom. 'Such a stunning colour too.'

He secretly hoped that out of the two cars, this woman picked the Audi because the Lexus was the one he used when going to Maidenhead. He didn't want to turn up in a different car the next time he picked Teagan up. Besides, he preferred the Lexus.

Feeling his mobile buzz in his trouser pocket, Heath smiled at the woman once again. 'I'll give you a few moments to think about it. Please let me know what you decide.' He nodded towards the office. 'I'll be in there when you're ready.'

Walking across the showroom, he pulled his mobile out and looked at the screen. *Talk of the Devil – a text message from Teagan*:

```
You won't believe this – Helen has given me the
night off. Is it too short notice to go out
tonight? X
```

Grinning, Heath walked into the office and held his phone up. 'Bingo! Helen's only gone and given Teagan the night off, which means only one thing – she's going in for a mega look around. We may be in luck. I've a good feeling she'll find those bloody lovely jewels.'

Mike looked up from the pile of bills spread over the desk. 'Then I suggest you get yourself up there and take her somewhere for the evening. She needs to be out of the house. Do me a favour though – somewhere less pricey this time, yeah?'

Heath tapped out his reply:

```
Fantastic! No, not too short notice. I'll pick
you up at 7. Can't wait. Xx
```

Pressing send, he smiled. *Today was the day – he could feel it.*

Scrolling through his contacts, Heath found Helen's mobile number and paced around the office as it rang out, eventually going to voicemail. 'Helen, it's Heath. I hear you've given a certain someone the night off. I'll be round at 7 to collect her, giving you a free run for the evening, ok? Any problems or you need to change the time, call me. Speak later.'

Ending the call, Heath smiled at his father. 'Right, I'll go and see if I can shift that red Audi onto that woman and then I'd best go home and get myself spruced up ready to get on the road.'

• • • •

JOE RESTED HIS HEAD against the moth-eaten upholstery of the Plough and Harrow and closed his eyes momentarily in the hope that the room might stop its never-ending spinning.

Some idiot had put Black Sabbath's *'Paranoid'* on the jukebox for the fourth time in a row and he was feeling even more deranged than he had when he'd first come in, which took some beating.

Rancidly hungover from yesterday's blowout, Joe was surprised he'd even woken up at all this morning, but somehow he had. He couldn't even recall getting home last night, let alone anything else, but being as he'd woken up in his own bed, albeit fully dressed, including his trainers, he'd obviously got back somehow.

At least Dave had been up for coming for a drink today so he didn't have to deal with the hair of the dog on his tod. It wasn't like Dave was a barrel of laughs though. He'd been miserable as sin since they'd got here a couple of hours ago and Joe would have thought the many pints they had so far would have cheered him up a bit, but no – Dave was still as moody as ever and it was starting to get on his nerves.

Opening his eyes, Joe waited for the bar to come into focus and then glanced at Dave staring forlornly into his pint. Sighing inwardly, he grabbed his drink and slugged three-quarters of it down in one go – it was already flat as buggery. 'Come on, Dave. Get that down your neck. It'll cheer you up.' *Hopefully…*

'Doesn't it bother you?' Dave said. 'Doesn't it bother you that we haven't got enough to give Alan a decent send-off? Because it bothers me.'

Joe frowned. *What was Dave talking about?* He vaguely remembered him saying something about getting the loan for the funeral.

Dave rolled his eyes in despair. 'For fuck's sake, Joe. You're that wankered all of the time you can't remember anything. I told you last night and I've been talking about it for the last *hour* and yet you haven't taken a word of it in.'

'No, no… I have,' Joe said, quickly. 'I didn't mean it like that.' *Shit. Quick. Think. What had Dave said?* He wracked his brains only to find no memory whatsoever.

Dave pursed his lips. 'Make a fucking effort! I know this has got to you, but you're not the only one.' He necked the rest of his pint. 'I said, we're five hundred quid short for the funeral and there's nowhere else I can ask.'

Joe blinked. 'The bank didn't give you the loan?'

'Of course they did, but they'd only give me two grand. You said the funeral's going to cost two and a half?'

Joe felt a rush of nausea run over him. He slapped a ten pound note on the table and shakily stood up. 'Get another round in. I just need a piss.'

Staggering off to the Gents leaving Dave staring bemusedly after him, Joe slammed the door of the one and only cubicle and leant against the wall, choosing to ignore the scrunched up dirty toilet roll on the floor, precariously close to his feet. He also averted his eyes from the toilet itself, suspecting that looking into that would cause the contents of his stomach to evacuate his body – not that there was much in there, apart from beer. He couldn't remember the last time he'd eaten anything.

Aside from that, toilet bowls reminded him of having his head shoved down one not that long ago. An experience he was not happy to be reminded of. But what had surged from his memory was worse than that. A *lot* worse.

Fumbling in his pocket, Joe pulled out the envelope the nutter had given him yesterday. Finding it empty, his heart raced. *The money must be loose in his pocket. It couldn't have disappeared.*

Shoving his hand into his inside pocket, Joe was relieved to find a load of bunched up notes. Pulling them out, he frantically straightened them one by one, his stomach plunging. *Where was the rest? Where was the fucking rest?*

He quickly thumbed through the twenties. *Oh, shit. No! Come on!*

Pushing his hand back into his pocket, he felt around, growing sicker by the second. He rummaged through all his other pockets, finding one lone tenner and a mangled betting slip. Totting up what he had, Joe swallowed hard. *Jesus wept!* That envelope had contained two grand yesterday and he knew that because he'd counted it in the pub toilet before he'd started at the bar. How could he only have seven hundred left?

Slowly the dregs of what he could remember of yesterday afternoon, which had morphed into the evening and then most of the night, slithered into his mind. He knew he'd spent a shed load in the pub and also knew, by what was on his bedside table this morning, he'd bought fags and more beer from the offy, as well as scoring a decent amount of weed from a dealer he didn't care to recall. *But 1300 quid? He'd spent 1300 quid?*

Ah, but then there had been that bet. He had hazy recollections of putting an extortionate amount on a horse, the name of which escaped him. He could only presume he'd lost…

Fuck. Fuck. FUCK.

Sweat ran down the back of Joe's stained T-shirt as he took a hundred quid worth of grubby twenties from the pile, shoving the rest back in the envelope. At least he still had enough money to make up what was needed for the funeral costs. But how would he tell Dave that the nutter had given him two grand and he'd inadvertently blown most of it? Shit – Dave would go apeshit.

Coming out of the cubicle, Joe stared at his reflection in the piece of mirror attached to the wall above the lone rusted-up sink. He looked like shit as well as feeling like it. A fucking tramp, that's what he looked like. *Christ, he needed to sort himself out.*

Joe walked back into the bar and stumbled his way across the room, pleased to see Dave had got another round in. Sitting back down, he scraped the change off the table and shoved it into his jeans pocket. *This would work.* 'Don't worry about the shortfall for the funeral,' he said, managing to manoeuvre his face into a smile.

'How can I not worry?' Dave moaned. 'It's alright for you – nothing bothers you anymore.'

'That's not true,' Joe countered. More stuff bothered him than Dave could ever realise, but he wouldn't tell him about it. If he knew those blokes were still on the scene, he'd go batshit. *Completely* batshit.

What he didn't know wouldn't hurt him, but it would hurt *all* of them if he got any of it off his chest and then Dave, the prat, opened his gob. 'That's why I've been so long in the bogs. I was just checking before I said anything cos I didn't want to get your hopes up.'

Dave frowned. 'What are you going on about?'

Joe leaned across the table, keeping his voice as low as possible. 'I've got the rest of the money for Al's funeral. With the loan you've got and this, we'll be able to make the bill.'

'What? How?' Dave eyed Joe suspiciously.

Joe shrugged. 'Thought I'd chance my luck on a little bet yesterday. Must have been the luck of the alcohol. Anyway, I ran a bit of an accumulator and pulled in – wait for it, 700 quid!'

Dave nearly choked on a mouthful of lager. '700 quid? Are you serious?'

'Absolutely!' Joe grinned. 'It's in my pocket. 500 quid to make up the funeral costs, 100 quid to buy us some new clobber for the funeral itself, which leave 100 quid to get bladdered tonight, plus a curry on the way home. What do you reckon?'

Dave beamed. 'Fucking hell! Thank God for that! That's really generous of you, mate. I know you're strapped for cash.'

Joe waved his hand dismissively, also to help mentally diffuse his raging guilt. 'Nah, it's nothing. It's all cool and the least I can do. So, let's drink up and get the next round in.'

'I'm up for that,' Dave smiled. 'You're a good mate.'

Joe grinned. *No he wasn't, he was a shit one*. He felt bad, but not bad enough to do anything about it. He'd also remembered that he was supposed to be calling Teagan last night and was fairly sure he hadn't got around to it. He could hardly do that now with Dave here.

He'd wait until Dave next went for a slash and then he'd call and see when she next had a night off.

THIRTY NINE

NERO WATCHED KEITH help himself to a handful of delicately cut sandwiches from one of the many plates arranged on the huge buffet tables and nudged him sharply. 'Pack that in! Jonah and Lena aren't even here yet.'

Keith shoved a crustless quarter of bread containing the finest Wiltshire ham and Dijon mustard into his mouth and pushed the edge in with his fingers. 'Aw, fuck off. I'm starving. Jonah won't mind.'

Nero scowled. *Jonah would mind.* He'd mind very much. Not about Keith's rudeness over the food. Keith may have only had eyes for the grub and the open bar since he'd arrived, but *he'd* noticed the rest. And judging by the on-edge looks on the faces of the rest of the firm dotted around the room, they had too.

Jonah would *definitely* notice and he wouldn't be impressed.

Nero nodded in acknowledgment to a man smiling in his direction as he passed. It was that bloke off EastEnders; he couldn't remember the guy's name, but it was him all the same. Not that he'd watched it for years.

In addition to members of the firm, their wives or

girlfriends and a healthy assortment of dancing girls, there were also many faces he recognised from the TV. His eyebrows furrowed. Lena must have enjoyed seeing how many famous faces she could use Jonah's clout to invite, but would bet his bottom dollar Jonah wouldn't have a clue who most of these alleged celebs were. He didn't either.

Half of the security and the majority of the dancers were still at work in the main club downstairs. It wasn't like *everyone* could be up here, but this shindig would undoubtedly be running well into the early hours, so they'd have time to join in after the show, no doubt.

Nero glanced at his watch. Jonah and Lena should be here anytime soon. The press was assembled ready by the door, so it wouldn't be long.

He was still confused as to why Jonah would be doing any of this with Lena, but hey – none of his business. He glanced around at the décor once again and sighed.

Spotting Gwen mingling with the guests, Nero dragged Keith away from the buffet then made his way over to Gwen. 'You look nice,' he smiled, then nodded towards the tables. 'I take it Jonah isn't aware of the party's theme?'

Gwen rolled her eyes and gave Nero a tight smile. 'I only hope he keeps it together when he sees it. You haven't seen the cake yet either…'

'Don't tell me that's a diamond too?' Nero gasped. 'Jesus Christ. Could Lena have picked anything more insulting? Is she taking the piss?'

'I don't think she's got the brains for that.' Gwen grabbed the arm of Nero's tuxedo sleeve. 'I don't trust her.'

Nero grinned. 'She's a bimbo - harmless enough, just thick as shit.' He glanced around the room once again. 'Clearly thick as shit.'

Sensing a sudden change in the atmosphere, Nero watched the press scuffle to get into prime position. 'I'm guessing the guests of honour have arrived?'

. . . .

HELEN PUT HER FOOT DOWN as she sped along the road towards home. She wasn't looking forward to putting up with James' whinging face, but she had no intention of allowing that to drag out any longer than necessary. She was only going back to grab those pills, so she'd listen to what he'd got to bleat on about and then get over to Footlights.

She glanced at the clock on the dashboard. *Already 6 o'clock, damn it.* She rarely spent a full day at work on a Saturday, but she had so much paperwork to catch up with. All this other business had made her slack with the admin side of things lately, so she'd had to make the effort to bring that up to date.

At least one of her sales had unexpectedly closed, meaning a nice bit of commission was finally coming her way.

Besides, she was in no rush to get home early as that meant more time with James. The longer she spent listening to the rubbish coming from his mouth, the more likely she'd lose her temper and waste time arguing when her time was much better spent looking for what was important at Footlights.

Her face cracked into a smile, tinged with smug satisfaction. She was definitely the shining star in Teagan's book. The stupid girl could hardly believe she was getting an extra evening off. Helen had turned the charm on, alright. She'd promised to be at Footlights by 7 o'clock and Teagan had been both pleasantly surprised and grateful when Helen had insisted it was the 'least' she could offer for all her hard work.

Her face cracked into an even wider smile. It all fitted in nicely. The voice mail Heath had left matched perfectly with her plans and she didn't need to rearrange anything at all.

He was another thick bastard. Thinking that he and his idiotic father would benefit from anything she found. *Would they hell?*

All she had to do now was to make sure her mother buggered off to bed out of the way and she'd be sorted. Every second spent with that woman and not screaming that she knew the sordid truth got harder all the time, but she'd keep it together.

On the up side, she'd also managed a quick call in to Robert and the completion date for the Oak Apple apartment was next week. *Wonderful.* He hadn't mentioned anything else about James, so it looked like her prat of a husband had quit with his snooping around as well, which was good. However, she was still going to have it out with him about that.

Pulling into her driveway, Helen leapt out of the Mercedes, spotting James' car. Irritation shot up her back and her neck became tense as she headed straight for the garage. She'd grab those extra pills before going into the house.

Closing the garage door behind her, Helen got to work moving the toolboxes and workbench. *Where was the box? Where was her goddamn box? She'd put it back the other day, so where had it gone?*

'Looking for these?'

Helen swung around, seeing James holding a box. *Her box. What the hell?*

'All that time...' James stepped from the house into the garage through the adjoining door. He put the box containing the tablets on the workbench. 'I spent days terrified that you were ill. I thought you were depressed – these... these pills... these antidepressants and anti-anxiety drugs... Then after what the chemist said, I realised one of these... well, I was terrified you had Parkinson's.'

Helen was rooted to the spot, processing what James was saying. *How long had he known about this? He'd asked the chemist? Jesus. Ok, think. What could she say?* 'You thought I had Parkinson's?' A huge rush of annoyance flooded her. '*Parkinson's*? Do I look like I've got bloody Parkinson's?'

James screwed his face up as he fought to keep his emotions under control. 'I was horrified, Helen. I thought you were self-medicating and I was gutted that you hadn't come to me with your problems.'

Helen's eyes narrowed. *The stupid prick.* 'You've been going through my things? How dare you! How bloody well dare y...'

'But then I found *this.*' James pulled a copy of the remortgage documentation from his pocket and watched his wife's face morph into pure rage. 'You remortgaged our home and ploughed the money into Shepherd, Percival and Proctor? Do you not think you should have discussed that with me?'

'With *you*?' Helen shrieked. 'Why? It's not like you've ever contributed anything! I've worked my backside off for years whilst you sat there and...'

'We're supposed to be married, Helen. It almost destroyed me thinking you were unwell and it really hurts that you don't think me worthy of being included when you've basically given all of our money to your business.'

Helen eyes flashed and she slammed her handbag down. '*Our* money? It's mine. *I* earnt it, not you. I don't have to discuss anything with you. And, oh my heart bleeds that you felt hurt and distressed.' She scowled venomously, looking James up and down with contempt. 'And married? Yes, that was another mistake I made. A *massive* one. You're ridiculous and can't be trusted. I want a divorce.'

She moved forward to snatch up the box, jumping back when James slammed his hand down on the top of it.

'It took me ages to work it out, but it's *you* who can't be trusted.' James studied Helen. 'I looked for every excuse in the book, but I couldn't ignore what I'd seen with my own eyes.'

Helen laughed shrilly, her eyes cold. 'Oh and what did you see, you fount of all wisdom? What conclusion did you reach?'

James paused. *He hadn't wanted it to be like this, but she'd left him with no choice.* 'Dulcie hasn't got dementia. You've been fabricating her illness, I know you have.'

Helen laughed again, but this time not quite so loudly. James couldn't know that. He was full of shit. 'Don't be so ridiculous!'

James smiled weakly. 'I saw you, Helen. I saw you putting

those tablets into a vitamin bottle. The vitamins you've been insisting your mother takes.'

Helen felt cold and buzzy. Suffocation rose up from her feet, encompassing her in a black shroud.

'I've done my research and the combination of those pills can mimic dementia-like symptoms,' James continued, seeing Helen's mind whirring. 'You've set it all up. You're ill, Helen – just not in the way I thought. You need help.'

Helen trembled with unbridled fury. 'Ill? I'm not ill! You don't know what you're talking about.'

'Yes I do and it stops here!' James moved to stand into front of Helen.

'Get out of my way. You're ridiculous. This is all in your head. And you've been hassling my brother too? Asking him about money, no doubt? Trying to catch me out, you stupid prick?' she spat. 'And what a surprise... he hasn't got back to you? That will be because he things you're a fucking brainless twat as well!'

'Robert loves his mother – unlike *you*!'

Helen laughed sarcastically. 'You don't know the first thing about anything!'

'I've sent Robert copies of everything. He deserves to know what you're doing. He'll phone the police, I know he will. You're crazy, Helen, *crazy*!'

Helen froze. *He'd written to Robert?* Her anger morphed into white rage. 'How dare you threaten me! How dare you interfere.'

Grabbing a wrench from the workbench, she lashed out, hearing a sickening thud as it connected with James' skull.

As he dropped to the floor, screaming loudly, his hands raised over his head, Helen continued striking out, her eyes wild. 'Shut. The. Fuck. Up. SHUT UP!'

JONAH RESISTED THE URGE to push Lena down the flight of stairs they'd just climbed and instead forced himself to smile at her.

Stopping outside the entrance to the VIP suite, Lena turned, picking something invisible off Jonah's tuxedo shoulder with one of her talons. 'Do I look nice, babe?' she fished, running her hand over the front of her skin-tight diamante encrusted dress. 'You don't think anyone will be able to tell I'm pregnant, do you? We don't want to give the game away.'

Jonah ran his eyes over Lena, the shimmering dress looking like it was painted on. Cut in a deep 'V' down to the waist, her huge breasts scaffolded into place with strategically placed invisible tape holding them against gravity and the shimmering material outlining the pert and perfectly rounded shape of her countless implants, giving a cleavage to die for.

Her oversized bust was at odds to her tiny waist and narrow hips, the dress clinging to her figure perfectly, only accentuating her washboard stomach was still that – completely flat. The dress also showcased her long legs, one visible through the high side split at the left and despite his daily increasing hatred for her, Jonah could not help his body reacting to the sight of her.

Almost able to read Jonah's thoughts, Lena lightly traced her hand over his crotch. 'Hmm, like I thought... I look more than fine!'

Irritated by his body's lack of control, Jonah rearranged himself so that his fast-growing erection wouldn't be visible to the hordes of press photographers waiting for them to make their entrance through the double doors.

Lena took Jonah's arm and whispered, 'After the party you won't be able to help but to fuck me senseless, baby.'

Hating himself slightly more than he hated Lena, Jonah gritted his teeth, his throbbing arousal strong. 'Let's just get this done,' he growled, stepping forward to push the double doors open.

Standing with Lena on his arm, Jonah could see little apart from the explosion of flash bulbs going off around them. He kept his accustomed smile in place as they posed for photographs, the raucous cheering deafening and then moved forward amidst a host of congratulations and well wishes.

The heavy bass from the top of the range music system cranked up and Jonah wished he was anywhere else but here. Aside from this party which had been foisted on him, he was still smarting over the ring he'd bought for Lena. Wanting no part in it, he'd feigned that she should choose one herself to ensure she liked it. He hadn't been at all surprised to see the size of the rock she'd picked. *Nor the price.* Not that it made any difference. She'd always cost him a fortune and now he was marrying her, the bill would run for eternity.

Catching the eye of Nero as he moved into the room, Jonah silently questioned the man's expression, then froze noticing the twice-lifesize image of him and Lena behind the stage. His irritation escalated. Lena knew things like that made him cringe. He may well be well known around the city, but he didn't want to be on a humongous billboard like in Piccadilly Circus and that's how all of this felt. *A fucking circus.*

He watched Lena air kissing random people who he had no

clue who they were and was about to get a drink when he saw them.

Freezing to the spot, his eyes narrowed at the diamonds making the centrepiece of a table. His eyes darted to the next table and there were more. *Every* table was the same...

Feeling his blood boiling, Jonah snatched a flute of champagne off the tray of a waiter. It was only then that he saw balloons printed with a diamond logo and banners emblazoned with the naff statement; *'Congratulations to the city's most sparkling couple'.*

'Take it you don't like the theme?' Nero muttered as he approached.

'Is she winding me up?' Jonah spat out of the side of his mouth, his face still outwardly neutral. 'Did you know about this?'

'Not until I got here.' Nero could only hope Jonah would keep it together. 'Just let it go over your head.'

'It's bloody difficult,' Jonah hissed. 'Any news?'

'Keith had words with the stoner. He's arranging for the girl to be out of the house.'

Jonah nodded, his eyes watching Lena make the most of the circle of women surrounding her and fawning over the huge diamond on her finger. *More diamonds...* 'What day will it be?'

'Waiting for confirmation of that,' Nero said, noticing Keith still making his way through the buffet.

'Jonah!' Lena screeched, tripping towards him in her sky-high glittering stilettoes. 'The press wants a photo of us in front of our big picture.' She proudly pointed to the embarrassing oversized image. 'Isn't it great? It took me ages to find somewhere able to produce one of such a size.'

Jonah glared at Nero, seeing him swallowing his smile.

'Wait until you see the cake!' Lena gushed. 'You'll *love* it!'

Nero took this opportunity to wander off in search of a proper drink. He couldn't deal with this champagne lark. *A pint would do, thanks.* He also wanted to make himself scarce before Jonah saw the cake and only hoped he'd have calmed down a bit by that point.

. . . .

SHAKING VIOLENTLY, Helen scrubbed at her body, frantically ridding herself of her husband's blood and closed her eyes as the jets of water from the shower cascaded over her head.

She'd watched James' face as she'd hit him. Seen the shock register with the first blow, immediately changing into fear as his legs buckled under him and he'd dropped to the floor to cower beneath her.

He'd tried to protect himself from the second blow. Oh yes, she'd seen him doing that, but it didn't work. Of course it didn't. And furthermore, she wouldn't have allowed it. He'd gone too far, the stupid, *stupid* bastard.

The image of that chunk of something, presumably brain, which shot out, sticking to her face, the rest going down her blouse, as the wrench had connected with his skull the second time was etched in her mind.

Helen scrubbed at her hair, her face. *Got to get it off. Got to get it off*, she chanted to herself, feeling bile rising.

Oh, but he couldn't even attempt to protect himself from the third or the fourth hit, could he? No, he couldn't. Because he knew it was over.

The bloody moron, the idiotic fool. He'd fucked everything up.

Stepping out of the shower, Helen kicked her blood soaked clothes to one side and grabbed a fluffy towel from the warmer rail. Quickly drying herself, she wiped the condensation from the bathroom mirror and stared at her reflection. She'd have to reapply her makeup now. *Christ, come on!*

The shrill ringing of Helen's mobile made her swing around violently, almost slipping on the wet tiled floor. 'Yes?' she snapped. *At least it wasn't James. It would never be James again. Ha ha.*

'Oh, Teagan... hello. No... no, I'm still coming.' Helen

glanced at the clock. *Shit. 7.15.* 'No, no... I'm fine... I just got a bit held up...'

Jamming her mobile in her neck, Helen stepped into some fresh knickers and quickly pulled on clean trousers. 'Look, don't worry. My mother will be perfectly fine for twenty minutes or so without you.' *Just go, Teagan for God's sake.*

Helen dragged a comb through her towel-dried hair and rolled her eyes forcing herself not to scream at the girl. 'I appreciate you're uncomfortable with leaving her... Yes, I know... but you don't need to worry.'

She was wasting precious time and she had to get out of here away from... from what was down in the garage. And Robert? If Robert read that letter, he'd be here like a shot. Although she knew he tended to leave his post to mount up and read it at the end of the week, like the weirdo he was, she still had to accept that it was a possibility.

That was of course if James had been telling the truth about writing to Robert in the first place.

Realising that Teagan was still procrastinating about leaving the old bat on her own, Helen gritted her teeth. 'Look, Teagan, she's my mother so I'm hardly going to let her down, am I? It's your well-deserved night out, so I insist you go as planned. It's not your fault I'm running late.'

No, it's James' fault. Fucking James, always James...

'I'll be there in less than half an hour ok, so stick her in front of the TV and give her a cup of tea. I doubt she'll even notice you've gone. I'm about to leave now, so off you go.'

Walking into the bedroom, Helen hung up, slinging the mobile onto the bed. She didn't need Teagan flapping and making things even worse.

Not even bothering to sit down, she grabbed her makeup, rapidly slapping on a bit of foundation and powder, along with a slick of lip gloss. *That would have to do.*

Shoving a selection of clothes into her weekend bag, Helen pushed her makeup bag in too, then ran back into the bathroom to grab her toiletries and toothbrush. There was no other way around it now. She had to locate those diamonds tonight and then get out of the country. *Damn James and his interference.*

Everything was ruined. *Everything.* All she'd worked for all her life she'd have to leave behind: her business, the house, the money from Footlights, the lot…

Rushing back into the bedroom, Helen opened the wardrobe and fumbled with the code for her small safe. Grabbing her passport and the small wad of cash in there, she crammed the lot into her handbag.

But wait… Maybe she was panicking? She needed to calm down and clear her head. Once she'd located those diamonds, she'd be in a better position to think straight. It was perfectly feasible that someone could have come into the garage and attacked James whilst she was out, was it not?

Teagan would witness she'd spoken to her at this time, which proved she was doing something else. Helen looked at the bag she'd packed. *Maybe she shouldn't take this after all? It would look suspicious.*

Quickly emptying it, she placed everything back where it had come from and kicked the bag back under the bed. If James hadn't sent that letter, or Robert hadn't yet read it, then she could 'discover' James' body when she returned later and deal with losing Robert's letter, if there was one, another time.

Helen flapped her hand in front of her face to get herself some air. *Stop panicking.*

Taking one more glance in the mirror, Helen hurried downstairs, walked past the adjoining door to the garage, leaving it purposefully open without looking in. Grabbing her jacket, handbag and car keys, she left the house.

FORTY ONE

HEATH HOVERED in the hallway at Footlights. 'What did Helen say?' he asked when Teagan returned. He was surprised Helen was late. He'd heard nothing from her to say the time he'd suggested wasn't convenient.

Teagan glanced through the door into the sitting room at Dulcie unmoving in one of the wing-back chairs. 'Helen said to carry on and go and that she wouldn't be long.'

'Right, let's do exactly that,' Heath grinned, moving to the front door. The sooner they got out of here, the sooner Helen could get on with searching.

'I don't know...' Teagan faltered, lowering her voice. 'Dulcie's really out of sorts. I'm worried about leaving her and feel I should stay until Helen arrives and...'

'You'll do no such thing!' Dulcie silently appeared behind Teagan. 'Go on. Off you go. I'll be fine. I'd be even finer if Helen wasn't coming to babysit.'

Teagan saw Dulcie studying Darren intensely and hoped she wouldn't ask him anything. The way she was wordlessly scrutinising him was painful and she didn't have the first clue how she would explain something like that to him.

Heath awkwardly soaked up the intense stare emanating

from the tiny woman in the doorway – the root of all his problems, as well as equally the answer to them. The way she was looking at him was... it was strange – like she could see through him. 'If you're sure you're going to be alright, Mrs Adams, then we'll make tracks.'

'You even sound like him...' Dulcie said quietly, her voice far away.

'Sorry? What?' Heath glanced at Teagan as she took Dulcie's arm and gently steered her back into the sitting room. *What had the mad old cow just said?*

Sitting back in the chair, Dulcie stared up at Teagan. 'He does. He sounds just like him. That boy sounds like...'

'Dulcie, *please*?' Teagan begged, glancing over her shoulder, hoping Darren hadn't heard. 'Now, can I get you a drink or put the TV on?'

Dulcie flapped her hand. 'No, nothing. I'm fine. Go and have a good evening.'

'Ok, if you're really sure?'

'I'm sure.' Dulcie's ice-blue eyes rested on Teagan. 'Don't keep your man waiting.'

As Teagan left the sitting room, Heath opened the door, holding it for her to pass through. Following her down the stone steps to the road, he glanced over his shoulder back at the house and shivered seeing Dulcie Adams at the large bay window, watching. *That woman knew – he could feel it. He didn't know how, but she knew...*

Glad to reach the Lexus, he opened the passenger door for Teagan, then moved around to the drivers' side and fired the engine. 'Where do you fancy going? Dinner? Drinks? Both?'

'I'm not hungry, so unless you are, drinks somewhere is fine.'

'Ok.' Heath knew his father would be relieved about that. Although he was bloody starving, drinks would have to suffice.

Hearing her mobile buzz, Teagan fished it from her bag, hoping it wasn't Helen saying she couldn't make it after all. Having to ask Darren to turn the car around now they'd finally got out would not be good. On top of that she felt awkward, unsure whether she should kiss him or hold his hand? He'd made no attempt at physical contact, so she didn't know where their relationship, if they had one, actually stood. One shared kiss before she'd screwed up last time was one thing, but where did things go from here?

Unlocking her phone, Teagan's heart sank to see a text from Joe. Whatever it was, whatever had happened, she wasn't dealing with it. *Not tonight.*

She reluctantly opened the message:

```
Hi Teag, when r u next free? Wld like to tk u
for a drink to say soz. J x
```

Teagan frowned. All the years she'd wanted Joe to make an effort and now they weren't together, he was. But it didn't matter – she wouldn't go out with him again, even as friends. Although she didn't hate him, his behaviour over his drugs and those men had put paid to any lurking residue of hankering after him. Joe had killed off the remnants of any feelings for him, so in some respects, his shitty ways had done her a favour:

```
Let's just leave things as they are. I'm out
at the mo. Have a good night. T x
```

She stared at the kiss she'd placed at the end of the text, wondering whether she should delete that or not. She'd also thought about saying she was out with her new boyfriend, but was that even true?

'Trouble?' Heath took his eyes off the road for a second to look at Teagan.

Pressing send, Teagan shook her head. 'No, not anymore. All the hassle is over now.'

With what Joe had very nearly involved her with, hassle was a bit of an understatement, but she wasn't about to embarrass herself telling Darren her ex was a stoner who'd inadvertently made her out to be a drugs mule to a pair of dodgy dealers. *No thank you.*

'I thought we'd go to one of those nice wine bars in town, if that's alright with you?' Heath said. He'd looked up a few bars in Maidenhead on the internet and there were a couple that looked decent. 'How about The Sommelier?'

Teagan frowned. 'The Sommelier? Wasn't that the pub which used to be called, oh what was it now? It was that place with the big fireplace.'

Heath bit his lip. *How would he know? He'd never been to bloody Maidenhead before all of this. What was a common pub name?* 'Erm, was it The Swan?'

'The Swan? There's never been a pub called that in town. Not to my knowledge anyway.'

Heath laughed nervously. *Bollocks.* 'I must be getting mixed up. It's been several years since I've been here.'

'Whatever it used to be called, let's go there. Hey, I wonder if we'll bump into anyone from school?' Teagan would have been very concerned if she knew how much Heath was hoping they wouldn't bump into anyone from a school he had never attended.

• • • •

JOE HADN'T HAD SUCH A GOOD TIME IN AGES. Lying face down on the green covering of the pool table, he laughed hysterically. His attempt to pot the black had resulted in him drunkenly following the cue, ending with him faceplanting.

Dave bent over, leaning on his thighs in an attempt to control his mirth. Many pints and several joints had lifted both of their maudlin spirits, but they were now having difficulty in controlling themselves.

'Oih!' the barman yelled. 'Get off the fucking pool table. You'd better not have ripped the felt!'

Still laughing, Dave dragged Joe upright. 'Come on, we'll get chucked out at this rate.'

Helping Joe to the edge of the table, Dave laughed again as

Joe's right leg folded as he stood up, resulting in him tipping half his pint down his T-shirt.

Wiping the tears of laughter from his face, Joe staggered towards the toilets. 'Gotta have me a leak before I piss myself,' he shouted loudly.

Ignoring the dirty looks from the barman, he bounced off the walls in his pursuit to reach the Gents. The miserable sod could glare all he liked, but if he knew what a shit couple of weeks him and Dave had had, then he wouldn't begrudge them having a laugh.

Opening the toilet door into his own face, Joe staggered inside, walking straight into another man trying to get out. 'Sorry, mate,' he muttered, weaving out of the way.

Dear God, he was *steaming*. He had no idea how many pints he'd sunk, but it was way too many. He'd feel rough as fuck come the morning, but sod it, he needed this blow out. Swaying from side to side, he aimed at the urinal, hoping not too much piss was going on his trainers.

At least Teagan wasn't giving him any grief. Ok, so she wasn't interested in going out for a drink, which was a better result than he could have hoped for. More importantly, she didn't seem suspicious of him having anything to do with her missing keys.

Joe frowned. She'd got a new fella by the sounds of it, poor bastard. Wonder how long it would take her to nag him to death or stalk him day and night? Yep, it was all good. Everything he wanted to be over, now was.

Oh shit! He was supposed to call that nutter and let him know when Teagan was next out.

Joe wobbled as he did his flies up. He'd got distracted with that quiz game Dave had been playing, then got involved with pool. Calling that psycho had, well… it had slipped his mind.

Shit, shit, shit. Pulling the burner phone from his pocket, it slipped from his fingers onto the filthy floor underneath the urinals. 'Christ!' he muttered, swaying as he picked the phone up, wiping it down his jeans.

Pressing the only contact on the phone – Alan, Joe tried to concentrate whilst the phone rang out. *If the bloke couldn't be arsed to answer, it was hardly his fault, was it?*

'Yeah?'

Joe winced, barely able to hear the gravelly voice of the man over the deafening music. *Where the hell was he? A fucking rave?* 'It's Joe.'

'And?'

'The girl's out. You said you wanna know when she's gonna be out. Well, she's out,' Joe slurred.

'What, now? Tonight?' The gruff voice barked. 'And you've only just thought to fucking tell me?'

'I've only just found out,' Joe lied.

'And the old girl's on her tod?'

Joe paused. *How did he know? Did Teagan say that? Did he even ask? He couldn't remember.* 'Yeah, as far as I know.'

The call clicked off and Joe stared at the phone, four copies of it swimming in front of his face. Shrugging, he stuffed it back into his pocket and made his way back to the bar, hoping Dave had the sense to get another round sorted in his absence.

FORTY TWO

AS MUCH AS SHE DIDN'T WANT TO, checking on Lena was the decent thing to do. Now Jonah had appeared back in the VIP suite – alone, Gwen knew she had to make sure Lena was ok. She'd seen Jonah's face when the cake was wheeled out. The expression was only fleeting before he'd concealed it behind his trained mask, but she'd seen his fury if only for a split second.

Shortly after the cake debacle and the accompanying photos, Jonah had disappeared, taking Lena with him. Gwen had whispered to him not to lose it, but she'd been watching him all night and could see his rising anger clear as day. *Maybe she should have warned him about the cake?*

Slipping down the staff corridor off the rear of the VIP suite, Gwen guessed Jonah could only have taken Lena to either *her* office or his. And she suspected it was hers. Pushing open the door she saw Lena busy texting. 'Lena?'

As Lena turned, black rivulets of mascara down her cheeks, Gwen's heart sank. 'Come now, don't upset yourself. You can fix your makeup.'

Lena eyed Gwen malevolently. Putting her mobile down, she started cutting a fat line of cocaine on the desk.

'What do you think you're doing?' Gwen yelled, all concern for Lena going out of the window. 'You can't do that! You know how Jonah feels about that on the premises. I came to check you were alright, but I can see I needn't have bothered.'

After running a rolled-up twenty pound note along the line, Lena sniffed hard, then expertly wiped all traces of residue from under her nose. 'I'm perfectly fine. Jonah just wanted a word, that's all.'

It had been more than a word. The minute he'd told her he needed to talk, she'd thought his resolve to wait until later before ripping her clothes off had failed him, but this was quashed the second they'd got around the corner and he'd dragged her into the office by her hair.

She wouldn't lie and say she hadn't panicked. He'd been mad – like *really* mad. And he'd scared her. His eyes had been feral as he'd gripped her around the throat. Lena swallowed uncomfortably, her neck still raw from Jonah's hands. *Maybe she had pushed things a little too far?*

People might think she had the IQ of a Pond Skater, but how wrong were they? They could think what they liked, but all that mattered was marrying him. Once she'd done that, then the world was her oyster, but she needed to get him down the damn aisle first.

Luckily, she still had the baby pawn to use, so turning on the tears, she'd apologised profusely, pretending she hadn't meant to upset him, but it was only when she'd screamed to think of the baby had he released his grip.

She'd allowed her actions on planning the party run away with her. She should have been more careful. But as far as Gwen sticking her nose in, pretending she cared; pretending to come and see if she was ok? *Yeah, right…* The old bat was trying to set her up.

'Lena? Did you hear what I said?' Gwen snapped, her sympathy having well and truly dissolved. 'You're not to do that here.'

'I think you'll find I can do what I like! This...' Lena waved her arm around the office. '...will soon be my domain.'

Gwen couldn't help but quietly chuckle – a short, yet sarcastic laugh. *This girl had a screw loose.* 'Is that so?'

After inspecting her nostrils again for good measure, Lena closed her compact case. Gwen Vella had no idea she was screwed. *Finished.*

Remaining silent with nothing but the trace of a sneer as a response, Lena savoured the moment for as long as possible. See how long it took to rile the oh, so perfect Gwen. She perched on the edge of the desk; one stiletto dangling from the end of her foot as she crossed her long legs.

Gwen sighed. 'I don't know what you're playing at, young lady, but it won't wash. You're causing problems for everyone, ructions with the girls and this theme for the party? Well...'

'The girls?' Lena tapped a false nail on the desk in a steady rhythm. 'Oh yes, the *girls*. You mean, me separating the wheat from the chaff? You mean, me wanting to get this side of the club running like clockwork, rather than the shabby way *you* run it? The way you've been *allowed* to run it because you think being here so long gives you the right to do a shit job?'

Despite lighting a slow-burning fuse, Gwen refused to rise to the bait. She wouldn't give the silly tart the satisfaction. 'If I'd been doing such a bad job, The Feathers wouldn't be as successful as it has been the past thirty years!'

Lena casually picked at one of her long talons, inspecting the varnish for any chips. 'If believing that makes you feel better, sweetie, that's fine. If you're happy to keep your job based on pity and inherited loyalty, then your self-respect is more lacking than I thought,' she jibed, her eyes sparkling with malice. 'Aw, bless you. Has no one ever had the heart to tell you that you couldn't organise a piss-up in a brewery? All of the girls can't wait for you to bugger off to pastures new or, by the looks of you, an old folks' gaff.'

She laughed shrilly, her mouth forming a scarlet gash, her white veneers glinting brightly in the light from the desk lamp.

'Jonah's too polite to say, but he tells me all the time. Not an evening goes past without him moaning about something else you've fucked up. And as for the party theme – how was I to know?'

Gwen's expression didn't waver. *Lena was lying.* She and the girls – apart from *this* one – always had a huge amount of respect for one another. And Jonah – well, Jonah was anything but too polite. He'd have said a long time ago if he was displeased with how she ran things. Furthermore, *everyone* knew about the history with the diamonds. 'What's your game?'

Lena arched her brows. 'Game? What makes you think there's a game? Not everyone is so manipulative to play games, Gwen. All I'm saying is that I think it's about time you let fresh blood take over from your antiquated ways. You should suggest it to Jonah.'

This time Gwen really did laugh. 'You want me to suggest to Jonah that you should have my job?' She rolled her eyes. 'Stay out of things, Lena. You've caused enough problems with the girls and the party and now you're trying to mess with me?' Her eyes narrowed. 'Jonah may have not got around to speaking to you about it, but I will.'

Lena smiled sweetly. Gwen would expect her to shout and scream. Normally she would, but this was different. This time she had the upper hand. 'Ah, but that's where you're wrong. Jonah *did* tell me to keep out of things.' She looked towards the ceiling in mock distress. 'Right upset me, it did. I couldn't understand why he would say that to me. ME – his fiancée. Apparently I was upsetting everyone. Oh wait… not everyone – just to the tune of two fat birds and some old has-been, which would be… ooh, let's think… you…?'

Gwen frowned despite not wanting to visibly react. *Still playing her hand, the stupid girl?* She didn't believe Jonah had spoken to her for a minute. He had so much on his mind lately, what with Dulcie Adams coming out of the woodwork, but that was ok – she had no problem giving Lena what for. She had no intention of falling for her bullshit either.

Gwen changed her frown into a smile and made a point of closing the dance rota book. 'Regardless of your misplaced delusions of grandeur, even *you're* not so thick to think if Jonah told you not to interfere, you'd defy him and do so anyway. You're talking out of your arse, girl and you know it. You're pushing your luck with him in general.'

Lena's laugh resounded loudly in the small room. 'Oh no, that's where you're wrong.'

Gwen sighed loudly. *She'd had enough of this.* 'That's enough of this stupidness. Fuck off back to your party. This time you're lucky – I won't mention our conversation to Jonah, but pull anything like this again and I will.'

Standing up, Lena folded her arms across her inflated chest and sidled closer. 'Being as you've decided it's the right time to retire from the industry, don't forget to suggest to Jonah that he should think about letting me take over from where you're leaving off.'

Gwen stared at Lena. 'Oh for God's sake. Really? Come on, I'll humour you. Pray tell me why I would do that?'

With a wide smile, Lena helped herself to the large bottle of vodka on the side, taking her time to fill a crystal glass. *Thanks, Uncle Ron!*

Taking a long swig, she placed both hands on the desk and stared directly into Gwen's eyes. 'Because if you don't, then I'll tell Jonah all about what you and his father did behind his beloved mother's back.'

FORTY THREE

'ALL I'VE DONE is make you a second cup of tea,' Helen said, her hands still shaking as she poured herself a gin from her mother's cabinet. She might have known the old cow had a stash of drinks in here, but at least there was no sign of Robert, so that was something.

Knocking the drink back in one, having been unable to find a mixer, she ignored the sour taste of the gin. She just wanted to turn down the speeding in her head. She glanced at her mother, barely able to look at the woman whose fault all of this was. Every single thing that had gone wrong in her life was Dulcie Adams' fault.

Helen's rage bubbled again. Three tablets she'd given her since she'd arrived and there was no sign of her becoming tired. She'd take matters into her own hands if something didn't happen soon because there was no time to waste.

Dulcie's eyes bored into the back of her daughter's head. 'You're very jumpy. Is there something wrong?'

Helen gritted her teeth. *Yes, there were lots of things that were wrong. Was it any wonder?*

'And you don't look like you usually do. Have you changed your makeup or hair?'

Helen self-consciously touched her face. 'I'm just tired.' *Tired of you, so shut up and go to sleep. Just go away and let me do what I need to do.* 'Are you not drinking that tea?'

'I might do later,' Dulcie smiled, her eyes glittering mischievously. 'Why are you so adamant I should drink it?'

Helen forced air into her lungs but despite the large amount of air, her breathing was shallow and laboured, making her dizzy. She knew her mother was trying to antagonise her and it was working. She wasn't in the frame of mind to keep a straight head – not after what had happened. Running late getting here had piled the stress on, not to mention the *reason* she was late. Damn James for messing up her carefully laid plans up. At least the girl and Heath Pointer had done as she'd said and gone out.

'See! You're jumpy. What's going on, Helen?' Dulcie pressed.

Helen's rage built higher. *She couldn't take this anymore.*

'Why are you pacing up and down?' Dulcie's voice held a tinge of mockery.

Helen span around. 'You should go to bed.'

Dulcie raised an eyebrow. 'Go to bed? Why would I want to do that? It's only 8 o'clock.'

Helen bit down so hard on her lip she tasted blood. 'Because you're tired. Right, I'm going to tidy up.'

'What is there to tidy up?' Uncrossing her legs, Dulcie stood up and walked over to the stereo. Flicking through the LPs, she placed one on the turntable.

Cringing as the needle made a hideous scraping sound, Helen stared at her mother in disbelief. 'What are you doing?'

Dulcie smiled nastily. 'I'm playing music. This is my house and you're free to leave if you don't want to listen to it.'

Helen rolled her eyes, her jaw clenching and her fists balling. 'I'm hardly going to leave you on your own.'

Dulcie laughed loudly. 'No, you wouldn't want to do that. It would ruin all of your plans. So, what exactly are you looking for, Helen?'

'I'm not looking for anything,' Helen spluttered.

Dulcie smiled. 'Oh, I think that you are.'

. . . .

BACK AT THE PARTY, Jonah chatted to one of the dancing girls, her sweet unassuming nature distracting him from the rolling pent-up rage and the urge to walk out of his own club, away from this 'wonderful' engagement party and set fire to the damn place. *Lena and her ridiculous ideas.*

Oh sure, he'd gritted his teeth about the ring. He'd also suffered Lena whining about clothes, nails, fucking hair extensions – whatever she spent her bastard time doing, as well as giving her free rein to do what she liked regarding the party – he'd just signed off the bill and turned the other cheek at the expense. It was worth every penny to give her something to concentrate on other that the weird penchant she'd developed for wanting to be more involved with the club. He didn't want her to be more involved. Correction – he didn't want her there at all, but that was out of his hands now his baby was growing inside her.

For that and that alone, he'd put up with her. Having a family of his own was top priority. Family, the club and levelling the score with what Pointer had done were the only things which mattered. And any child of his would be even more important. It was just *Lena.* The engagement party might have kept her out of his hair, but he hadn't thought her so fucking stupid to have the theme of bastard *diamonds.*

Everybody knew of his antagonism for that subject, thanks to Pointer and that Irish bastard, O'Hara, and Lena expected him to swallow it? What utter bullshit. Lena knew about the diamond heist – *everybody* did, so there was no other explanation, short of her wanting to wind him up. And she'd done that with bells on.

Jonah scowled, his jaw hurting with the amount of time it had been clenched.

He'd even put up with her inviting a host of non-entities to give her kudos. If she'd had it her way, they would have been the only people, apart from the press, here tonight. Luckily, Gwen had made sure the staff, the firm - people that *really* mattered, got an invite as well.

Jonah had also swallowed the never-ending photographs Lena arranged to be taken at every possible opportunity. Photos when they arrived, photos posed with a growing selection of reality and TV 'stars', photos of him standing with Lena: *'Can you look at each other adoringly?', 'Just one more next to the pile of diamonds on the table.', 'Can we have one with you presenting Lena with the engagement ring?'*. On and on and fucking ON it had gone, his face cracking with the effort of having to pretend he wanted to be there, wanted to be with *her*, wanted to get fucking married...

Jonah had also let Lena answer the trifling questions accompanying the photos; *'When's the wedding date?'. 'Any patter of tiny feet on the horizon?', 'Mr Powell, when did you first realise you wanted to marry Miss Taylor?'*

Easy – never...

Jonah knew he would blow eventually. The massive hanging billboard, along with the diamond table centrepieces and shitty banners had lit the fuse well and good, but there had still been a small chance of making it to the end of the evening, but that hadn't happened. Just when he thought it couldn't get any worse, out came the cake. A covered monstrosity, he'd guessed it would be bad, but had underestimated just *quite* how bad.

A four-foot diamond-shaped cake with 'Jonah and Lena 4Eva' emblazoned on the side in glittering stones had done it. But it hadn't just been a diamond-shaped cake. Oh no, it had been a *pink* diamond-shaped cake.

Feeling like his jaw might snap clean in two, he honestly didn't know how he'd stopped himself from pushing Lena's face deep inside the sponge of the fucking cake and suffocating her.

The words Gwen whispered as he'd headed past her, his hand tightly gripped on Lena's arm had been the only thing that had saved him from really losing it. The words, *'don't be too hard on her - remember yourself'*, repeated in his mind as he'd wrapped his hands around Lena's neck and what had stopped him from finishing her. Because he'd wanted to. *Christ, he'd wanted to.*

That and remembering she was carrying his child had smacked him between the temples, stopping him in his tracks. Oh, she'd bleated out all of the expected apologies amid the tears – proclaiming she had no idea, but she had *every* fucking idea why. She'd picked the one theme guaranteed to insult him more than anything in the fucking world.

Realising the dancing girl was still talking, Jonah chugged down his glass of champagne and turning on his legendary smile like a light, managed to continue the small talk, making out that he was as happy as Larry. *If only they knew.*

As for Lena... she was a master of deceit. Half an hour after he'd left her sobbing in Gwen's office, she'd reappeared, looking not at all ruffled – such was her ability to turn on the charm. Despite him having roared at her and wrapping his hands around her throat, she looked unperturbed, her ruined makeup now as perfect as it had been at the start of the evening. Her regeneration complete, she'd flitted around the room, mingling, flirting and laughing and he'd wanted to punch her beautiful face.

Grabbing two fresh flutes of champagne, he handed the dancer a glass, watching her blush at his close proximity, but when an arm suddenly snaked around his waist, he tensed. He knew who it was and the urge to rip those taloned hands away and cast Lena to the floor was strong.

'Hello darling,' Lena purred, before looking the dancing girl up and down, not bothering to hide her disdain. 'Janice, you're too late to get your claws into this one. Jonah's all mine...' Smiling maliciously, she wiggled her oversized diamond ring in the girl's face. 'My man only has eyes for me.'

The girl turned scarlet. 'I-I wasn't... We were just...'

'Yeah, yeah.' Lena slithered in front of Jonah, pressing her lips against his.

Jonah cringed at Lena's rudeness towards the girl and fought the need to scrape the residue of her sticky lip gloss from his mouth. Pulling her to one side, he kept his smile as the dancer scuttled away, thoroughly mortified. 'You nasty bitch,' he hissed from the corner of his mouth.

Lena beamed. 'I was only joking to cheer myself up after your dreadful behaviour. I'm putting your actions down to you being overstressed, but don't ruin the night any more than you have already, Jonah. I've put a lot of effort into this.'

Jonah needed to change the subject before he publicly throttled her. 'Have you seen Gwen?'

Lena pursed her inflated lips and wobbled slightly on her sky high heels. 'No. Should I have?' she lied.

'How many have you had?'

'Only one,' Lena traced her fingers along Jonah's jaw.

Removing Lena's hand from his face, Jonah saw Nero making his way over, his expression not one that he liked the look of. 'I need to speak to Nero.' Untangling himself, he made himself peck her on the cheek.

'Keith's just had a call on the burner from that stoner. The girl's out and Adams is on her own,' Nero muttered as Jonah approached.

'What? Tonight? Are you sure? When?' Jonah felt his adrenalin pulse and glanced at his watch. It was almost 9 o'clock and it would take at least an hour to reach Maidenhead. Probably longer getting through London with the Saturday night traffic.

'About twenty minutes ago.' Nero nodded towards Lena. 'I couldn't get your attention and I didn't want to make anything obvious.'

'And the stoner's sure the girl is out?'

Nero shrugged. 'Keith said he's as pissed as a rat and could barely work out what the cunt said, so your guess is as good as mine. But he seemed to think so, yes,'

'Fuck,' Jonah spat. 'We'd best get on the road.'

'But what about the party? What ab…'

'What about it? Tell Keith to bring the car round. We need to move on this, even if it turns out the old thief isn't alone. We'll spec it out when we get there, but it's worth a punt.' Jonah looked at his watch again. 'It might be the only chance we get for a good while and I'm sick of fucking waiting.'

. . . .

DULCIE'S HIGH-PITCHED LAUGHTER hurt Helen's ears. It left a ringing sound to match the all over buzzing coursing through her body. The Fats Domino record was sticking, the same line going over and over for half an hour. She was going to scream. She would scream and scream and *scream* and then she was going to kill the old witch.

'Did you not hear me? I said, you've always been a disappointment. You were then and you are now.'

Moving to the bureau, Helen yanked the writing flap down and began rooting through the contents. She'd heard what her mother had said, of course she had, but she was ignoring it. She'd decided to crack on with searching in full view because she had little left to lose and time was running out. She'd been through the entire sideboard, as well as several drawers in the sitting room and achieved nothing, apart from the consistent vitriol spewing from her mother's spiteful mouth.

'Look all you like. You won't find anything. You'll *never* find anything. I know exactly what you're looking for – I don't know how you found out and I don't really care, but I'll never let you get your hands on what you're after. They're not for you - they're Robert's.'

Unable to take it any longer, Helen span around. 'Oh, yes, Robert. The Golden Boy. Well, of course, it *would* be Robert – your favourite.'

'You've always been a jealous, nasty little cow.' Dulcie spat. 'Unlike Robert.'

Helen's eyes narrowed. *It was too late – the old bitch could just shut up.* 'The child of the man you preferred, right?' She got deep satisfaction watching her mother pale. 'Yes, I know all about that too. You didn't expect that, did you?'

Moving closer, Helen refrained from scratching her mother's eyes out. She'd save that until later if needs be. 'You owe me, so tell me where the diamonds are, mother. The ones you were given by your *lover*, Michael Pointer.'

Wobbling at hearing Michael's name, Dulcie quickly pulled herself together, masking the shock of Helen's unexpected words. She lowered herself into the armchair next to the little table with the drawer holding her treasured and only picture of the man she'd loved. 'I owe you nothing.'

Helen shrugged as she sifted through the bureau, her confidence returning. 'Oh, but you do. You've lied to me all my life, but say what you like - no one will believe you because you're crazy.' She smiled maniacally. 'And guess what? Next week you're off to an apartment. One in a home for people like *you* – for *mad* people.'

Helen grinned. She could still do this – she knew she could. Despite the nagging worry of what might stem from James' demise, she was confident she could deal with that without it adversely affecting her. There was no proof she'd had any hand in it. Besides, she'd been here and had proof of that.

Dulcie laughed. 'You think I didn't weigh you up a long time ago? Oh, Helen, you're so predictable, I almost feel sorry for you. You really think I'd be so stupid to take those 'vitamins'? I just let you and everyone else believe I was taking them and acted accordingly. Let's face it, I'm a damn fine actress. That's why I was so good at The Feathers and at just about everything else I've ever done.'

Helen was shell-shocked. *She hadn't been taking those pills? She'd put it on? But, why...? Why would she want to do that?*

Her brow furrowed as the truth dawned. Her mother had been playing her. Been making out she had no idea when she knew all along.

A sneer slid across Dulcie's face. 'Yes, that's right. I can see by your expression you're getting the gist. I wanted everyone to believe I was mad because I knew it would give you the confidence to play into my hands and show your true colours. You're a greedy, selfish, deluded person – just like your imbecile father.'

Helen's rage spiked. What she had was better and it wasn't going to stop her. Nothing would stop her from getting her hands on what she was owed. 'My father... funny you should mention him. I'm surprised you can remember. Oh, yes – you'd hardly be likely to forget, being as you went to great pains to arrange his *murder*. Car accident, my arse. You and your lover, Robert's father, arranged it, didn't you? Just admit it!'

Dulcie shrugged. 'And so what? You can't prove it. No one can.'

Helen refused to let her mother's admission bother her. She knew it was true, but it still grated to hear her admit it with such little care. *Rise above it, Helen.* 'I wonder what Golden Boy will think when I tell him that his father killed mine? I wonder how he'll feel about being lied to all his life too? I wonder how he'll take it knowing his mother is a manipulative old tart as well as a thief!'

Dulcie laughed once again. 'Robert doesn't believe anything you say. And...,' she casually played with a string of beads, 'he won't allow you to put me in a home.'

It was Helen's turn to smile. She dropped down on to her haunches in front of Dulcie. 'Actually, it was his idea...' She giggled at the look of horror washing across her mother's face. '*Robert* bought the apartment for you. He bought it himself.'

She watched her mother's face with growing satisfaction. 'Sinking in, is it? I have many witnesses as to your lunacy. So *so* many – all of whom who will truthfully say you're barking mad and demented as hell.'

Helen moved closer. 'Tell me where the diamonds are, you lying old slut – the ones your lover stole and the ones you've been hiding ever since. If you're really lucky I'll tell you who else is after you too.'

Folding her arms, Dulcie shook her head. 'They're mine and mine alone. And eventually they'll be Robert's, not yours. *Never* yours.'

Helen sneered. 'I think you must be confused again, mother. Why don't you sing Blueberry Hill to yourself and have a little dance around whilst I go and have a good look upstairs.'

FORTY FOUR

ROBERT STARED AT HIS COMPUTER SCREEN, unable to concentrate. He'd got a massive amount of work to finish but he just couldn't get his head into gear. Getting up from his desk, he finished what was left of his coffee and decided to make another one. He walked towards the kitchen, glancing at the items of post he'd walked past earlier.

Bending down, he scooped two envelopes from the floor and moved into the kitchen to flick the kettle on.

Plonking himself down at the kitchen table, he thought he might as well concentrate on something else, short of that bloody coding, for five minutes. Having a break might, with any luck, unstick his brain and give him the impetus to dream up a fresh way of addressing the problem flagged up in the computer script. He hoped so anyway because he'd got to get the program fixed in time for a big rollout of a system upgrade. He'd be up all night at this rate.

Tearing open the first envelope, Robert flicked through the contents. Information from the solicitor including copies of the land registry and all the associated bumph for the purchase of that apartment. His eyes scanned the accompanying letter, seeing the completion was confirmed for next week. He smiled to himself. Helen had been pleased to hear that when she'd phoned earlier. The solicitor had already called to tell him the news, but he liked to have things in writing too. It was sad with how things had developed, but at least his mother would be properly looked after by specialists soon.

Shoving the solicitor's paperwork back in the envelope, Robert picked up the second letter – a large, thick one. He almost threw it back down on the table, thinking it looked like one of those stupid catalogues about Tupperware and thermal vests, but something made him open it.

Tearing open the brown envelope, he pulled out a sheaf of paper. Frowning, he scanned the note. *From James? What was Helen's husband writing to him for?*

Irritation bubbling, he glanced over the letter uninterestedly. *'I tried to call you several times… No answer… Hope you receive this… I had no choice… Didn't know what else to do…'*

Robert frowned, his eyes running down the typed words and fear jangled. Frantically moving to the next page, he read a print out of something from the internet, followed by a copy of remortgage documents and bank transfer requests.

Robert's heart raced. *Was this for real? It couldn't be possible, could it?*

Jumping up, he raced back to his desk, knocking the mouse to bring the computer back to life. Opening a new Google tab, Robert furiously entered bits of information from James' notes. *He had to see for himself.*

Returning several pages of results, his eyes scanned up and down the words on the screen in record time. *It was true…* These drugs – these drugs that James reckoned were in the garage and the ones Helen was swapping out for vitamins, could cause those side effects when combined.

He scrolled his mouse down the pages of text: *'anticholinergics… block the effect of the brain chemical, acetylcholine… Temazepam… Fluoxetine… combination… confusion… memory disturbances… agitation… delirium… altered cognitive function…'*

Sweat beaded on Robert's forehead. '... *acts on neurotransmitters... levels deplete naturally with age... medication can accelerate deterioration and effects... mimics dementia...*'

Mimics dementia…?

Robert put his head in his hands and pulled his shaking fingers through his hair. *The bitch. The fucking bitch. She'd done this.*

Helen had set this up. *Helen.*

Robert jumped to his feet. He would go there now. He wanted to see this stash in James' garage for himself before he'd believe it. If James was correct in his suspicions and Helen really had done this, then he'd wring her neck with his bare hands.

And then he was going to go and get his mother. He'd take her to hospital and get them to flush all of that shit out of her system. *He'd sort this. He could sort this.*

Grabbing his car keys, Robert's face was red with rage. Helen would pay for this. How could she do this? How could she systematically poison their mother and make out she was going insane. And for the money? Holy Mother of God, this couldn't be right. It just *couldn't.*

Helen would go to prison for this if it were true. He'd make sure of it. That's if he didn't kill her first.

Slamming the door to his flat, Robert rushed to his car.

• • • •

NERO'S FOOT WAS PRESSED TO THE FLOOR as the car raced up the M40. They'd made good time and he desperately hoped they didn't get a tug. He glanced in the rear view mirror at Jonah, his face set like stone, patiently loading his Glock. Even more reason not to get pulled over.

Sensing Nero's interest, Keith looked over his shoulder at his boss in the back seat and felt hopeful. Saul would feel better about things if Jonah finished off the bitch who'd helped ruin Jacky. 'What's the plan then, boss?'

Jonah glanced up, his eyes cold, impatient to get to Maidenhead. His concentration fully honed onto how he would do this had thankfully paled the events of tonight's engagement party debacle to the back of his mind – the part reserved for irrelevant matters.

He would be finishing this tonight.

Warm, fizzing blood pumped in his veins in anticipation of finally closing the door on this chapter of his life which had caused so much stress and upheaval and get the answers he'd waited so long for and retrieve what was his father's.

'I'll let myself into the house.' Jonah tapped his inside pocket where the keys to Footlights were safely secured. 'Then I'll confront Adams. Finally, I'll be lifting my stuff back.'

Keith's irritation bristled. He was still planning to talk to the old bitch? Saul wanted vengeance not conversation and wouldn't be happy if Jonah let the thieving cunt walk, regardless of whether he retrieved the goods or not. His arm brushed against the gun concealed in his waistband. He'd promised Saul he'd take the old bag out himself if Jonah didn't.

'You planning on using that?' Keith nodded to the gun in Jonah's hand.

Jonah placed his Glock back in his inside pocket and smiled coldly. 'Planning on it, no.' *But he would if he had to.*

· · · ·

'HELEN?' Robert banged on the front door. 'Helen! Open the door. I know you're in there.'

He glanced around, not caring if any of the neighbours were watching. It was doubtful because the nearest was a few hundred yards away. Besides, he didn't give a toss. He had to have it out with Helen and if what James had said was right, get his mother to the hospital.

'Helen? James?' Robert thumped on the door yet again. The lights were on - one in the front sitting room and one in a bedroom – he'd seen that from the drive. James' car was here too, but Helen's wasn't – unless it was in the garage?

Peering through the letterbox, Robert could see all the way down to the kitchen and the light in there also on. He squinted to the left, noticing the door to the garage from the house was open. *Maybe they were in there?*

Running briskly around the side of the house, Robert brushed the sweat from his brow. Reaching the garage, the large double shutters were down, but there was a side door... Despite his eagerness to locate his bitch of a sister, he felt strangely reticent. *He had a bad feeling about this.*

Reaching the door, Robert tried the handle, finding it unlocked. He pushed it open with trepidation, the hairs on the back of his neck bristling. 'Helen? James? You in here? Hello?'

Stepping into the garage, he fumbled for the light switch and clicked it on. Rooted to the spot, he blinked several times as his brain processed the crumpled mess of James' body on the floor in front of him.

He didn't want to look at it, but found he couldn't drag his eyes away from the unholy sight of his brother-in-law's caved in skull – the cranium visibly dented. *And, oh Christ! A piece of it was missing... There was actually a piece missing!*

Robert dragged his eyes away from the ghastly sight, spotting clods of bloody tissue-like flesh near the body, surrounded by thick purple blood. James Shepherd's eyes stared sightlessly at the garage ceiling, his mouth twisted in a horrible grimace.

Who had done this? Had Helen been butchered too?

Heart pounding, Robert moved towards the door leading from the garage into the house. His leg was poised, raised to step over James' body, when he stopped.

It was Helen. Helen had done this. Jesus Christ! And she wasn't here?

Robert's mind whirred frantically, panic spiralling. *No! She'd said on the phone earlier that she was planning on spending the evening at Footlights with their mother.*

Robert shook as a horrible concept dawned. Helen had killed her husband and now she was going to kill their mother?

Nausea rushed over him and doubling over, he vomited violently over the concrete floor.

FORTY FIVE

HEATH CASUALLY GLANCED AT HIS WATCH. Almost 10.30. Helen should have had a good look around by now. *Had she got them yet?*

His heart raced with the prospect of her having located the diamonds. He was *this* close to getting his hands on them, he could almost smell it.

His father had wanted him to remain whilst Helen searched – convinced she might be tempted to run off if she found them, leaving them in the lurch, but Heath believed this a bad idea. Firstly, how would he justify his presence with Teagan there? Teagan would understandably want to know why and furthermore, she needed to be out of the way, so it would have never worked.

As he'd explained to his father several times before now, there was no way Helen could shift the jewels, and that was something else he'd need to look into now they all but had their hands on them.

He glanced at Teagan. The evening had been a bit tricky in places when she'd talked about more stuff from the 'old days', but he didn't think she'd suspected anything. But the conversation hadn't been as easy as the last couple of times he'd spent with her and he hoped this would be the last time he spent an evening with the girl because it was apparent she was reading a lot more into what was between them than there was.

'Fancy another drink?' Heath asked, for want of something to say. Maybe if she had a couple more she'd loosen up a bit – make the conversation flow.

'I'd better not. I've already had a fair few,' As much as Teagan had been looking forward to the unexpected evening out, Darren seemed preoccupied – on edge. She got the niggling feeling he didn't want to be here, yet she couldn't put her finger on why. He'd done and said all the right things – there was just something that felt stilted.

No matter how much she tried to relax, she was on edge. She wasn't comfortable leaving Dulcie alone – even if it had only been for a very short time before Helen arrived. Since then she'd felt consistently compelled to glance at her phone just to make sure she hadn't missed any calls.

In the two weeks she'd been at Footlights – despite the troubles, she'd grown to love Dulcie dearly. The thought of not being around after next week was playing on her mind more than she'd realised and hoped this specialist place Dulcie was moving to allowed visitors, because she'd very much like to remain in contact.

A frown crossed her face. What if Dulcie blamed *her*? If Helen told her the decision had been made primarily because of what *she'd* reported regarding her deteriorating behaviour, then it stood very likely that Dulcie would hold her responsible.

Despite herself, Teagan felt the beginnings of tears burning at the back of her eyes. Although it was most unprofessional of her and a big no-no to get emotionally attached to clients, she just couldn't help it where Dulcie Adams was concerned.

'Are you alright?'

Teagan looked up sharply. 'Yes... No... Oh, I don't know... I'm sorry... I know I haven't been much company tonight.' She smiled weakly. 'Do you mind if we go back?'

'Go back?' Heath yelped. 'What? Already?' *Shit.* He'd

been hoping to drag this out until the best part of midnight. 'Shall we just have a couple more? It seems a shame not to take full advantage of an evening off, being as you don't get that many.'

Teagan finished her wine. 'I'll be having a lot more evenings free now Dulcie's leaving,' she said sadly. 'But I would like to go back. I-I just want to make sure everything's alright.'

Heath frowned. *God, she was like an old woman.* 'Why wouldn't it be?'

Teagan shrugged. 'No reason. Oh, I don't know. I'm sorry.' She got to her feet and pulled her jacket on, leaving Heath little choice but to do likewise.

• • • •

'GO ON THEN. SMASH THE PLACE UP!' Dulcie screeched. 'You're a joke, Helen. A joke!' She waved the newspaper clipping of Michael Pointer in front of Helen, her face screwed up with rage. *This* is who I should have married, not that worm who somehow had it in him to father *you*.'

With tears of anger and frustration, Helen swiped one of the many higgledy-piggledy collections of ornaments from the top of the sideboard, the splintering and crashing noise as glass, pottery and crystal shattered into a thousand pieces over the polished floor of the sitting room, loud.

'You should be dead you evil, lying old witch!' she screamed. 'I wish those pills had killed you!'

Dulcie laughed. 'But you couldn't even manage that, could you? Now get out of my house. Go on – GET OUT!'

Helen breathed heavily, her chest heaving. Snatching the newspaper cutting out of her mother's hand, she screwed it into a ball and threw it onto the floor. 'You vindictive slag. At least your lover had the sense to disappear, rather than hang around. I'm going to find those diamonds. You know – the ones you and your lover stole and I'm taking them with me. You won't be able to do a thing about it because you'll be locked away with all the other demented old crones.'

Turning on her heels, Helen pushed past Dulcie and stormed out of the room.

Dulcie stared at the scrunched up newspaper cutting on the floor as Helen pounded up the stairs, before quickly rushing after her.

With surprising agility, Dulcie rushed up the stairs, catching up with Helen as she ran into the pink bedroom, shutting the door in Dulcie's face.

Pushing the door back into Helen, Dulcie stormed into the room. 'Get out of this room, do you hear me?' she roared, her eyes icy. 'I said, GET OUT!'

Helen's eyes lit up. 'Ah, so this is where they are? I thought as much. The infamous pink bedroom that you never wanted anyone going in. All throughout my childhood you didn't like us coming in here and now I know why.' She pulled at the drawers in the dressing table, yanking out perfectly folded, but very old lacy negligees. 'Wear these for *him*, did you?'

With eyes like slits, Dulcie grabbed Helen's arm, her bony fingers digging into her skin. 'You vile creature!' she screamed. 'I never wanted you. *Never*. I wanted rid the minute I found out I was pregnant. I've never stopped hating you!'

Twisting around, Helen shook her mother's arm off. 'The feeling's mutual. Now get the hell off me so I can find what I want in peace. You're a pathetic excuse for a woman and even more of an embarrassment as a mother.'

Raising her hand, she backhanded Dulcie around the face, the force splitting her lip and sending her flying backwards into a cheval mirror. Hitting her head on the corner of the wooden surround, Dulcie slumped to the floor.

Helen glanced over her shoulder at her mother lying unconscious and smiled serenely. Pulling out an array of boxes from under the bed, she tipped the contents on the floor. 'I've already killed my husband tonight, mother, so killing you too will be no skin off my nose.'

. . . .

THE CAR PULLED UP OUTSIDE the big old house and Jonah glanced out at the ramshackle façade and overgrown garden. 'This is it? Are you sure?'

'Definitely - we've been here enough,' Keith said.

Jonah glanced at Keith, the tone of impatience in the man's voice not going unnoticed. He'd pick him up about that later. Pulling the keys from his inside pocket, he opened the car door. 'I'm going in. Stay here - you know the drill. If anyone who shouldn't come back, does, call my mobile – let it ring just the once. I'm not sure how long I'll be.'

Nero glanced at Keith. 'We'll be here.'

Slamming the door, Jonah raced up the overgrown front steps. Whatever Dulcie Adams had done with the spoils from Pointer's thieving, she hadn't spent it on this house.

His heart pounded in his ears as he risked a glance in the front bay window. The curtains were shut, but there was enough of a chink to see the light was on behind the heavy maroon drapes. It didn't look like anyone was in there, but they could be out of sight.

Hoping he'd picked the right key from the two on the keyring, Jonah pushed it into the lock of the outer door. Stiff as copied keys are initially, his heart was in his mouth as he waited to see if it turned the barrel.

And it did.

This was it – he was about to come face to face with the woman who had helped turn his father over and had been the bane of his life since he could remember.

Jonah opened the door and winced as the old hinges creaked loudly. Slotting the second key into the inner door, he opened that, quickly shutting both doors behind him. All the lights were on, but it was very quiet. *Too quiet.* Perhaps the old bag was asleep?

Treading softly along the hallway, Jonah stuck his head around the door of the first room and froze, his hackles bristling as he surveyed the pile of smashed ornaments across the floor. *Who had been in here and done this?*

Ears alert for any sound, the big old house was completely silent, except for the sound of his own breathing.

Jonah glanced warily around the rest of the space, clocking the plentiful framed photographs – many of which contained pictures taken at The Feathers – his father's club. *His* club.

Aside from the pile of smashed and broken ornaments on the floor, the drawers from a chest in the corner were open, their contents scattered over the floor too. His eyes then darted to a mahogany bureau, the writing flap pulled down with a jumble of paperwork and odds and ends littered over it, but the rest of the room was intact, including several pieces of antiques that he could see straight away were valuable. *This was not a burglary.*

A wave of cold rushed over him. Whoever had done this hadn't come to trash or burgle the place, they'd come *looking* for something… And he suspected he knew exactly what that was. And he was damned if they would beat him to it! Over his dead body. *But who the fuck was it?*

Pulling the Glock from his inside pocket, Jonah moved to start checking the rest of the house for intruders.

FORTY SIX

KEITH OPENED HIS SECOND MARS BAR and crammed it into his mouth.

Nero looked at Keith in disgust. 'How can you possibly be hungry? You ate half the fucking buffet!'

Keith shrugged and stared out of the car window. He'd have preferred to still be at the party. He'd had his eye on a tasty little redhead, who if she did a good a job in the sack as she did on the stage, he'd have had a fine time. Yeah, judging by the looks she'd been giving him he would have been on to a winner had he hung around, rather than having to come back to fucking Maidenhead.

This could have been done and dusted ages ago. If it had been up to him, the minute they'd confirmed where the old trout lived, he'd have been straight in there, turned the place upside-down, retrieved the goods and removed Dulcie-fucking-Adams from the face of the planet, the thieving cunt.

Keith's face screwed into a scowl. Instead, they'd been fannying around for what seemed like *months* with dickheads like that stoner and that ponce estate agent bloke.

He was of the ilk to go straight after Adams' bastard son - the one with the gambling problems – the one the suit had mentioned. As well as getting another client for a lucrative loan on the books, he had the distinct feeling the man in question was Pointer's kid. From what he'd learnt over the years, Pointer had got his mistress up the duff, but the woman – Helen Shepherd, wasn't Pointer's - that much was obvious by looking at her. But Jonah had only wanted that to happen if the stoner failed to come up with the keys.

Keith shook his head. He'd have done things a *lot* differently to Jonah. For a start, had he been around when all of this had happened, he'd have sorted the rest of those O'Hara wankers out too.

Ok, so Saul had finished Sean O'Hara, but he would have had the wanker's brother Ron and his fucking wife, Noeleen, whilst he was at it too. He wouldn't have given a fuck if that Ron prick was in the loony bin – he'd have dragged him out of his straitjacket and finished him off all the same. He certainly wouldn't have let him walk away. And Saul wouldn't have either, had he not got banged up.

But then Jacky Powell did things differently and although Keith readily admitted he both liked and respected Jonah, the man had a very similar take on things to his father - ruthless, but a bit too fair, with definitely too many morals.

Whereas Saul… Saul thought the same way as him - that's why they'd worked so well together. Had Saul been running the ship, as he should have been, had it not been for O'Hara, then things would have turned out a lot differently. *Better.* There would have been none of this dilly-dallying about.

Keith crammed the last bit of his Mars bar into his mouth and sucked his sticky fingers.

He'd do it though. He'd promised Saul he'd sort it if Jonah didn't. If Jonah didn't finish Dulcie Adams off, then he'd step in. *Enough was enough.*

Keith had received another VO from Saul only this morning for a couple of weeks' time and it would be good to give his old pal the news he'd been waiting on for so long.

Sensing Nero stiffen, Keith glanced up seeing a Lexus

coming down the road towards them. 'This anything, do you reckon?'

Nero's forehead furrowed, his eyes trained on where the car would stop. 'Not sure, but if it is, then it will balls up everything. Jonah's only been gone ten minutes.'

Keith raked his fingers through his hair in frustration. It would more than balls things up. If this Lexus was anyone returning to the house, then they'd have to warn Jonah. That meant any chance he had of getting in there and making sure the old girl was stone dead was down the bog too.

Gritting his teeth, he watched the car pull up a few doors down from Footlights.

• • • •

TEAGAN COULD TELL Darren wasn't happy. She was disappointed he'd made her feel bad about coming back. He'd tried several times to cajole her into having a couple more drinks before finally accepting defeat, acting almost annoyed when she'd stood her ground.

Her wish to return had really bothered him and she couldn't understand why, but then again, she'd misread lots of things where Darren Harding was concerned. She didn't need a control freak or a man with a yo-yoing personality in her life again.

Despite this, she still felt the need to apologise again and hated how she felt bestowed to justify and explain every single part of her existence all of the time. Shouldn't the fact that she was worried about Dulcie and wanted to go back have been enough?

'I'm sorry about cutting the evening short, Darren,' Teagan said. 'Would you like to come in for a cup of tea?'

Heath glared at Teagan. *Cup of tea? What was he? Sixty?*

How fucking typical was this? It wasn't even pub kicking out time. He dearly hoped returning early wouldn't hinder anything. Hopefully by now Helen had done the business and found the stash. He had tried calling her while Teagan popped to the loos on the way out of The Sommelier. He'd wanted to give Helen the heads up they were on their way back, but she hadn't picked up.

Heath frowned. He hadn't left a message and wondered if he should have?

The nagging disquiet of whether there was any plausibility in his father's paranoia of Helen doing a runner with the jewels filtered into his mind.

No. He was being daft. Helen was still here because he'd spotted her Merc as they'd driven down the street. It was parked well away from the house, but it was definitely her car. *Stop panicking, Heath.*

'Darren? I said, did you want to come in for a cup of tea?'

Heath quickly remembered to drop his inner rage from being visible. 'Oh, erm… no, I'd better not. I'll leave you to it.' He couldn't go in. He might put Helen off and there was no way he wanted to arouse Teagan's suspicions. On top of that, Dulcie Adams gave him the creeps and he'd rather not be around her.

Teagan swallowed her disappointment with Darren's attitude for the second time that evening, which quickly turned into a third time when he leant over, depositing a chaste kiss on her cheek. That alone signified that whatever she thought she and Darren may have, they didn't.

Forcing a smile, she grabbed her handbag from the footwell and opened the car door. 'I'll text you, ok?'

• • • •

IT HAD TAKEN JONAH a lot longer than he would have liked to check every room on the ground floor was clear due to the combination of the size of the place and the maze-like layout. Several rooms he'd had to meticulously check, whilst simultaneously watching his back as well as the door to ensure no one slipped past while he was inside.

This was easier said than done being as some of the rooms had L-shaped layouts as well as alcoves. He'd also had the unenviable task of checking the cupboards. It was a hoarder's paradise. *Christ, there was enough stuff in this place to keep*

Antiques Roadshow going for centuries.

Pointing the Glock up the hallway whilst doing a final double check behind him, Jonah looked at the staircase in front of him. Spotting the threadbare carpet runners, he made a mental note to watch where he put his feet. Lying at the bottle of that staircase with a broken neck wasn't the best way to resolve this business.

He hadn't checked any outhouses – if there were any, but couldn't risk going outside. Someone could be upstairs, which would give them a clear run down to the ground floor. He turned the key of the door leading to the cellar. If there was anyone down there, then they could stay there. *Better to be safe, than sorry.*

Pausing, with one foot on the bottom stair, Jonah listened intently. Still nothing; not a sound. He started thinking that as well as the girl being out, so was Dulcie Adams.

Ascending the stairs as quietly as possible, Jonah gritted his teeth as one of the stairs made the loudest groaning noise. Hastily moving to the next step, he paused and listened again. *Still nothing.* He'd wasted a lot of time searching the ground floor, but he'd had no choice. Someone had been here – and by the looks of it, searched for what he wanted.

But who else could know? Who else could know this old woman was harbouring some of the rarest and most expensive diamonds?

He was pretty sure no one was lurking in the house. Surely he'd have heard a noise, at least *something*, however slight by now. He'd have a quick scan around upstairs and then make a start searching through the place. If Dulcie Adams wasn't here, then he could at least look for his stuff. He'd also get Nero and Keith in on that as three pairs of hands was better than one.

Walking across the landing, Jonah winced at the loud and almost blinding busy wallpaper - a classic Victorian pattern with a dark background, covered with a multitude of tiny flowers and swirls. As well as making the high ceilinged landing feel depressingly gloomy, it hurt his bloody eyes. *Jesus.*

A light spilled from a room along the corridor. All the other doors were shut. He knew he should probably check them, but the one with the open door had to be the first priority.

With his back against the wall, Jonah slid along the migraine-inducing wallpaper, holding the Glock out in front of him. Slowly and carefully he peered around the side of the door jamb and froze. 'What the fuck?' he muttered, the rest of his body, gun poised, following him into the bright pink room.

Lying on her back over by the window was the body of a woman. The bloom of red across the left hand side of her white blouse showcased where a bullet had entered. Her glassy eyes stared upwards, her face contorted in a terrified expression and blood spread in a wide pool over a rug bunched up underneath her body.

Fuck. Whoever had been here had a gun. And it was the daughter on the floor – he recognised her from that web clip. The clip which had led them to uncover where Dulcie Adams was hiding in the first place.

Jonah's eyes darted around the room. Again, like downstairs, the room was pulled apart, the contents of a chest of drawers turned out, the dressing table in chaos. Most of the wardrobe had been emptied. *Fucking shit.* Whoever had been in here must have killed the daughter, taken the diamonds *and* Dulcie Adams because she wasn't anywhere to be seen.

Fuck. Shit. Fuck.

Heart hammering, Jonah yanked his mobile from his pocket and fumbled with his gloved fingers.

'Nero, it's gone tits up!' he panted, his mouth dry. 'Shepherd's here and she's dead... No, it wasn't me... The house has been turned over and Adams has gone. At least, I mean I haven't found her yet.'

Sweat poured down Jonah's back, the crisp cotton of his white dress shirt sticking to him underneath his tuxedo jacket. 'I'm deadly serious... Whoever's been here has turned the place over, found the stash, offed Shepherd and fucking lifted the old cow, taking her somewhere – possibly for leverage. I don't know?'

He couldn't believe this, he just couldn't believe it.

'I'm going to search now, yeah an… What? Shit! Ok.' Jonah's heart lurched into his throat. *Tonight was going from bad to worse.*

Still holding the gun out in front of him, he shoved the phone back in his pocket. Nero hadn't said who had just arrived, but someone had and he had to get out of here. *Now.*

It could be the girl or the Old Bill. Maybe a neighbour had heard a gunshot? It made no difference. *Shit, shit, SHIT.*

Swinging around, Jonah legged it along the landing and down the stairs two at a time, taking the chance that his shiny dress shoes wouldn't snag on the loose threads of the runner.

389

FORTY SEVEN

THE ONLY SPACE TO PARK WAS SEVEN HOUSES UP. Screeching to a halt, Robert yanked on his handbrake and jumped out of the car, not wasting a second by locking it.

He sprinted along the road, heart thundering, *If Helen had done anything to their mother... If she'd touched her he'd...*

Seeing a figure nearing the house, Robert raced on. *That was Teagan! Jesus Christ, what was Teagan doing out?*

Reaching her, he grabbed her shoulder. 'Teagan? What are y...?'

Teagan's terrified scream froze Robert in his tracks.

'Christ, girl! It's me – Robert!' he barked.

'R-Robert?' Teagan stammered, her pulse rate through the roof. She looked at Robert, his rugged face waxen. 'You scared the life out of me! What's happened? What are you doing here?'

'I could ask the same of you, but there's no time to explain,' Robert panted, out of breath. 'My mother's in danger. I've got to get in there.'

Teagan followed, her mind in overdrive as Robert moved off rapidly towards the house. *Dulcie was in danger?* 'Robert? What's happened?' She rushed to catch up with him. 'Oh God, I knew I shouldn't have gone out. I sensed something was up, that's why I came back. Out of the blue Helen gave me the night off an…'

Robert swung around, causing Teagan to run straight into his chest. He gripped her by the shoulders. 'Helen gave you the night off?'

Seeing Teagan nod, Robert looks skyward. 'Christ! I knew it! Oh Jesus! Come on, we've got to get in there. We've got to stop Helen.'

'Helen?' Teagan followed Robert again. *Stop Helen? Stop Helen from what? What was Robert going on about?* Her brain churned. In all the occasions she'd seen Robert, he'd never looked anything but controlled and aloof, yet here he was running about like a madman, abject terror behind his eyes. The knot of growing fear increased in her gut. *Something was very wrong.*

Turning into the path for Footlights, Teagan didn't even see it coming it happened that quickly. The large figure barging into her, knocking her clean off her feet took the breath clean out of her lungs.

'OIH!' Robert roared, turning to chase after the man.

Teagan scrabbled to her feet just as Robert reached the road, seeing a well-built, tall man open the door of a car which screeched up from nowhere. The man jumped in and the car roared away.

Panic spiralled. She hadn't seen the man's face, but there were three men in that car and she knew somewhere in the recesses of her mind that they must be the men connected with Joe. She raised her hands to her mouth in terror, watching wide-eyed as Robert steamed back up the path.

'Are you alright?' Robert glanced at Teagan whilst fumbling to get his set of keys into the lock.

'Y-Yes, I'm ok. T-Those men… They…'

'I don't know what the fuck is going on here, but we need to get mother away from Helen.' Robert panted, wrestling with the door. 'Fuck it, come on damn you!' With a final struggle, he turned the key and rushed into the hallway.

Teagan followed, her mouth dry, terrified to what she would find. If anything had happened to Dulcie because of what Joe had done... That man... those ones in the car... They had to be the ones that had been terrorising Joe; the ones who had murdered Alan... *Oh Jesus*... She could scarcely think as she rushed after Robert into the sitting room.

'Mother?' Robert yelled, his voice panicked.

Teagan stared in horror at the room – empty, apart from the smashed glass, pottery and scattered paperwork all over the floor.

• • • •

'I'M TELLING YOU, IT WAS *HIM*,' Heath babbled, narrowly missing running someone down on a zebra crossing. *Shit – that wouldn't be good. Pay attention!*

He tried to concentrate on the 101 questions his father was firing at him, but he couldn't untangle his mind from what he'd seen and how at that precise second, he knew he'd had to make a sharp exit.

Once Teagan had got out of the car he'd been planning on hanging around in the hope Helen would shortly emerge, but as his eyes followed Teagan towards Footlights, he hadn't expected a man to run up to her. He'd scrabbled to get out of the door, initially thinking Teagan was about to get attacked, then stopped when it became quickly obvious that Teagan knew him.

It was only then that Heath had seen the man's face. Although he'd never seen this person before in his entire life, he'd also seen him virtually every single day. *The man was a double of his bloody father.*

Heath concentrated back on the voice which yelled at him from his Bluetooth hands free speakers.

'Trust me, Dad, it was Robert. Robert Adams – your brother. I know Helen said he was dead the other day... Yes, I know... But he isn't. It was definitely him. It *had* to be. He looks *just* like you. So much like you that I thought it *was* you for a second.' His father was slightly less well built, but apart from that they could have been twins. The likeness was uncanny. 'Like I said, he looked in a right state. Very upset.'

Heath swallowed uncomfortably. He had no idea what had gone on, but whatever it was, it had set the cat amongst the pigeons. 'No, he didn't see me.' Neither the man, nor Teagan had even glanced in his direction, they'd just hurried off towards the house.

'I-I'd planned on waiting – even after that. Seriously, I had, but I had no choice but to disappear, surely you can see that?' Heath said as his father's voice raised pitch. 'What do you mean why? What else was I supposed to do? Someone ran out of Footlights, barged into Teagan, knocked her flying then jumped straight into a fucking car!'

And he hadn't even noticed the car until it had screeched up outside. It must have been there all along, watching...

'No, they didn't see me,' Heath said. At least he hoped they hadn't. Ducking down in the driver's seat as the car had sped off past him and up the street, Heath didn't think any of the three men had clocked him. But he hadn't wanted to hang around in case they had.

Pulling on to the motorway, Heath felt a rush of relief, grateful to be out of Maidenhead and on the route back home. 'No, Dad. I didn't get their registration. And I really don't know. I didn't get a very good look at him. All I know is he was a big fucker.'

In answer to his father's question, Heath wasn't sure whether he would recognise the man he'd seen running from Footlights, but this was only because he didn't think he wanted to.

He normally dismissed his father's wild and usually cynical theories, but this time he had a horrible lurking feeling that on this occasion, he could be right. And that wasn't good.

The big man leaving Footlights in a rush could well have been one of the Powells. And if it was, then his long awaited dreams of getting his hands on those jewels was down the toilet.

And that was something he didn't want to consider a possibility. But either way, he couldn't go back there now. At least not yet. He would just have to wait and see what happened when Helen called him – *if* she called him or when he next called Teagan.

Ending the call to his father, Heath turned the music up on his car stereo in the hope that it would drown out the clamouring in his head.

• • • •

NERO SLAMMED HIS FOOT to the accelerator as he navigated the road out of Maidenhead. 'I couldn't be sure it was her until she got out.'

Jonah's face was white with rage, his piercing eyes staring blindly out of the window, adrenalin pumping mercilessly through his veins.

'So what fucker has lifted the gear and the old witch?' Keith asked, scarcely able to believe what Jonah had told them.

When they saw that man running down the pavement to catch up with Teagan they'd reached the house just in the nick of time. Nero reckoned the man was the same one he'd seen a few weeks' ago whilst they'd been watching the house. He reckoned it was the son – the bloody *son*. What the hell he was doing there, Keith didn't have a clue, but he'd known they literally had split seconds to spare before the girl and that bloke ran headlong into Jonah on his way out. *Christ, he'd been cutting it fine.*

'Did the girl see your face when she ran into you?' Nero asked.

'How the fuck do I know?' Jonah muttered, his jaw set in pure anger. *This was a disaster.* 'All I know is that we need to get out of here, pronto.'

He could scarcely believe how events had unfolded. His teeth gnashed in pure, unbridled rage. Some fucker had come in, lifted his goods and took the old woman; there was no other explanation for it, but it had left *him* bang in the middle, standing next to the corpse of Helen Shepherd.

Clenching his fist, he punched the back of the driver's seat. 'Bastards!' he roared. *He was back to square one. Where the hell did he go from here?*

'And you didn't shoot her?' Keith said, looking over his shoulder at Jonah.

'How the fuck could I shoot her when she wasn't there? And if you mean, did I shoot the other one, no I did not. Some other fucker did. If Dulcie Adams was there, then she was hiding or fucking dead elsewhere. I barely had chance to do anything before I had to shift out of there,' Jonah spat. Keith's stupid questions made him want to punch the big man repeatedly in the back of the neck. *Stupid, stupid questions.*

Jonah's mobile rang again and he ripped it from his pocket. Seeing Lena's name on the caller display he felt like his head would explode. Ignoring the call, he shoved his phone back in his pocket. Listening to her whining voice would push him well over the edge of the precipice he was clinging on to.

'That was Lena – no doubt having just noticed I've been missing from my own engagement party for the past two hours,' he muttered. 'We need to think of a reason as to where we've been.'

'I'll sort that,' Nero said. 'We'll all need an alibi by the sounds of it. An alibi for something that, for the first time in history, we've had fuck all to do with.'

· · · ·

PANIC SURGING THROUGH HER BODY, Teagan raced up the stairs hearing Robert clattering from room to room below roaring loudly for Dulcie.

She couldn't afford to speculate on what had happened or what she might possibly find. All she could do was something functional – something, *anything* locate Helen, and more importantly, Dulcie.

'Helen?' Teagan shouted, her voice hoarse. 'Dulcie?' Reaching the top of the stairs, seeing the door to the pink bedroom open, she raced towards it, stumbling on the loose fitting carpet.

Rushing into the room she immediately saw Helen lying on the floor and an ear-splitting scream escaped from her mouth. 'Oh my God, oh my God,' Teagan panted, nausea and fear rushing through her like anaesthesia. *Helen was dead. She was DEAD. Oh Christ… Dulcie? Where was Dulcie? Please not Dulcie too?*

Tears pouring down her cheeks, Teagan inched towards Helen's body, clearly able to see she was past saving. Her hands shook violently and she dithered from foot to foot, not able to decide what to do or even *know* what to do.

'Robert!' she screamed. 'Robert! Call the police! Call the police!' *Oh God, where was Dulcie? Where was she?* 'Dulcie? Are you here?'

Almost having a breakdown on the spot as she heard movement from under the bed, Teagan froze. Holding her breath, she squatted down and saw one of Dulcie's bony arms poking out from under the old bedframe. 'Oh, thank God!' She grasped Dulcie's hand. 'Are you alright? Dulcie, are you hurt?'

Robert crashed into the room, physically swaying as he took in the body of his sister, the gunshot wound to her chest as obvious as the sunrise. 'Fuck! FUCK!' he shouted, his frightened eyes meeting Teagan's.

'Robert, Dulcie's here, she's under the bed. Help me.'

Robert rushed around to where Teagan squatted, helping her pull Dulcie's tiny body out from under the bed. He wrapped his mother in his arms, anger exploding at the sight of her cut lip.

'Get Dulcie out of here, Robert,' Teagan whispered, nodding towards Helen's body. 'She can't see th…'

'Helen's dead, isn't she?' Dulcie said, her voice tiny. 'I-I…'

'Come on,' Robert soothed, leading Dulcie out of the room, leaving Teagan to close the door behind her.

Robert kicked open a door of another bedroom – one Teagan had never seen before; a dark-painted room with a single bed in the centre covered with a dust sheet.

After being sat upon the bed, Dulcie looked up at her son, her blue eyes wide. She gripped his hand with shaking fingers. 'I-I couldn't stop her... I... Helen... She's... I... We were having an argument... She's been trying to poison me. She was going to sell Footlights... She admitted everything an...'

Teagan squeezed Dulcie's hand reassuringly. 'We've been through this, Dulcie. Helen wasn't trying t...'

'But she's right.' Robert interrupted, looking Teagan straight in the eyes. 'Helen *was* poisoning my mother. I only found out tonight – that's why I came over.'

'W-What?' Teagan's mind swam. 'H-How? How was sh...'

'Those vitamins. They weren't vitamins. They were tranquilisers, anti-depressants... lots of different medication. They can mimic the effects of dementia.'

Teagan's mouth dropped open. So Dulcie wasn't losing her mind? Helen had been doing it on purpose? And *she* had been giving Dulcie those pills? Giving her them faithfully morning and night? Oh God... 'But why? I...'

'Money,' Robert barked, wincing hearing his mother sobbing loudly. 'It's all about money.' Cradling his mother in his big arms, he sighed. 'I raced over to Helen's house. James told me what was going on. He found stuff in their garage and wrote to me... I got there... she... she's killed him.'

Teagan wobbled and leant against the bed's wooden footboard for support. *This was too much.*

'I'm guessing Helen killed James earlier tonight. She staved his head in and then came over here. I think she was planning on...' Robert jerked his head towards his mother.

Teagan couldn't comprehend this. Was he saying Helen was planning on killing Dulcie too? Was that why she was here?

'She was so angry with me,' Dulcie whimpered, clinging on to Robert like a child.

Teagan moved to sit next to Robert and Dulcie on the bed. *If Helen had planned to kill Dulcie...?*

'We were in here arguing,' Dulcie murmured. 'Helen hit

me… She was saying the most dreadful things… I fell… banged my head.' Her voice became quiet, almost inaudible. 'I was on the floor behind the bed. Then… then I heard a man. He was screaming at Helen, saying… oh, I don't know what he was saying.'

Dulcie wiped her shaking hands across her eyes. 'He didn't notice me… I crawled under the bed whilst he tipped out all my drawers. Helen was shouting, calling him a liar. The next thing I heard the gun go off and that was it. I must have passed out.' She threw her hands up in the air. 'Oh God, my daughter, my beautiful daughter is dead. He killed her! I should have been able to protect her… I…'

'Sshh, you couldn't have done anything,' Teagan soothed, her mind racing. She looked at Robert. 'We need to call the police.'

Robert nodded. 'I'll do that now.'

Dulcie gripped onto Robert as he got up from the bed. 'Don't let them take me away! Don't let them take me to the hospital. I want to stay here with you. I…'

Robert held his mother's face in his big hands. 'Don't worry, you won't have to do anything you don't want to do. I'll make sure of that. This isn't your fault, mother. Helen was involved in a lot of things none of us had the faintest clue about. This man must be something to do with her and whatever she was involved in. Her luck clearly ran out. I'm just so glad you're safe.'

Kissing the top of Dulcie's head, Robert staggered from the room, dialling 999 on his mobile.

FORTY EIGHT

SITTING DOWNSTAIRS WAITING for the police to arrive, Teagan shook with both nerves and shock. The relief that Dulcie was ok was immense, but she couldn't get her head around what Helen had done and her mind was knotted into a thousand different tangles.

When seeing the man had rushed from the house she'd immediately thought he was something to do with those despicable people Joe had got himself involved with, but from what Dulcie had said, it was all to do with something Helen had been involved in. This was *nothing* to do with Joe.

Relief poured over her – as much as that was possible in a situation such as this. The knowledge that this hadn't happened off the back of anything inadvertently connected to her made the awfulness marginally more bearable.

But she was also angry. Angry, hurt and incredibly sad.

She looked at Robert sitting outwardly calmly, but locked inside his own head with his own collection of tumbling thoughts.

'How could I have been so stupid?' Teagan whispered. 'I believed Helen. I believed she was worried sick about Dulcie and genuinely trying to do her best, but all along... all along...'

A fresh wave of tears poured down her face.

'She fooled all of us. I believed her too,' Robert said. 'I fought Helen for a long time over her claims that mother's behaviour was getting worse. I never wanted to believe mother had dementia. It was only recently when she told me what you'd said...'

'See! I gave Helen the ammunition to get Dulcie into that home. I thought I was doing the right thing... I thought...'

'Teagan, you *did* do the right thing. What else were you supposed to do or think with the way those tablets were making my mother act?' Robert countered. 'This is not on you.' His eyes narrowed. 'This is on Helen. She's always been cold, but I never dreamt she'd do this. Any of it! She did it so methodically too; so well planned... And James... the poor bastard.'

The image of James' caved-in skull flashed vividly in Robert's mind. He didn't think he'd ever be able to erase it from his memory. He didn't think he'd ever be able to erase *anything* from this day from his memory.

Teagan smiled weakly. She'd got Robert all wrong. She'd chosen the wrong sibling to suspect. It hadn't been him, it had always been Helen. 'Do you think we should have allowed Dulcie to go back into the room? The police... it's a crime scene.'

Robert shrugged. 'I can't see how it will make much of a difference. You didn't see the guy's face, as neither did I and mother said all she saw was his feet and his gloved hands holding a gun.' His eyes grew cold. 'Personally, I don't know why she wants some time alone with Helen before the police cart off her treacherous body.'

'Helen's still her daughter.'

'Yeah, a daughter who had been poisoning her for months and planning to rip her off by selling her house from under her. It's obvious my sister was involved with unscrupulous people and she'd pissed them about. To top it all off, she murdered her own husband because he'd worked her out. She knew the game was up.'

'What are we going to do if the police insist Dulcie goes to hospital to be checked over? You heard what she said, she wants to stay here – she's terrified, bless her.' Teagan wrung her hands together in despair.

Robert pursed his lips. 'My first thought was to get her to the hospital and get all of those drugs Helen's been shoving into her out of her system, but now I'm thinking that would do more harm than good.'

Teagan nodded. 'I think you're right. They'll be completely out of her system within a day or two anyway. It's not like she's had an overdose and you don't know what they'll want to do. They might want to pump her stomach or subject her to countless blood tests.' She looked at Robert, worry reflected equally in his eyes as her own. 'I-I don't think she'll be able to take it. She's already had too much to deal with.'

'Don't worry. I won't let them take her anywhere. She's been through enough.'

Teagan placed her hand on Robert's arm, the sensation feeling at odds after all the time she'd spent thinking so little of him. 'But what will happen? She can't stay here – probably not for a few days. The police will need to remove... remove the body, then do their investigation and...'

'I know I didn't want you here, but I have to say that I'm glad you were!' Robert placed his hand over Teagan's. 'You'll both come and stay with me – at least until we know what's going on.'

Teagan smiled weakly. 'Thank you. I think Dulcie will need you around – especially tonight. And I'll feel so much better knowing you're around too. It's so much to take in. My head's spinning, so I hate to think how Dulcie feels. Imagine your daughter doing something like that to you?' Teagan shook her head wearily watching Robert do the same in a mixture of despair and anger. 'I'd better go and get her. The police will be here any minute.'

Robert nodded. 'Do you mind? I really don't want to set

eyes on my bitch of a sister again. I hope she fucking rots in hell.'

. . . .

DULCIE STARED AT THE BODY of her daughter, a slow smile spreading across her face. 'Thought you'd got away with it?' she whispered, her beady eyes fixed on Helen's lifeless face. 'But you didn't, did you?'

Getting down on her hands and knees, she reached under the bed, blindly feeling around, her ears finely tuned for any movement signalling Teagan or Robert were coming upstairs. Satisfied they were respecting her wish to spend a last few moments saying goodbye to her 'darling daughter', her fingers probed further until they closed around the barrel of the Beretta she'd pushed behind the furthest foot of the bed.

It was fortunate Teagan hadn't spotted it when she'd crouched down to help her out from under the bed, but thankfully she'd been too busy concentrating on getting her out unharmed to notice anything else.

Scrabbling back up from the floor, Dulcie rubbed her knees, scowled at her ripped tights, courtesy of getting under the bed in such a rush in the first place when she'd heard that man coming. That and the split lip where her bitch of a daughter had backhanded her. She'd already got a lump forming on the back of her head, courtesy of whacking it on the mirror, but it had all been worth it in the end.

She glanced at Helen again. *More* than worth it.

Dulcie stared at the gun in her hands. Something else Michael insisted she kept in the event she should need it. His words of that day from very long ago resounded clearly in her mind. *'Just in case, babe, just in case. You never know when you might need it'.*

Well, Michael was right. She *had* needed it – albeit forty years on and not for what she'd thought she'd need it for. But she'd enjoyed finally putting it to good use. *Enjoyed it very much indeed.*

With a grunt of effort, Dulcie prised the floorboards back up, exposing her secret hiding place. Wrapping the gun back in a towel, she carefully placed it back in its wooden box, glad she'd relied on her instinct that this day was fast approaching and got it out ready.

Helen really had been stupid to think she hadn't noticed what she'd been planning. Dulcie smiled. She hadn't even been completely sure that Helen was swapping out those vitamins, but she *did* know her daughter well enough to know that she'd been doing something. She knew she wanted her out of the way so she could have Footlights.

Her wrinkled forehead furrowed, unable to work out how Helen had found out about the stash and about Robert's father, but now it all made sense.

When that man had turned up, *everything* had made sense.

Before replacing the floorboard back in its correct position, Dulcie removed another box – a small wooden one and held it in her hand, smiling once again.

'I promised you Michael and I haven't let you down. They're still safe and will remain so.' She'd have to change her plans a little now because something had become very obvious. It was imperative she covered all bases.

Dulcie shoved the small box into her pocket and replaced the floorboard carefully. She stared at her daughter's lifeless body once again. *You little bitch*, she thought acidly. *You should have gone years ago.*

But at least one thing Helen had done before she was removed off this mortal coil was to unknowingly give her a heads up.

Helen knew Dulcie was in possession of the diamonds – those beautiful pink diamonds – *Michael's* beautiful pink diamonds, because someone had told her. And the only people that could have told her were the Powells. She knew they'd been looking for her for years, but she was too clever. *Oh yes, she was far too clever.*

Dulcie knew she was lucky to be in the position where she'd

had time to scramble under the bed before that man had reached the bedroom. It was all very fortunate all round.

After despatching Helen she'd been wracking her brains to think of a reason – a plausible reason as to why *she* had shot Helen. Self-defence? Although not without its many problems, Dulcie knew she'd have to use that one. She'd say it was Helen's gun; that she'd pointed it at her – tried to kill her and then it had just gone off. She'd have thought of something, but now she didn't need to.

When she'd heard it – that floorboard – the one half way up the stairs that sounded like the whole staircase would collapse, she'd known someone was coming.

From where she'd hidden under the bed, she'd watched the man, his face livid to see Helen's body on the floor and the turned over state of the room and had obviously come to his own conclusions. She'd seen his face only briefly, but she'd known straight away who he was. She didn't know his name, but she knew he was a Powell.

She'd seen those eyes, that jawline and that expression many years ago on more than one occasion. And she knew exactly who that man's bloodline was. That man was a Powell. She'd seen Jacky Powell himself on several occasions whilst working at The Feathers and whoever had been standing at the foot of her bed tonight was, it was a Powell. A son, presumably. And he was here for only one thing. *Those diamonds.*

Well, he wasn't having them. She'd seen his expression as he'd surveyed the scene and Helen's body. It must have been *him* who'd told Helen about the diamonds in the first place; cut a deal with Helen to get her dear old mother out of the picture and then lift the jewels, but he must think Helen had involved someone else, because she'd single-handedly in her rage made it look that way, the idiotic girl.

Dulcie tried not to laugh. The Powell man also presumed that, judging by what he'd said on the phone, she had been kidnapped, along with the diamonds. Oh yes, she'd heard his conversation. He thought he'd been turned over. *It couldn't be better.*

Dulcie smiled serenely. Luck was definitely on her side. If he hadn't got that phone call warning him that Teagan and Robert were coming he would have discovered her under the bed. *Bless their perfect timing.*

Dulcie's smile dropped. But there was something else. As well as the Powell man that was here tonight, there was that other one – that Darren Harding. She couldn't leave *him* out of the equation.

Something was going on there too. Whoever he said he was, there was an unmistakeable link to Michael there. Something about him, his eyes – *something*. It was there and it was clear.

That man hadn't been here because of his interest in Teagan, she'd bet her life on it. He was here because of the diamonds too.

Dulcie's eyes narrowed as the pieces of the jigsaw slotted into a feasible place.

That boy must be to do with Michael's *first* family – the one he should never have had. That boy was something to do with Sophie Pointer, she was sure of it. It was the only thing that made sense. How he had found her or discovered about the diamonds was another mystery, but not one she could afford to ignore.

One thing was certain and that was she couldn't risk hanging on to the jewels. Not on her person and not in this room. She needed someone else to take on that burden just in case Powell returned and she suspected he would. Perhaps not next week or next month, but he'd be back now he knew where she was and when he found out that she was still about.

That was unless she could frame him for Helen's murder. Robert and Teagan had certainly believed her when she'd said the man had shot Helen and the police had no reason not to either. It all depended on whether they could link it back to him. But she could hardly give his name without dropping herself in it. Neither did it help her where the Harding boy was concerned.

Dulcie frowned. She had to make sure that if Teagan was to

continue seeing the man, then she only spoke to him of things that *she* instructed. Actually, it could be imperative that Teagan remained seeing Harding – that way she could control it.

The trick was how she would do this without the girl knowing.

It was ok. She had a plan. She just had to keep up the pretence that she'd taken those pills and act the part of the distressed mother and all would be good. There was no way she was going to the hospital. It wouldn't take them long to discover there were zero traces of any of those drugs in her system and never had been. She couldn't have that, it would ruin everything.

Teagan was imperative in the next phase of keeping her prized possessions safe. That girl soaked everything in, like a sponge. She'd been able to see that from the off, which was why she was just so perfect. And Teagan would continue to being just that if she worked this the way she needed to.

Dulcie grinned. She had ultimate faith in her own ability. It hadn't let her down yet.

• • • •

DULCIE'S HEAD SWUNG UP with the tapping at the bedroom door.

'Dulcie? It's me,' Teagan's voice came through the thick door.

Dulcie knelt back on the floor, adopting a convincing position next to Helen. Grabbing one of her daughter's cold hands, she put on a shaky, distressed voice. 'Come in.'

Teagan moved into the room, her eyes immediately moving to Helen's body, even though she'd told herself repeatedly all the way up the stairs that she wouldn't look at it again. She quickly averted her eyes, moving them to Dulcie, her heart aching for the desolate expression on the old lady's face, tears running down her cheeks.

She swallowed the lump in her throat. *This was awful – so unfair.* 'It's time to come downstairs now, Dulcie. The police will be here any minute.'

'I can't... I can't leave her...' Dulcie sobbed. 'She's my daughter.'

Teagan gently pulled Dulcie to her feet. 'Please. I know it's hard.'

Dulcie stared at Teagan and grasped her hand. 'I'm sorry for acting the way I have half the time towards you,' she said. 'I...'

'Oh, Dulcie,' Teagan cried, pulling her against her chest and wrapping her arms around her tiny frame. 'It wasn't your fault. It wasn't you – it was those pills. You're going to be just fine.'

Leaning against Teagan's body Dulcie smiled, then pulled away. 'I need to ask something of you.' She fished the small box from her cardigan pocket. 'I want you to look after something for me. Just for the time being.'

Teagan stared at the small box. 'What is it?'

Dulcie placed the box in Teagan's hand and gripped her arm, staring up at her pleadingly. 'The police will want to go through this room and... and Robert will know... He'll find out. This is something Michael gave me. But please don't tell anyone I've given it to you. I want to be the one to tell Robert about his father. I don't want him to find out like this and certainly not now. Not after what's happened... what's happened with his sister. He's got enough to deal with right now.'

Dulcie gripped Teagan's arm harder. '*Please* don't say anything. I will tell him, just not yet.'

Teagan smiled kindly. 'I understand. I won't say anything, I promise. Is this something important?'

Dulcie smiled weakly. 'Only to me. It contains my heart.' She looked down at the box. 'All that's in there are a handful of letters from Michael. Worthless to anyone, but priceless to me,' she lied.

Teagan smiled. 'Don't worry, I'll keep them safe for you.'

'You won't make me go to the hospital, will you?' Dulcie

said, grasping at Teagan's sleeve. 'I don't want to go. I can't take it, I…'

'You won't be going anywhere.' Teagan soothed, pulling Dulcie into a hug. 'Robert agrees and we won't let anyone make you do something you don't want to do, I promise.'

Dulcie smiled weakly. 'And your young man, Darren. You won't tell him about all of this… about the poisoning? I'm so embarrassed… Things I said…'

'Please don't worry. You're the most important thing here. No one will be saying or doing anything you don't want them to,' Teagan said, squeezing Dulcie's hand. Pulling away, she held Dulcie at arms' length, looking down with concern. 'You do know that you won't be able to stay here at least for a few days, don't you?'

'But where will I go? I don't want to go. I don't want *you* to go.' Tears cascaded down Dulcie's cheeks again. 'I've already lost my daughter and you… you're…'

'I'm not going anywhere. I'm staying with you and will do for however long you'll have me. In the meantime we're both going to stay at Robert's – his suggestion. I'm not leaving you, ok? And neither is Robert. Everything will be fine, but we really do need to go downstairs now and I'm afraid you'll have to tell the police everything. Everything you told us about what happened.'

Dulcie nodded sadly. 'I know…'

She waited until Teagan turned her back to walk out of the bedroom. She had no problem telling the police everything she needed them to know. It was, however, a different story where the Powells were concerned now she knew without a doubt that they were back on her tail.

But all in all, things were going very nicely. Robert and Teagan were playing exactly the way she'd orchestrated it. *All was good.*

Smiling widely to herself, Dulcie followed Teagan out of the pink bedroom.

Epilogue

KEITH TRIED VERY HARD TO PAY ATTENTION. He knew it was vital to keep his ears to the ground – now more than ever, but he was absolutely bush-whacked after virtually every hour that should have been spent getting shut-eye, had instead been taken up snorting coke and shagging the feisty little tart offering him a taster of her services in the hope of landing a job at The Feathers.

Oh, she'd been up to the job, alright – there was no question about that. It was just a pity, for her at least, that it wasn't up to him to say if she'd got a job or not. But she hadn't known that and he certainly hadn't been in any rush to correct her assumptions.

If he remembered, he'd put in a good word for her, although the way things were going, it could well be him that *did* get the say-so about which girls worked here and which didn't. And he didn't have the time or the inclination for that. He wanted to get on with his own fucking job.

Bloody Gwen. Things had gone pear-shaped where the show side of the club was concerned since she'd gone AWOL and it had put Jonah in an even worse mood than he was already in.

Four days since the engagement party and the Dulcie Adams debacle and if he said they weren't all on tenterhooks waiting to see if what happened at the old bat's gaff led back to them, he'd be lying. As yet nothing had come of it, but Keith knew the Old Bill were on it because Jonah was following Maidenhead's local news like a stalker, but so far, so good. It wasn't like Jonah could be pulled in for the killing of that snotty Shepherd bird anyway. Well, he could, but it would never stick – it wasn't like he'd done it, but his very presence could lead back and then uncover the ins and outs of the diamond heist. And it was *that* which was eating away and bothering all of them.

Keith glanced at Jonah, the stress of the last few days clearly visible on his face. The man should have sorted it properly in the first place, like *he* would have. Buggering about had got him precisely nowhere – apart from in the shit. And despite him putting out some careful feelers, there was nothing on the grapevine about who had lifted and cashed in on this behind their back.

But then it was unlikely that would ever come out because anyone worth their salt knew who'd they be taking on. Some fucker had it though and everyone was determined to find out exactly who that was. *When the heat died down...*

Always when the heat died down, Keith thought angrily. *Walk straight into the fire and get it done.*

'Can Lena not deal with this?' Nero said, jolting Keith from his ponderings.

Jonah placed Gwen's black dance rota folder down sharply on the desk. 'No she fucking can't!' he spat. 'We might be up to our necks with this being as Gwen's off sick, but I'm not involving Lena.'

Nero shrugged, whilst Keith grimaced. 'When's Gwen back?'

'I don't know. I'll go and see her. Find out what's going on.' Jonah wanted to know where Gwen was too. In all the years he'd known her, he could barely remember her *ever* having a day off sick, let alone four. And even then she still phoned in.

No one had heard anything and he was extremely concerned. It couldn't have happened at a worse time either. As well as being worried about Gwen, he wanted her take on what had happened.

His head was mashed trying to work out who had swiped the stash from under their noses and set him up to be framed at the same time. Oh, he knew what they'd done, he just couldn't work out who the fuck it was. *But when he did....*

Jonah glanced up irritably when Keith's mobile rang out loudly. Unless an emergency was underfoot, it was always the code to have the mobiles set to silent during the daily meetings. *No disturbances.*

Embarrassed, Keith fished his mobile from his pocket and glanced at the screen. *Shit.* 'Sorry, got to take this,' he mumbled, hefting himself up from the chair and out of Jonah's office.

He glanced over his shoulder as he hurried through the lobby. 'Yeah, I'm still here. Give me a second.'

Nodding at Jim on the door, Keith rushed down the entrance steps to the street outside, then darted down an alley at the side of The Feathers. 'Sorry, I had to get out of the club.'

Catching his breath, he leant against the wall. 'I'm glad you've called. I know I'm due to come in next week, but you need to know th...'

Keith was cut off by Saul's insistent voice and he listened avidly to what was being said. He hadn't needed to fill him in with what had occurred at Dulcie Adams' place – Saul had already seen the news. But that wasn't what surprised him, and Keith could scarcely believe what he was hearing.

• • • •

ENDING THE CALL, Saul placed the phone he'd acquired back under his mattress in his cell and smiled.

Although Keith confirming what he'd read was correct was nothing to smile about – he'd fully expected his brother not to pull off anything in a proper way to exact complete vengeance, but conversely, neither had he expected it to go so horribly wrong.

So, some other fucker had beaten them to it and fucked off with what was theirs. *Again.* But whoever it was, they hadn't got the old bat – that newspaper report citing she was unharmed and recovering at an 'undisclosed' location made that crystal clear. As clear as the detailed description and photofit of his brother the old bitch had pieced together for the Old Bill.

How had Jonah, the stupid fucker, missed a doddery, demented old woman hiding under a fucking bed? Was his brother purposefully winding him up?

Saul gnashed his teeth. If any of this had kicked off in a few weeks from now then he'd be laughing, but it hadn't. Whether he liked it or not, he had to swallow that his brother had let this slip through his fingers.

But that would be changing soon. *Very soon.*

Getting unexpected early parole was a surprise, but a good one. A very well-timed one, too.

In two days from now he would, after 17 years, be out of this shithole to take up the place which had always had his name on it. He'd had to concede his rightful place because he'd had to serve time for the family, but now he was getting out. And when he got out, he would be head of the family firm, just like his father would have wanted and, as the eldest son, what he was due.

And then he'd go and get the jewels back from whichever fucker had been stupid enough to lift them and Keith would be helping.

They'd be doing it *their* way – the way that always worked and Jonah would just have to accept it.

THANK YOU!

Thank you for reading *An Old Score*. I hope you enjoyed reading it as much as I did writing it!

If so, would you please consider leaving a review on Amazon and/or Goodreads.

Reviews from readers are SOOOO helpful and especially important to us authors and without you we would have nobody to write for!

Thank you once again and hope you enjoy the rest of my books.

Edie xx

MORE FROM THIS SERIES

RETRIBUTION SERIES:

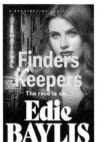

#2: FINDERS KEEPERS

The race is on…

When Saul Powell is released early from prison, it causes mayhem for the family firm. His brother, Jonah, has enough problems trying to keep semblance amidst the chaos, not to mention his fast approaching unwanted marriage.

But even Jonah's problems pale into insignificance compared to what Robert Adams is discovering about his mother, Dulcie – the woman he's always put on a pedestal.

In the meantime, Teagan Fraser is also facing a dilemma – one which could ruin her life completely.

Can anyone come out of this nightmare unscathed?

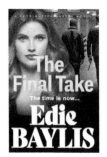

#3: THE FINAL TAKE

THE TIME IS NOW…

Even knowing Ron O'Hara is somewhere in the vicinity, Jonah Powell feels it's time to finally get rid of the diamonds which have haunted his family for decades and caused so much trouble.

However, other problems start to arrive from unexpected and additional sources, some of which Jonah didn't expect.

Neither did he expect Teagan Fraser to be playing on his mind so heavily.

But what does it all mean? It may be apt to call time on the curse plaguing his family and of those around him, but how can this be achieved while so many other things are at stake?

More From this Author

ALLEGIANCE SERIES:

#1: TAKEOVER

Samantha Reynold hadn't bargained on unexpectedly needing to step into her father's shoes and take over the family casino business and known nothing about the rules of this glamorous but deadly new world. But she won't let her family down, especially when it looks like they could lose everything to their biggest rivals – the Stoker family.

Eldest son Sebastian hasn't got time to pander to pretty girl Samantha as she plays at being boss. Rumours are swirling around the streets of Birmingham that have the power to rip the Stoker family apart and destroy everything they've built.

#2: FALLOUT

With the odds stacked against her, Samantha Reynold is determined to prove she's tough enough to be the boss. But when a secret from the past threatens to ruin Sam's reputation, she suddenly feels very alone in this dark new world. There's only one man she can turn to – rival club owner, Sebastian Stoker.

Seb knows first-hand how secrets and lies can tear a family apart. He wants to protect Sam at all costs, but siding with her could threaten his own position as head of the Stoker family and risk accusations of betrayal.

With loyalties divided and two families at war – the fallout could be deadly.

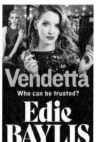

#3: VENDETTA

Once bitter enemies, Samantha Reynold and Seb Stoker's powerful alliance enables their firms and casinos to go from strength to strength. With the families no longer in opposition, it seems that Sam and Seb are untouchable…

But not everyone is happy with the new power couple of the club world.

Unbeknownst to everyone, someone new wants to see Sam's perfect life ruined. And they will stop at nothing to seek their revenge – even if it means destroying everything - and everyone - in their path.

MORE FROM THIS AUTHOR

HUNTED SERIES:

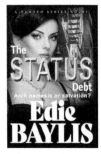

#1: THE STATUS DEBT

Lillian Morgan would do anything to regain the status she lost by marrying beneath her and to cover the sordid details of her husband's death. This includes blackmail and the hand of marriage of her own daughter.

Tori thought her life couldn't get much worse, but someone is not being honest and secrets have the power to rip everyone to shreds.

Especially when life is built on lies.

#2: THE FAMILY LEGACY

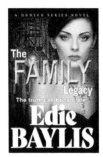

Unsure of whether Matt or Hunter has fathered the child growing inside her, Tori's unwanted wedding to Matt grows closer, but is there light at the end of the tunnel? Unfortunately, Tori hasn't counted on another man present in her life. One who is more instrumental in her misery than she realises.

Sometimes the truth is too late in coming and makes bad things happen and sometimes a hidden legacy can cause the most horrific thing of all…

#3: THE TARGET OF LIES

Neil Sparks has a score to settle. In fact, he has several… His first port of call when returning from France after a five year exile is to catch up with his estranged wife. Secondly, Neil wants to even a score with the people instrumental in his departure and thirdly, he wants an explanation from the man who promised his marriage would be free from hassle. The trouble is, he's not the only one with an agenda…

There are too many people about to become caught in the crossfire and everyone could become a target.

** This series contains written depictions of graphic violence, sex and strong language. It also contains some themes that may be uncomfortable for certain readers. **

MORE FROM THIS AUTHOR

DOWNFALL SERIES:

#1 - UNTIL THE END OF TIME

Dive into Seth and Jane's train wreck of a life, where drugs, alcohol and obsessional love means this downright dangerous pair will do *anything* to ensure nothing gets in their way.

They do bad things. *Very* bad things and their promise to love each until the end of time turns into a war against each other.

A war neither of them can win.

#2 - ESCAPING THE PAST

Things have changed and Jane has got on with her life.

Well, not *entirely…*

Embroiled in a bitter feud between two rival firms, it is clear that not everyone is who they proclaim to be.

The net is closing in and some things just can't be changed.

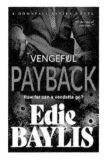

#3 - VENGEFUL PAYBACK

There is something missing. Something *very* important and no one is above suspicion.

Past vendettas are gaining pace and it is vital that whoever is behind this never-ending stream of cleverly engineered payback is discovered before it is too late and everything held dear is ripped apart.

** This series contains written depictions of graphic violence, sex and strong language. It also contains some themes that may be uncomfortable for certain readers. **

ABOUT THE AUTHOR

Over the years Edie has worked all over the UK as well as in several other countries and has met a lot of interesting people - several of whom have supplied ideas for some of the characters in her books! She has now settled back in central England with her partner and children, where she is pursuing writing her gritty gangland and urban fiction novels.

Edie is currently signed to Boldwood Books for a 5-book gangland fiction series set in Birmingham. The first three in the *Allegiance* series, *Takeover*, *Fallout* and *Vendetta* have been released and the fourth in the series, *Payback*, is due to be released in January 2023. She is also concurrently writing the *Scarred* series - the first titled, *Mirrors Never Lie*.

Edie's other series are the *Retribution* series, the *Hunted* series and the *Downfall* series - all trilogies.

When she isn't writing, Edie enjoys reading and is a self-confessed book hoarder. She also enjoys crochet and music as well as loving anything quirky or unusual.

Visit www.ediebaylis.co.uk for the latest news, information about new releases, giveaways and to subscribe to her mailing list.

CWA MEMBER

CONNECT WITH EDIE

https://fb.me/downfallseries

https://www.goodreads.com/author/show/17153586.Edie_Baylis

https://twitter.com/ediebaylis

https://www.amazon.co.uk/Edie-Baylis/e/B075FQHWCZ/

https://www.bookbub.com/authors/edie-baylis

https://ediebaylis.co.uk/

info@ediebaylis.co.uk

https://www.fantasticfiction.com/b/edie-baylis/

https://www.instagram.com/ediebaylis/

https://www.tiktok.com/@edie747

https://www.pinterest.co.uk/ediebaylis/

JOIN EDIE'S MAILING LIST

Subscribe to Edie's mailing list for the latest news on her books, special offers, new releases and competitions.

https://ediebaylis.co.uk/signup.html

Edie Baylis

gangland | crime | urban

THRILLER AUTHOR

ACKNOWLEDGEMENTS

I would like to thank Sue John – a wonderful lady, that courtesy of my books, I am privileged to know. Thank you Sue for your unwavering support, help and feedback, as well as your faith in me.

Special thanks also goes to the people (you know who you are) - who were brave enough to allow their names to be adopted by some of the characters in this story (I must point out that these characters are in no way anything to do with, or connected to, their namesakes in real life!) ☺

Printed in Great Britain
by Amazon

25668841R00239